DREAMING IN COLOR

At last, she coiled the hair back atop Alma's head and carefully pinned it in place. "There!" she said, stepping to one side to give the woman a smile. "All set."

Alma looked up at her for a long moment, then said, "What a kind little person you are."

Bobby felt her smile get wobbly on her face, like something that'd been stuck over her mouth with glue and was about to fall off. She thought she might cry, but managed to choke out, "Thank you," and busied herself returning the hairbrush to the bureau. Clearing her throat, she said, "I guess it's time to go downstairs now," and waited for Alma to get the wheelchair aimed at the door.

The compliment had rattled her, Alma saw, and felt a sadness blossom in her chest. It was all too obvious that Bobby was far more accustomed to abuse than praise. How very sad, she thought. Three disenchanted females under one roof. But then she was forgetting Penny, that charming sprite. It really was lovely to have a child in the house again. M___ ___ ___ ___, she'd been ___ ___ ___ ___

CHARLOTTE VALE ALLEN

DREAMING IN COLOR

MIRA BOOKS

ISBN 1-55166-030-X

DREAMING IN COLOR

First published by Doubleday, a division of Bantam Doubleday Dell Publishing Group, Inc.

Copyright © 1993 by Charlotte Vale Allen.

MIRA and the star colophon are trademarks of MIRA Books.

Printed in U.S.A.

For Dina Watson,
who always makes
me smile

One

She stayed where she was even after the front door slammed. Sometimes he came back. So she waited until she heard the car go roaring off down the street. Then she sat up against the cupboard door, looking around at the mess. She hadn't cried this time, hadn't tried to reason with him, or to defend herself. It hadn't made a difference.

Her face hurt. So did her hips and the backs of her thighs, where he'd kicked her. She looked at the spaghetti sauce splattered on the wall, the pieces of broken plate, the chair lying on its side by the sink. Spaghetti all over the floor, some of it mashed into the linoleum.

Her heart wouldn't slow down. It kept rapping too fast in her chest. She had to breathe through her mouth and it made her lips sting. Blood ran down her chin, dropped into her lap. Penny had slept through it this time, thank God. Last time she'd come running in and Joe had slapped her, sent her flying all the way into the hall. It was bad enough the things he did to her but she couldn't let him start hitting Penny. And if she'd awakened this time, he'd've hit her again. Next time, though, she might come running in and Joe would hurt her. That couldn't be allowed to happen. It was one thing for him to hit her. She was used to it by now. But Penny was only six years old; she hadn't done anything wrong; she deserved better.

She staggered into the bathroom, ran cold water in the sink, and bathed her face. No more, she thought, her heart still going too fast. If she didn't take Penny and get out of there he'd wind up killing both of them.

She ran to the bedroom, got the old suitcase from the back of the closet, and started shoving her clothes into it. Then, moving fast, she got the duffel bag and went to Penny's room. She wasn't going to waste any time thinking about it. They were going, and right away, before he came back.

"Honey, get up," she said softly, touching the sleeping child on the shoulder. "Get up and get dressed."

Opening her eyes, Penny murmured, "Where we goin'?"

"We're leaving. Get dressed fast as you can."

"Where we goin'?" she asked again, sitting on the side of the bed and watching for a moment as her mother emptied drawers, pushed clothes into the bag.

"Away," Bobby told her, running her tongue over her split lip, feeling the sting. "Get dressed now. We've gotta hurry."

"Are we running away?" Penny wanted to know, pulling her nightgown over her head.

"That's right," Bobby said, at the closet now.

"Good," Penny said, reaching for her jeans. "I hate it here. Where we goin' to?"

"I don't know," Bobby said breathlessly. "Hurry up. And don't forget Mr. Bear."

"What about Mr. Rabbit and all my other books and toys?"

"Listen." Bobby dropped down in front of her, fumbling at the buttons on Penny's shirt. "We can't take everybody, just Mr. Bear. We've got to go right away, now, before Daddy gets back. Okay?" She got up and handed the child her sweater, then grabbed the pillow and comforter off the bed. Arms laden, she tore through the house, out the back door to the car. After tossing the bedding on the back seat, she got the trunk open and threw in the duffel bag before running inside for her suitcase and their coats, Penny's boots and backpack.

Grabbing up her handbag and the keys, she did a quick check of the house. The envelope with all their important papers. She got it from the desk drawer in the living room. What else? Think! There was nothing else she wanted, and the urgency was singing in her ears. Go, go, go! She opened the freezer compartment of the refrigerator and grabbed the foil-wrapped package from under the stack of frozen pizzas. Her secret savings. Nickels and quarters she'd saved for months on end, converting the change into bills until she'd amassed almost three hundred dollars, all she had in the world.

Penny was standing in the kitchen doorway, thumb in her mouth, taking in the mess.

"Come on, honey." Bobby lifted the child onto her bruised hip and picked her way through the shards of crockery, the slime of spaghetti. "We're going now."

She got Penny settled in a makeshift bed in the back, then climbed into the driver's seat and got the car started. The old Honda was falling to pieces. The valves were about shot and it had an oil leak. Just get us away from here, away from him, she prayed. Tasting blood in her mouth, she reversed out of the driveway and headed down the street. Knees shaking, hands slick on the wheel, she drove automatically. She had no idea where they were going. Just as far away from him as they could get.

"What about school?" Penny asked, startling her.

"You'll go to a new school when we get where we're going," Bobby told her. "Lie down now and go to sleep."

"But where're we goin'?"

"I don't know," Bobby said tiredly, feeling the bruising deep in her legs. The pain in her face throbbed in syncopation with her heartbeat. "Somewhere nice, somewhere far away."

"Daddy's a bad, bad man," Penny said, her chin resting on the back of the passenger seat. "He'll be sorry we're gone."

"Yeah," Bobby sighed, one eye starting to swell closed. "Real sorry," she said, imagining his rage when he returned home to find them gone. He'd probably smash up the whole house. Then he'd collect his guns, get in the car, and go looking for them. First he'd go to Lor's house and wake everybody up, demanding to see his wife and kid. That's what he'd done the last time. He'd made such a screaming fuss Lor wound up calling the cops. They'd booked Joe again for disturbing the peace. And after the cops had taken him away, Lor said, "I'm real sorry, hon, but you're gonna have to go." She'd had no choice; she'd taken Penny home. He'd behaved himself for two weeks after the cops let him out. Then he'd started all over again.

"You lie down now and go to sleep," she told Penny. "We've got a long way to go." They were on highway 17, headed east. She'd always wanted to see the ocean. If the car held up, she'd drive it right to the Atlantic, find some seaside town where they could start fresh. Someplace small and clean, just a couple of rooms. She'd get a job, settle Penny in a new school. "Don't fall apart on me," she whispered to the car, hands tight on the wheel, eyes straining in the dark.

Penny lay down cuddling Mr. Bear and began to sing herself to sleep. Bobby listened to the small voice singing "Mr. Sandman." Penny got through two verses before her voice thinned, then stopped. Bobby put the radio on low and concentrated on the road.

At first she kept checking the rearview mirror, expecting him to come racing up behind them in the Firebird. It didn't happen, and after a while she stopped looking. She got all the way to Elmira, where she just had to stop. Her head ached so badly she could scarcely see, and a steady pain radiated up and down her thighs. She pulled into a twenty-four-hour service center and gassed up the car, then drove around back to where all the long-distance trucks were parked. Putting the seat back as far as it would go, she wrapped her coat around herself and closed her eyes. Every few minutes she jerked awake, her heart hammering as she surveyed the area. No one came anywhere near them. At last she fell into a kind of half sleep.

Rain drumming on the car roof roused her at just after six the next morning. Penny was already awake, looking out the window, Mr. Bear in her arm.

"Hungry, hon?" Bobby asked.

"Where are we?"

"Outside Elmira," Bobby told her. "We'll get some breakfast, then go on."

"I gotta go to the bathroom."

"Okay." Bobby held her breath and turned the key in the ignition. The car started. Relieved, she let out her breath and drove back around to the front of the service center. Then she and Penny ran through the rain, following the signs to the ladies' room. A couple of women on their way out gave her a look, and Bobby lowered her eyes. A glance in the mirror showed her how bad she looked: her right eye purple and swollen almost shut; her lips puffed out, her nose swollen too. No amount of makeup would cover the damage.

After she and Penny had used the toilet and had a quick wash, they went into the restaurant, where she sipped at some coffee while Penny ate scrambled eggs and toast. Mr. Bear had to eat too. Penny shared every bite with him, telling him what a good boy he was after each forkful of egg. Bobby kept looking over at the door, expecting to see Joe come charging in with his shotgun. She imagined people diving under the tables for cover as Joe let go with both barrels, then changed guns and started firing one of his handguns. Glass shattering, screams, her body bouncing as the bullets tore through her flesh. Was it the fear? she wondered. Or was the coffee actually bitter?

Penny wanted some Jell-O, but Bobby couldn't stand the thought of staying there another minute. She got an order of cherry Jello-O to go and another coffee. Five minutes later they were on the road again. The rain made it slow going. It was hard to see in the downpour, especially with one eye almost closed. They crawled along at forty while everything on the road went past sending sheets of water splashing over the little car. Her arms ached from her fierce grip on the wheel. In the back seat, Penny ate her Jello-O, telling Mr. Bear he couldn't have any because he hadn't eaten all his breakfast.

After Binghamton the rain let up, and she made good time all the way to the interchange at Interstate 84. They stopped so Penny could have a grilled cheese sandwich and Bobby took three aspirins with another cup of coffee, then looked at the map, trying to choose which way to go. She decided they'd take 84 to 684, then cut along secondary roads into Connecticut. She'd heard of Stamford but none of the other towns. So they'd stop in Stamford and she'd buy the local newspaper, see what kind of jobs were available. If they got lucky, she might get a job right away and then she wouldn't have to waste money on a motel. She'd rent them a room and get Penny started in school. Things would work out. They had to.

It was late afternoon by the time they arrived in Stamford. She found an inexpensive motel on Route 1 and bought a newspaper at the front desk. While Penny sat in front of the TV set eating a burger and fries from the McDonald's drive-thru, Bobby circled ads in the Stamford *Advocate*. First thing in the morning, she'd start making calls. If anybody asked, she'd say she'd been in a car accident.

Penny watched *Sesame Street,* an old episode of *I Love Lucy,* and a repeat of *Happy Days.* Then Bobby got her into the tub and sat on the toilet while Penny blew soap bubbles between her hands and sang the theme song from *Happy Days.* Bobby got down on her knees beside the tub and washed Penny's hair, then sat with the towel-wrapped child on her knees and dried her hair.

"Your eye's all big and purple," Penny said, touching the tip of one tiny finger to her mother's temple.

"I know."

"Does it hurt?" Penny's small face twisted sympathetically.

"A little."

"Poor Mommy," Penny said soberly. "Daddy's bad. Is he gonna come find us?"

"No," Bobby said strongly, her throat starting to close. "We're never going to see him again. Tomorrow I'll find a job, and then we'll look for someplace to live. We're going to stay here."

"Right here?"

"In this town."

"Do they have schools here?"

"Sure they do."

"Where're we gonna live?"

"We'll find a place."

"Where?"

"Maybe by the water," Bobby said. "Wouldn't you like to see the ocean?"

"Yeah." Penny grinned. "We could go swimmin'."

"In the summer we could."

"Did you bring my storybook?"

"Damn! I forgot. I'll get you another one tomorrow. Okay?"

"I like *that* storybook. I don't *want* another one."

"We'll get another copy of that same book, Pen. Don't fuss, please."

"What'm I gonna read before I go to sleep?"

"I don't know," Bobby said tiredly, fitting Penny's nightgown over her head. "How about if I let you watch one more TV show instead?"

"Okay." Penny ran to turn on the set and began changing channels until she found a show that captured her attention.

Bobby checked the door again, making sure it was double-locked and the chain was in place. Then she tried the window and, satisfied it was locked, sat down in the leatherette chair by the desk and lit a cigarette. Penny made a face and waved dramatically at the air, but didn't complain as she usually did. When the show was over, she announced, "I'm going to sleep now."

"That's my good girl," Bobby said, settling the blankets around her. "I'll take a shower now. I won't be long."

"Leave the door open," Penny said as Bobby turned off the light.

Bobby kissed her, then went into the bathroom, leaving the door ajar. Penny was afraid of the dark. The bathroom light would have to stay on all night.

There were large bruises on her hips and thighs and one on her breast. She stood under the hot shower, with the curtain pulled partway back, her eyes on the door as she soaped herself. She thought of Joe bursting into the room and her heart began racing. She had to keep telling herself he didn't know where they were; they'd never see him again. Over and over, she told herself they'd never see him again; he'd never find them.

In bed, with Penny deeply asleep, she lay on her side facing the door. Once she had a job and they'd found a place to live, she'd call her aunt, let her know they were all right. Aunt Helen would never tell Joe where they were. And he knew better than to go anywhere near her. Helen would call the police if she so much as saw his car pulling into the driveway.

Bobby closed her eyes but couldn't relax. Her body still hummed to the motion of the car on the road. And the slightest sound from the parking lot made every muscle in her body go tight. It was almost worse fearing Joe from a distance than it was facing him in the same room.

She turned over, her bruised hips protesting, felt too vulnerable with her back to the door, and turned back. She was wide awake. Slipping out of bed, she went to sit at the desk and smoked another cigarette while she watched Penny sleep. Finally, she lay down again and gazed at the ceiling. Eventually, exhausted, she slept.

It wasn't until they were at McDonald's the next morning, while Penny was having an Egg McMuffin and she was having a coffee, that she realized most of the job ads she'd circled were out of the question. Who was going to look after Penny after school? She knew no one in the area, which meant a full-time job was impossible. What had she been thinking of? She'd have to try to find some kind of live-in work. The domestic ads offered half a dozen possibilities. Cautioning Penny not to move, she went to the restaurant pay phone and began making calls, keeping an eye on Penny and checking the door every few seconds.

Three of the people listened until she mentioned Penny. A child was out of the question. End of call. Two said they'd see her. She got an answering machine at the last place and didn't bother leaving a message. She sat down again and went through every single one of the help wanted ads from start to finish, in every category, even office work for which she had no qualifications. Aunt Helen had been after her and after her to take typing, but Bobby never had. She should've listened to her aunt.

There was an ad for a live-in practical nurse. She didn't have any training but she'd nursed Grandpa until he died, dealing with the bedpan and the medications. She knew how to look after sick people. And the worst that could happen was they'd say no.

"Stay here, hon. I've got one more call to make."

Pen nodded, preoccupied with feeding Mr. Bear the last of the Egg McMuffin.

The woman who answered said, "I can see you this afternoon at four. Let me give you the address."

Bobby wrote it down, then asked for directions.

"You're not from this area?" the woman asked.

"No, ma'am. We're new to the state."

"I see. All right." She gave the directions.

Bobby got them down, then said, "I'll be there at four. Thanks very much."

The woman hung up without even bothering to say good-bye, and Bobby returned to Penny's side, not holding out much hope for that interview. The woman had sounded like the impatient sort, and kind of snooty. God, she was scared. Her money wouldn't last more than a few days. She had to get settled somehow. She couldn't go back to Joe. He'd kill her this time. And she couldn't go to Aunt Helen's again. Not after all the trouble Joe had caused over the years.

"I love you dearly," her aunt had said. "But I can't have that man coming here, threatening me with guns. You've got to get right the way away, Bobby, far enough so he can't find you."

The neighbors had called the police on Joe the last time and after they'd taken him away, they'd said she and Penny could go to a shelter. She'd never even known there were places like that, or people who cared, and she'd wondered why nobody had ever told her about them before.

She'd been amazed to see so many other women with their kids, a lot of them black and blue like her. It was a secret place, and you couldn't give anybody the phone number or say where you were, in case the husbands found out and came around making trouble. It was going to that shelter that first gave her the idea of running away. She'd gone back home to Joe after five days because she'd had no place else to go, but in the back of her mind she had the idea. And that was when she'd started saving, keeping back her change, hiding it in a jar under the back stairs. She'd never actually planned anything. It was just there in her mind in a place she called One Day. And months went by before One Day arrived, and she and Pen got in the Honda and drove away. One Day was now.

Please let one of these people want us, she prayed silently, running a hand over Penny's hair. We really need a miracle.

At the first place the woman who came to the door took one look at her and Penny and said, "I'm sorry. The job's been filled." She took a step back and quietly closed the door.

The woman at the second appointment invited them in and talked baby talk to Penny, who refused to say a word and sat with her arms folded tightly across her chest. Bobby was told what the job entailed: cooking and cleaning for a family of five; they were shown a small room next to the kitchen that would be theirs. Finally, the woman said, "I've got three other women to interview this afternoon. I'll have to let you know."

Bobby gave her the motel number and took Penny back out to the car. She wasn't a bit optimistic about her chances. The woman had never once looked her in the face.

It was too early for the practical nursing appointment but she decided to go along anyway in case she had trouble with the directions. She found the house pretty easily and sat parked at the top of the driveway to wait until four o'clock. It was a lovely house. The lawn out back went right to the water's edge.

"I've got to go to the bathroom," Penny announced.

"You'll have to wait, hon."

"I *can't!*" Penny insisted. "I've got to go *now*."

"Oh, damn. All right. Come on." She and Penny got out of the car and went up the walk to the front door. Bobby felt depressed and frightened and oddly defiant. No one was going to give her a job looking the way she did. Who was she kidding? She and Pen would spend another night in the motel, then use the last of their money to go back home. And maybe for a week or two Joe would be real sweet and sorry. But in a month or six weeks, maybe two months, he'd break some more of her bones and then he'd kill her. All she could do was beg Aunt Helen to take Pen. Joe didn't care enough about Pen to want to kill her. He wouldn't care if Pen went to Aunt Helen's.

The woman who came to the door stared at Bobby's face and said, "What on *earth* happened to you?"

"I was in a car accident. Ma'am, I know I'm early for our appointment but Penny's got to go to the bathroom real bad."

The woman looked down at Penny for a long moment, then sighed and said, "Come on in. The bathroom's at the end of the hall on the right. Can she go alone or do you have to take her?"

"I'll take her, if that's okay."

"Would you like some coffee?" the woman asked, frowning slightly as she looked again at Bobby's face.

"That'd be great. Thanks a lot."

"Fine. The living room's here," the woman pointed. "I'll just get the coffee."

It was the prettiest house Bobby had ever seen. Even the bathroom was pretty with flowered wallpaper and yellow fixtures, bright yellow curtains on the window.

"Who's that lady?" Penny asked, as Bobby helped her to get her jeans down.

"Damn!" Bobby whispered. "I forgot to ask her name. I didn't even tell her mine. She'll think I'm some kind of moron."

"Are we gonna visit?"

"I hope maybe she'll give me a job and let us live here."

"I'd love to live here," Penny said. "It's *nice.*"

"Keep your fingers crossed, hon. It's about time we had a bit of halfway decent luck."

Two

Upon opening the door, Eva's initial reaction was dismay. Over the telephone the woman had sounded strong and capable. It was an impression created by her husky voice and by the directness of her manner. In reality, the husky voice belonged to a tiny woman of no more than five feet, with battered features, dyed blond, badly permed hair, and a child in tow. Eva couldn't imagine this undersized woman tending to Aunt Alma. But she felt sorry for her, and the child had to go to the bathroom, so she invited them inside.

The woman's bruised and swollen face brought Deborah to mind. Eva had blocked off memories of her old friend, of the island and the plantation high on the mountain. It rattled her to think of all that now—her mind racing over the past like a machine speed-viewing a film. She pushed it forcefully away, wanting to keep the past safely distant.

She put coffee, cream, sugar, and two mugs on a tray and carried it to the living room, where the woman and her little girl were sitting side by side on the sofa, waiting.

"I didn't tell you my name," Bobby said at once. "I'm Bobby, and this is Penny."

The woman was, Eva thought, a nervous wreck. Her hands trembled as she accepted a mug of coffee, and her unblemished eye was wide and unblinking.

"I'm Eva Rule. Help yourself to cream and sugar." To the child, she said, "Would you like some juice?"

Penny nodded.

"Say yes, please," Bobby prompted.

"Yes, please," Penny parroted.

"We've got apple, orange, and cranberry," Eva said. "What kind would you like?"

"Apple."

"Say please," Bobby told her, daunted by Eva Rule's good looks and good clothes, by her alternating impatience and kindness.

"Once was enough," Eva said curtly, on her way to the kitchen. The sight of that battered face was painful; it made her angry. She shook her head as she poured the juice. She knew a beating when she saw one. And again an image of Deborah flashed on her mental screen, heightening her irritation. She did *not* want to think about any of that.

"What sort of experience have you had?" she asked Bobby after giving the child the juice.

"I nursed my grandpa until he died," Bobby said. "Fifteen months. I did everything. I'm not afraid of hard work or sick people."

Eva sat back with her coffee, asking, "How long ago was that? And how old are you?"

"Grandpa died eight years ago. I'm twenty-seven. And Penny's six. She's in the first grade."

"I know how to read," Penny announced. "Have you got any books?"

Taken off guard, Eva laughed and said, "Plenty."

"C'n I see them?"

"Hush, Pen." Bobby put a hand on the child's arm. "Just drink your juice."

"When was it you had this 'accident'?" Eva asked.

"Last night," Penny piped up. "Daddy was bad. We're runnin' away."

Bobby lowered her eyes miserably. She should've known she'd never get away with that story of a car accident. Any fool could see she'd got herself beat up. She felt queasy with shame.

Eva nodded. "How far have you run?"

"From Jamestown, New York."

"Why here?" Eva asked, curious.

"I've always wanted to see the ocean," Bobby said, too nervous to drink the coffee. "It's real pretty around here, just like I imagined it."

"What previous work experience have you had?" Eva asked.

"I worked part-time at the Burger King a year and a half, since Pen started school. Who is it needs the nursing?" Bobby looked around as if expecting to see the invalid.

"My Aunt Alma. She had a stroke last year. I came back from the city to be with her."

"The city?"

"New York."

"Oh!" Bobby attempted to smile and her lip split again, a bead of blood welling. She at once opened her bag for a tissue saying, "Sorry," as she dabbed at her lip.

"Why didn't you go to a shelter or something?" Eva asked, both sorry for her and somewhat annoyed by the woman's apologetic attitude.

"It wouldn't've done any good," Bobby said. "We went once, and wound up having to go home. We're never going back to Jamestown," she said with determination. "No matter what happens, we're not going back." She placed a protective arm around the child's shoulders.

"Where are the books?" Penny asked.

Eva looked at the little girl. She was a delicate, very pretty child, with long brown hair caught up in a ponytail; a dainty nose, immense, thickly-lashed deep blue eyes.

"Upstairs," Eva said. "Come on. I'll show you."

"Please don't go to any trouble," Bobby protested.

"It's no trouble." Eva held out a hand and the child at once scooted off the sofa and took hold. "Be right back," Eva told Bobby. "Make yourself comfortable."

"You don't have to..."

"She can look at the books while we talk," Eva said firmly. "Drink your coffee."

Intimidated by the woman's authoritative manner, Bobby took a sip of the strong flavorful brew. She wanted the job so badly she felt like weeping. She wished she knew what to do to convince this woman she could look after her ailing elderly aunt. She couldn't help thinking she'd have more of a chance if she weren't so beat up.

On the way up the stairs, Penny said, "I like it here. What's that?"

"A chair lift so my aunt can get up and down the stairs. Why do you like it here?" Eva was very taken with the directness of the child's manner. Whatever else she might be, Bobby was clearly a good mother. Penny's natural inquisitiveness had obviously been encouraged.

"It's nice. And I like the colors. It's really big," Penny said, looking down the hallway. "What's down there?"

"Bedrooms. We're going in here," Eva said, taking the girl into the small sitting room at the front of the house. "All these are children's books," she told Penny, indicating the bottom three shelves of the bookcase.

"Whose room is this?"

"It's a sitting room," Eva explained.

"Do you have a little girl? Where is she?"

"My little girl's grown up and away at school," Eva said. "Now I'm going downstairs to talk to your mother. Okay?"

"Okay."

Penny was down on her knees, already pulling a book from the shelf as Eva went to the door.

Bobby looked over anxiously as Eva came back into the room, and tried again to smile. "It's real nice of you to let her look at your books. She's a good girl and she'll be real careful with them.''

"How do you feel about old people?'' Eva asked, wishing Bobby would stop apologizing for every last thing. It was an effort to be ingratiating that only served to raise Eva's hackles. She preferred people who possessed a healthy degree of self-confidence. She was, in her own way, as frequently intolerant as her aunt and had no doubt she'd acquired her attitudes as a result of growing up under Alma's guidance. It was inevitable, she'd long thought, that Alma's convictions would have infiltrated her own subconscious. Until her stroke, Alma had been a powerful woman. And while she may have lost some of her physical capabilities, fortunately her mind remained intact.

"I feel okay about them. Is your aunt real old?''

"She's sixty-seven.''

"That's not so old. My grandpa was seventy-four.''

"No,'' Eva agreed, "it's not. You know, I really don't think you'd be up to the job...''

"Please give me a chance,'' Bobby rushed in. "I'm a real hard worker and I don't mind cleaning up messes, or tending to sick folks. I've got a strong stomach.''

"I'm sure you do,'' Eva said, bothered by Bobby's wild, permed hair. She wondered how anyone could find it attractive. Then she chided herself for being so uncharitable, so judgmental. This young woman was poor. Her clothes were cheap, her leather shoulder bag was splitting at the seams. But the child was well dressed and clean. "The final decision will have to be Aunt Alma's,'' she said. "We've had a number of nurses this past year. My aunt is not easy.''

"I'm used to that,'' Bobby said. "It takes a lot to rile me. Please, Mrs. Rule, at least let me meet your aunt. If she doesn't take to me, that's that. But I've got to work, and we need to find someplace to live. I can't go back.'' She was begging, and hated herself for it. But what choice did she have? If she went back, Joe would kill her, maybe kill Penny too. She couldn't let that happen. Begging wouldn't kill her.

Eva thought Aunt Alma would probably eat this little creature alive, then spit out the bones. But you never knew. Alma was the essence of unpredictability. "Sit here a minute while I go have a word with my aunt."

"Sure," Bobby said. "That'll be fine."

Eva went back upstairs. Glancing into the sitting room, she saw the child sprawled on her stomach on the floor, slowly turning the pages of a large picture book. Satisfied, Eva continued on to the master suite at the far end of the hall, knocked, and opened the door.

Alma was in her wheelchair by the window, staring out at the Sound. Eva went to stand beside her, placing a hand on her aunt's jutting shoulder. Alma had lost at least twenty-five pounds since the stroke. Her former roundness was gone, revealing her angular bone structure. "Water's rough today," she observed, looking out. "I've got someone downstairs about the job."

"Another bossy bitch," Alma growled, her s's slurred.

"Just the opposite," Eva said, looking at her aunt's distorted features, the left side permanently downturned from the stroke. "You'll probably scare the hell out of this one." She smiled at her aunt.

"That's no good to me, either," Alma said.

"We've got to have someone," Eva said reasonably. "I can't manage alone and get my work done. We've discussed this until we're blue in the face. And we're running out of applicants. It's been almost two weeks since Freda quit. Much as I love you, I'm falling behind schedule."

"I know." Alma raised her right hand, and Eva grasped it. "I know," she repeated, giving Eva's hand a squeeze, then releasing it. "All right. Bring her on. Let's get it over with."

"She reminds me of Deborah," Eva said, and at once wished she hadn't.

"She's English?"

"No, no. She's nothing like her, really. Forget I said that. I'll go get her. You can be the one to say no. I don't have the heart to do it."

"Oh, Lord." Alma fixed her shrewd eyes on her niece's face. "What's this one, a charity case?"

"In a way. You'll see for yourself."

Eva went halfway down the stairs and summoned Bobby. The young woman got up, clutching her shoulder bag to her side, and hurried to the stairs. Eva led the way along the hall, able almost to feel Bobby's apprehension. "In here," she said, standing to one side to allow the young woman to enter the room. "Aunt Alma," she said, "this is Bobby."

"Good grief!" Alma muttered, eyes widening at the sight of Bobby's face. "Well, come in," she said after a moment. "You'd better sit down."

Bobby went to sit on the edge of the armchair by the window. Eva perched on the side of the bed, interested to see what would happen.

"How'd you get in that condition?" Alma asked bluntly, looking Bobby over from head to toe.

"Her husband," Eva said, thinking to spare the woman further embarrassment. Her aunt was notoriously outspoken, always had been.

"A woman who gets herself beaten's a damned stupid woman," Alma declared. "I can't have someone around here in worse shape than I'm in."

"I've left him," Bobby said quietly. "And my face'll be better in a couple of days. Otherwise, I'm fine. There's nothing wrong with me."

"What're you good for?" Alma asked. "You don't look up to any heavy lifting."

"I can cook and I can clean..."

"We don't need you for that," Alma cut in. "We've got a cleaning woman who comes twice a week. And Eva likes to do the cooking. She finds it therapeutic, for some reason. I always hated cooking.''

"I looked after my grandpa until he died."

"What'd he die of?" Alma demanded to know.

"Stomach cancer," Bobby said. "I cleaned him and fed him and gave him his medicine right till the day he died. There wasn't anybody to help me, either, except for the doctor who came once a week. I'm real strong. I can help you do whatever needs doing."

Alma was about to fire off a remark having to do with her doubts about that when Penny appeared in the doorway, a book in her hand. With a smile, she said, "Hi," and went directly over to Alma. "How come your face goes up and down?"

"Penny!" Mortified, Bobby moved to take hold of the child, but Alma put up a hand to stop her.

"Who're you?" Alma asked the girl.

"My name's Penny Salton and I'm six years old. Are you a granny? Is this *my* granny?" she asked her mother. "I don't have a granny," she told Alma. "Buddy Atkins has two and so does Amy, but I don't have a single one."

"Penny, hush," Bobby said.

"Let her alone!" Alma said. "What's that you've got there?" she asked Penny.

"It's that lady's book." She pointed at Eva, then held the book out for Alma to see. "It's called *Where the Sidewalk Ends*. It's a good story. You want me to read it to you?"

"You can read?"

"Uh-hunh. Want to hear?"

Alma croaked out a laugh. "Come here," she beckoned the child closer. "Let's have a look at you."

Penny held onto the book while Alma studied her face, then asked, "Want me to read it now?"

"Maybe later. Right now I'm talking to your mother. Can you stand here and keep very quiet?"

Penny closed her mouth tightly and nodded firmly.

To Bobby, Alma said, "I raised Eva from the time she was this one's age. I like children. You've got a bright girl here."

"Yes, ma'am," Bobby said politely.

"Frankly, you don't look strong enough to help me in and out of this chair, or my bed, or the tub. I also happen to think that a woman who gets herself beaten more than once is a woman with not a lot of self-respect."

Refusing to be insulted by what, after all, was only the truth, Bobby said, "Nobody's going to touch me or Penny again, no matter what. If I have to, I'll carry you over my shoulder. You're not all that big. My grandpa was twice the size of you. Give me a chance," she pleaded. "Say, two weeks' trial. If it doesn't work out, then we'll go."

Alma studied her for several moments, then turned to Penny. "You want to stay here?" she asked the girl.

"Uh-hunh. You got lots of nice books. You got a TV?"

"You watch a lot of TV?"

"Not a whole lot," Penny said. "My mom doesn't let me."

"Your mom's right," Alma said. "Reading's better for your brain."

"I like reading. I can read all kinds of things."

"All right," Alma said, her eyes still on the child. "Two weeks. When can you start?"

It took Bobby a few seconds to realize Alma was speaking to her. Then she had to swallow before saying, "Tomorrow?"

"Fine. Eva, take her downstairs and work out the details."

Bobby thanked the formidable woman, then moved to take Penny's hand. Penny tucked her hands behind her back, saying, "I wanna stay and visit. C'n I stay?" she asked Alma.

"We'll visit tomorrow," Alma told her.

"Okay." Penny leaned forward and looked into Alma's face, asking, "Are you smiling at me?"

Alma gave another croaking laugh.

"Are you?"

"Penny, come on!" Bobby took hold of her arm. "Thank you very much," she said, following Eva out. "You won't regret it, I promise."

"I'd better not," Alma said, already turning her motorized wheelchair away to face the window.

"You get room and board and two-fifty a week," Eva explained back in the living room. "There's a self-contained apartment downstairs. You can park your car on the far side of the driveway next to the garage. I'll fill you in on Aunt Alma's routine when you get here in the morning."

"What about schools?" Bobby asked. "I'll have to get Penny enrolled."

"We'll take care of everything tomorrow. Be here by nine."

"We gonna live here, Mom?" Penny asked.

"For a little while anyway," Bobby told her. "You leave that book here, Pen."

"She can take it with her," Eva said.

"Are you sure?"

"Quite sure," Eva said, impatient always with people who questioned her stated intentions. "Just take good care of it," she told Penny.

"Oh, I will," Penny promised solemnly.

"Good. Can you find your way back?" Eva asked Bobby.

"Yes, ma'am. Thank you."

"Okay. We'll see you in the morning." Eva went to the front door while Bobby quickly got Penny into her coat. "I hope you're not biting off more than you can chew."

"No, ma'am," Bobby said, looking her directly in the eye. "I don't think so. I'll work hard for you and take real good care of your aunt. And Penny won't be any trouble at all."

"My aunt loves children," Eva said. "She was head mistress of a girls' school for thirty years." Penny was the only reason Alma was willing to go for a two-week trial, but Eva knew it would be cruel to say so.

"We'll be here right at nine," Bobby promised, and hurried with Penny up the driveway to where she'd left the Honda.

Eva stood in the open doorway until the pair had driven off. It was going to be a disaster, she thought. She simply couldn't imagine that tiny female bearing the brunt of Aunt Alma's weight or of her sharp tongue. "We'll see," she said to herself, closing the door. "We shall see."

Bobby got Penny's seat belt fastened, then folded her arms over the steering wheel and let her head drop onto her arms. She was being given a chance. Those two women were going to let her and Penny stay. Yes, it was only a two-week trial, but she knew she could do the work and win them over.

"What'sa matter, Mom?"

Bobby turned to look at her daughter. "Nothing, honey. I'm just real happy."

"You don't look happy." Penny's features drew together into a puzzling frown.

She'd wanted a miracle and she'd got one. It made her want to break down and cry. "I am, honest, Pen." She felt shaky all over, her fingertips buzzing. Too much coffee and no food. "You hungry, honey?"

"Yeah."

"Me too," Bobby said, sniffing back incipient tears. "Let's go eat." She looked over at the white clapboard house with its black-painted shutters, and the Sound beyond. Tomorrow, they'd be starting over. Hoping the Honda wouldn't let them down now, she fit the key into the ignition. The engine turned over at once. She patted the steering wheel, then put the car into gear. Joe would never find them here.

He was more surprised than mad when he'd come home to find the house empty, the kitchen still a mess. After checking the bedrooms, he stood in the kitchen doorway, staring at the footprints in the spaghetti on the floor, feeling his pulse beating in his temples. The stupid bitch had run off again. He'd have to go after her, drag her back home. He could almost feel his fingers grabbing hold of her hair, see her head pulling to one side. Goddamned bitch couldn't do one thing right. He imagined hearing her bones crack as he drove his fists into her. It gave him a momentary high that swelled his chest, made the muscles in his arms tighten and bulge.

"Look at this fuckin' mess!" he muttered, kicking a piece of broken dish halfway across the room. "Son of a bitch."

He thought about having a beer, looked at the shit all over the floor, and changed his mind. He was tired. The hell with it. He turned and went into the bedroom, threw off his clothes and flopped on the bed. Tomorrow after work he'd go over to that goddamned Lor's place, get the bitch and the kid, bring 'em home. He was getting sick and tired of her running off every chance she got. Maybe it was time to teach her a lesson once and for all. But first he'd make her clean that goddamned kitchen on her hands and knees, lick the floor clean with her tongue, boot her in the ass a couple of times while he had her down there.

Maybe she'd found herself a new boyfriend. He wouldn't put it past her. She was always coming on to guys, like the way she sucked up to that weasely nerd who managed the Burger King. Thinking he wasn't clued in to what she was up to, the dumb bitch. He caught her with another guy, he'd whack the both of them, shove the double-barreled up the guy's ass and blow him to kingdom come. Then he'd break every bone in her fucking body before he made her eat his .38. Closing his eyes, he saw a radiant slow-motion explosion of blood. It got him hot, picturing it. If the bitch had been there just then, he'd've put her down on her hands and knees and fucked her brains out.

Tomorrow, he thought, feeling sleep turn his body heavy. Tomorrow five on the dot he'd get in the car and go to Lor's, get the bitch and drag her home by her hair. He'd fix her but good, teach her once and for all who was boss, teach her to say how high when he said jump.

Three

Eva was remembering Montaverde. It was the last thing she wanted to think about, but the memories had more strength just then than she did. It was almost two in the morning and she'd awakened from another in a series of bizarre black-and-white dreams she'd been having lately. They were scenarios spawned, she knew, by anxiety and had started a few months earlier, soon after Melissa had a minor accident with the car. A broken headlight and a mashed fender; no one had been injured, yet the incident triggered the dreams. Her interrupted sleep and the additional workload—caring for her aunt full-time after the departure of the last nurse, as well as trying to keep on schedule with the latest book—was wearing her down. Which was why, perhaps, she lacked the energy to push away these scenes from the past.

Very vividly it all came back: the sagging armchair out on the wide veranda where she'd so often sat and gazed at the tangled, wildly overgrown brush in the immediate foreground and, beyond, at the mountainside sloping downward to the sea. The air had, for much of her stay on the island, been heavy with unshed rain, yet cool because of the altitude. In the kitchen to the right beyond the veranda she could once again hear Deborah slamming pots on the tiled counter and muttering angrily to herself; she could feel the dense air weighing her down as scurrying noises in the underbrush made her heartbeat quicken. She saw the tall grass bend in the wind, and felt once more the overwhelming confusion and helplessness that had gripped her almost from the moment she and Melissa had arrived on the island.

Deborah. She moved into center stage in Eva's mind, and Eva felt anew the pain she'd successfully buried for so long. She remembered with perfect clarity their first meeting. She'd been spending a semester of her senior year at college in London, living in a bed-sitting room in a big old house in West Kensington. On a Friday afternoon about three weeks into her stay she'd gone down to the ground floor to use the telephone but had to wait because the most beautiful girl she'd ever seen was making a call. Eva had sat down on the stairs, trying not to gape when the girl turned, gave her a brilliant smile, and signaled she'd be finished in a minute or two.

Deborah. Tall and slim but with an aura of strength; wide-eyed, enormous brown eyes above pronounced slanting cheekbones, full lips over flawless, very white teeth, dimples in her cheeks; skin the color of creamy coffee; thickly curling black hair cropped almost to her well-shaped skull. She had radiated health and energy and extraordinary self-confidence.

The call had lasted another four or five minutes. Then the girl put down the receiver and, with another dazzling smile, said, "Sorry. He did rather go on and on."

"Oh, that's okay," Eva had said, taken by her low mellow voice and charming English accent.

"You're American?"

"That's right."

"What part of America?" Deborah had asked with interest.

"Connecticut."

"My dad was American," Deborah had told her. "From Virginia. He was in the navy and Montaverde was one of his ports of call. I never knew him, actually," she said thoughtfully, leaning on the banister.

"That's too bad," Eva said, assuming the man had died.

"He already had a family in America," Deborah explained. "But he did evidently care very much for my mum. And he sent money for my care for years. Until Mum and I came over here, actually." She was silent for a moment, then gave a soft laugh and said, "Here I am nattering away at you and we haven't even met. I'm Deborah," she'd said, extending her hand.

Eva introduced herself, then, unable to suppress her curiosity, asked, "Are you a model?"

"Model, singer, actress, what-have-you." Deborah had glanced at her watch, then said, "I must run. I've got an audition in the West End in forty minutes."

"I'm in room five," Eva said. "Let's get together sometime."

"Lovely. Sorry about taking so long on the blower." Deborah started up the stairs, then turned back. "What about a drink later at the pub over the road?"

"Great. I have a class this afternoon but I should be back by five."

"So should I. Perfect. I'll come knock you up then."

And that was the beginning.

Remembering was like ripping the stitches from a newly-made incision. Eva couldn't bear it. She threw off the blankets and went into the bathroom, switched on the light, and stood shielding her eyes with one hand, blinking rapidly. Why was all this coming back to her now? The sight of that small battered woman and the knowledge that she was going to be living here in the house had unblocked her memory. She grabbed a Dixie cup from the wall dispenser, ran the cold water, drank down a cupful, then turned to the mirror.

She looked like hell, the shadows beneath her eyes deepening with each passing day. Every night she prepared for bed, longing to lose herself in seven or eight hours of untroubled sleep. And instead she found herself dreaming in black and white, like some film noir from the late forties—all slanted shadows and sudden unsettling pools of blinding light. And now Deborah. It was too much.

With a weary sigh, she turned off the light and went downstairs to the kitchen. In the dark, she filled the kettle and put it on to boil. While she waited, she sat, head in hand, at the table and, unable to help herself, studied mental snapshots of her old friend.

Anticipating having a child in the house again led Alma to thinking of Randy Wheeler. Her eyes fixing on an indefinite point in the darkness, she saw the two of them sitting on the glider on the porch of the old house in Greenwich, holding hands and rocking gently. It was 1948, she was twenty-four years old, and she and Randy were discussing their plans for the future. He'd gone back to Yale shortly after being released from the army, and he'd be graduating, finally, in a few weeks' time. He already had several job leads, one in Hartford, two in the city. As soon as he secured a position, they'd steal away and get married. And she'd stop feeling immoral and guilty. They'd be able to sleep together in the same bed for the rest of their lives. There would be no more furtive lovemaking in dark places, no more seedy cabin courts, no more secrecy. She'd never been happier. The years of anxiety were over, ended with the war. He'd come home intact, an answered prayer. She had her teaching job. Soon he'd be working, too. The very air was rich with promise, scented with the fragrance of lilacs. His hand was large and finely shaped, the long fingers laced loosely through hers.

The glider swayed gently back and forth in her recall. She sat on the darkened porch with her head on Randy's shoulder, breathing in his scent and the sweetness of the lilacs. Music from the radio drifted through the living room window where her parents and her sister were talking quietly, and she hummed along softly. She was young and healthy, and felt incredibly fortunate. The future was waiting, its invitation in the breeze, in her veins. She lifted a hand and touched it to Randy's face, her fingertips reading the strong angle of his jaw, the smooth plane of his cheek, the uptilting corner of his wide mouth. "I love you," she whispered, willing herself to remember forever each detail of this quiet moment. "I'll always love you," she told him, "always."

She shook her head suddenly, shoving aside the memory. Why bother rehashing ancient history? It was pointless, self-defeating. Yet, in the past year she'd been caught up in a review of her life that occupied quite a number of her late-night hours. The stroke had forced her to reevaluate, to look backward, trying to pinpoint critical moments, trying to find the juncture at which she might have taken another direction in order to have arrived at an altered present.

It was ridiculous. The stroke had been her destiny. Nothing she might have done earlier in her life would have prevented its happening. Yet, arbitrarily, she couldn't stop conjecturing on the possibilities. It did no good reminding herself that she was satisfied with the course her life had taken, because on a certain level that simply wasn't the truth. Yes, she'd had a successful career. And, yes, she'd derived pleasure from her single lifestyle. But because of Randy Wheeler she'd made choices that had taken her in a direction she'd never thought to go. If she'd been asked upon turning twenty-four about her expectations, she'd have quickly replied she was looking forward to being a wife and a mother. Having a career that spanned forty-five years wasn't at all what she'd anticipated.

She and her younger sister, Cora, had grown up in a happy household. Father was a transplanted Scotsman who'd come to America as a young man hired to teach English at a private boys' school in Greenwich. Mother had been a secretary at the school. They'd met within days of his arrival, married six months later, and become parents just over a year after that, in 1924, when Alma was born. Mother continued to work until she got pregnant again when Alma was three. Thereafter she remained at home to take care of her girls, while Father went on to head the English department of the school and, ultimately, to take over as headmaster.

It was a household filled with books and music and laughter, even through the Depression years. Father was a cheerful man who seemed perpetually surprised by his good fortune in having a trio of females under his wing. He would, without warning, suddenly burst into song and scoop up one or both of his daughters to go dancing around the room. Mother was a clever, imaginative woman, whose thinking was ahead of her time. She encouraged her girls to be independent and self-reliant, to stand firmly on their own two feet. There was never any doubt that both girls would go to college and acquire marketable skills.

"You never know," their mother often told them, "when you'll need to provide for yourselves. With a good, solid education, you'll always be able to work."

Alma was the more academic of the two sisters, invariably to be found curled up in some corner with a book in her hands. Cora had a romantic nature, was given to long idle hours spent on the window seat, humming to herself and dreaming of the wonderful husband she'd one day have. She did well enough in school but not nearly so well as Alma, who, while harboring somewhat romantic dreams of her own, was too pragmatic by nature to place her faith entirely in some nebulous fantasy of the future. She wanted to be like her tall, strong-featured father, whom she so much resembled: principled yet fair, dedicated but open-minded, generous but not foolish, fun-loving but not frivolous.

She and her sister got along well as youngsters, but when Alma turned thirteen she began to be at first irritated and later contemptuous of what she perceived as serious flaws in Cora's character. Cora had a tendency to be lazy, both physically and mentally, and she spent what Alma considered an inordinate amount of time studying herself in mirrors. Cora was vain, and Alma had no time for vain, silly girls. Cora was small, like their mother, with their mother's tidy features and milky skin. Cora took pride in ridiculous things, like her tiny feet and narrow wrists. Alma would have found her altogether unbearable had it not been for Cora's contagious laugh and her adventurous nature. Cora was good company, always ready to go off on the spur of the moment, always willing to give in to impulse. There were countless occasions when Alma's displeasure was eradicated by Cora's suddenly, in the midst of an argument, exclaiming, "I know! Let's go get the train into the city and see a show," or, "Let's bundle up and go tobogganing." They could be ready to tear each other's hair out when Cora would suddenly smile and say, "Let's do some baking. I have a craving for peanut butter cookies." Alma could never resist her sister's impetuosity. And most of the good times they had growing up were a result of Cora's sudden inspirations.

But they continued to grow further apart during Alma's high school years. The three years separating them were almost unbridgeable by the time Cora was a freshman and Alma was a senior. Cora's concerns were primarily social. She worried aloud over crushes she had on this boy or that one, while Alma studied college brochures and worked to keep her grades at the highest possible level. Since Alma had never had anything remotely resembling a crush on any of the boys she met prior to her departure for college, she deemed Cora's behavior to be addle-headed and female in the worst possible sense. And Alma's contempt for cute female behavior was limitless. She disliked simpering, coy, helpless-acting women, and Cora was becoming one of them. By the time Alma began college, the sisters had nothing left in common; they'd evolved into politely interested strangers who maintained a civilized attitude toward one another out of deference to their parents.

By twenty-two, Alma had attained her Bachelor of Arts degree, had completed her teacher's training, and had secured a position teaching English at a private girls' school in Stamford. Her parents were proud of her. She was proud of herself. Cora was sweetly congratulatory but primarily jealous, because Alma, who'd never had the least interest in boys, was engaged to Randy Wheeler, whom she'd met through mutual friends during her senior year at Barnard.

From the instant she set eyes on him, Alma was lost to Randy Wheeler. It wasn't just his looks that pleased her, although that's what drew her initially. What captured her utterly was the combination of his deep, baritone speaking voice and the wonderfully intelligent things he had to say. He was well-bred and effortlessly charming; he was handsome, and attentive, and he, too, fell in love, he claimed, at first sight. They saw each other whenever he could get a few free hours to drive down from Yale.

In the meantime, there was Alma's career. To her surprise, she not only loved teaching, she also loved the girls. She felt a powerful affinity for the youngsters who came under her supervision. She saw these children as individuals and was interested in every one of them, even the difficult ones. Like her mother, she was clever and imaginative, and she was able to interest her students in learning. She felt no qualms about deviating from the accepted classroom behavior and encouraged the girls to open their minds to new ideas. She kept control, but with a gentle hand. She was able to give the very best of herself without hesitation, without fear, in almost the same way she gave herself to Randy Wheeler. Her reward came in the form of well-written essays, and in the discovery now and again of a girl with special ability. In the end, her job was her salvation.

Cora, who favored their mother in looks but not in temperament, found college too demanding, and dropped out after her freshman year to go to secretarial school.

Subsequently she went to work for an insurance agency in Greenwich, where she met Willard Chaney and fell madly, hopelessly in love. Alma privately doubted it would last, convinced Cora had set her sights on Willard only because she was so envious of her older sister. But Alma was later forced to concede that Cora's affection for the man was genuine. Cora baked special treats for him, knitted him somewhat misshapen sweaters and argyle socks; she tended to him when he came down with a cold and treated him with tender deference. She confided to Alma that she liked the feeling she had when she was with Willard of being small and in need of protection. This confidence turned Alma's stomach, but she merely smiled and allowed Cora to prattle on. Her sister was happy. Alma would never have begrudged her that.

They married after an engagement lasting two years, in 1946, and in 1948, shortly after Randy Wheeler left Alma's life forever, Cora gave birth to her only child, Eva.

From the moment of her birth, Alma was devoted to her niece. Eva brought the sisters together again by providing them with a common focus. At that point, having lost all faith in men and having secretly vowed never again to permit herself to be vulnerable to any man the way she had to Randy Wheeler, Alma saw her relationship with Eva as being the closest she was ever likely to come to motherhood. It also provided her with an outlet for all the loving instincts that had been so abruptly stifled with Randy's departure from her life.

To her credit, Cora never gloated over the collapse of Alma's romance. Alma had expected it; she'd steeled herself to cope. But Cora, upon hearing of the broken engagement, simply said, "I'm so very sorry," and gave her sister a hug that was so caring and consoling that Alma came dangerously close to behaving like a silly female by breaking down and weeping in her younger sister's arms. Fortunately, she managed to contain herself. And Cora had the wits never again to refer to the subject. Instead, she shared her child, insisting that Alma knew far more about children than she ever would. Which, in retrospect, Alma knew was a kindly gesture prompted by a magnanimous spirit. Cora had been a truly generous woman.

Alma's devotion to her niece had been a very good thing, as fate would have it. In many ways it eased matters considerably when circumstances forced her to take on the role of Eva's mother, a role she'd enjoyed pretending to play on those occasions when Cora entrusted her child into Alma's care for a weekend so that she and Willard might get away for a brief holiday.

In the darkness, Alma sighed, thinking of poor Cora and remembering the little girl Eva had once been. It eased her, thinking of that trusting child and her strong, capable thirty-year-old self, and she closed her eyes, picturing Eva constructing a fort with old cartons and some towels on the back lawn.

Bobby thought she'd heard a noise in the parking lot. Slipping from the bed, she tiptoed across the room to peer out between the plastic-lined drapes. Nothing. A dozen cars sitting under the orange overhead lights that illuminated the area. A white cat with black patches on its fur sauntered across the lot toward the dumpster at the far end. Bobby let the drapes fall closed and looked over to where Penny lay sleeping. No one was ever going to hurt her baby. *No one, not ever again.*

Opening her bag, she got out a Marlboro, lit it, and sat down on the leatherette chair by the desk. Tomorrow morning their lives would begin again. She took a puff of the cigarette and inhaled deeply. Only a few more hours and she and Pen would be moving into that fine old house. Oh, she knew they'd never have hired her if it hadn't been for Pen. Everyone loved her girl. Ever since she'd been a baby people had been stopping to fuss over her, saying what a beautiful child she was, what a clever child she was.

What was that? She dropped the cigarette into the ashtray and moved to the window to look out again through a crack in the curtains. The cat was walking daintily around the rim of the dumpster. A shadow to the left. Bobby's eyes darted in that direction. Someone was out there. She held her breath, waiting, scanning the lot. Suddenly a figure rose up from between the cars, and her heart gave a massive leap in her chest. Joe. With his shotgun.

Frantic, she flew across the room, lifted Penny into her arms and carried her into the bathroom, turning the lock as, with a roar, the shotgun went off and the motel room door flew clattering off its hinges. With Penny clutched to her chest, she huddled in the shower stall as Joe began shouting. "Get the hell out here, bitch!"

They were going to die. The doorknob rattled. Then the door shuddered as he kicked at it. She cradled Penny's head to her breast. Nowhere to go. Another kick at the door. Then the distinctive crack of the gun barrel as he opened it and reloaded. Please God don't let us die this way please God. A tremendous crash as the door exploded into the room. Somebody help us, please don't let this happen. Joe stepped over the threshold, grinning, his teeth seeming to glow in the darkness.

"When're you ever gonna learn?" he asked, grinning, grinning, as his hand wound itself into her hair and he gave a mighty yank that sent her spilling to the floor, half-in half-out of the stall, Penny squirming fearfully beneath her weight.

Please God please God please . . .

Fueled by terror, she groped her way upward through the dense layers of sleep, fighting off the ropy tentacles of exhaustion, and burst awake like a diver surfacing into the early morning emptiness of the ugly motel room, gasping, her heart drumming painfully against her ribs.

A quick look to reassure herself Pen was okay, sleeping soundly, Mr. Bear secure in the bend of her arm. Then she lifted her legs over the side of the bed and let her head come forward until it was resting on her knees. She concentrated on controlling her breathing, slowing it down, down, until the panic subsided. After several minutes she reached for her watch on the bedside table and tilted it until she was able to read the time. Almost five. The hair at her forehead and on the back of her neck was wet. Sweat ran down her sides, collecting in the folds of her belly. She returned the watch to the bedside table and stood up, holding the nightgown away from her body. Groggy, she walked over to the desk, opened her purse for a cigarette, then sat down in the chair, the leatherette cool against the backs of her legs.

Holding the unlit cigarette, she thought about the two women in that house. The younger one hadn't wanted to hire her. She didn't like me, Bobby thought. Yet she'd been kind, offering coffee, taking Pen up to see her books. I'll make them like me, she promised herself, one hand lifting the damp hair off her neck. They'll never be sorry they gave me a chance.

Alma was already awake when Eva came up with her breakfast tray.

"You're up early," Eva said with a smile, setting the tray on the bureau while she went to help her aunt to a sitting position.

"Bad night," Alma said. "And from the sound of it, another rotten day."

"According to the forecast, it's supposed to clear up by midday." Eva set the tray across her aunt's lap, took her own cup of coffee from it, and went to sit in the armchair by the window. "How do you feel?"

"The same as every other day: handicapped, angry, bored witless."

"I can't help thinking we're making a mistake taking on this woman."

Alma stirred cream into her coffee, then set the spoon down carefully. "I like the child," she said. "The child is special."

"She's very bright, I agree."

"She'll keep us on our toes," Alma said, getting a firm grip on the cup before lifting it to her mouth. "We could use a bit of that."

"I don't know about that. It's not as if I'm short of things to do."

"You wouldn't be happy unless your dance card was full."

Eva laughed as Alma picked up a strip of bacon and aimed it at the right side of her mouth, then took a healthy bite. "Do you dream in color or black and white?"

"What?"

"You heard me."

"Color, naturally." Alma gave her a sharp look. "Is this some kind of imbecilic psychological test?"

"No, I'm serious. I've been dreaming lately in black and white. I think it must mean something."

"Maybe it means you're too lazy to fill in the mental colors."

"Maybe," Eva allowed with a smile. "Whatever it means, it's strange."

"You're just missing Mellie."

"No, I honestly don't. We need time apart. It's good for both of us. She's become very much her own woman since she started college last year. We no longer argue the way we used to. When she's home now, we're able to appreciate each other."

"All right," Alma relented. "I'm missing her." She lifted a triangle of toast and took a bite. "I miss all the children."

"I know you do," Eva said quietly. "It's why you agreed to give that waif a two-week trial: because of the child."

"It's probably why you let the woman in in the first place," Alma countered. "All this talk about Mellie being her own woman doesn't fool me. You miss having a child around the house as much as I do."

"No, I honestly don't," Eva said, holding her cup with both hands and gazing into its depths. "Oh, I admit that first week of her freshman year I had some trouble believing my little girl was gone forever. That was kind of rough. But I don't miss picking up after her, or the arguments, or her sleeping until one in the afternoon. I think what I actually miss is her dependency. And she hasn't been dependent for years."

"I always thought it a great pity you didn't have more children."

"We probably would have," Eva said, as she always did when they had this particular conversation.

"You should've married again."

"What about you?" Eva asked. "It wasn't as if you didn't have chances."

"I lost interest in the state of marriage long ago. Being in love takes too much out of a person. The emotional investment's too big."

"You know I agree, so why do you keep telling me I should have married again?"

"Because you should have," Alma said implacably. "It worked for you."

"It would have worked for you too. But you chose not to try."

"We've wandered very far off the topic. I thought we were discussing the child."

With a laugh, Eva said, "We were." She got up, saying, "I'm going to go down and get the place ready for them. I'll be back in a while for the tray."

"Eva?"

"What?"

"That's a very frightened young woman. Let's try not to make things difficult for her."

Surprised, Eva paused in the doorway. "You liked her, didn't you?"

"I admire her courage," Alma said. "It took genuine grit for her to show up here looking that way."

"Or genuine stupidity," Eva snapped.

"I don't think so. I think she's a brave little thing."

"I can't believe this is you," Eva declared. "You've never had anything but contempt for weak women. You can't stand stupid people, people who are slow to catch the conversational fastballs you throw, people who get themselves into trouble then go back for more."

"Listen!" Alma said. "Anyone who'd offer to carry *me* over her shoulder has grit." She gave one of her croaking laughs and waved her toast in the air.

Eva smiled, and said, "I thought that was pretty good too. I'll be back shortly."

On impulse, Eva stopped in the sitting room and pulled several of Mellie's old favorites from the bookshelf. She'd put them downstairs for the child to read. As she went down the stairs, she tried to think of polite ways of suggesting to Bobby that she should do something about that ungodly mess of frizzy bleached hair.

Alma ate slowly, chuckling to herself between mouthfuls of toast and egg, as she recalled the way the child had offered to read to her. Oh, yes, she thought with satisfaction. This was a child with enormous potential. And regardless of what Eva thought, the mother did have grit. If nothing else, it was bound to be an interesting two weeks.

Four

Bobby had expected at best a small room she'd share with Penny. But Eva led them downstairs to an entire self-contained apartment, with a living room, a good-sized bedroom with twin beds, a bathroom, and a kitchen. There was even a small color TV set in the living room.

"It's real nice," Bobby said softly, giving Eva a shy smile.

"Really, not real," Eva corrected her. "Leave your bags for the moment and let me show you the rest of the house."

"This is *my* bed!" Penny stated, depositing her backpack and Mr. Bear on the bed nearest the wall.

"Okay, honey," Bobby agreed. "Come on with me now."

Eva led Bobby and Penny back to the first floor, where she pointed out the laundry room off the sunny spacious kitchen, and the utility room adjacent. After a quick tour of the second floor, which consisted of four bedrooms and the small sitting room at the front of the house, Eva said, "Let's have some coffee and get the paperwork out of the way. Then I'll drive you over to the school."

"C'n I visit with Granny?" Penny asked, hanging back at the top of the stairs.

Bobby was about to say no, but Eva preempted her, saying, "Knock first. Then go in."

"Okay." Penny scooted down the hall to knock at Alma's door.

Bobby wanted to say that she hoped Penny wasn't being a nuisance but decided to keep silent. These women would be quick to let her know if and when Pen was making a pest of herself.

In the kitchen, Bobby sat as directed at the round white table while Eva got them both coffee.

"I'll need your Social Security number," Eva said, putting on her reading glasses and reaching for a file folder before settling opposite Bobby at the table.

Bobby recited the number and watched Eva make a note of it, deciding this was a woman who didn't waste time on idle chitchat. Bobby had never encountered anyone quite like her, or like her aunt. She'd always thought well-to-do people didn't come right out and say things straight to your face. She'd imagined them to be subtler, to have less direct ways of making themselves understood. Obviously, she'd been wrong. If anything, the two women of this household said straight out exactly what they thought. Like the way the both of them had asked first thing what happened to her. Lor or Aunt Helen would've pretended not to notice, waiting for her to tell them.

"Eventually, you'll have to reregister your car," Eva was saying, "and transfer the insurance coverage. Do you have health insurance?"

"No, ma'am."

Eva looked at her for a moment over the rims of her glasses. "You should have some," she said. "Children do get sick."

"We couldn't ever afford the premiums," Bobby said.

"If things work out and you stay on, we'll have to make arrangements to get you some health coverage. In the past, we've shared the cost with our nurses."

"Yes, ma'am."

"Call me Eva," she said somewhat impatiently.

"All right."

"And call Alma by her name. Neither of us cares overly for formalities."

"All right," Bobby agreed, not entirely certain she knew what the woman meant.

"You'll have to keep track of your income for taxes. If you stay, I'll introduce you to my accountant and he'll get you set up to pay quarterly estimated taxes as a self-employed individual."

"Okay," Bobby nodded.

"Right," Eva said, closing the folder. "Now, Alma's usually awake by seven-thirty, and I take up her break-fast. At eight, you'll be expected to help her out of bed to the bathroom. She prefers to manage the toilet on her own, but she needs help in and out of the tub, and she can't dress without assistance."

"Okay."

"Once she's dressed, she likes to come downstairs. At this time of the year she spends the morning in the living room, reading and listening to music. Since I work from roughly nine until two or two-thirty, you'll be responsible for fixing lunch for the two of you. Otherwise, I do all the cooking. After lunch, Alma takes her nap. At four she gets up and comes downstairs again until dinner. Some eve-nings she'll watch a bit of television. She prepares for bed between ten and eleven. And that's roughly her day. You're free in between times to tend to your own affairs, al-though we'd prefer you to let us know in advance if you're going to be out of the house." What a bleak recitation, Eva thought. No mention of friends because Alma had cut everyone off in the past year. And, aside from Charlie, Eva hadn't seen many of her own friends since her aunt's stroke. There hadn't been time.

"That sounds fine."

"You and Penny will dine with us in the evening. You'll help Alma cut her food and so forth."

Bobby smiled. "I do that for Pen anyway."

"Alma's entire left side is critically weakened as a result of the stroke," Eva continued, as if Bobby hadn't spo-ken. "That affects her balance and, of course, her ability to move around. Which is where you come in. She's fairly mobile in the wheelchair but otherwise requires assistance in getting from one place to another. We have a van that's equipped with a ramp, and I try to take her out at least once a week for some fresh air. The physical therapist comes on Thursdays, and she sees her doctor in Greenwich every other Monday. Saturday afternoons she spends an hour in the pool at the Y. It helps her keep her muscles toned to a degree. She looks forward to her swim. Until she had the stroke, my aunt was a very active woman. She played golf and tennis and traveled extensively. Anyway, I usually take her to the pool, but there may be an occasion when I'm not free. Then you'll have to go with her. Can you swim?"

"Yes, ma ... Yes."

"Good."

"You'll get into the swing of our routine fairly quickly. Now, if you haven't any questions, I'll take you and Penny over to the school."

"How's she gonna get there and back every day?"

"School bus," Eva said. "It'll pick her up and bring her back to the top of the driveway."

"Is she gonna need lunches?"

"You can either make it for her or buy lunch tickets for the school cafeteria. My daughter hated school food. Penny probably does too."

"She hates it all right. How old's your girl?" Bobby asked.

"Twenty."

"And she's away at school?"

"She's at college in New Hampshire."

"Oh! That's real nice."

"Really nice," Eva corrected automatically.

"Were you a teacher or something?" Bobby asked.

At this, Eva laughed. It changed her entirely. She was suddenly no longer austere and business-like, but friendly and very pretty. Bobby smiled in response.

"I'm a writer," Eva explained. "I'm forever correcting people. You'll get used to it."

"What d'you write?" Bobby asked with genuine interest.

"Novels," Eva answered flatly, setting aside her glasses and the folder, then glancing at her watch. "Why don't you get Penny while I put on my coat?"

It was all so easy Bobby could hardly believe it. Penny was whisked off to join the first grade class within fifteen minutes. The principal assured Bobby the driver on that route would be notified of the additional stop and Penny would be dropped at the top of the driveway by three-fifteen that afternoon.

Clutching her lunch tickets, Penny waved everyone good-bye and happily went skipping off with one of the secretaries to meet her new teacher and classmates.

A few forms were completed, and that was that. Bobby was back in the car with Eva, who took a somewhat circuitous route home in order to point out the nearest shopping center and supermarket, the post office, and the bank.

"You'll probably want to open an account," she told Bobby. "I'll be paying you by check."

"I guess so," Bobby agreed, wondering what to do about her mail. Not that she got much. Maybe she'd have the post office forward it to Aunt Helen, and Helen could send along anything important. She'd call her later and ask if that was okay. She glanced over at Eva, admiring her smartly-cut tweed coat. This woman and her aunt had money. A nice house, a special van, and this cushy car that was some kind of import. Joe would've known right off what kind of car it was. He'd always been crazy for cars. Thinking of him, she scanned the oncoming traffic, fully expecting to see the Firebird cruising the streets, looking for her.

Trying to push away her sudden fear, she turned her attention back to Eva. She had a pretty profile, with a rounded chin and kind of a pointy nose, big gray-green eyes, long dark hair tied at the back of her neck with a black bow. She wore a wedding band on her left hand and a big diamond ring on her right.

"You divorced?" Bobby asked, surprised by her own boldness.

"Widowed," Eva answered, looking over briefly.

"Oh, that's too bad."

"It's been a long time," Eva said with a slight shrug. "My husband went off on a business trip sixteen years ago and had a heart attack in his hotel room."

"He must've been real young."

"He was thirty."

"That's awful," Bobby said with immediate sympathy. "It must've come as a terrible shock to you."

"It was awful," Eva confirmed. "Melissa was four at the time. She kept asking for him for months. Eventually, she seemed to forget. But when she turned twelve, she asked to have a photograph of him. She's kept it with her ever since."

"It must've been hard on her, a little girl with no daddy."

"What about you?" Eva asked. "How has it been for Penny with a father who likes to use his fists?"

"Joe's never cared much about Pen," Bobby said quietly. "See, he never wanted her in the first place. It's 'cause he started hitting her too that we ran away. Long as she stayed out of his way, it was okay. But lately, the past few months, if he started in on me and she came in, he'd slap her around. I couldn't let him do that."

"No," Eva said soberly, "you couldn't. Does he have any idea where you've gone?"

With alarm, Bobby said quickly, "No! I don't ever want to see him again."

"Really?" Eva's eyebrows lifted as if she didn't believe what Bobby was telling her.

"I don't," Bobby enunciated carefully, "*ever* want to see him again."

"I'll make the lunch today," Eva said, "then I'll come up with you to get Aunt Alma, show you how the chair lift works."

It was Bobby's job to shift Alma from the wheelchair to the lift. It wasn't difficult. The woman was tall and big-boned but not especially heavy. Since the lift was on the right-hand side of the stairs, it was simply a matter of Bobby's positioning herself on Alma's weakened left side, draping the woman's lifeless arm across her shoulders and, with an arm around her waist, directing Alma sideways and down into the chair lift. She could feel Alma helping, could smell the woman's perfume, and at the moment Alma was safely deposited into the conveyance, Bobby felt a wrenching pang of sympathy for her. It had to be terrible to lose control of yourself that way, to go from being someone strong and in charge to someone needing help with almost everything.

Eva showed her how to collapse the wheelchair, then carried it down the stairs and reopened it at the bottom. When the slow-moving lift arrived, the procedure was repeated again in reverse. From that point, Alma insisted on driving herself along the hallway to the kitchen, where the table was set for lunch.

It was a simple meal of soup and sandwiches, but Bobby was embarrassed to eat in front of these women. She was convinced they'd find fault with her table manners just as they found fault with the way she talked. She took tiny bites of the baked ham and Swiss cheese sandwich, finding it hard to swallow. Her mouth was still very sore and this, combined with her uneasiness, made her even more self-conscious. Neither of the women appeared to take any notice of her. Alma started in asking Eva about some guy named Charlie, and Eva said they'd be going out Saturday night. Charlie had tickets for a play at the Long Wharf Theater in New Haven.

Bobby pretended to be busy with her food, not wanting to appear as if she were listening. But she couldn't help hearing, and wondered if Charlie was Eva's boyfriend. The possibility that Eva had a boyfriend lent the woman a new dimension, and Bobby again covertly studied her, as she had earlier in the car. Men would probably find her attractive, Bobby thought, even if she did like to correct everybody's grammar. She was slim but had a good shape, with a nice small waist and quite a big bust.

Every few minutes Bobby looked over at the back door, imagining Joe charging through it with a shotgun under one arm, a handgun in the other, a grin on his face. It kept her stomach in knots. It didn't matter that there was no way he could know where she was, she couldn't stop expecting him to come crashing in.

Eva had the impression that Bobby was trying to hide behind the frizzy curtain of her hair. She watched her take tiny bites of her food, saw the way her eyes kept going to the door, and knew she was afraid. Deborah had been angry and defiant, her dark brown eyes wide with challenge, her spine straight as a rule. She'd never cringed or cowered. Yet she'd appeared to tolerate the beatings. Now, as then, Eva couldn't help wondering if there were some cultural aspect to Deborah's behavior that she'd failed to perceive or comprehend. After all, despite her British public school education, Deborah and her mother had been West Indians, and Eva knew all too little about social customs in the islands. During her stay on Montaverde, it had seemed to her to be a male-dominated society. It had been another era as well, a time when wife-beating wasn't something discussed on talk shows and on the front cover of *Newsweek*.

Eva had gone to the island knowing very little about Deborah's relationship with Ian. She'd met the man only twice before, once soon after his and Deborah's hasty marriage when Melissa was a newborn, and again just before she and Ken left England when Mellie was six months old. Both times Eva had felt uncomfortable, in part because Ian seemed so unlikely a partner for Deborah. For one thing, he was almost fifteen years older than she and appeared deeply set in his ways, while Deborah had always been spontaneous, a free spirit. The fact that he was white didn't faze Eva in the least. Deborah had dated any number of white men, and Eva didn't believe in any form of racial discrimination. No, what bothered her about him were his protracted silences when he contributed almost nothing to the conversation, and his penetrating, somehow judgmental sidelong stares. His elongated features seemed to have been shaped into a perpetual sneer.

At the time, she had told herself she was being hypocritical, but she couldn't help feeling there was something about Ian that smacked of contrivance. For Deborah's sake, she'd wanted to like Ian. But his three-piece suits, his club tie, his sports car, his mannerisms, and his constantly referring to himself as "one," all struck her as pretentious. One said, one did, one thought, one would rather. It irritated Eva, and after that second meeting with Deborah and Ian at their new house in Newington Green, when she and Ken were back in their denuded flat, the baby sleeping in her carry-cot while they packed the last of the boxes, she'd had to ask Ken what he'd thought.

"He's a pompous jerk," Ken had said. "I can't figure out what the hell Deb's doing with him."

"Neither can I," Eva admitted. "There's more to it than her being pregnant. But what?"

"Don't know. Maybe it's money," he offered. "Maybe it's security."

"From what I can gather, they bought the house with her savings."

"Well," Ken had said with a grin, "maybe it's love. You never can tell what attracts two people."

Just like Ken, she thought then and now. He'd been living proof of her secret conviction that men were far more romantic than women. And all at once, added to the discomfort of remembering Deborah was the pain of missing Ken. No longer acute, but pain nonetheless at recalling his sweetness and humor. It was a reawakening of the same sorrow that had prompted her finally, more than six months after the fact, to write to Deborah on the island, telling her about Ken's death.

Deborah had written back at once, sympathetically suggesting that a change of scene might do her good. Why not bring Melissa and spend a month on the island? Melissa would have Deborah's little boy, Derek, to play with, and Eva could help with the children while Deborah and Ian oversaw the construction of their new house. "Ian's as keen as I am to have you come," Deborah had written, "and the island's beautiful. I'd forgotten just how beautiful. As I told you ages ago, I was only eight when Mum took me to England, so I scarcely remembered it after so many years. When my uncle Alfred died and I inherited the land last year, Ian felt it was the perfect time to return. He was fed up with practicing law and wanted to make a new start. So here we are, and I'm longing to see you. I haven't seen Melissa since she was a baby, and you've never seen Derek. It's been too long. Getting on for five years. Please say you'll come, darling. I miss you."

The invitation had seemed providential. Eva had been emotionally paralyzed by Ken's death. She needed a break. An island in the Caribbean sounded idyllic. Mellie would have a playmate and open spaces to run around in, and Eva would finally see Deborah again. Without stopping to think about it, she wrote back saying she'd love to come in eight weeks' time, when Melissa's play school group closed down for the summer.

There followed an exchange of letters while they worked out the details, and Eva actually became excited about something for the first time since Ken's death. It wasn't

until the plane had landed and she saw Ian standing at
Deborah's side, watching her and Mellie cross the tarmac,
that she remembered her dislike of the man. And by then
it was too late.

"So, tell me," Alma was asking Bobby when Eva turned
back to the conversation. "What does this husband of
yours do?"

"You mean Joe?" Bobby asked stupidly.

"If that's his name."

"He's a welder. He's got a job in a machine shop, earns
good money." Why did she make it sound as if she was
proud of him? she wondered. It was what she'd always
done, not wanting people to know she was unhappy.

"And how did you come to be married to this welder?"
Alma asked, taking a spoonful of the cream of mush-
room soup.

"I met him when I was in high school," Bobby said
quietly. "Me and my girlfriend Lor used to hang out at the
pizza parlor. Joe came in one night with his friends and
asked me out. We started going together. After my
grandpa died, we got married."

"And was he abusive from the beginning?" Alma
asked, slowly turning to look directly, piercingly into
Bobby's eyes.

"You mean did he start hitting me right away? No."
Bobby thought for a moment, the last bite of her sandwich sticking in her throat. "That didn't start till after Pen
was born."

"Why did you stay?" Alma asked. "I've never understood that about women like you."

Women like me? Bobby bridled at that. What did these
two know about women like her? "Everybody's different," she said softly. "Even women who get beat up're
different from each other." Her eyes filled and she sat in
silence, vowing she'd die before she shed a tear in front of
these women.

"Don't take offense," Alma said in a softer tone. "I'm simply trying to understand."

Bobby looked over. It was hard to read the woman's expression, what with the way her face sagged on the left side. "This one time," Bobby said slowly, feeling her way, "I tried complaining to Joe's mom, thinking maybe she could talk sense to him, get him to stop. She made out it was only what I deserved, that men had a right to go hitting their wives. That's the way marriage worked. She didn't see nothing . . ."

"Anything," said Eva.

"She didn't see anything wrong with it." Bobby lowered her eyes, feeling like a freak. These two probably thought she was trash. Maybe she was. How could she explain Joe to them when she couldn't understand him herself?

"Woman was a fool," Alma growled, glaring down at her plate.

"Did you love him?" Eva asked surprisingly.

Taken off guard, Bobby looked across at her. "I don't know," she said thickly. "I thought I did. He was real good-looking, and I was only eighteen when we met. I guess I was stupid." If they were going to question her this way all the time, she didn't know how she'd last more than two weeks. She felt naked and ugly.

"Eighteen is very young," Eva said, and gave her quite a gentle smile. "No one would blame you."

"What about your mother?" Alma asked. "Where was she?"

"I never knew my mother," Bobby said almost in a whisper. "She ran off when I was a baby. She was seventeen and not married. Nobody ever saw her again. She left me with my grandpa and Aunt Helen, and she never came back. See, my grandma died a long time before, so it was only Grandpa and Aunt Helen, and they didn't really want the responsibility of a baby. They talked some about sending me away for adoption, my aunt told me. But they didn't. They kept me." Bobby's voice faded out and she sat gazing at her plate, hoping they wouldn't ask her any more questions. She didn't like the way her story sounded.

"Let's give Bobby a break," Eva said to her aunt. "We're embarrassing her." To Bobby she said, "You'll have to forgive us. We're in the habit of dissecting everything, analyzing endlessly."

"I don't understand that," Bobby admitted.

"You'll get used to it," Eva said with confidence. "It isn't personal."

How, Bobby wondered, could it not be personal when it was her they were talking about? This must be the way educated rich people conversed. It sure was a far cry from going over the K-Mart flyers with Lor, or visiting Aunt Helen with the TV going the whole time. She sat with her hands folded in her lap and waited for the meal to end.

At ten past three Bobby was waiting at the top of the driveway. And when Pen came off the yellow school bus, Bobby threw open her arms, relieved to see her. With Penny, she knew who she was.

"My teacher's name is Mrs. Corey and I like her a whole whole lot," Penny said as they walked up the driveway. "We did printing and we had a story. It's a good school. C'n I go up'n see Granny?"

"Hold on a minute," Bobby said, stopping her outside the front door. "Alma's not really your granny, you know, Pen."

"She c'n be my granny if I want her to."

"She might not like you calling her that. You call her Aunt Alma, and don't go making a pest of yourself. Old people like to stay quiet."

"She told me I could read to her this afternoon. She *said* I could."

"Okay," Bobby said, standing upright. "But we're just hired help here, honey. You've gotta remember that. Don't go acting like it's your place."

"But we live here now," Penny said, frowning.

"We live here, but it's not our house. Okay?"

"Okay." Penny looked unconvinced as they entered the foyer. "I'm going up now," she told her mother, dropping to her knees to open her backpack for *Where the Sidewalk Ends.*

"Take off your coat and boots," Bobby told her quietly. "I don't want you dirtying the carpet."

Penny obeyed, then ran to the stairs. Bobby remained in the front hall watching her go, and winced at hearing Penny knock at Alma's door and sing out, "Granny, I'm home from school."

Alma's gruff voice replied, "I've been waiting for you. Ah, you've got your book. Good."

Exhaling slowly, Bobby went downstairs to unpack before dinner. She didn't know *what* to make of these people, and couldn't begin to imagine what they thought of her. But as long as they did their dissecting and analyzing about somebody else, she figured she could survive it. And Pen was settling right in, making herself a granny out of that tough old bird.

Five

"Where're you at?" Aunt Helen asked.

"We're in Connecticut," Bobby told her. "I got a live-in job in a real . . . really nice place."

"Joe came here looking for you."

"I figured he probably would. What'd you say?"

"I told him to get off my property, that I wouldn't tell him even if I knew. He didn't believe me, but I said I'd call the cops and he took off. You and Pen gonna be all right?"

"We're gonna be fine. Listen, would it be okay if I give the post office your address for my mail? That way, anything important comes, you can send it to me."

"I guess," Helen said. "Lemme get a pencil."

Bobby gave her the address, then said, "Hide it somewhere safe."

"Don't you worry. Just let me hear from you once in a while."

"I will. And thanks, Aunt Helen."

"About time you got yourself away from that man. He's gonna wind up killing somebody one of these times."

"Yeah," Bobby said. "I know."

After dinner, Eva worked in her office over the garage for a couple of hours, making up for some of the time she'd lost getting Bobby oriented to their routine.

At eleven, she stored her chapter and turned off the computer. She jotted down a few points she wanted to remember for the next day, then switched off the lights, locked up, and walked through the dark garage to the kitchen.

She unloaded the dishwasher, set the table for tomorrow's breakfast, laid out Aunt Alma's tray, and finally filled the coffeemaker and reset the timer. She automatically checked the downstairs doors and windows before heading upstairs. Seeing the light still on in her aunt's room, she tapped lightly then opened the door. Alma laid her right hand across the page she'd been reading and looked up.

"What do you think?" Eva asked, crossing to sit on the side of the bed. "Will she work out?"

"She's afraid of her own shadow, but she didn't misrepresent her physical strength. She seems to have no problem at all with this old carcass. And it's nice being a granny again. I like that child. What do you think?"

"She keeps reminding me of Deborah," Eva said, staring off into space for a moment. "They're not remotely alike, but I can't stop comparing them."

"It's the psychology that fascinates you," Alma said cannily. "It always has."

"I hadn't thought about her for years before Bobby came along. D'you suppose her real name is Roberta? Bobby is so... I don't know. It's so *rural.*"

Alma rasped out a laugh.

Eva smiled at her. "Well, it is. Bobby's a name from the Appalachians or the Okefenokee Swamp."

"Bitchy and elitist," Alma accused.

"Both," Eva agreed. "And I'm longing to do something about that hair. Granted, it's hard to tell what she looks like, given the condition of her face, but I suspect she's actually quite pretty. She'd look infinitely better with a decent haircut."

"Her hair has nothing to do with her capabilities," Alma insisted.

Thinking aloud, Eva said, "It's almost like a self-imposed class barrier: women defining themselves by their hair."

"Go to bed," Alma said, "and let me get to sleep."

Eva leaned forward to kiss her aunt's cheek, then got up asking, "Anything you want before I go?"

"Not a thing. I'll see you in the morning."

Penny dreamed that she climbed onto the school bus and every single child was dressed up like a clown, with round red noses and big red mouths and little black teardrops painted on their white cheeks. The bus driver said, "Hurry up now and sit down. You know I can't start this bus until you're in your seat." Penny looked up and down both rows, unable to see anywhere to sit. She turned to tell the driver but when she tried to talk, nothing would come out.

"You'll have to get off," the driver said.

But how was she going to get to school? Penny asked her mutely.

"If you can't find a seat, you can't ride the bus."

Penny looked again at the rows of clown-suited children, all laughing and honking squeezy horns. Way at the very back was one empty seat, and she started toward it, smiling at the little clowns as she moved down the aisle. Maybe it was a special day at school and she was supposed to have a clown costume too. Why hadn't her mom known about it?

Sliding into the seat, she held Mr. Bear to her chest as the bus lurched forward, feeling mad at her mom.

"Keep it quiet, you kids!" the driver called back over her shoulder.

The children turned to each other, giggling.

Penny held Mr. Bear and smiled politely, her eyes on the front of the bus. She wished she had a clown suit and a red nose and a big painted smile, a polka-dot costume with puffy sleeves and a white ruffled collar. It was because it was a new school, she decided. And nobody had told her mom. Now she was going to be the only one in the whole school wearing dumb old jeans and a sweater. But maybe, she thought, feeling a sudden hope, maybe the teachers would be wearing everyday clothes too, and then it'd be okay.

Bobby lunged awake into the darkness, not knowing where she was. Heart hammering, she reached out blindly, groping for the light on the bedside table. Got it on. Looked around. Penny had kicked off her covers. Taking short, shallow breaths, Bobby got out of bed and drew the blankets up over her daughter. Then she went into the bathroom and splashed cold water over her face, touched her wet hands to the back of her neck, shivering. Turning off the water, she straightened, her neck and shoulder muscles tight and aching.

Sitting in the kitchen with a cigarette, head resting on her hand, she tried to remember when she'd last slept through the night. It had been so long she couldn't remember. She thought it was probably sometime before Grandpa got sick. A long, long time ago.

Eva looked at the telephone on the bedside table, realizing another day had gone by and Melissa hadn't called. Nothing unusual. During the first few weeks of her freshman year, Melissa had phoned every other night. But after that, once she'd settled in, she'd let weeks go by before she called home. Eva wished she could hear from her more often, but she accepted the reality that her daughter's life was no longer tied to hers. She herself had been equally casual about calling home during her own college years. Now she wondered if Alma hadn't privately worried about her just as she couldn't help worrying about Melissa. Being young meant being self-absorbed. Perhaps Alma had always understood that, having spent most of her life dealing with the young.

Eva had wanted to commute to Sarah Lawrence in Bronxville, but Alma had persuaded her to go to Bennington. "It'll be good for you," her aunt had insisted. "You need to get out on your own, fend for yourself, become accustomed to living alone." She'd made it sound as if she expected Eva to remain single for life, the way she had. And she would have argued, but her aunt's failure to marry was a sticky subject, one that Alma had usually dismissed as being unworthy of discussion.

"I made my decision many years ago," her aunt said whenever Eva broached the subject, "and I have yet to regret it." She wore a particular expression at these times that cautioned Eva against pursuing the matter. And having spent all but the first six years of her life in her aunt's care, she'd learned to recognize the warning signals. Alma would discuss men only in the abstract, never in the specific. She worked with them, socialized with them, even, Eva suspected, went to bed with some of them, but she never talked about them. And when Eva began dating, at thirteen or so, she sensed it would be wise to follow her aunt's lead and keep the details to herself.

Eva could vaguely remember a conversation she'd had with her mother when she'd asked why Auntie Alma didn't have a husband. Her mother had sighed and said, "My sister had a very unhappy love affair. The young man married someone else, and now Alma holds every man she meets responsible."

It hadn't made much sense to a five-year-old, but the brief conversation stayed with her, and as she grew older the explanation seemed ever more viable. Some awful man had broken her aunt's heart and ever afterward she was skeptical and somewhat jaded where men were concerned. But her aunt didn't seem especially unhappy with her life, and Eva had concluded that while she herself aspired to marry and have children, it wasn't necessarily a given that all women would feel that way. Whether it was intentional or unwitting, Alma had taught her niece to understand that some women simply elected to live alone. She saw nothing wrong with it.

When she met Ken Rule she knew she was going to be one of the women who married. He was destined to be her partner, and she was very comfortable with the knowledge that her life would be different from her aunt's.

They met during her semester in London, at a pub in Chelsea where she'd gone with Deborah for a drink one evening. He'd been sitting with some friends at the next table and, upon hearing her accent, turned with a smile and said, "Hi. I'm from D.C. Where're you from?"

She'd liked him immediately. He reminded her of her grandfather, who'd died when she was fourteen. Ken Rule was tall and soft-spoken, with heavy eyebrows like her grandfather's, and wonderfully open. She told him she was from Connecticut and introduced herself and Deborah, who smiled at Ken while giving Eva's knee a significant nudge under the table.

Ken had worn a tartan vest that night and Eva had said, "That vest's just like my grandfather's."

With a grin, shifting his chair so that he was now sitting at their table, he'd said, "As a matter of fact, this *is* your grandfather's."

She'd laughed delightedly, and they'd started talking, exchanging information, until the barmaid called, "Time, ladies and gentlemen."

While Deborah was in the loo, Ken said, "Give me your number, and say you'll go out with me Saturday night."

He insisted on seeing the girls home in a taxi, told Eva he was looking forward to Saturday, told Deborah how happy he was to have met her, then went off, whistling, back to the waiting taxi. As they were climbing the stairs to their rooms, Deborah said, "I expect to be Maid of Honor, darling. Just, please, don't ask me to wear anything pink."

She and Ken made love in her room after that first date. Thereafter they saw each other two or three times a week.

In order to accomplish this, Ken put in extra hours at the office, trying to stay on top of his workload. His degree was in civil engineering but he'd been offered a job straight out of college working for an international carrier. At the time they met he'd been in London for a year and a half. He didn't say much about his work. "It would bore you to death," he told Eva at the beginning. "But it's a good jumping-off point. There's going to be room upstairs for someone like me."

She had implicit faith in him. By the end of her semester she'd consented to marry him, and he flew back with her to meet Alma. They had only two days together before he had to fly back to London. Her last semester at Bennington went by in a blur. Somehow she got her work done, but all she wanted was to get back to London to be with Ken, and with Deborah.

If Alma harbored misgivings, she never once expressed them, showing only satisfaction in Eva's choice of husband. She came over to London a week early, shopped with Deborah and Eva for a simple wedding dress, and footed the bill for the wedding.

Almost a year to the day after they were married, Eva learned she was pregnant. Ken wept when she told him.

"I've always wanted to be somebody's father," he'd said.

"You're only twenty-six, for heaven's sake," she'd said, laughing. "How long is always to you?"

"You know what I mean," he'd said. And she had, because she'd always wanted to be somebody's mother. She'd grown up without a father, and she'd wanted one. Ken's parents had been divorced when he was eleven, and he too had wanted a father. By creating this child they were each satisfying a deep-seated need to correct what they considered historical errors.

Alma sounded awed when Eva telephoned to give her the news. Awed and possibly wistful. She declared she was overjoyed and wished there were some way she could be in

London when the baby was born. But school was in session and it was impossible for her to get away.

Deborah was on the road with the touring company of a musical but hoped to be back in time for the birth. "And," she'd announced momentously, "I may have some rather fabulous news of my own." She'd refused to elaborate, promising to tell all upon her return.

As it happened, the baby arrived three weeks early. Ken was present for the birth, standing to one side of the midwife, holding Eva's hand at the moment Melissa left her mother's body. And the first thing he said upon seeing the infant was, "We'll have to do this again."

"Give me a minute or two," Eva had gasped. And everyone had laughed.

Melissa was six weeks old by the time Deborah got back to town, pregnant and with Ian in tow. And things were never quite the same afterward between Eva and Deborah. Although Eva made herself available, suggesting outings, there were no more lengthy rambling conversations over lunch or dinner. Just occasional chats on the telephone and, finally, that last visit to the house in Newington Green. Deborah's letters in the intervening years were reassuring; they constituted proof of their continuing friendship. And Eva elected to focus on her friend, setting aside her mixed feelings about the man Deborah had chosen to marry.

When Ken was transferred back from London, Alma contributed to the down payment on the co-op apartment in Manhattan where Eva had continued to live until Alma's stroke the previous year.

Oddly enough, in the aftermath of the stroke, Alma became quite loquacious about her early life and spent several afternoons in her hospital room telling Eva all about Randy Wheeler. She spoke without bitterness but slowly, enunciating carefully, recited the facts of the affair, and Eva listened, correctly suspecting that the only reason Alma was revealing her history at this juncture was because she believed she was going to die. Eva was certain that she'd live and, possibly, at some future date, regret making this confession. But for as long as it lasted, Eva drank in the details of her aunt's early life, as eager to hear it as Alma was to tell.

Alma had never again mentioned either those hospital conversations or the young man she'd once intended to marry, and Eva guessed that her continuing silence was the only indication her aunt was going to give of her regret. Which was typical of Alma. She'd never been one to cry over spilt milk. She simply got on with things, putting whatever displeased her to one side.

It was this ability to forge ahead, Eva believed, that had made her both a splendid teacher and a wonderful, albeit somewhat eccentric, parent. She expected Eva to learn from her mistakes and never rehashed past incidents in order to make her points. Eva sometimes wondered how she might have turned out if she'd grown up with her natural parents, but in view of the fact that she could scarcely remember Cora and Willard Chaney, it was usually a short-lived exercise. The fact was, Alma was her mother and had been for the past thirty-seven years. And Eva was devoted to her, perhaps more than she might have been to her actual mother who, so far as Eva could remember, was a little dithery and given to playing the helpless female. There was no question that her writing career was a direct result of Alma's long-term encouragement and support. Alma had always been her fiercest ally and severest critic, urging Eva from the age of eleven to commit her thoughts to paper. "You've got the gift, Eva," her aunt had said over and over. "Don't be afraid to use it." So she had. She'd taken the things she'd seen and heard and thought about and shaped them into stories that her aunt had edited and critiqued. And, finally, a year after Ken's death, she'd published her first book. Since then there had been five more, and she attributed her success to her aunt's powerfully positive influence. Now she wished she could find a way to restore to her aunt some degree of the gusto she'd lost with the stroke; wished she could repay even a little of what Alma had given her.

"I've fixed breakfast for you," Eva said. "This afternoon, while Alma's napping, you might want to take a trip to the supermarket, stock up on some food."

"Okay, thank you," Bobby said, getting Penny settled at the table. "Anything I can do to help?"

"Everything's done," Eva said. "I usually have coffee upstairs with my aunt. Just help yourself."

Bobby arranged a plateful of bacon, eggs and toast for Penny, poured her some orange juice from the pitcher on the counter, and sat down with a cup of coffee while Penny ate. When she'd finished, Bobby got into her coat and boots, pulled on her own coat, and walked with her to the top of the driveway to wait for the school bus.

"You got your lunch tickets?" Bobby asked her.

"Uh-hunh." Penny's eyes were on the road, brightening when she saw the bus approaching.

"Okay. Starting tomorrow I'll make your lunches. You be a good girl, and I'll see you this afternoon." She bent to kiss Penny's cheek, then straightened as Penny clambered into the yellow bus. Bobby watched it out of sight, turned, and hurried back down the driveway to the house. There was snow in the air. It'd probably start falling sometime soon, and winter would set in for real.

She rinsed the dishes, put them in the dishwasher, and stood by the window to finish her coffee while she waited for Eva to come down. It gave her a thrill to see the water right at the bottom of the property. Where the grass ended there was a drop like a little cliff down to the eight or ten feet of rock-strewn sand, and then the water stretching off to forever. She could hear the waves washing in even from inside the house. The sound made her feel clean and strong.

"You can go up now," Eva said, coming in with her aunt's breakfast tray.

"Okay."

Bobby moved to the sink to rinse her cup, but Eva said, "Just leave it." For some reason, Bobby's eagerness to help irritated her this morning. She snapped at the woman, then at once felt badly. But she couldn't clear a space in her mind that would allow room for an apology. All she wanted was to get to the computer and go to work.

Shaken by Eva's abruptness, Bobby left the cup on the counter and headed for the stairs. She couldn't get a fix on Eva, thrown by her friendliness at one moment, her coolness the next.

Alma merely grunted in response to Bobby's "Good morning."

Bobby waited, prepared to take her cues from the older woman, and watched Alma as she struggled to shift herself to a sitting position on the side of the bed. She had to lift her dangling left arm and then her leg, her strong right side doing all the work.

Instinctively, Bobby came forward to assist her into the wheelchair. Once in the bathroom, and out of the chair, Alma said, "You can take the chair. Leave it to one side of the door. I'll let you know when I need you."

Bobby backed away to wait, turning to look at the room. There was a fireplace on the left-hand wall. Directly ahead was a wide window, in front of which was the armchair where Bobby had sat for the interview. To the right of the window was the bed. It was a pretty room, with pale blue carpet and sheer white curtains swagged over the window; an embroidered blue coverlet on the old-fashioned bed, and flowered wallpaper with a dark blue background. Books were stacked on the bedside table and in a row on the mantelpiece. There was a long, narrow bench at the foot of the bed, its top covered in hand-done needlework.

Alma called to her, and she hurried across the room.

"Get the water started. Not too hot," Alma told her, clutching one of several stainless steel rails affixed to the walls of the room. "Now," she said, when Bobby had done that, "help me out of this damned thing."

Pretending she was undressing Penny, she got Alma's nightgown off, keeping her eyes averted. The tub had filled very quickly and she turned off the taps, then braced herself to bear Alma's weight as she helped her into the water.

"I bathe myself," Alma told her. "But I don't mind company. Sit down there." She indicated a white enamel stool in the corner.

Bobby sat. While Alma busied herself with the soap, she stole a look at the woman. It was nowhere near as bad as Bobby had thought it'd be. Alma was thin, but not down to skin and bones, and she had a better shape than Bobby had imagined someone her age would have. Her shoulders were wide, but her back tapered in at the waist; she had small breasts that didn't sag too much, and a bit of a pot belly. She had a nice long neck, something Bobby had always admired in a woman, and real long arms and legs. Once upon a time, Bobby decided, she'd been very good-looking. Half of her face still was. The other half looked good and mad all the time.

"I'll do your back, if you want," Bobby offered, feeling awkward sitting there not doing anything.

In answer, Alma handed her the soap, then took hold of the handle fastened to the wall above the tub.

It was just like washing Pen, Bobby thought, lathering up a washcloth and breathing in the fragrance of the soap. She rubbed the cloth up and down and across, humming to herself under her breath.

"You're good at this," Alma said, her head bent forward, lulled by the pleasurable motions.

"Can you feel it on this side?" Bobby asked, rinsing the left side.

"Some," Alma murmured.

"What about your hair? When d'you wash it?"

"That, my dear, is a production worthy of Cecil B. DeMille. We do it in the wheelchair at the sink twice a week. Mercifully, today's not one of those days."

"But you could do it right in the tub," Bobby said. "You've got one of them shower spray contraptions. It'd be real easy. Really easy," she corrected herself. "We'd lean you back and get it done one, two, three."

"I don't think you realize just how awkward that would be."

"It wouldn't," Bobby disagreed. "You'll see. We'll give it a try when it's time."

"You'll probably wind up drowning me."

Bobby smiled and reached for one of the big towels on the rack. "I won't go drowning you," she said, bracing herself to assist Alma out of the tub. "I want to keep this job."

It wasn't that hard at all, getting the woman shifted from one place to another. In some ways, Bobby thought, it was like handling a great big child. But one who could say some wicked hurtful things.

Wrapped in the towel, Alma sat on the side of the bed and told Bobby what she wanted to wear and in which drawers of the bureau she'd find things. A silky pair of what Lor called tap pants, a slip, and knee-high stockings; a skirt and blouse and sweater. Simple as pie. She'd thought she'd be bothered handling a naked woman, but she wasn't. She felt a surprising kind of closeness in dressing her new employer, in drawing the stockings up her legs, getting those tap pants tugged up over her lean hips. All in all it was pretty satisfying; it made her feel in charge and competent.

Once dressed and settled into her wheelchair, Alma opened the drawer of the bedside table and got out her cologne. She sprayed herself and Bobby breathed in the pleasant scent. As Alma returned the bottle to the drawer, Bobby had the idea that from now until forever she'd associate the flowery fragrance with this woman.

"How about if I brush your hair?" Bobby said, reaching for the silver-backed hairbrush on the bureau top.

"I'd love it," Alma said, and Bobby was pretty sure the woman gave her a smile.

So Bobby felt around for all the pins, smoothed the long hair with her fingers, then brushed the silky gray mass, gratified by Alma's soft contented sigh. The sun shone warmly in on them and from moment to moment Bobby glanced out the window at the water. She actually felt happy. She liked the crackling thickness of Alma's hair sliding under her hand as she drew the brush through it, liked the fragrance of her cologne and the pool of warm sunlight that contained them. Time dissolved. She would have been content to stand forever, watching pinpoints of sunlight dancing on the water out there beyond the window, her hands at work.

At last, she coiled the hair back atop Alma's head and carefully pinned it in place. "There!" she said, stepping to one side to give the woman a smile. "All set."

Alma looked up at her for a long moment, then said, "What a kind little person you are."

Bobby felt her smile get wobbly on her face, like something that'd been stuck over her mouth with glue and was about to fall off. She thought she might cry, but managed to choke out, "Thank you," and busied herself returning the hairbrush to the bureau. Clearing her throat, she said, "I guess it's time to go downstairs now," and waited for Alma to get the wheelchair aimed at the door.

The compliment had rattled her, Alma saw, and felt a sadness blossom in her chest. It was all too obvious that Bobby was far more accustomed to abuse than to praise. How very sad, she thought. Three disenchanted females under one roof. But then she was forgetting Penny, that charming sprite. It really was lovely to have a child in the house again. More than anything else, she'd been missing the children.

After two days he swept all the shit off the kitchen floor, shoveling it directly into the trash can out back. The stuff on the wall could stay there. No way was he gonna touch it. Anyway, it kind of kept him focused. He cracked a Coors, his eyes on the wall. The way he figured it, she'd gone with the kid to one of them shelters, and she'd come dragging her ass back as soon as the shelter people threw them out, just like the last time.

There wasn't a woman alive you could trust, wasn't one of them wouldn't sneak around on you the minute your back was turned. Bobby was no different. Only way to get hold of their attention was to smack 'em good, show 'em who was in charge. He squashed the Coors can one-handed and dumped it in the garbage. Not a goddamned thing to eat in the fridge. Fuck it! He'd head on down to Garvey's, grab a couple of brews and a burger. Then he'd cruise by that Lor's place again, make sure the bitch and the kid weren't there after all.

The phone rang. He picked it up, willing to bet it was Bobby begging to come home. But it was that weasely nerd from the Burger King wanting to know was Bobby going to be showing up for work. "She quit," he told the nerd and slammed the phone down. "Asshole!" He looked at the phone. Maybe it was their way of being cute, making out like she wasn't showing up when she was actually shacked up with the nerd. He'd check that out, he decided, jamming the .38 in the back of the waistband of his 501's. He'd wait till closing then nail the nerd in the parking lot, shoving the .38 up under his nose and see what fell out of his mouth.

Six

Thursday morning as Bobby was walking back to the house after seeing Penny off on the school bus, a dusty black Buick turned into the driveway and parked behind the Honda. A trim middle-aged black woman climbed out and stood for a moment, eyeing Bobby.

"You the new nurse?" the woman asked doubtfully, approaching.

"Uh-hunh."

"Looks like you had yourself some kind of accident."

"Uhm, yeah. I'm Bobby." Uncertain of the protocol, she held out a hand.

"I'm Ruby," the woman said, with a bemused expression, giving Bobby's hand a quick shake.

They entered the house together and Bobby stood in the foyer for a moment, appreciating the warmth. She'd gone out with only a sweater. Ruby busied herself hanging away her coat, and Bobby headed for the kitchen. She had a few minutes before she was due upstairs, and she wanted to tidy up her apartment. She quickly stacked the breakfast dishes in the sink, then made the beds. Planning to get to the dishes later, she went up to the kitchen to have another half cup of coffee before starting the day with Alma.

Ruby came out of the utility room wearing an apron and carrying a bucket filled with cleaning gear in one hand, a mop and broom in the other. "When'd you come?" she asked.

"Started Tuesday morning," Bobby told her, standing by the counter with her coffee.

"How you finding it?"

"It's fine," Bobby said. "They're real nice folks."

"Uh-hunh." Ruby started rinsing dishes, putting them in the dishwasher.

"You been working here long?" Bobby asked.

"Nine years."

"That sure is a long time."

"Seen a lot of nurses come and go this past year," Ruby said, closing the dishwasher door.

"Is that right?"

"Six or seven, at least."

"I'm hoping to stay," Bobby said, as Eva came in with Alma's breakfast tray.

Eva said good morning to Ruby, nodded over at Bobby, then started in telling Ruby it was time to clean out the refrigerator. Bobby left her cup in the sink and headed for the stairs.

While she was helping Alma from the bed to the wheelchair, she said, "I was thinking maybe you'd like me to take you out for some air. You know, in your chair."

"I think not," Alma said curtly.

"Why not?" Bobby asked.

"I'd prefer not to be paraded in front of the neighbors. Leave me now." Alma pushed the bathroom door closed. Chewing on her lower lip, Bobby retreated to the bedroom to wait. She'd slipped up that time, she thought, wandering over to look at the titles of the books on the mantel. Better be careful, she told herself. It was real easy to rile these people. From the look of her this morning, she'd already done something to get Eva's back up. But she couldn't think what. Now that she'd opened a checking account and put in a change of address with the post office and stocked up on some groceries, she didn't want to be told she'd have to go. So she'd keep her mouth shut, keep her ideas to herself.

While Alma was in the tub, Bobby sat on the enamel stool with her hands folded in her lap, not sure if she should again offer to wash the woman's back. But Alma looked over at her and said, "Today's a hair-washing day."

"Okay," Bobby said, and pulled off her shoes and socks, then rolled up her pant legs.

"What on earth are you doing?"

"I'm gonna sit on the side of the tub, while you lean yourself back against my legs."

"You'll get soaked. What's the point of that?"

"No, ma'am. It'll be fine, you'll see. It's how I washed my grandpa's hair. All that'll get wet're my feet. It's bound to be way more comfortable for you than tipping your head back in that chair."

Bobby removed all the hairpins, reached for the hand shower, got the water going, then with Alma hanging on to the support bar, she eased the woman back. "It's real...really easy," Bobby said, wetting the long hair thoroughly before applying the shampoo. She took care to be gentle, massaging the suds into the woman's scalp before rinsing it clean. "See," she said, "that didn't take but a couple of minutes." She eased her upright again, then wrapped a towel around Alma's head, folding the sides under so it stayed secure. "You got a blow dryer somewhere?"

"Under the sink," Alma said, amazed by how effortlessly the job had been accomplished, and wondering why none of the other nurses had thought to do it that way. Probably they hadn't wanted to get their feet wet, she thought, and then had to smile at the metaphor. This young woman was remarkably resourceful. "I think I'm going to enjoy having you around," she said, as Bobby assisted her out of the tub.

She was rewarded with a shy smile. "I sure do hope so," Bobby said. "I like tending to you."

"Now, why is that?" Alma asked.

"I like looking after people," Bobby said, enfolding the woman in the big bath sheet. "We'll sit you down right here on the stool and get your hair dry now," she said, locating the hair dryer and plugging it in. "You okay there?"

"I'm fine."

"Good."

With a brush in one hand and the dryer in the other, Bobby set to work. Alma looked down at the young woman's bare feet. They were small and beautifully shaped, with high arching insteps. Alma wondered if she had trouble finding shoes. She doubted Bobby wore anything bigger than a size five. Her hands were small too. Altogether she was the size of some of the twelve-year-olds Alma used to caution about racing through the school corridors. Thinking of the girls gave her a pang. She missed their animation, their restless energy and barely contained impatience. She missed the small ones from the kindergarten classes, with their uniforms always askew and soft toys tucked under their arms, their socks forever crumpled around their delicate ankles. She didn't miss the parental interference, or the squabbling among the teachers, or the annual drives to solicit funds from alumnae. But the girls danced constantly through her mind, their laughing chatter a pleasurable echo. Occasionally, there'd been a girl who'd touched her in a particular way; something about her demeanor or her looks brought Randy to mind and she thought the two of them might have had just such a girl. She'd never imagined she'd live out her life as an unmarried woman, mother to no one. For years she'd expected someone to come along to replace Randy, to make her a wife and mother. But on the several occasions when the opportunity had been there and all that had been required of her was to say yes, she'd said no instead. Something of great magnitude had been lost, some fundamental ability within her had shut down for good, leaving her incapable of risking commitment. She'd given herself to a select few men with temporary abandon, deriving great sexual satisfaction from those encounters, but her brain—or was it her heart?—had remained out of bounds. They could touch her body—God knows she'd had few compunctions about that—but they could not touch that scarred-over area within her.

Perhaps, unconsciously, she'd made the decision to live out her life alone on the day she'd withdrawn her savings to make the down payment on this house. Her mother had been greatly dismayed at Alma's announcement of her plans, and had come up to Alma's bedroom to talk to her, asking, "Why are you doing this?"

"To have a home of my own," Alma had said, as if that should have been obvious.

"But if you marry..."

"I won't," Alma had declared, surprising herself and her mother. Until that moment she'd still believed there was a man out there who'd partner her, be her live-in companion and lover for the rest of her life. But she was taking a stand she hadn't expected to take and, oddly, she found some grim measure of satisfaction in it. She was making a choice that would to a great degree determine the course of her future, and she reveled in her ability to make decisions and take action.

"Not all men are like Randy," her mother had said, looking saddened. "He was weak-willed and foolish. I know he broke your heart, but..."

Alma cut her off, despising the image of herself as something weak and shattered. "I'm certainly not brokenhearted," she'd insisted, denying the monstrous ache that resided permanently deep in her bones. "I'm not Cora, you know," she said, determined to make it clear to the entire world that she wasn't romantic at heart, or dependent, like her sister.

"There's not a thing wrong with Cora," her mother said, frowning.

"I didn't say there was. I'm simply telling you I'm not like her."

"I know what you're like," Margaret Ogilvie assured her eldest daughter. "Your pride may one day be your undoing, my dear."

Alma had laughed at this, and in an excess of fondness for her small, practical mother, hugged the woman, saying, "My pride will be my saving grace. It's what keeps me strong. It's what will get me ahead in the world."

"Your intelligence will do that," her mother disagreed. "Your pride will only misdirect you. You, more than most women, more even than your sister, should have a husband and a family. You may be a big woman," her mother said cannily but with kindness, "but you have the soul of a more fragile being. I know you, Alma, and I know when you're doing something just to prove you can, not because it gives you any lasting satisfaction. But I can see I'm not going to get anywhere arguing with you. It's clear you've made up your mind and nothing's going to change it, so I'll give you this and have done with it." She'd reached into her pocket then to give Alma the check. "Your father and I have discussed it and we've agreed, since you're determined to go ahead with this, to help you get started, just as we helped Cora and Willard with their first house."

Right then, Alma had wanted to call it off, to get on the telephone to the real estate agent and say never mind, she wasn't going to be buying the house after all. But the loss of face would have been more than she could bear. So, all but choking, she'd accepted her parents' money, whispered a thank you, and gone forward on her chosen path. She would have a home of her own and her own income. She only wished that those accomplishments could balance out the secret and terrible longing she sometimes felt to be part of a pair, to belong to someone. Yet more than anything else, she feared ever again turning herself over, heart and mind, as completely as she had to Randy Wheeler. She'd learned that even the people you thought you knew best were capable of astonishing acts of treachery.

While Bobby was gathering her clothes for the day, Alma asked, "How much education have you had?"

Carefully removing a blouse from its hanger, Bobby said, "I had to quit my senior year of high school to care for my grandpa."

"Did you do well in school?"

"About average, I suppose." Bobby laid the clothes on the bed, then knelt in front of Alma holding her undergarments. "I was never smart, like Pen. Pen's real . . . ly smart."

"Yes, she is," Alma agreed. "She's an exceptionally bright child."

"She's real . . . ly taken with you."

"It's mutual," Alma said.

While Bobby brushed her hair—something else none of the other nurses had ever done with such attentiveness—Alma gazed out the window, noting the massed clouds over the Sound. It was bound to snow any time now, and she'd spend her second winter trying not to be depressed, trying to believe that being handicapped was preferable to being dead.

In the afternoon the physical therapist came. Alma introduced him to Bobby as Dennis Forster, saying, "Dennis is now going to subject me to an hour of exquisite torture." But Bobby could tell she liked him, and he liked her, too. He was tall, with carroty red hair and brown eyes, and he wore white like a doctor. Bobby thought he had a nice smile.

"I'll bet Alma didn't tell you she has exercises she's supposed to do," he said to Bobby but with his smile directed at Alma.

"It's pointless," Alma declared. "You can't resurrect what's dead."

"Stay and watch," Dennis told Bobby. "I'll show you the drill."

Bobby stood by and watched obediently as Dennis worked the older woman's body, urging Alma to make more of an effort with her essentially paralyzed left side. For forty minutes, they went through exercises that visibly frustrated and angered Alma as she grappled with limbs that no longer felt as if they belonged to her and complained volubly about the pointlessness of the procedures.

Dennis was soft-spoken, good-humored, and remarkably patient. He wouldn't let Alma quit, despite her repeated threats to do just that. "You can do it," he said again and again. "You're doing fine." And finally, when Alma was winded and a bit red in the face, he looked over at Bobby and said, "See if you can't get her to do even twenty minutes a day. It'll make a big difference."

"I'll do my best," Bobby promised, and left when Dennis told her that the rest of his time would be taken up with massage, after which Alma would have her nap.

Ruby was running the vacuum cleaner in Eva's bedroom as Bobby went downstairs. She poured herself some of the coffee left over from lunch, and sat down at the table with the pad and pen from beside the telephone, making a note of the exercises.

"Mind if I have some of that coffee?" Dennis asked from the doorway a short time later.

"I'll get you a cup," Bobby said. "You usually have coffee before you go?"

"Only if it's already made. I take it black," he said, sliding into a chair. "So, are you from around here?"

"Jamestown, New York," Bobby said, setting the cup down in front of him and resuming her seat. She wondered if they were supposed to be in here, and imagined Eva storming in from the garage demanding to know what they thought they were doing, making themselves at home in her kitchen.

"Don't know it," Dennis said.

"It's upstate, near Lake Erie, about seventy miles west of Buffalo."

"Mind if I ask what happened to your eye?"

She looked down at the tabletop. "I'd rather not say."

"Right," he said. "So what brings you to this neck of the woods?"

"I like the ocean," she said, feeling awkward and stealing a glance at his hands. They were large and very clean, the backs covered with freckles. He wasn't wearing any rings.

"It's as good a reason as any," he said, then took a large swallow of his coffee before checking the time. "I'd better get going. I've got another client up in Norwalk." He got up, carried his cup to the sink, then went to the refrigerator, lifted aside a magnet, and took the check Eva had left there for him. Tucking it into his pocket, he said, "See if you can't get her to do those exercises. They'll help, if she'll only do them."

"I'll try my best."

"Okay. See you next week." He went along the hall to get his coat and let himself out.

After the door had closed behind him, Bobby let out her breath slowly and carried her coffee downstairs, planning to clean up the breakfast dishes. But Ruby had already done it. The carpet showed vacuum tracks, every surface had been dusted, and the countertops were wiped clean. Bobby looked around, amazed. Nobody had ever cleaned for her. She wasn't quite sure how to react.

Ruby looked surprised when Bobby thanked her, and finished stowing the cleaning gear in the utility room before saying, "You're welcome, but it's my job. There's no need to go thanking me."

"Well, thank you anyway," Bobby said, slipping on her coat. "I'm going to meet the bus now," she explained as Ruby untied her apron.

"You got a child with you?"

"My girl, Penny."

Ruby smiled, showing brilliant white teeth. "Bet Miss Alma's pleased about that. She sure do love children."

"Penny's real taken with her."

"I'll bet she is. Be seeing you Monday," Ruby said, getting her check from the refrigerator door just as Dennis had done.

"See you then," Bobby said, wondering as she started up the drive if her own check would be stuck with a magnet to the fridge.

Eva stared at the computer screen seeing Crescent Bay stretching silver in the afternoon light. Overhead the sun was a blinding hole in the white sky. She saw herself sitting near the water's edge at the apex of the bay, powdery sand slipping through her fingers as she watched the children splash in the shallows. To her left a trio of boats sat tilted on the beach, and to her right, about fifty yards distant, Deborah stood talking to a group of seven or eight Montaverdeans. Some of them, Eva had been given to understand, were relatives—cousins and uncles—and some had been hired to work on the house.

Deborah, long legs planted firmly, arms folded across her chest, stood stony-faced with anger as she listened to one of the older men. The construction was, weeks, even months, behind schedule, and Deborah was furious. Rough seas and rains were responsible for some of the delay, lackadaisical work habits were evidently responsible for the rest. So far, only the foundation had been laid: rectangles of concrete block that would be the ground-level utility and storage areas. On the hillside above, an area had been cleared for the catchment that would capture and store rainwater—a raw black area surrounded by dense brush.

Eva and Mellie had been on the island for four days. And each day, when the weather permitted, they all traveled by boat through the barracuda-infested waters to arrive at the bay. Day after day, Deborah's anger grew as she stepped ashore in her bright orange life vest—to her astonishment, Eva had discovered that Deborah couldn't swim—to find that little or nothing had been accomplished in her absence. And every evening when they returned to the plantation, Deborah accosted her husband, demanding to know why he refused to take on the responsibility of overseeing the construction.

Her English accent having subtly become more West Indian, she'd confront Ian. "Man, you *know* these people don't respect women. It's *your* bloody house too. *Why* won't you get off your scrawny white ass and take charge?"

Invariably, Ian fingered his silver Dunhill cigarette lighter, turning it over and over in his hands, as if waiting for Deborah to run out of steam. Eva still was unable to determine if he was smiling to himself or if that sneer was his normal expression. Either way, his silence fueled Deborah's anger. After twenty or thirty minutes of fruitless badgering, she'd march into the kitchen to begin the evening meal.

At the outset, Eva had offered to help with the cooking, but Deborah had given her a pained smile and said, "No, thank you, darling. Just keep an eye on the children." So Eva had stopped offering. It made her feel guilty to be sitting idle while her friend worked, but she'd decided there was no point continuing to offer when she knew she'd be refused. So she supervised the children, watching with fascination their complicated games.

They played either in the vast, empty lower room that in another era had been the living room, or in the grassy area beyond it that was partially enclosed by the L-shaped house. It wasn't until their third day on the island that Eva commented on the peculiarity of the location of this grassy area, and Deborah explained it had been a swimming pool which, for some unknown reason, the owners had filled in. "I expect they were afraid one of their children might have an accident," Deborah said, doubtfully eyeing the expanse of green.

The house altogether was odd. Four bedrooms were situated side by side along the bottom of the L, and the upright consisted of two enormous rooms defined only by the steps that separated them. The front door opened into the middle of the upright, and to the left, up two wide steps, was what had originally been the dining room but was used by Ian and Deborah as the living room. Fronting the living room, overlooking the mountainside, was the veranda. To the right of the front door, down two more steps, was the empty former living room, at the bottom of which was the door leading out to the bedrooms.

Built sometime in the late forties, the house reminded Eva of a motel. Constructed of concrete block, with the interior walls plastered and whitewashed, the place was cool and characterless. It belonged to the friends of one of Deborah's uncles, who were away in Europe for an undisclosed period of time. The owners' furniture was evidently in storage, which accounted for the unremitting emptiness of the rooms. The bedrooms contained only beds, nothing else.

The children took turns riding a tricycle across the hardwood floors of the echoey lower room. Aside from several wooden chairs and a bench in the living room, there was only a rickety table that held the telephone and sundry papers. And on the veranda was the sagging armchair in which Eva often sat, and an equally sagging two-seater sofa. They all gathered each evening on the veranda to eat the food Deborah prepared. She usually sat on the railing with a plate propped on her thigh, staring narrow-eyed into the distance, one leg braced on the floor for balance.

Her thoughts returning to the beach, Eva remembered how she'd sat most days watching the children run in giddy circles, in and out of the water. Their boundless energy in the tremendous heat had amazed her. From early morning until eight in the evening, they'd skipped or jumped up and down, playing incomprehensible games. Derek and Mellie were happy together, for which Eva was tremendously grateful, because from the moment she'd arrived, she'd been aware that Ian and Deborah were not. The tension between them was constant and unrelenting. Eva tried very hard to pretend that everything was normal, but the atmosphere in the house alarmed her. She spent most of her time with the children, trying to behave normally but feeling like a fraud, getting through the days while thinking constantly about leaving.

Once washed and put into bed, the children closed their eyes instantly and plunged into sleep like tiny divers. Scarcely moving, their bodies dark against the bed linens, their chunky limbs were stilled for the duration of the night.

And it was at night that things happened. The tensions of the day seemed to reach the breaking point when darkness fell. Sitting out on the veranda, Deborah would start in again on Ian, demanding to know why he was letting all the work fall on her shoulders. "You're to come to the site with me," she'd insist, "and not go off for hours in the car without letting anyone know where you are."

He'd shrug and toy with his Dunhill lighter, smirking at her.

"You're bloody fucking useless!" Deborah would rant, puffing furiously on her cigarette.

Eva would sit in silence, ignored by the two of them, trying and failing to think of some way she might mediate. She sensed that Deborah wanted her there, possibly as a witness, or possibly for her support. As far as Ian was concerned, Eva might as well have been invisible. So she'd smile now and again at Deborah, signaling her support, and then, at last, not having been acknowledged in even the slightest fashion, she'd excuse herself, saying, "I guess I'll head off to bed now."

At this point, both Deborah and Ian would click in, as if belatedly realizing she was there. "Sleep well, darling,"

Deborah would say, but with an expression almost of relief that Eva was going. And Ian would clear his throat, stop turning the lighter for a few moments, and direct his sneer/smirk/smile at her, saying, "Hmn, yes. Good night, Eva."

"See you in the morning," Eva would say, and then escape to her bedroom, feeling positively traitorous because she wanted so badly to take Mellie and get the hell off the island. She'd sit on her bed and tell herself there was nothing wrong. Deborah and Ian simply had a different kind of marriage. Not every marriage was like her and Ken's had been. Some people thrived on discord. Perhaps Deborah and Ian were happy in a negative way. Eva didn't know what to think. Exhausted both from a day's play with the children and from her efforts to decipher precisely what the hell was going on with Deborah and Ian, she'd get into bed, promising herself that tomorrow she'd find some way to talk to Deborah and clarify matters.

She'd read for a time and then, calmed and distracted, she'd turn out the light and settle down to sleep. The darkness would suddenly be cut by the light going on in the kitchen across the way, and through the open louvered windows, she'd hear the harsh low notes of discord. Or she'd hear the sounds of their grunts and scuffling traveling out through the rear windows of the master bedroom, wafting into her own. She would lie on the unyielding mattress with her eyes tightly closed, wishing she could shut it all out. But she couldn't.

On the fifth morning, Deborah appeared with a bruise under one eye, and at least one of Eva's suspicions was confirmed. But Deborah behaved in her usual, angry fashion, allowing Eva no opening for conversation. And subsequently, on the few occasions when the opportunity for a private talk presented itself, Ian appeared as if directed by personal radar, to shut down the opportunity. On these occasions, Eva noticed, Deborah actually seemed relieved, as if she'd been dreading having to deal with whatever Eva might choose to say. As a result, Eva's confusion grew, and so did her ambivalence.

In the following days Deborah appeared with angry red swellings on the backs of her calves, or the visible bruised impressions on her mid-arm of Ian's fingers. Deborah steadfastly said nothing. Eva wanted badly to speak, to help, but had no idea how to deal with the situation. She wished she'd never come to this place, yet out of loyalty to her friend she felt she should stay. She had the arbitrary notion that as long as she did stay nothing truly terrible could happen. But even as she thought this, she knew it was absurd. She had no control over what might or might not happen in this motel-like house. And repeatedly she wondered why, given the warring circumstances of their marriage, Deborah had invited her in the first place. Nothing made sense.

"Whatcha doin'?"

Eva started, her heart slamming once, violently, against her ribs. She looked over to see Penny standing in the doorway, holding her bear by one arm.

"Working!" Eva barked, annoyed, staring at the child for a moment before turning back to the screen.

"Doin' what?"

"Writing!" Eva said, trying to get a grip on herself as she looked at the half-finished sentence on the screen. Feeling guilty, as if she'd been caught in some illicit activity, she typed several words, then looked over her shoulder to see that Penny had come halfway across the room. "I'm working now," she said sternly. "You shouldn't be here. Where's your mother?"

"She's with Granny. We're exploring," Penny said, the bear now held to her chest. "You mad at me? You look mad."

"No one's allowed to come up here when I'm working," Eva explained firmly, wondering why the child wouldn't leave.

"Okay." Penny tentatively backed up a step or two.

"Damn it!" Eva said under her breath. Why was she being so hostile? Swiveling around in her chair, she said, "Come here."

Penny stood her ground, asking anxiously, "You gonna hit me?"

"No, I am not." Eva held out her hand. "Come here."

Penny reluctantly crossed the room and stood at Eva's side. Eva had a sudden, all but ungovernable, desire to hug this child. She looked so scared, Eva felt like a monster. "This is my computer," she explained.

"I know," Penny whispered. "We've got computers at school."

"Well, this is mine and it's what I use to do my work. And when I'm working I can't talk to anyone because I'm trying very hard to think. If I try to talk I get distracted and forget what I'm doing. Do you understand?"

Penny nodded soberly. Eva put an arm around the child's waist. "When I'm not working, I like to talk to people," she said, admiring the long lashes framing Penny's deep blue eyes. She really was a lovely-looking girl. "Okay?"

"Uh-hunh. You gonna tell my mom I was bad?"

"No. We won't talk about it. But you have to promise not to come up here again. Okay?"

"Okay."

"Good. Now you run along downstairs and I'll see you in a little while."

To her surprise and dismay, Penny laid her head on Eva's shoulder and said, "I'm sorry."

Eva surrendered to her impulse and hugged the girl. "I'm sorry too," she said. "I shouldn't have snapped at you."

"Are we friends again?"

"Yes, we're friends," Eva said thickly, undone by the child's sensitivity.

"Okay," Penny said, and slipped away, tiptoeing to the door. "Bye."

"Jesus!" Eva whispered, so rattled by the brief incident that she knew she'd be unable to do any more work. She stored the partial chapter, then sat looking at the blank screen. She wanted all at once to talk to Mellie, to hear her voice. But of course she'd hold off and wait for Mellie to call. Instead, she picked up the telephone to call Charlie.

"Are you home tonight?" she asked when he came on the line.

"I'll be in. Why? What's up?"

"Mind if I drop by after dinner?"

"Sure," he said, a smile in his voice. "Great. I'll see you, what, around eight?"

"Maybe earlier. I need to get out of here for a while."

"You know I'm always glad to see you," he said.

"Thanks," she said, and hung up.

Still on edge, she went over to the old armchair in the corner and sat gazing at the door. At times like this she missed her life in New York so terribly it was like a physical craving. Thank God, she thought, for Charlie. Without him, she didn't know what she'd do. She'd never dreamed when she agreed to move back to this house that she'd have to contend with quite so much. Instead of becoming more adept at dealing with her aunt's stroke and the resulting disability, as the months passed she felt she was almost daily losing more of her emotional equilibrium. How could she have spoken to the child in that fashion? It was reprehensible. She'd have to make a concerted effort at dinner to compensate for her sharpness with Penny and for the way she'd all but ignored Bobby that morning.

Taking a deep breath, she got up and headed for the kitchen. Cooking would help her put things back into perspective. It was the one activity, next to reading cookbooks, that gave her any real degree of peace.

Seven

Her mom was doing laundry in the bathtub and Penny didn't feel like watching television. With Mr. Bear tucked under her arm, she wandered into the living room and waited for Alma to stop reading and notice her.

When Alma looked up from her book, Penny went over and leaned against her knees, asking, "C'n I sit in your lap, Granny?"

Sensing that something was troubling the child, Alma said, "Climb aboard," and used her good hand to assist Penny into her lap. At once, Penny settled her head against Alma's breast and popped her thumb into her mouth. "What's the matter?" Alma asked, intensely gratified by the feel of the child.

"Nothin'," Penny murmured around her thumb.

"Feeling a bit blue?"

"Uh-hunh."

"Did something happen to upset you?"

Removing her thumb from her mouth, Penny sat away and looked up at Alma, whispering, "I'm not supposed to tell."

"Tell me," Alma invited, "and it'll be our secret."

Penny thought about that for a moment as she looked over at the doorway. Then, still whispering, she said, "Auntie Eva yelled at me 'cause she was workin', but I didn't know I wasn't supposed to go in her workin' room."

"Ah! I see," Alma said.

"She yelled like my daddy does. I got scared."

"She didn't mean it. I'm sure you just startled her. Eva's very fond of children."

"My daddy doesn't like children," Penny said, her eyes fixed on Alma's.

"He's a foolish man."

"He didn't like *me,* " Penny confided.

"That makes him a *very* foolish man," Alma declared. "Anyone with half a brain would like you. You're a fine child, a splendid child."

"Yeah?" Penny began to smile.

"Positively!" Alma said. "And you're not to be upset about your little run-in with Eva. I promise you, she didn't mean to be cross with you."

"That's what she said. But my mom always said Daddy didn't really mean it when he got mad, only I know he *did* mean it. He was always bad, hurtin' everybody." Again, she looked over at the door, fearful of being caught tattling.

"Well, Eva really *didn't* mean it. I know for a fact that she likes you very much."

"I like her, too," Penny said, her confidence returning.

"Good. So we'll forget about what happened, won't we?"

"Uh-hunh."

"But I want you to know that any time something bothers you, any time at all, even in the middle of the night, you can come and talk to me about it. Okay?"

"Okay." Penny settled again with her head on Alma's breast and was quiet for a time. Then, shifting, using both hands to do it, she lifted Alma's deadened left arm, draping it across her shoulders. "There!" she said, when she was done. "That's better, isn't it, Granny?"

Unable to speak, Alma merely nodded.

Eva just couldn't help herself. Bobby came in offering to set the table and Eva said, "Please don't be offended, but will you let me set up an appointment for you with my hairdresser?''

Bobby touched a hand to her hair. "It's too long. Is that it?"

"It's too long, and whoever gave you that perm shouldn't be allowed anywhere near hair. You'd be so much more attractive with it returned to its natural color and condition."

Bobby felt heat flooding her face. "Joe wanted it blond," she said, eyes downcast.

She was so visibly distraught that Eva reached up to put a hand on her shoulder and the smaller woman flinched, audibly sucking in her breath.

"Sorry," Eva said, quickly pulling back her hand.

"That's okay," Bobby murmured, her heart racing. For a second there she'd thought Eva was going to hit her.

"I was thinking you could go Saturday afternoon while I'm at the pool with Alma," Eva went on, as if nothing had happened. "My hairdresser's very good. He'll give you a cut that'll suit you."

"I don't know," Bobby hesitated. "I don't have too much cash left."

"My treat," Eva said quickly with a coaxing smile. "Have I upset you? If I have, I'm sorry. I know I have a tendency to be sharp with people. It doesn't mean anything, except that I'm distracted."

The woman was apologizing to her and Bobby didn't know how to deal with it. No one had ever treated her the way the women in this house did: prickly one minute, nice as pie the next. They kept her feeling anxious. "It's all right," she said.

"Good," Eva said, smiling more widely. "I'll make the appointment tomorrow." She turned away to the stove and Bobby stood a moment, then took the dishes and cutlery into the dining room.

As she set the table, she wondered if by Saturday she'd be able to conceal her bruises with makeup. She hated having people ask what had happened. Lining up the salt and pepper shakers, she listened to Penny chattering away to Alma in the living room. Bobby stood by the swing door hoping Pen wasn't getting on the old woman's nerves. But Alma was laughing at something Pen had said. So that was good. She returned to the kitchen to ask if there was anything else Eva wanted done.

"Nothing, thank you. I'll be going out after dinner. If you wouldn't mind loading the dishwasher, I'd appreciate it."

"Sure, be glad to," Bobby said.

"By the way, feel free to use the washer and dryer. I know how kids can go through clothes."

"Thanks a lot. I was wondering about that."

"When Mellie comes home for Thanksgiving, she'll bring an entire carload of dirty clothes," Eva said, making a face. "Her excuse is she never has any quarters for the machines at school. I think she's just lazy. I shudder to think what she'll be like when she has a place of her own."

"She'll probably be fine," Bobby said. "People change when they get on their own."

Eva glanced over. "Did you?"

"I haven't ever been on my own. I went from caring for my grandpa to being married to Joe. What about you?"

"I spent a semester of my senior year in London. Then, after I graduated, I went back and we lived there for another year and a half."

"Is that where you met your husband?"

"That's right. Mellie was born in London. We came back when she was about six months old."

"So he was English, your husband?"

"No, American," Eva said, checking the potatoes with a fork. "Ken was from Washington, D.C. If you want to get everyone, dinner's ready."

Eva was so restless she could scarcely eat. She picked at her food and watched Bobby cut up Alma's meat and then

Penny's. She did it quickly, with no fuss whatsoever, then sat back to eat, with one hand holding the hair away from her face. Penny jiggled about in her seat, moving from one side to the other, as if to music no one else could hear. Eva had forgotten that about small children: the way they were constantly moving. It was as if they had motors inside them that ran in overdrive until they were about nine or ten, at which time the motor settled in to idle at a more reasonable rate.

"How do you like school?" Eva asked the child.

"It's a very good school," Penny said with seriousness. "Mrs. Corey's really nice. She let me read the story to-day. Out loud," she added, then looked to Alma, who nodded approval. "She said I did ver-y well." She aimed her fork at a slice of carrot, missed and took aim again.

"Have you made some new friends?" Eva asked.

"Uh-hunh."

"You'll have to invite your new friends over to play sometime," Eva said.

Penny started to speak with her mouth full, and Bobby shushed her, saying, "Swallow what you've got in your mouth first, Pen."

With exaggerated motions, Penny finished chewing, swallowed, and said, "Emma Whitton said her mom's going to call my mom"—she looked over at Bobby—"and see if I can come to her place to play on the weekend. I wroted down the telephone number and gived it to her this morning."

Alma set down her fork and put her right hand on Penny's arm. "You *wrote* down the telephone number and *gave* it to her this morning."

Happily, Penny said, "That's *right!*"

Eva burst out laughing.

Bobby smiled behind her hand.

Alma stroked the child's arm briefly, then retrieved her fork. She *was* smiling this time, Bobby could tell.

"It was very clever of you to write down the phone number," Eva said.

"I haven't had time yet to teach it to her," Bobby explained.

"I already learned it," Penny said proudly. "And I learned the address too. Granny learned me."

"Taught me," Alma corrected her.

"Right," Penny said. "And she taught me all about nine-one-one, too."

"I never thought to do that," Bobby said, feeling perhaps she'd been remiss.

Eva looked at her aunt with respect. It would never have occurred to her to teach the child the emergency number, but it was obviously a sensible thing to do. She took a bite of potato, thinking about the book she was working on. The two weeks without a nurse had set her behind schedule, and she was putting in extra hours attempting to get caught up. In part that was why she'd been so ill-tempered the past few days. Seeing Charlie would, with luck, calm her down, and get her back in control. She couldn't wait for the meal to be over so that she could leave.

Charlie came to the door barefoot, wearing an old gray track suit, his hair still damp from a recent shower. He said, "Hi," and gave her a kiss, then held out his hands for her coat. "You look a little frazzled," he observed as he turned from the closet and took hold of her hand. "Drink?"

"Hmmm. Something strong but not incapacitating," she said, breathing in the smell of his cologne. He liked Obsession. So did she. She had bought him the whole Obsession for Men line the previous Christmas.

He laughed and said, "Jack Daniels."

"Perfect. Straight up."

"Things must be bad," he said, heading for the kitchen.

Following after him, she said, "Actually, we've got a new nurse. Well, she's not really a nurse but Alma seems happier with her than with any of the others. And she's got a child."

"How's that working out?"

"Aside from the fact that I behaved disgracefully to the poor little girl this afternoon, it's working out very well." She leaned in the doorway as he poured the drinks. "She wandered into my office while I was daydreaming and I shrieked at her." She shook her head in disgust. "She thought I was going to hit her. The mother's a battered wife on the run."

Eyebrows raised, drinks in both hands, Charlie said, "Let's go into the den. A battered wife?"

"She's black and blue," Eva said, settling next to him on the sofa and accepting the glass he held out to her. "She's scarcely five feet tall and can't weigh more than ninety pounds. I went to touch her in the kitchen this evening and she literally cringed."

Charlie gave a knowing shake of his head. "I see more of them than you'd care to believe," he said.

"Do you?" She shifted to face him. "You never told me that." In the nearly ten months they'd been seeing each other, they'd covered quite a wide range of conversational topics, including his work. Their conversations were, in fact, one of the most appealing aspects of their involvement. It was something they'd fallen into almost effortlessly in the aftermath of Alma's stroke. He'd been Alma's doctor for years and she'd spoken of them to each other so that when they finally did meet they both felt as if they'd known one another for a long time. Once Alma was home from the hospital, he'd called to ask Eva out and she'd accepted without hesitation. They were, from the start, very relaxed together. Charlie was the only man, aside from Ken, in whom Eva had ever had complete confidence. He didn't play games and said exactly what he was thinking. He also admitted to the guilt he still felt about breaking free of his marriage. She very much admired his truthfulness.

"It's not something I talk about," he said. "Most of them tell me tales about walking into open cabinet doors, or accidentally slamming car doors on their hands. I patch them up and try to let them know I'm willing to listen if they want to talk. They rarely do. How is this titch of a woman managing with Alma?"

"She's evidently strong as a horse, although you'd never believe it to see her."

"You don't like her," Charlie guessed.

Eva hesitated, swallowed some of the Jack Daniels, then said, "I don't *dis*like her. It's just that she bothers me."

"Why? Because she got beaten?"

"Partly. And partly because she's so…lower class. God! What an appalling thing to say! But her hair, and her clothes, the way she talks… Alma says I'm an elitist bitch. I think maybe she's right. I should be able to accept Bobby as she is, shouldn't I? But I want to change her, make her over. I'm treating her to a haircut on Saturday. And over dinner tonight I was actually trying to think what I had in the way of clothes that might fit her." She gave a hoarse laugh and said, "If I keep this up, you'll never want to see me again."

"If you keep it up," he said wisely, "you might figure out why she bothers you so."

She studied him for several moments, thinking how much she liked him, liked his face. He didn't look fifty. He had few wrinkles and there was just a bit of gray threaded through his hair. His hazel eyes were exceptionally clear. "Why don't you look your age?" she asked with a smile.

"Oh, I do," he said easily, extending his arm along the back of the sofa. "And what does fifty look like, anyway? What does forty-three look like, for that matter?"

"Forty-three looks like me," she said, still smiling. "Am I an elitist bitch, do you think?"

"Maybe a little. There are worse things to be. You did take the woman in and give her the job."

"That's true."

"With a child."

"True, too."

"So you're a little on the critical side. It's forgivable."

"You think so?" she asked, her head tilting to one side.

"I think so."

"I came over hoping you'd want to make love."

He grinned. "I think I could accommodate you. Did you have a specific time in mind?"

"Now?"

"You don't want to finish your drink first?"

"We could bring them with us," she said.

"We could do that."

"Okay." She got up and started toward the bedroom.

He sat for a few seconds watching the sway of her hips, then got up to follow her. She was pulling off her sweater by the time he got to the door. After setting his drink down, he shed his track suit, then perched on the end of the bed, enjoying the sight of her removing her clothes. When she got to her underwear, he stood up behind her and ran his hands over her back, bending to kiss her shoulder.

"That's nice," she said, untying the ribbon from her hair.

He unhooked her brassiere, reached around and closed his hands over her breasts.

"That's very nice," she said, her voice lower as she leaned back into him.

"*You're* nice," he said into the side of her neck, "even if you don't think so."

She let her head drop onto his shoulder, her hands on his hips, savoring his warmth. There'd never been anyone, aside from Ken, she'd enjoyed making love to more than Charlie Willis. She wondered now and again if it had anything to do with his being a doctor, or if it was simply because he was one of the rare men who actually liked women. Whatever the cause, she'd quickly become addicted to his lovemaking. "*You're* kind," she said, turning inside his arms. "Or maybe you're just attracted to bitchy elitist women."

"That's possible. God knows, Bets certainly qualified."

"I'm glad I never met her."

"I sometimes wish *I* hadn't," he said, maneuvering her to the bed. "Still, she made three damned decent kids." Adroitly, he put her down on her back and eased off her bikini pants, dropped them to the floor.

"I've been thinking about this for hours," she said as he lowered himself into her embrace.

"I think about this all the time," he said, laughing. "You tend to interfere with my practice."

"Good," she murmured, holding him tightly.

"You really were thinking about this for hours," he said, his hands delving between her thighs.

In answer she brought his mouth down to hers and spread her legs.

He'd become very adept at reading her signals and recognized that this was one of the times when extended foreplay wasn't expected or required. She was already lifting forward, fitting herself to him. The connection was made with such smooth fluidity that for a moment he lost all sense of himself, awed by their ability to join so perfectly. Eva without her clothes was an altogether different woman, utterly uninhibited and completely aware of how her body worked. When he'd asked her about that awareness early on in their involvement, she said with rare candor, "I've been a widow for a very long time. It was either learn to satisfy myself or go crazy." He fell in love with her when she said that. He'd never known anyone so honest.

With Charlie's head resting on her breast as he dozed, Eva's brain traveled back to the island, and she remembered sitting with the children on the living room steps, reading to them from a storybook. Mellie sat on one side of her, Derek on the other, both of them listening attentively. Behind them, on the veranda, Deborah and Ian were arguing in fierce undertones. Outside, a torrential rain obscured the view. The open door at the bottom of the room rattled against the wall with each gust of wind. Suddenly, Eva heard scuffling sounds, the thud of some piece of furniture overturning. Frightened, she forced herself to go on reading, striving to keep her voice under control. She was anxious that the children shouldn't be upset. The unmistakable sound of a hand meeting flesh. A muted cry—of rage or despair? Running footsteps. A blast of inrushing air as the front door was flung open. A few seconds of silence. The roar of the car engine starting, tires spitting up gravel as the car reversed into the driveway then went squealing off down the mountainside. Another brief silence, then the pad of bare feet as Deborah traveled across the living room, pausing to shut the door. She came down the living room steps and continued straight through the room where Eva sat with the children and out the door, into the master suite. The bedroom door closed noiselessly. Eva drew a shallow, ragged breath and went on reading.

With no warning, Derek began sobbing. Grinding his rather grubby small hands into his eyes, his sturdy little body curving inward, he wept in gusting cries. Eva moved to put an arm around him, but he blindly ducked away. Shooting to his feet, he ran pounding through the empty room, out the door to the master suite. Finding the door locked, he banged on it with his fists, crying for his mother. Both Eva and Mellie watched as Derek, in a fury of stormy passion, kicked and beat at the door. After a long minute, the door opened and the boy launched himself at Deborah's legs, wrapping his arms around them and burying his face in her thighs. Deborah said something low, then the door closed.

Dry-mouthed, Eva swallowed as Mellie looked up at her, her face wreathed in confusion, asking, "Mommy, what's the matter with Derek?"

Taking her daughter on her lap, she said inadequately, "He's upset," and slowly rocked Melissa as she tried to think what she could do to help matters. She did very much want to help, but not only did Ian pop up every time she went to talk to Deborah, she was also fearful of becoming another of his victims. And there were the children to consider. More than anything else, she wanted to protect them. Were she to leap to Deborah's defense, all hell might break loose. The thought of the children being firsthand witnesses to mayhem held her back, as did the realization that she didn't actually know what was going on here. No one would talk to her. And even though she longed to say or do something in her friend's defense, on a deeper level she felt the wisest course of action would be to hold back while actively shielding the children as best she could from what was going on. Her combined fear and confusion had her constantly on edge, feeling guilty for her failure to do anything positive and, at the same time, justified in her concern for the children.

God! This was intolerable. She dragged her thoughts back into the present, gently slid out from beneath Charlie, sat up, and reached for her glass.

"What is it?" he asked cannily, as adept at reading her moods as he was at lovemaking.

"I'm reliving ancient history," she said, wishing she'd asked for ice in her drink. She'd have liked something cool now to hold to her forehead. She took a mouthful of the Jack Daniels, swished it around in her mouth, then swallowed. A glance at the clock radio informed her it was nine-fifty. "It's early," she said.

"You sound surprised. Did you think it was much later?"

"Uh-hunh." She put down her glass and turned to him. "Do you ever feel conflicted?"

"Why, because I'm your aunt's internist? No. Now, if I were your internist, that would be a whole other matter. That is what you meant, isn't it?"

"Yes." She took the glass out of his hand and leaned over him to put it on the table. "Do you dream in color, Charlie?"

"Don't you?"

"Not lately. Does it mean something?"

"I'm not qualified to answer that," he said, his hand on her waist. "I doubt it's anything to worry about. If you weren't dreaming at all, that would signify something. What, I couldn't say. But I do know dream deprivation is considered a form of psychological torture." His hand covered her breast, the thumb stroking gently, the fingers applying a slight pressure.

"I thought that was sleep deprivation."

"There's dream deprivation too. Although I can't imagine how that could be accomplished. I imagine they're one and the same thing. So you're reliving ancient history?"

"Uh-hunh." Reluctant just now to talk about it and knowing he wouldn't push her, she trailed her fingers back and forth across his chest, then put her hand to his face, came forward, and kissed him. "You smell wonderful," she said, shifting her face to his neck.

"*You* smell wonderful," he said.

"I smell of you." Smiling, she straddled his lap and sat back on her knees.

"Then we both smell wonderful," he said equably, both hands on her thighs.

"I suppose I should think about going home," she said, leaning back against his upraised knees.

"I never like to have you think about going home. Maybe now that you've got another nurse you'll spend a night now and again. It's been a couple of months since the last time."

"Maybe. I do like sleeping with you. You're a very tidy sleeper."

"You're not, cupcake." He grinned. "You're all over the place."

She laughed and said, "When I was little, Alma used to call me a windmill."

"I'm sure she'd be gratified to know you haven't changed."

"You could just arrive on Saturday night with a sign that says you and I are lovers."

"Your aunt would probably love that," he said. "Alma's no dope."

"No dopes in our family," she said. "Time to go home, chief." She kissed him again, then climbed off the bed and began collecting her clothes.

As she was leaving, he caught hold of her hand and said, "I love you, you know, Eva. If you want to talk about that ancient history, I'm always willing to listen."

"I know that, Charlie. Thank you. I'll get to it eventually, but right now I'm still trying to sort it out." She kissed him a final time. "And you know I love you, too. I'll see you Saturday."

She waved to him before driving off. He waved back, then went inside and closed the door. She sighed deeply and headed for the turnpike, wishing he lived a little closer than Old Riverside. But she thought that every time she left him to drive the six exits up to Stamford. One of these nights she was going to have to stay with him again, enjoy an entire night at Charlie's side. For now, though, she felt much better.

Eight

At ten Saturday morning a station wagon with fake wood paneling pulled into the driveway and the horn honked.

"I gotta go now!" Penny said, pulling away from her mother before her coat was buttoned.

"You hold on a minute," Bobby said. "Let me finish doing up these buttons. They'll wait for you."

A moment later the doorbell went and Bobby opened it to see a small girl with long blond pigtails and eyeglasses, clad in a forest green duffel coat.

All smiles, Penny said, "Hi, Emma. I'm coming right now."

"I need the phone number of where you're gonna be," Bobby said.

Emma Whitton recited it on the spot.

"Is that your mom in the car?" Bobby asked the girl, mentally storing the number.

"Uh-hunh." Emma took Penny by the hand and the two of them started running toward the station wagon as Emma's mother opened her door and called out, "I'll have her back by five. Okay?"

"Okay." Bobby waved.

The children climbed into the back seat. Mrs. Whitton slid behind the wheel, refastened her seat belt, then the car reversed out of the driveway. Bobby closed the front door, wondering why Emma's mother hadn't come up to introduce herself, then decided that the people around here probably didn't bother with things like that, so long as the children knew each other.

Coming down the stairs at that moment, Eva said, "Don't worry. She'll be fine. And next week, it'll be your turn to go pick up Emma and bring her back here for the day. Your appointment's in half an hour," she said, checking her wristwatch. "Are you sure you know how to get there?"

"Yes, ma'am...Eva."

"Good. All you'll need is two dollars to tip the shampoo girl."

"Okay." Bobby looked down at her feet.

"Don't be nervous," Eva said. "Bruce is the best hairdresser in the area. He'll do a wonderful job."

Bobby nodded, her eyes still on her feet.

"Is there something else?" Eva asked.

"I was just wondering what day I get paid."

"Oh, right. Did I forget to tell you that? I usually pay the nurses on Mondays, unless you need money now."

"No, that's okay. I was just wondering. Monday's fine. How do you manage on Sundays?" Bobby asked, thinking Eva seemed different this morning, friendlier and more relaxed. She really was very good-looking, especially when she smiled. And she dressed better than anyone Bobby had ever known. Today she was wearing navy slacks and a blue and white striped blouse, with a short sleeveless white wool sweater. Her hair ribbon was striped red, white, and blue. She looked real sharp, Bobby thought, feeling shabby in her old Lee jeans and a baggy green sweater.

"I look after my aunt on Sundays," Eva explained. "After all, you've got to have a day off."

"I don't mind," Bobby said.

"You mean you'd work Sundays too?"

"Sure, if it'd help."

Eva was thinking quickly. If Bobby was willing to be on call seven days a week, she'd be able to get her writing back on schedule. The other nurses had been strictly by the book, claiming Saturday afternoons and Sundays for themselves. "That might work out very well," Eva said. "Let's talk about it later this afternoon. Of course, you'd be compensated."

"I don't mind about that," Bobby said, glancing over to the living room, where Alma was in her wheelchair, reading the New York *Times*.

For a second time, Eva was prompted to put a hand on Bobby's shoulder. The smaller woman jerked slightly, but this time Eva made good on the gesture, in a lowered voice saying, "You really like her, don't you?"

Bobby nodded.

"I'm so glad," Eva said fervently, then withdrew her hand from Bobby's childishly narrow shoulder, saying, "You'd better get going or you'll be late. And Saturday's a zoo at the salon. We'll sort out the details when Alma and I get back from the Y."

The receptionist gave Bobby a smock and showed her where to get changed. In the closet-sized room, Bobby took note of the clothes people had left hanging and added her own coat and sweater to the tightly packed rack.

When she emerged, the receptionist indicated the rear of the salon, saying, "Go on back and Peggy will get you washed."

Self-conscious, convinced everyone was staring at the bruises she'd tried to conceal with makeup, she made her way to an area that had sinks on both sides.

The girl used shampoo that smelled of apples and gave Bobby's hair a good washing. Then she applied a minty conditioning cream, rinsed it off, wrapped a towel around Bobby's head and with a smile told her she could sit up now. "That's Bruce's chair," the girl said, pointing. "Go on over and sit down. He just ran next door for coffee. He'll be right back."

Bobby sat in the chair and tried to avoid looking at herself in the wall of mirrors. She could smell cigarette smoke and was dying to light up but didn't dare in case there was some special smoking area or something. She looked over to the front of the salon and saw an amazing-looking man with long black hair pulled back in a ponytail and a black leather jumpsuit festooned with silver chains come hurrying in with a container of coffee in one hand and a lit cigarette in the other. He bumped the front door closed with his hip and came striding forward in silver cowboy boots, his expression changing several times as he saw her. Removing the lid from his coffee, he said, "So you're Bobby. Eva said you were in desperate need and, sweetie, I can see she wasn't kidding." He took a swallow of the steaming coffee, his eyes never leaving her face, then set the cup and his cigarette down and came around behind her so that Bobby was forced to look at him in the mirror.

"Honey," he said, holding up her hair with both hands, his expression one of greatly exaggerated dismay, "who *did* this to you?"

"I had it done back home," she said in a small voice.

"It's a disaster, sweetie."

"I guess so," she agreed wretchedly.

Parting her hair with his fingers, he gazed at her roots, then looked at her in the mirror and said, "Medium brown with red highlights. Am I right?"

"That's right."

"Well, dearest, here's what I think," he said, bunching the ends of her hair in one hand, his eyes on hers in the mirror. "I think first we'll get rid of all this Brillo on the ends, and bring it up about here." He laid the side of his hand next to her jaw. "Give it some shape that'll go with what's left of the perm. Then we'll tint you back to medium brown. The tint'll take a lot of the dryness out. So," he said, reaching for the cup and taking another swallow of coffee, "what d'you think? Are we together on this?"

"I uhm . . ."

"Course," he went on, holding the cup now with both hands as he studied her face in the mirror, "we could straighten and condition it before we do the tint, get rid of that atrocious perm altogether." Freeing one hand, he looked at the enormous watch on his wrist that had an airplane's wings on the face instead of hands. "Let's do that, shall we, sweetie?" he said decisively. "I had a cancellation, so we've got the time. And God only knows you need my help." He put the cup down again and reached for a huge comb with long teeth and began drawing it through her hair. "Someone as petite as you shouldn't have such long hair. Your face is too small." He suddenly swiveled the chair around and bent to look at her close-to. "Honey," he said sadly, "that makeup only makes it look worse. If it was me, I'd just say, 'Fuck it!' and let them take me as I am."

Bobby didn't know how to react. She thought he was being kind but couldn't tell for sure. She risked a smile and he smiled at her conspiratorially, then swiveled the chair around again and reached for the scissors, saying, "You'll be gorgeous, sweetie!"

The cutting took more than forty minutes. Then the straightening solution had to stay on her hair for half an hour, followed by a rinse, then twenty minutes for the conditioner. After that Peggy washed her hair again with the fragrant apple shampoo, before leading her to the extreme rear of the shop where Bruce, his jumpsuit protected by a pale green smock, tinted her hair, the mixture cold each time it touched her scalp. When her entire head was covered with thick dark goo, he placed a rim of cotton batting all the way around her face, from one ear to the other. He set a timer, peeled off his rubber gloves, said, "I'll be back in thirty-five minutes, sweetie," and went to his chair in the middle of the salon to cut another woman's hair.

Bobby sat reading an old issue of *People*, her scalp itchy, and feeling as if trickles of the dye were inching down the sides of her face. The level of noise in the place was high, what with the dryers going and everyone talking, the front door opening and closing, women coming and going. Between shampoos, Peggy got a wide-bottomed broom and walked between the chairs, sweeping up the hair. The itching of her scalp almost unbearable, Bobby resisted the temptation to plunge her fingers into the goo and give her head a good scratch. She read a piece on Madonna, then an article on some couple who'd written a best-selling diet book. At last, spotting an ashtray on the counter, she lit a cigarette and inhaled deeply, thinking this was going to cost Eva a lot of money and wondering why she was willing to do it. Maybe it was just that she plain hated Bobby's hair. She hadn't much liked it herself. But Joe had told her to go get herself fixed up blond and curly, like the women on TV, and she'd done it because she knew if she argued he'd get mad and beat her up.

The bleach had burned like crazy. Then the setting-lotion burned on top of what the bleach had already done. She'd had to sit under a hair dryer with dozens of tiny rollers pulling the hair out of her scalp, her entire head on fire. And when the woman had finally removed the rollers and rinsed her hair, the relief had been tremendous. Until Bobby saw herself. She looked like one of those little troll dolls she'd had as a kid, a tiny squash-faced creature with hair twice as long as its body. Instead of the curls she'd anticipated, she'd come away with pure frizz. But Joe thought it was great. He got so excited he put his hand up her skirt, pulled down her pants right in the kitchen, bent her forward over the table—she knew better than to protest—and did it to her right there, where anybody could've looked in and seen. He'd grabbed hold of her hips and pushed himself into her and pumped away for what felt like forever until he'd finally finished. Then he'd pulled out of her, slapped her naked bottom, laughed, and gone off to Garvey's to grab some beers with the boys.

The timer shrilled, and she jumped.

Bruce came over and used a Q-tip to check her roots. "All done, dearest," he said, and summoned Peggy to give her hair yet another wash. More apple shampoo and more peppermint cream rinse. A fresh towel around her neck and another over her hair, and back to Bruce's chair, where he whipped the towel off her hair, presenting her with her image in the mirror.

"Heaven!" he declared. "I knew it would be."

With a round brush and a blow dryer, he began drying her hair a section at a time, side-parting it and curving it under at the very bottom. She didn't recognize herself. Her hair was glossy and sleek, with just the slightest bit of wave left from the perm. When he'd finished, he turned the chair around again so he could talk to her eye to eye. "Sweetie," he said, "don't *ever* let anyone do that to you again. *This* is what you're supposed to look like. You've got an absolutely adorable little face, and a mouth I'd *kill* for, I swear to God. Come back and see me in six weeks for a trim. Okay?" He chucked her under the chin, kissed the air in front of her nose, and said, "And use brown eyeshadow, dearest. You'll be divine."

She said, "Okay. Thanks very much."

"Half a tick, sweetie," he said, and swept the loose hairs off her neck with a soft brush.

Even though Eva hadn't said anything about it, she tipped him five dollars. He tucked the money into one of the dozens of pockets of his jumpsuit and said, "Don't forget! Six weeks. Give my love to darling Eva."

She gave Peggy two dollars, then went to the changing room, deposited the damp, stained smock in the bin, pulled on her coat and sweater, and left the salon, surprised at the freshness of the air after the ammonia smell she'd been breathing for hours. Her head felt light. The wind seemed to drift through her sleek new haircut. She felt altogether renewed, and wanting to make some gesture of her appreciation to Eva, she bought a bouquet of big yellow mums at the market.

Alma was napping when she got home, and Eva was evidently up in her office. Leaving the flowers in the kitchen, Bobby went down to the apartment to admire herself in the bathroom mirror. Bruce was right about the makeup. It just called attention to the bruises. She washed her face, relieved to see the swelling was gone from her eye. What remained was a greenish yellow stain encircling the entire area, even the lid. She healed fast, thank heavens. Another few days and she'd be back to normal.

She collected the laundry and carried it upstairs, got the first load of whites going, then went downstairs to fix herself some coffee, and had a cigarette while she drank it. Looking around, she wished she'd thought to take some of the photographs before she went running off. Aside from Pen's books and Mr. Bear, this place had no personal touches. On her way home she'd seen a sign advertising a flea market in the bowling alley parking lot every Sunday. Maybe she'd take Pen over tomorrow while Alma was napping, see if she couldn't pick up a thing or two.

While she sat sipping her coffee, enjoying the Marlboro, she thought about all the ways Joe had hurt her, and wondered why it had taken her so long to run away from him. She'd never made love until she started going with Joe, and when they'd only been fooling around in his car it'd been okay, even kind of exciting. But she should've known after the first time they did it for real that he was someone who'd hurt her. The minute they were married, he'd stopped using rubbers. "It's like taking a shower with your goddamned socks on," he'd said, forcing her legs so far back that it hurt. He liked to do it that way, with her knees almost touching her shoulders so that it was nothing but pain and shame. And it wasn't enough for her to let him do that. He complained she was like wood. So she had to pretend she liked it, breathing hard the way he did, while the whole time she felt as if she was being battered inside. It amazed her every time that she didn't bleed from the way he went at her. And there were always bruises on the insides of her thighs; they never got a chance to heal. He came at her every day except when she had a period.

Then he made her use her mouth on him, holding handfuls of her hair and whispering, "Come on, bitch. Do it."

Sometimes after he hit her—because she forgot to iron his shirt, or she burned the bacon, or she only had time to heat up a frozen pizza because she was late getting home from work—he'd drag her into the bedroom, not caring that Penny was in the house, and throw her on her hands and knees on the floor and ride her until she collapsed. She bore it in silence, careful not to make a sound because that only got him going worse; the blood dripping from her nose and mouth onto the floor, pain throughout her body, until he finished and he'd give her a kick before zipping himself up and slamming out of the house. She was always terrified Penny was going to see, scared to death Penny would come wandering in and he'd keep right on with what he was doing, forcing the baby to watch. It had never happened, but a couple of times it'd been close. Penny had come to the door calling for her and Bobby had had to keep her voice steady, calling back, "Go play, hon. Mommy'll be there in a minute." Inside her mind, she'd prayed Pen would listen and go away. She didn't want her baby growing up with terrible pictures in her head. But Pen had seen Joe hitting her; she'd heard him shouting and cursing. She probably had plenty of terrible pictures in her head. The thing was, she was still little. Maybe she'd forget. That was all Bobby wanted, for Penny to forget.

When she went up to the kitchen to start the second load going in the washer, Eva was standing looking at the flowers. "Where did these come from?" she asked.

"They're for you," Bobby said.

"Let me *look* at you," Eva exclaimed, breaking into a wide smile. "You look *wonderful!* Didn't I tell you Bruce was good?" She circled Bobby, saying, "Now, that's more like it. You look *so* pretty. Are you pleased?"

Bobby returned her smile. "The flowers are to say thank you."

"You didn't have to do that," Eva said.

"I wanted to."

"Well, that's very sweet of you. I'll just put them in water before I start dinner." She turned away to open the cupboard for a vase, and Bobby went to put the whites into the dryer before loading the coloreds.

The front door opened and Penny came flying into the kitchen clutching a handful of drawings.

"Honey, go back and wipe your feet," Bobby told her.

Penny's mouth dropped open. "Mom," she said. "You look so *different.*"

"You like it?" Bobby asked, bending to unbutton Penny's coat.

"Isn't it great?" Eva said.

"Yeah," Penny agreed. "It's great, Mom." Then, remembering the handful of drawings, she said, "Wait till you see! We played Nintendo and Emma's got a great big dollhouse and a zillion Barbies and we had turkey sandwiches and chocolate chip cookies and we did Etch-A-Sketch and watched cartoons and..."

"Slow down," Bobby smiled. "Let's get these things off you, first."

"Auntie Eva," Penny said, "look what I drawed!"

"Drew," Eva corrected her. "Come show me."

Penny ran over to lay her drawings on the countertop, and Eva admired each of them, saying, "They're very good. Do you think I could have one to put on the refrigerator?"

"Sure! You pick one."

Eva selected the drawing of an immense yellow flower with pointy green leaves and made a small ceremony of fastening it to the refrigerator door with several magnets. Bobby watched, with the sense that something special was happening. A family feeling was growing in this house. She saw the way Eva patted the top of Penny's head, saw the easy way Penny asked if she could have a piece of the green pepper Eva was slicing, and felt the beginning of closeness. And right then she knew it was going to be okay to keep the refrigerator downstairs stocked with food, and to lay in a supply of Pen's favorite cereals, because they were going to be staying on.

Penny announced, "I'm gonna go up and show Granny my pictures," and went running off with a piece of green pepper in one hand and her drawings in the other, calling as she went, "Granny, wait'll you see what I drawed for you!"

The nerd came to the end of the counter, asking, "Something I can help you with?" and Joe said, "Yeah. I wanna talk with you. Outside." The nerd's eyes slitted a bit and he said, "You're Bobby Salton's husband, aren't you?" Joe said, "You got that right. And I wanna talk with you." The nerd looked over at the lineups of people waiting to be served and said, "Could it wait? We're pretty busy right now."

"This'll just take a minute," Joe said. He waited a second to be sure the creep got his meaning, then pushed out the side door to the parking lot. He touched the .38 in his waistband, then fired up a smoke, ready for action.

The side service door opened and the nerd came out carrying a goddamned baseball bat. The guy marched right over and said, "What do you want? I'm busy. I've got a business to run."

"Where's my wife at?" Joe demanded, flicking his cigarette in the direction of the dumpster.

"How should I know?" the nerd said, the bat hanging loose in his hand. "She's your wife."

"Don't play cute with me. I know what the two of you're up to." Joe reached around under his jacket.

"Keep your hands where I can see them," the nerd said, firming up his grip on the bat.

"Hey!" Joe grinned and held his hands out to the sides. "Don't get your balls in an uproar. I'm just asking did you see Bobby."

"I don't know where your wife is. But if she's smart she's probably a thousand miles away from here. Now if that's all, I'm going back inside. Don't come here again. People like you make my stomach turn."

"Watch your mouth!" Joe said, wishing he'd planned this better.

The nerd just gave him another look and went back in through the metal service door, letting it slam after him. Furious, Joe raced back to the Firebird and burned rubber, fishtailing as he hit the road. He was so mad he wanted to torch the whole fucking place.

Fuck it! he thought, pounding his fist on the steering wheel.

All at once he remembered that Easter Sunday so long ago. Three years old and excited 'cause after church they were going to have a special dinner with the grandparents. He's ready to go, sitting waiting, and all of a sudden his guts start making these wet gurgles and before he can do a thing, he's done a job in his pants. It's a stinking mess and he goes running to his mother in the kitchen, crying, because his guts're still rumbling and the mess is burning. The old man laughs and says, "Never mind," but she goes nuts, yelling, "What d'you mean, never mind? Son of a bitch!" Right there in the kitchen she hauls off Joe's clothes, takes the reeking mess and rubs Joe's face in it. The old man goes, "Jesus, Ruth! Don't do that to the kid!" and she goes, "Shut the hell up!" She gives Joe a shove, going, "Get the hell out of my sight, you filthy little pig," and Joe's sick and sobbing, three years old, it's not his fault. The old man goes, more quietly, "You didn't have to do that."

Goddamn it! Why'd he have to think of that now? He hated remembering that. It made him want to go out with an AK-47 or an Uzi and shoot up everything he saw, made him want to burn things down, smash things to pieces, break bones, blow away everybody in sight.

His hands were shaking, the car was all over the fucking road. Get a grip, for chrissake! He rolled down the window, let in a blast of cold air to take the stink of shit out of his nostrils, get him past the feeling like he was drowning.

Nine

Bobby dreamed she and Alma were walking across the back lawn toward the shore. The air was warm and scented with freshly mown grass, the sky was a flawless blue. Alma was wearing a lovely white silk dress with a full skirt that lifted lightly in the breeze. Her hair, pure silver in the sun, was coiled atop her head in a perfectly symmetrical circle. Bobby couldn't get over how beautiful she looked. She was tall and stately, with a fine strong profile and a pretty mouth that Bruce would've said he'd kill for. She walked the way Bobby imagined a dancer might, holding herself real proud with her shoulders back and her legs taking long easy strides. There was a bench at the bottom of the lawn, and she and Alma sat down and looked out over the water. The day was so clear they could see all the way across to Long Island. And sailboats rode the waves, white against the marbled green of the water.

Bobby looked down to see they were holding hands, and she felt like a child, her hand surrounded by Alma's much larger one. Alma wore a ring on her middle finger and Bobby wondered why she'd never noticed it before. It was magnificent, old-fashioned, with a big diamond surrounded by a circle of smaller ones. The sun glanced off the big diamond's facets, creating little rainbows in Bobby's eyes. She inhaled, tasting the salt in the air and smelling the seaweed the tide had washed up on the shallow strip of beach.

"I used to swim here," Alma said. "Years ago, when I first came to live in this house, I'd get up very early in the morning and swim for half an hour. The water was so cold it made my lungs seize up and for the first minute or two I always thought no one had ever done anything sillier than to swim in this water. But then I got used to it and I went out a ways and swam back and forth until my arms and legs ached. Then I'd come in and shower and feel the heat restoring my circulation. That was a very long time ago, when I was young."

"You're still young," Bobby said, not intending any flattery.

Alma turned to look her full in the face and Bobby was shocked to see a twitching in the woman's cheek. "It's already happening," Alma said with sadness and anger. "Don't tell me you can't see it for yourself."

"We'll make it stop," Bobby said, unable to look away from the muscle that seemed to be clenching and unclenching in the woman's cheek.

"Just sit back and enjoy the day, Barbara," Alma said, facing the water again.

"You never called me Barbara before," Bobby said, so hot now she'd begun sweating.

"It's your name, after all." Alma's shoulders lifted and fell in a slight shrug.

"My mother named me Barbara," Bobby said, firming up her grip on the older woman's hand.

"I know that."

"She didn't want me. But it didn't really matter. Grandpa and Aunt Helen were real good to me." Holding tightly to the hand enclosing hers, she said, "I'll take good care of you, I promise."

"It's time to get the chair," Alma said, her words oddly misshapen, and turned her head to reveal her cruelly distorted features.

Bobby began crying as she tried with her hand to lift Alma's face, to restore her beauty.

"Let the old bitch be!" Joe said, standing with his back to the sun so that she couldn't make out his face. "Clear out of the way, Bobby!" he ordered, raising the barrel of the shotgun.

"NO!" she cried, and flung herself in front of Alma.

"Okay," he said, "if that's the way you want it," and pulled the trigger.

Charlie turned off the ignition and put a hand on the back of Eva's neck. "A nightcap, cupcake?"

"I'd rather have some coffee."

"Coffee and Courvoisier?"

"Sold," Eva said, and slid out of the car.

While she got his coffee machine going, he poured an inch of Courvoisier into two balloons, then went to the den to put on some music. He looked over the rack of CD's and decided on volume one of Ray Charles's greatest hits. A few moments and "Georgia on My Mind" eased from the speakers.

"Oh, I love that," Eva called from the kitchen.

"Good," he said, crossing the room to hug her from behind, winding an arm around her waist and lifting her hair aside to kiss the back of her neck. "I want you to be happy. Care to dance while we're waiting for the coffee?"

She turned and fitted herself into his arms, and he led her gracefully around the kitchen. "How did you get to be so good at everything?" she asked, her arms looped around his neck.

"Practice," he said, smiling. "Lots and lots of practice."

"When? You were married to Bets for twenty years."

"I've had five years since then to hone my skills."

"I'll bet you had women coming out of your ears."

"Some," he said, his lips moving against her ear. "A few. And what about you? Were they beating down your door?"

"Men have no concept of female reality," she said. "You don't know the way it works. If you're a young widow, the men you meet think you're desperate for sex. It stands to reason you would be. After all, you've just lost a virile young husband who had to be putting it to you at every possible opportunity. So they believe, they'll ease some of the infamous sexual tension suffered by every young widow. The fact that they're utterly unattractive in countless ways has no bearing on their libidos. They've got the necessary equipment, therefore they must be capable of doing the job. They think women are dictated to by their genitals, the way they are."

"You mean you're not?"

She pinched the back of his neck and laughed softly. "No, we are not. We're dictated to by our brains. Common sense and emotions first, genitals last."

"Your recent heroines aren't," he said, as "Unchain My Heart" started.

"My recent heroines do *not* reflect my personal values. But it's my job these days to deliver starry-eyed young women into the arms of their true loves."

"I don't know how the hell you do it."

"We need the money, Charlie. Alma's insurance won't cover the nurse full-time or the physical therapist, or the medications. The insurance company insists she no longer requires those things. I don't happen to agree."

"No, neither do I."

"Right. So for the time being, I'm writing commercial women's fiction under three different names. Someday I'll get back to the real work."

"It's a shame," he said feelingly. "I liked the real work."

"The coffee's ready," she said, breaking away to get cups from the cabinet.

"Sorry," he said quietly as she poured the coffee.

"Hell, don't be sorry, Charlie. Nobody held a gun to my head. It was an offer I couldn't refuse, so to speak. I'm lucky I can do the damned things. It's not easy writing a book every three months, but the money's good. It pays for the extras.''

"Surely Alma has savings."

"Of course she does," she said, carrying her cup to the den. "But why should she use up her life's savings when I can carry the ball? Besides, I owe her."

"I guarantee you she doesn't see it that way."

"She wouldn't. But I do. Let's discuss religion or politics."

"You left out sex."

She laughed. "I thought we'd already covered that in the kitchen."

"Oh, right!" He slapped his hand against the side of his head. "Genital dictation. Silly old me!" He smiled and leaned over to give her a kiss. "Stay the night."

"I can't."

"Sure you can." He looked at his watch. "It's almost eleven. Call home and say you'll be back in the morning."

"I don't know," she said, wavering.

He reached across to the phone on the coffee table and set it down in her lap. "Call home, Eva."

"If I do this, she'll know for sure we're having an affair."

"She already knows that," he said. "She probably figured it out after our first date."

"I didn't sleep with you on our first date."

"No, but you thought about it."

"So did you," she countered.

"Damned right, cupcake. Now call home." He gave her another kiss, then sat back to wait.

Feeling like a guilty teenager, Eva dialed and listened to the ringing start on the other end. On the second ring, Bobby answered. Relieved, Eva said, "Hi. It's me. I hope I didn't wake you."

"Oh, no," Bobby said in a hushed voice. "I was just sitting here, reading."

"Well, good. I wanted to let you know I won't be home tonight."

"Okay."

"Would you mind locking up?"

"No, I don't mind. Anything else you want done?"

"No, thanks. I'll see you in the morning."

"Okay, bye."

Eva hung up out of breath.

"Now, that wasn't so bad, was it?" Charlie said.

"No comment." She returned the phone to the coffee table and drank first a swallow of coffee, then one of the liqueur. Ray was singing "You Don't Know Me." She pushed off her shoes, then swung her legs up and across Charlie's lap. "Well," she sighed. "Now Bobby knows as well as Aunt Alma."

"They'll have the sex police out after you," he quipped.

She laughed and took hold of his hand, threading her fingers through his. "Where do your kids go for Thanksgiving?"

"Home to Bets. Why?"

"Want to come to my house?"

"Sure. I'd love to."

"Okay. Good."

"So," he said, "care for another dance?"

She shook her head. "I'm too comfortable."

"I could put the speakers on in the bedroom."

"That'd be nice."

"Let's do it," he said, lifting her legs off his lap. Going over to the stereo system, he threw a switch, then waited as she got up carrying a drink in each hand.

Charlie dreamed he was at a convention in a huge hotel. Doctors crowded the corridors, filled the escalators going in both directions. Bored, he removed the badge from his lapel and dropped it into his pocket. He fished a room key out of his pocket and strolled toward the bank of elevators, thinking he'd pack his bag and catch a plane home. He not only hated conventions, he also hated hotels. There were always windows you couldn't open and heating or air-conditioning that made the room too hot or too cold and couldn't be shut off. He disliked water glasses in little inverted paper bags, plastic convenience packs of shampoo, diagonal strips across toilet seats, and hotel furniture, particularly the beds.

He got off on the fortieth floor and headed for his room, determined to call the airlines and get on the first flight back to New York. His car was parked in the long-term lot at LaGuardia. Traffic permitting, he could make it home in thirty-five or forty minutes. He'd call Eva and maybe she'd be able to come over.

Inserting his key in the lock, he turned the knob only to find the chain in place on the door. "What the hell?" he muttered.

"Just a moment," came Bets's voice from inside, and the door closed briefly.

The sound of her voice gave him a sick, guilty feeling. He heard the chain being removed, then she called, "Okay. Come on in," and he pushed open the door to see her sitting naked on the edge of the table by the window. The sight made his stomach clench like a fist. Why wouldn't she give up the fight and get on with her life? Why did she have to keep making these dismal plays to get him back? He hated to see her losing her dignity. "What are you doing here?" he asked tonelessly.

"I know how much you hate these things, Charlie," she said, her hands on her knees, which were slightly parted, her feet swinging gently. "So I came to take you home."

Closing the door, he turned and stared at her.

"Come here," she said, holding open her arms. "We've just got time to do this before our flight."

He kept his distance, trying to think how to get her to go. She was only doing this to compound his guilt.

"Bets," he said. "I thought we'd settled this a long time ago."

She leaned back, regarding him with calculating eyes. "It'll never be settled," she said, her thighs parting a little more.

"Don't do this," he pleaded. "You're only making things more difficult."

"We have fifteen minutes before you have to zip me into the suitbag," she said.

"Look, this is ridiculous," he said. "I've got patients to see."

It was true. He looked over his shoulder to see half a dozen people sitting in straight-backed chairs reading old copies of *National Geographic*.

"I've got to go home anyway," she said, slipping down off the table. She began dressing, and he felt relief easing the tension in his chest. He hated the way she insisted on clinging to something that was long dead. "I've got a cab waiting," she said, and went out, leaving the door open.

"Am I next?" asked an elderly woman, setting aside her magazine and getting to her feet.

His throat choking closed, he nodded, and the woman hobbled toward him. He shut his eyes and when he opened them he was standing in a deserted corridor trying to remember where Eva had said she'd be waiting. He started walking, badly needing to see Eva. Please be there, he prayed.

Glancing over at the luminous dial of the clock on her bedside table, Alma saw it was nearly midnight. She folded her right arm back, tucking her hand beneath her head, and contemplated the darkness. It felt odd without Eva in the house. It was one of the few times she'd spent an entire night with Charlie. Alma didn't mind. After all, Eva was a middle-aged woman, not some naive teenager. What bothered her was the way Eva's life seemed to be mirroring her own. Being witness to another woman's evolution was now acutely painful to her. It made her miserably aware of all that had once been and could never be again. It required considerable effort not to become envious and bitter when confronted by that other woman's still-firm flesh, by the multiplicity of possibilities that still existed for her. What made it bearable, of course, was the love. But even so, it wasn't easy to look into that empty mirror, knowing it needn't have been that way.

And once again she found herself reviewing that so well remembered evening forty-three years before, scanning it as if for details she might have missed.

They'd been sitting on the glider, talking quietly so as not to be overheard by her parents and Cora in the living room only a few feet away. Then, abruptly, Randy had said, "Let's take a walk. There's something I have to tell you." And with a sense of dread, she'd followed him off the porch.

In the darkness of the cool summer evening they walked along the road, the music from the radio thinning, then disappearing, the farther they got from the house. She felt an icy stabbing in her heart, an apprehension that was so palpable she could almost see and taste it. It was strange, but she'd never until that moment realized that fear could leave a metallic taste on the tongue, or that it could envelop one like a heavy second skin.

Randy was talking, but she didn't hear the individual words so much as she absorbed an overall sense of their meaning. "Something I never meant to happen... You have to believe I'd never hurt you... It just *happened*..." His words hovered in the air between them like frozen crystals, and all she could think was that she'd been played for a fool. And it hurt. There'd never been a pain quite like this, not even when, as a child, she'd fallen down the flight of stairs leading from the attic and had fractured her arm. That had been a localized pain. She'd been able to view it objectively, even with awe. At the age of five it had never occurred to her that the interior of her body was capable of being broken, that inside her flesh were countless fragile bones. She'd thought of herself as all of a piece. But the cracked radius proved graphically that she was comprised of many parts, any of which could sustain damage.

At twenty-four she was no longer a child. But she was as shocked and dismayed by this new form of pain as she'd been by that old injury. No one had ever warned her of anything as vicious as the damage she was suffering internally as a result of what Randy had to say.

There was another woman, and he'd made her pregnant. He had no alternative but to marry her. He'd been making love to both of them. Alma had had the wits to take precautions, the other woman had not. Did that make Alma the better or wiser of the two? Perhaps. But there was no satisfaction to be gained from being better and wiser. She felt simply foolish. And coupled with the pain was a gathering rage at the realization that she'd been used and was now being discarded.

"You have to believe... How sorry I am... I swear to God I never... You're the one I really love..."

She was unimpressed by his tears, by his apologies and explanations; she scarcely heard them. She was all at once actively engaged in the process of ripping from her interior the roots of her considerable affection for this feckless young man.

Without a word, she turned and ran, leaving him alone on the dark road with his seemingly limitless supply of words. She ran, feeling the impact jarring her spine, rattling her teeth. Her jaws clamped shut, she ran and ran.

Her father had taken one look at her and he'd known. It still amazed her that the person she'd deemed least likely to perceive any change in her, knew instantly that her world had been upended. Saying nothing to disturb the newly pregnant Cora or her mother, who were playing a game of rummy, her father set aside his newspaper, got up, caught Alma at the foot of the stairs, and directed her to the kitchen.

"I think a drink is in order," he said, sounding very like a doctor giving a prescription, and took a bottle of scotch and two glasses from the cupboard. He poured a measure of the liquor in each, handed one to Alma, and said, "Drink that. It'll help."

She obeyed like an automaton, then shuddered as the scotch seared its way down her throat.

"Would you like to talk about it?" he'd asked, his heavy brows drawn together in concern.

"I can't," she'd managed to get out, praying he wouldn't persist. If she had to speak, she'd go to pieces, perhaps never recover.

"I understand," he'd said, his sympathetic eyes boring holes in her resolve.

They'd stood in silence for a few moments, then her father had said, "I know right now you feel you've lost everything of consequence, but if you take the time to think about it, you'll see that you've actually gained something."

"What?" she'd asked hoarsely, unable to see any possibility of gains. All she could feel were the losses. She'd been carrying around mental portraits of her children and suddenly those images had been eradicated. She was in a state of mourning, as if actual children had died.

"You've gained a new insight," he said. "Consider it, Alma," he'd counseled. "There's a lesson to be learned in every experience."

"Oh, yes," she'd said bitterly, with a tremendous effort of will keeping her spine straight, her chin up. Her body wanted to collapse in on itself.

"We've all of us had our hearts broken, one way and another. It's part of the human experience. I know you don't want to hear any of this," he'd said, again demonstrating his uncanny awareness, "but in time I believe you'll see the truth of what I'm saying."

There was another brief silence as they gazed at each other. She was tempted to throw herself into her father's arms, allow him to comfort her, but she couldn't do it. She refused to display any hint of weakness. Her stomach roiling from the scotch, she'd said, "Thank you, Father. I'm very tired. I think I'll go up to bed."

"Of course," he'd said. And as he did every night, he kissed her on the forehead, then busied himself returning the liquor to the cabinet and rinsing the glasses in the sink.

She'd started for the door, telling herself to turn back and seek her father's embrace, take the comfort he was then, and always had been, prepared to offer. Go over and let him put his arms around you, she told herself. But she kept going. Her legs moved, taking her to the hallway, to the stairs, to the landing, to her room. Not bothering to turn on the light, she sat on the bed, feeling the marrow dry in her bones, going to powder. She was as hollow as a woodwind, the breeze making a faint moaning noise as it penetrated the dusty interior of her bones.

She did learn something that night, but it wasn't what her father would have wished. She'd discovered to her horror that, her contempt notwithstanding, she had the capacity to be a silly female. She'd been one with Randy Wheeler. She'd never do it again. Even if she found someone else to marry, she would never reveal herself completely. She would always, no matter what, keep a part of herself safely in reserve.

Ten

Ruby arrived Monday morning as the school bus was pulling away.

"Hair looks real nice," Ruby said, with a smile as they entered the house together. "Real nice."

Bobby thanked her, and went downstairs to make the beds while Ruby collected her cleaning materials and went off to Eva's office.

On her way up to get Alma, Bobby stopped in the kitchen to glance at the refrigerator. There was a check, but it was for Ruby, and Bobby scrupulously avoided looking at the amount. Eva came in with Alma's tray just then, instantly misinterpreted what Bobby had been doing, and said in frosty tones, "Ruby is paid roughly the same daily rate as you are."

"Oh, no," Bobby said, fairly stricken by the thinly disguised accusation that she'd been snooping. "I wasn't looking at that."

"It certainly *looked* as if you were."

"No, ma'am," Bobby said. "I was just seeing if there was a check for me."

Oh hell! Eva thought, setting the tray on the counter. *Why* was she such a bitch to this woman? "I'm sorry," she said, turning from the counter to see that Bobby was chewing on her lower lip, visibly upset. Eva wanted to take hold of her by the shoulders and shout, "Fight back! Don't just take this crap from people!" What she did say was, "I'll give you your check before I take my aunt for her doctor's appointment."

"Okay," Bobby said. "That'll be fine. I'll go on up now."

"I'm sorry," Eva said again. "It'll take us a while to get used to each other."

"Yes, ma'am," Bobby said, and fairly flew out of the room.

"What's the matter with you?" Alma asked at once.

"Nothing. I'm fine," Bobby said, moving the wheelchair over by the bed. "Did you have a good night?"

"What, in your opinion constitutes a good night?" Alma asked gruffly.

"That'd be one when I slept right the way through without waking three or four times."

"You do that?"

"Uh-hunh."

"Why?"

"I have bad dreams," Bobby said, getting Alma settled in the chair.

"Every night?"

"Uh-hunh. But I'm used to it. D'you sleep right the way through?"

"Usually," Alma said. "Mind you, I sleep at least two hours less a night than I used to."

"My grandpa did that, too. The older he got, the less he slept. Until he took sick. Then he woke up every couple of hours. I'll be right here waiting," she said, leaving Alma alone in the bathroom.

On impulse, she busied herself straightening the bedclothes while she waited, folding the top sheet back, then plumping the pillows. Alma called for her and she went to start the water going in the tub before getting Alma out of her nightgown.

"We oughta do them exercises," she said.

"We ought to do those exercises," Alma corrected her. "And to hell with it. They're pointless."

"But that Dennis said they'd help."

"Dennis is well-intentioned but misinformed."

"Well, I think we should do them anyway. It won't hurt."

"Feel free to do them, then," Alma said. "I'll watch."

Bobby shook her head with a smile as she eased Alma into the warm water. "You sure are stubborn."

"That is correct."

"Today's a hair-washing day, right?"

"I suppose it is."

"Okay," Bobby said, and slipped off her shoes and socks before rolling up her pant legs. Aware that Alma was watching her, she said, "What?"

"The hair makes a remarkable difference. You're really very pretty."

"Oh, no," Bobby said, abashed. "I'm real . . . really ordinary."

"When someone pays you a compliment," Alma said sternly, "accept it and say thank you. Don't twist it into a pretzel."

"Okay. Thank you. Would you like me to do your back?"

"I would, please."

Alma handed her the soap and Bobby knelt at the side of the tub to lather up the washcloth. "I dreamed about you last night," she admitted.

"Did you? What did you dream?"

"We were sitting out on the back lawn, and you called me by my real name."

"Did I? And what is your real name?"

"Barbara."

"That's an infinitely more appropriate name than Bobby."

"What does that mean?" Bobby asked.

"It means simply that it suits you better. It has more dignity."

Bobby shook her head and said, "I don't have any dignity."

"Of course you do."

"I had any dignity, I wouldn't've stuck with Joe for so long."

"Perhaps not. But that's self-esteem, not dignity. And I'd have to agree you're somewhat deficient in that area. It's hardly surprising, though."

"I guess I had it beat out of me."

"Beaten."

"Yeah."

"You assumed you were always in the wrong, I suppose."

"Uh-hunh. I was forever trying to do things exactly right, so's not to make him mad. It took me a long time to figure out there was never going to be any right way. I'd always be wrong, no matter what."

"What attracted you to this man in the first place?" Alma asked.

"I don't know. He's real...really good-looking. And he was older, you know. I thought I was special 'cause he chose me."

"Women always think that," Alma said with faint disgust. "*We* make ourselves special. No one else does that for us."

"I guess not." Bobby wrung out the washcloth, draped it over the towel rail, then sat on the side of the tub with her feet in the water. "Hair-washing time," she said, bracing her knees to bear the old woman's weight. "You sure do have nice hair," she said, adjusting the water temperature on the hand shower.

"Thank you."

There was a pause, then both women laughed.

Bobby looked at the check and said, "You paid me too much."

"No," Eva said. "You worked Tuesday through Sunday. That's a full week. And if you really don't mind working Sundays, I'll pay you three hundred for the week."

"I really don't mind," Bobby said, carefully folding the check and putting it in her pocket. It was the most money she'd ever been paid in her life.

"You'll want to set some aside to cover your taxes at the end of the year."

"Yes, ma'am."

"Please," Eva said impatiently. "Call me Eva."

"Okay."

"My aunt's appointment is at ten-thirty. We should be back by twelve-thirty at the latest, depending on the traffic on the turnpike. If you have errands to do, you might as well do them while we're gone."

"I was thinking I'd go to the bank."

"Whatever," Eva said, as if Bobby's plans were of no interest to her. She took a leg of lamb from the freezer and set it in a pan to defrost.

"You need anything from the supermarket?" Bobby asked, wondering what she'd done to make this woman dislike her.

"No, thanks."

"Okay. You want me to bring Alma down now?"

Eva checked the time and said, "Might as well. Thanks."

"I do something wrong?" Bobby asked, the pulse in her throat suddenly throbbing.

Caught off guard, Eva looked over and said, "No. Why?"

"I was thinking I must've done something to make you mad."

Angry with herself for not concealing her irritation, Eva said, "No. I apologize if I've given that impression. You shouldn't take things so personally." That was a stupid thing to say, Eva thought. Of course she'd take it personally. "What I mean is..." What did she mean?

"It's hard, people living together," Bobby said, trying to help. "Folks get on each other's nerves. If I'm doing something wrong, you should tell me."

"You're not doing anything wrong," Eva said, completely unprepared for this confrontation. "As I've said before, I get distracted."

"I know you work real hard," Bobby said, "all those hours you spend in your office. But the thing is, I like your aunt real well, and we seem to be getting on good together. I'd like to be getting on good with you, too."

Eva resisted the temptation to correct her. It was not the time to play English teacher. "I'm used to running my own household," she explained. "The past year has been a big change, for Alma and for me. There are times when it's hard to take."

"I can understand that."

"Sometimes, as much as I love my aunt, the situation makes me angry."

"It gets you down," Bobby said.

"That's right."

"It gets her down, too."

"Yes, it does," Eva concurred.

"The way I see it, my job's to make it easier for the both of you. And I'm happy to do that. Like I said, I'm getting real fond of your aunt."

"Yes," Eva said. "I can tell."

"So if you don't like me," Bobby went on, "it makes me feel bad. Because I like you. You've been real good to me'n Pen, taking us in, giving me this job. What I'm saying is, it'd be better if you came right out and said what's bothering you, so I could try to fix it. It makes me worry when you're acting mad at me and I don't know why."

"You've done nothing wrong," Eva said. "And I'd tell you if you had. I know I'm abrupt and distant at times. Try to ignore it. It really has nothing to do with you."

"Okay," Bobby said, thinking they were ending up right where they'd started, with nothing settled or any clearer than before. "I'll try to do that. I'd better go up and get your aunt now."

"Thank you."

Bobby left, her hands shaking, heart pounding. She'd never talked that way to anyone. But she'd had to do it. She couldn't stand the idea that Eva was finding fault with her, that Eva didn't like her. At any other time she'd have kept silent, the way she did with Joe when he started in on her. This time, though, she simply couldn't. It was too important. She wanted to be able to stay, therefore she had to be clear on where she stood.

Eva held on to the counter, feeling as if she'd just run a race, and lost. She hadn't expected Bobby to be so candid, and she respected her for it. But there seemed to be no way Eva could explain that her coldness was because of Deborah, because of things that had happened almost fifteen years ago; events that didn't necessarily have any bearing on anything that was going on in this house.

"Are you doing the exercises?" Charlie asked.

"They're a waste of time," Alma said flatly.

"They are not a waste of time," he disagreed. "You have some mobility in that left leg. If you worked at it, you could strengthen the muscles to the point where you might be able to get around with the aid of a walker."

"I have no interest in getting around with a walker, thank you."

"You've got a lousy attitude," Charlie said, smiling. "How are you feeling otherwise?"

"I'm alive. That's something, I suppose."

"That's a great deal," he said. "It could've been far worse."

"You have a talent for stating the obvious," she said accusingly.

His smile grew wider and he said, "I understand you've got a new nurse. How's it working out?"

"She's a damned sight better than the others," Alma said. "I suppose Eva told you this one has a child."

"So I hear."

"The child is a joy," Alma said, softening. "A positive joy." Trying to sound offhand and failing, she said, "She calls me Granny, for God's sake."

"You love it," he said.

"Do something for me."

"What?"

"Encourage Eva to give up writing that commercial rubbish and get back to serious work."

"I can't tell her what to do, Alma."

"You have influence," she said. "Use it."

"I can't do that."

"Why not?"

"Because it's not my place. Because I don't want to say or do anything that'll affect the status quo. It's Eva's decision. It seems to satisfy a need she has."

"A need to play martyr. I have more than enough money to pay for everything."

"She feels obligated."

"That's nonsense," Alma said heatedly.

"Tell that to Eva."

"She won't hear it."

"There's really nothing I can do," he said. "Maybe you'll just have to accept the gesture and learn to live with it. So, my dear, if there's nothing else, I've got to be moving on. I'll see you in two weeks. And do those exercises!"

"Go on and see to your other patients," she said with disgust.

"You knew I'd never agree to it, Alma," he said fondly with a hand on her shoulder. "I give you points, though, for trying."

"All men are useless," she said, her squared chin outthrust.

He laughed and kissed her cheek. "I'll send Eva in to help you dress," he said, and went out.

"Useless," Alma muttered, grabbing her blouse and trying without success to get it on.

After the bank, Bobby stopped at the bookstore in the shopping center to buy Pen a new copy of her favorite storybook. She looked at the display of newly released paperbacks, spotting several she'd have liked to read. But she didn't dare spend any of her money on such a luxury; she might wind up needing every penny if things didn't work out with the job. Maybe she'd join the local library. In Jamestown she had gone every couple of weeks, and she was used to having books to read.

After the bookstore she looked at the clothes in the children's store. There was a blue party dress she knew Pen would love, but it was way too expensive. She wondered how people could afford to spend ninety-five dollars for a dress a child would only wear a few times before she outgrew it. But it sure was pretty, with hand-done smocking, a full skirt, and puffy sleeves. She could just see Pen in it, with white stockings and shiny new Mary Janes. Reluctantly, she left the rack of dresses and had a look at the everyday stuff.

She selected a pair of Oshkosh overalls and some underwear for Pen and carried the items to the counter, where she waited for one of the saleswomen to serve her. Opening her new, temporary checkbook, she wrote out a check.

"I'll need a driver's license and a credit card," the saleswoman told her.

Bobby handed over her New York State license, saying, "I don't have a credit card."

"I can't accept an out-of-state license," the woman said, frowning at Bobby's license.

"But it's valid..."

"I'm sorry," the woman said firmly, handing back the license.

Feeling suddenly as if everyone in the store were staring at her, Bobby quickly counted the money in her wallet. She didn't have enough cash. Embarrassed, her face hot, she said, "You could call the bank. They'd tell you I've got enough in the account."

"If we had to do that every time someone wanted to write a check, we'd spend all our time on the phone," the saleswoman said irritably. "Do you want these things or not?"

"I do want them," Bobby said softly, hearing an echo of Joe's voice shouting how stupid she was, how incapable she was of doing the simplest things right. *But that's not true,* she defended herself. She could do all kinds of things, and this was one of them. "I'll go to the bank and cash a check," she told the woman, who shrugged, reaching around Bobby to take an outfit another woman was waiting to buy. "Will you hold these things until I get back?"

"They'll be here," the saleswoman said. Then, smiling brightly at the customer she was serving, she added, "It's not as if there's a big rush today on Oshkosh overalls."

Humiliated, Bobby said, "I'll be back," and hurried out of the store.

There was a line at the bank, and she had to wait ten minutes to get to one of the tellers. The whole time she kept telling herself it was no big deal, she'd get the cash and go back to the store, pay for Pen's stuff, and that'd be that. But she kept hearing Joe's voice telling her how stupid she was and she had to fight down a desire to forget the whole thing and go on home. She hated the idea of facing that snotty saleswoman again, but she'd do it. And until things were settled one way or another, she'd carry enough cash to pay for whatever she wanted. Once she knew for sure they'd be staying, she'd get a Connecticut license, and by then she'd have properly printed checks and no one would give her a hard time when she wanted to buy something. *I'm not stupid,* she told herself. She just wished she weren't so bothered by the incident.

By the time she got back to the children's store, she was geared up to deal with the bitchy saleswoman, but another, friendly woman found the underwear and overalls and accepted Bobby's money with a smile and a "Thank you. Come again."

It was almost noon when she got back to the house. The garage door was still open, the van not back. After taking her purchases downstairs, she decided to make herself useful and prepare the lunch. Eva had said at the start that Bobby should do it, but every day so far she was there in the kitchen making the lunch when Bobby came in to do it. This was Bobby's first chance to do it herself. She knew Ruby didn't stop to eat, so it was just food for three. She had a pot of vegetable soup simmering on the stove and a platter of tuna salad sandwiches ready by the time she heard the van pulling into the driveway.

Bobby held the back door open as Eva pushed the chair up the ramp, and said, "I'll take over, if you like."

"You made lunch?" Eva said, taking in the set table and the platter of sandwiches.

Oh, Lord, Bobby thought. She was going to take offense. "You told me I should," she said quietly.

"That's right, I did. I'd forgotten," Eva said, touched. Not one of the previous nurses had even a small degree of Bobby's conscience. When they'd seen Eva making lunches after she'd said they were expected to do it, they'd simply assumed there'd been a change of plans and let her go on doing it. And, out of habit, Eva had. "Thank you, Bobby," she said with a pleased smile.

"You're welcome." Relieved, Bobby helped Alma out of her coat. "How was your doctor's visit?" she asked.

"A waste of time, as always," Alma growled.

"He wants her to do her exercises," Eva said.

"We'll do them this afternoon," Bobby promised.

"The hell we will!" Alma barked.

"We'll do them after lunch," Bobby insisted. "I've got them all written down."

"Charlie and I both think you should stop writing that rubbish and get back to serious work," Alma pounced on her niece.

Eva emitted a disbelieving laugh. "He said nothing of the sort."

"He most certainly did!'

"You're blowing smoke," Eva said, carrying their coats to the front hall closet. "What he probably said was he wouldn't discuss it with you."

"He thinks you're wasting your time and talent," Alma said as she drove her chair to the table.

Bemused, Bobby followed this exchange, trying to make sense of it.

"You've been meddling," Eva said, getting bowls from the cupboard.

"I did my best," Alma said.

Laughing again, Eva began ladling soup into the bowls, saying, "Leave us both alone. I'm doing what I want to do."

"You loathe it, and it's changing you," Alma said. "Since you started writing those books you've become hardened in a way that doesn't suit you."

"That is *not* true," Eva argued, but had to wonder if her aunt hadn't actually scored a bull's-eye. "Besides, you weren't around to know what I was like when I was working on the other books."

"I saw you often enough to know you were happy. The only time you're happy now is after you've spent a few hours in bed with Charlie."

Eva blushed, exclaiming, "My God!" and looked to see how Bobby was responding to all this. Bobby kept her eyes lowered and fiddled with her spoon. "Why don't you take out a full-page ad in the *Advocate?*"

"Charlie," Alma said to Bobby, "is my doctor and Eva's inamorato."

"What's that?" Bobby asked, not sure she wanted to be drawn into this argument or whatever it was.

"We see each other socially," Eva said.

"Oh!" Bobby smiled and risked looking at Eva, who was still red in the face and visibly flustered. "That's nice."

Eva looked at the younger woman and saw only sincerity, even approval. "Yes, it is nice," Eva said, and then felt herself helplessly grinning. The amorphous animosity she'd had toward Bobby was suspended for a moment, and she was able to view her as a friend. "It is very nice," she stated, her eyes on Bobby, who smiled and reached to lift the platter, asking, "Want a sandwich?"

"Yes, thank you," Eva said, deciding there and then that Bobby would be staying. "These look good."

"It's my Aunt Helen's recipe," Bobby said, sensing there'd been a change. "She uses a tablespoon of vinegar along with the mayonnaise. I hope you like it."

"I'm sure we will," Eva said.

Picking up on the changed atmosphere, Alma decided to let the matter of Eva's writing drop, and helped herself to half a sandwich. She was well aware that Eva had conflicting emotions about Bobby and wished she knew why. She'd never seen Eva behave quite the way she did with this gentle little creature, and the only clue Eva herself had so far offered was the reference to Bobby's reminding her of Deborah. An oblique reference at best, in view of the fact that Eva had spared Alma the finer details of what had happened on the island that summer. Eva had been so distraught when she returned that Alma had chosen to leave her be, deciding she'd talk about it in due course. But, aside from revealing the bare bones of the matter, Eva never had. Curious, Alma thought, looking first at Bobby and then at her niece, both of whom had their eyes on their plates. For the first time in years, Alma wondered what it was Eva hadn't told her.

Eleven

Almost compulsively now, Eva was remembering Montaverde. A pattern had evolved. Each night she'd have monstrous monochromatic dreams from which she'd awaken feeling weakened and afraid. Then she'd lie still for a time, reviewing her weeks on the island.

Tonight she was recalling one afternoon in particular when the heat was so intense that the children had fallen asleep together on the two-seater out on the veranda. She paced back and forth in the living room waiting for Deborah and Ian to get back. They were in town, seeing government officials about some permits having to do with the house they were attempting to build. In the two weeks Eva had been there, not a lick of work had been done on the site.

She wanted to take Mellie and get on the first flight out. New York had an entirely new appeal after these two long weeks on the island. And she thought longingly, constantly now, of going with Mellie to spend a few weeks with Alma in the calm of Connecticut. She paced, waiting, her shirt wet with perspiration and clinging to her back. She was desperate to get away from what was going on inside this house. Deborah seemed to have evolved into someone she'd never known, someone who bore no resemblance to the woman who'd been her closest friend in England. This other Deborah was unapproachable, grimly silent, in a state of permanent rage—primarily over the lack of progress on the house, for which, however arbitrarily, she blamed Ian. Only at moments—when she paused to place a loving hand on her little boy's head, or she appeared briefly to remember Eva and there was a flash of her dazzling smile—was Deborah familiar. Yet Eva was convinced there had to be something she personally could say or do to help. Each day she hoped that Deborah would provide the opportunity for a dialogue. She couldn't believe Deborah didn't want to talk as badly as she did. She had to want Eva's help. Why else had she invited her to come? Yet she didn't give the slightest hint that she had any interest in discussing her problems. Every time Eva approached her to say, "Let me give you a hand with this or that," Deborah would look up distractedly and say, "No, darling. But thank you for offering."

The result was that Eva felt strangled by all the things she was yearning to say, but couldn't. She also felt like the world's worst hypocrite because she wanted so badly to take her child and get as far away as possible from the fulminating animosity between her former best friend and her best friend's odious husband.

Locked in place by her seesawing emotions, she was missing Ken. He'd been dead eight months and the shock was somehow even greater than it had been when she'd received the phone call from the Minneapolis police telling her he had, from all the evidence, died quietly in his sleep. With her husband eulogized and in the ground, she'd hidden from the loss in her work, doing rewrites in every free moment. She was consoled to a small degree by the fact that her book had been sold just prior to Ken's death. He'd been almost as overjoyed at the news of the sale as he'd been by Melissa's birth, and, playfully, he'd made wild predictions. "You'll be on all the talk shows. You'll become a household name."

"Right. Like Wonder Bread. I'll probably sell twelve copies," Eva had laughed.

"Fourteen," he'd said. "No, seriously. This is great, Evie, really great. I'm so proud of you."

When she was at the typewriter during those weeks following that shattering telephone call, she was able to focus strictly on the events unfolding in the narrative. The ache that the rest of the time felt crippling disappeared when she concentrated on the characters she was creating. The writing, and her responsibility for Melissa, prevented her from succumbing to complete emotional paralysis. Deborah's invitation to come to the island had given her something to look forward to. She'd anticipated six weeks of fresh air and sunshine, a happy reunion with someone who, having known Ken, too, would indulge with her in fond, funny recollections of those earlier, happy times in London. Instead, almost from the start, she'd found herself squarely in the eye of a hurricane and had diligently pretended that nothing out of the ordinary was going on. But the wild drive from the airport should have been her first warning, when Ian took them careening along the treacherous mountain road at a terrifying speed. Halfway up the mountain, Deborah's low-pitched cry of fear had resulted in Ian's slamming on the brakes, pulling the car to a stop with its front tires at the very edge of a sheer drop-off. And they'd had their first argument then; Deborah, in a low, shaky voice saying, "If you can't drive properly, move over and let me drive. You'll kill the lot of us, you feckless bastard!" In the back, weary from the flight and the heat and slightly queasy from the insane drive, Eva had sat with the two children, concentrating hard in order not to throw up, and offering quivery smiles to the children that were meant to be reassuring.

Right then she'd wondered what she had, in all innocence, stepped into; and right then she'd had a powerful intimation that her wisest course of action would be to spend the night, make some excuse in the morning, and take Melissa to a resort on some other island. But the idea of doing that seemed to her so cowardly, and so precipitously judgmental, that she dismissed it. She'd come all this way to see her old friend. She couldn't possibly pick up and leave after only one night. Deborah would think she was crazy.

Now it was two weeks later and she was frightened. For the first time she had doubts about her ability to raise Melissa alone. She'd depended on Ken. He'd been her best friend, her constant companion. He'd made her laugh when she was in a mood to kill. He'd been her sounding board, allowing her to bounce ideas off him, telling her in no uncertain terms when she was out of line. They'd had six and a half years together. It seemed like no time at all. In the immediate aftermath of his death, she'd found herself pausing to look at her watch, wondering when Ken would get home. Then his death would be new to her again, and she'd feel as if she were drowning in disbelief, as if her life with him had been nothing more than a dream.

Feeling trapped in this barren house, she missed him more every hour, especially since Deborah and Ian fought constantly, openly now. There were brief truce-like spells over dinner while the three adults sat with their food out on the veranda and something akin to civilized conversation took place.

Just two nights earlier, Ian had expressed great interest in Eva's forthcoming book, wanting to know what it was about and as much as she could tell him about the inner workings of the publishing industry. And despite her dislike of the man, in the interest of promoting peace, Eva had detailed her limited dealings with her publisher, then went on to outline the plot of her novel.

"One would think it would do jolly well," he said judiciously.

"Yes," Deborah agreed. "One would think so."

Perhaps there was some hope for the situation, Eva thought, relaxing a degree or two as the evening drew toward a quiet close.

Then, out of the blue, Ian said to Deborah, "One imagines tomorrow's trip to the site will be another wasted effort. Rather a bad idea hiring your uncle to oversee the construction.''

Instantly livid and defensive, Deborah said, "At least *he's* willing to do some bloody work. At least *he's* not hanging about in town, trying to impress the fucking *natives*.''

Ian leapt from the sofa, flew across the veranda, and backhanded his wife, knocking her from the railing where she habitually sat. Then he marched out.

"Bastard!" Deborah shouted at his retreating back.

"Evil bitch!" Ian bellowed, not even bothering to turn around.

Appalled, scared, Eva moved to give her friend a hand up.

"Leave me be, darling!" Deborah waved her off, rising to her feet and, without another word, walking toward the master suite.

Uncertain of what to do, Eva sat and waited, hoping Deborah would come back and talk. She didn't. Finally, after waiting on the veranda for close to an hour, Eva trudged through the cavernous spaces to her bedroom.

Their battles were epic, ceaseless, often going on late into the night. And Derek, bewildered, had to be distracted constantly in order to keep him from running to his mother in the middle of one of these sessions seeking to be reassured. On the few occasions when Eva was unable to hold him back and he flung himself, sobbing, at his mother's legs, both Deborah and Ian had rounded on the child, telling him to "Go off now and leave Mommy and Daddy be," pushing the boy away and then, without missing a beat, continuing their argument.

Fortunately, Derek and Mellie got along well together, and they took turns being the leader. One hour Mellie would be telling Derek what to do, the next he'd be fabricating complexly bewildering rules to some new game. They played with astounding energy and inventiveness while around them everything slid further out of control.

The day before, Eva had seen Ian standing in the driveway with a gun. Evidently he'd been keeping it hidden in the car. For some reason he'd taken it out to examine it and Eva had, in passing the windows, seen it in his hand. Since then she'd become, almost hourly, increasingly anxious to leave. She'd been debating telling Deborah about the gun, but Deborah was so preoccupied, and Ian, with that damnable radar of his, stuck so close to her so much of the time that no opportunity had presented itself for a private conversation.

She wanted to weep. Outside, the palm fronds rattled dryly in the heavy air. She went to sit in the armchair on the veranda and looked at the children. Their hair was wet, matted to their faces. They slept sprawled, like abandoned dolls. She let her head fall back, wondering if Deborah knew about the gun. Dread, like the heat, seemed to be saturating her. She couldn't imagine how she was going to survive one more day here, and, feeling sorry for herself, wished with all her heart that Ken were there to take control of the situation.

She *hated* this, couldn't abide a single minute more of it. Flinging herself forward, Eva sat up in bed, actively pushing it all away from her. After a minute or two she rose and went barefoot to the kitchen.

The door to Bobby's apartment was ajar. She could see a faint glow of light, could smell cigarette smoke. According to the clock on the stove it was three-twenty. She opened the refrigerator for the orange juice, glancing again at the apartment door. Bobby was awake down there, smoking a cigarette. Did she also have dreams and memories that ruined her sleep, had her getting up at random hours seeking escape? She poured some juice, then stared into space as she drank it, wondering why it all had ended as it had.

Penny sat up and rubbed her fists into her eyes, then looked over to see her mom curled up under the blankets, sleeping. Getting out of bed, she tiptoed over to read the numbers on the digital clock. Six-forty. Still on tiptoe, she crept out of the room.

She knocked very very softly at Granny's door and right away Granny said, "Come in."

Penny paddled over to stand by the side of the bed, whispering, "You said I could come see you anytime."

"That's right, I did."

"C'n I come in bed with you?"

"Yes."

Penny climbed up, asking, "C'n I come under the covers?"

In answer, Alma lifted the bedclothes and Penny ducked in beside her, saying, "I had a bad dream."

"Did you?"

"Uh-hunh." Penny snuggled closer.

"Would you like to tell me about it?"

"Uh-hunh."

"Okay," Alma said.

"I dreamed that me and Mom were in the car at night, drivin' fast. It was rainin' very very hard and I was havin' a peanut butter and jelly sandwich, tryin' to see out the window through the rain. My mom had her new hair but it was tied back like Auntie Eva's, with a big blue bow, and she said we were goin' to see Auntie Helen. Then all of a sudden the sun was shinin' and the trees were nice and green. So I said, 'I'm goin' swimmin',' and I opened the back door of the kitchen and started runnin' across the grass. It was all wet on my feet but it was warm outside and you were there, Granny, wavin' to me from down by the water. Auntie Eva was sittin' at a table on the grass with her computer and she said, 'I can't talk to you now. I'm workin'.'

"I stopped to watch and put my finger on one of the keys. Auntie Eva jumped up and started shoutin', and I wanted to touch the key again and make everything right but Auntie Eva wouldn't let me, and Mom came runnin' from the house. Everybody was mad at me and I was in big trouble, so I started runnin' again, down to the beach where you were.''

Penny snuggled a bit closer. ''You said to me, 'Come on, we'll hide in the water.' So I climbed on your lap and you drove the wheelchair right into the water. It rolled on top of the water just like a boat and you smiled at me 'n' said, 'Isn't this fun, Pen?' and I said, 'Uh-hunh,' and when I looked back Auntie Eva was diggin' up the grass with a big shovel and Mom was helpin' her bury the computer in a hole.''

Alma chuckled appreciatively. After a moment, she said, ''Go on, dear.''

''Is that funny?'' Penny asked.

''I can't begin to explain just *how* funny,'' Alma said. ''I apologize for interrupting. Go on, Penny. Tell me the rest of it.''

''Okay. So we're ridin' on top of the water and I told you I made Auntie Eva mad,'' Penny said, ''and you said, 'Auntie Eva likes being mad,' and you laughed.''

Again Alma chuckled. ''This is wonderful,'' she said.

''Yeah?''

''Truly,'' Alma said. ''I'm sorry I keep interrupting.''

''That's okay, Granny.''

''What happened next?'' Alma prompted.

''We saw a big white boat and Emma Whitton was standin' on it with a yellow flag, wavin' to us. I said I was gonna go play with Emma, but then I felt bad and said if you're gonna be sad, I wouldn't go. But you said for me to go ahead and play with Emma, and that you'd wait for me. So Emma and I played with the Nintendo and her mom made us tacos and we had cherry Cokes.''

''Then,'' Penny said with a tremor in her voice, ''all of a sudden it was late and I went to find you to say I was comin' home now, but you were gone and I was scared, Granny. I thought you were gone. I looked everywhere, but I couldn't *find* you.''

Alma reached for the child's hand, saying, "I don't intend to go off and leave you, Penny."

"Promise? Cross your heart and hope to die?"

"Cross my heart," Alma said.

"It was a real bad dream," Penny said earnestly.

"Yes, it was. I hope you're not scared anymore."

"No, I'm not. D'you have bad dreams sometimes, Granny?"

"Sometimes."

"Yeah. My mom does, too." Abruptly she sat up, worriedly asking, "What time is it?"

Alma turned to look at the luminous clock on the bedside table. "Almost seven."

"Oh, I better go back. I don't want my mom to worry."

"No, you wouldn't want that," Alma said.

Penny leaned over and gave Alma a hearty kiss on the cheek, then scrambled off the bed, ran to the door, stopped and ran back. "I love you, Granny," she said.

"Granny loves you, too," Alma smiled in the darkness.

"See you after school," Penny promised, then flew to the door.

"What kinds of books do you like to read?" Alma asked, from over by the bookcase in the living room.

"I don't know," Bobby said. "Ones with good stories."

Alma turned to the bookcase and came up with a book. "Try this," she said, handing it to Bobby. "I'd be interested to know what you think of it."

Bobby looked at the front cover, the back, and again at the front. Understanding suddenly, she felt her face grow hot. "Evangeline Chaney," she said. "Is this one of Eva's books?"

"That's right. One of the ones she wrote before she started grinding out this trash." Alma pulled two paperbacks from the shelf.

"She wrote those, too?"

"She's done three of them. The third one's coming out in a month or so, and she's working on number four. That's what she's doing every day up in the office." Alma made a face and moved to return the two paperbacks to the shelf.

"Maybe I'll have a read of them," Bobby said.

"One does not 'have a read of,'" Alma corrected her. "One reads."

"Okay. Maybe I'd like to give them a try."

"Suit yourself." Alma surrendered the pair of books and Bobby looked at the covers.

"She uses different names?" Bobby asked.

"Thank God for something," Alma said. "She'd have no reputation left if she signed her own name to that rubbish."

"So this is what you two were arguing about yesterday."

"That is correct."

"If she wants to do them, what does it matter?"

"It matters," Alma said with an exaggerated show of patience, "because her motives for doing them are questionable at best."

"Oh!"

"Why do you say oh, as if you know what I mean?"

"Well, I kind of think I do."

"And what precisely do you think you know?"

"Lots of people read these books," Bobby said. "They probably pay good money. Maybe not so many people read this other kind of story. So she's doing it for the money."

Grudgingly, Alma said, "You seem to have grasped the nuances of the situation."

"I'll read them all," Bobby said, quite excited. Eva was probably pretty famous. And Bobby was impressed to see there were a number of other Evangeline Chaney books on the shelf. "I've always loved to read," she said eagerly. "I read the whole of Dickens while I was going to school. I

liked *Great Expectations* best, especially Miss Havisham.
I could just *see* her in her ratty old wedding dress, and all
the cobwebs.''

"What else did you like?" Alma asked with interest.

"It's hard to think," Bobby said, sitting on the ottoman with the books piled on her knees. "Oh! I liked the
stories by that woman... What's her name? Kind of
spooky books. And there was one I thought was going to
be real... really scary but it turned out to be about a little
kid. *Raising Demons*, it was called."

"Shirley Jackson."

"That's right! I really liked her books. I read that one
and then I went back to the library and got every single one
of hers I could find. I like to do that with a good writer:
read all the books."

"Yes, so do I," Alma agreed. "I'm very pleased to learn
you like to read, Bobby. It's the sign of an inquiring
mind."

"It is?" Bobby said, flattered. "I didn't know that. I
just like to read so I don't have to think about things." She
remembered Joe coming in one time while she was sitting
in bed reading. He'd had too many beers, and he came
over and whipped the book right out of her hand, whacked
her across the side of the head with it, then ripped it to
pieces, even though she tried to explain to him that it was
a library book. He tore off the covers, ripped the thing to
bits, and threw the bits on the floor. And when he'd finished, he unzipped his pants and pissed all over the pieces.
She'd had to tell the librarian she'd lost the book, and pay
the library sixteen dollars and ninety-five cents to replace
it.

She was startled back into the present by Alma's hand
touching hers.

"Whatever it is," Alma said, "it's over now."

"Things are never over inside your head," Bobby said
soberly.

"That's true," Alma agreed. "But they can't happen again."

"That's what I used to tell myself every time Joe took his hands to me. I'd think, it's over now. It'll never happen again. But it always did."

"But you've changed things now. You've made a choice, and placed all that behind you. You don't ever have to go back."

"No," Bobby said softly. "I'd never want to."

"Then you won't," Alma said, and gave Bobby one of her sadly lopsided smiles.

Gripped by sudden gratitude and welling fondness, Bobby sat forward and kissed the old woman's cheek. Then, cowed by her own boldness, she sank back on the ottoman saying, "You make me feel real . . . really good about myself."

"And you've worn me out with those damned exercises," Alma said to mask her pleasure. "Get me upstairs now for my nap."

"Yes, ma'am," Bobby said, and put the books aside to accommodate her. While Alma had her nap, she'd start in right away on reading Eva's books. She was very curious to find out what kind of writer Eva was, and maybe what kind of woman, too.

He couldn't believe it, but Bobby really was gone. It kind of scared him, but he didn't know why. He got this empty sensation in his chest, and when he went through the deserted house he felt kind of the way he did as a little kid when the old lady would punish him for no goddamned reason whatsoever.

The house was a shit-heap. He sat in the living room with a brew, staring at the blank TV screen, half of him wanting to go after Bobby and kill her, the other half hurt that she'd abandon him this way.

The way he figured it, she wouldn't just up and leave without letting her aunt know where she was at. Bobby was real tight with that grizzly old bitch. She'd have been in touch with her. He was going to have to convince Helen one way or another to tell him where she was at so he could go after her.

The house was goddamned depressing. He couldn't stand being there. The sheets were starting to smell so he'd been sleeping on the sofa. No way was he going to do woman shit like washing sheets and towels. That wasn't his job. He held up his end. He went every day of his life to the goddamned factory, put in his eight hours. He had a right to come home to a decent hot meal and clean sheets on his bed. Now he was having to take his work clothes to the laundromat, doing his own stinking laundry like some pathetic loser. Feeding quarters into those goddamned machines, he wanted to rip the place apart, kick the shit out of the pasty-faced women sitting around on those goddamned plastic chairs waiting for their shit to dry. He hated it. He'd dump a load of his stuff into one of the washers, then go walk until it was time to come back. No way was he gonna sit there with those bitches smirking at him, like they knew he'd been dumped.

She'd probably run off with some weasel. The idea drove him nuts. He found her with another guy, he'd kill the both of them, put bullets right through their fucking brains. But first he had to find her. He'd just have to fig-

*ure some way to get it out of Helen. If it came right down
to it, he decided, he'd kill the old bitch if he had to.*

*He had to figure it out, make a plan. She'd have the law
on his ass she so much as saw his car in her driveway. So
he'd have to think it through real carefully, maybe get into
the house while she was at work. Yeah, he thought, starting to feel a whole lot better.*

*Imagining what he'd do to her when he caught up with
Bobby got him right back up again. He chugged the last of
his brew, crushed the can in one hand, tossed it into a corner of the room and got up to go over to Garvey's for
something to eat, maybe a couple of games of pool.*

Twelve

Bobby got so caught up in Eva's book she couldn't let go of it, and stayed up way past midnight, curled into a corner of the sofa, reading.

Then, lying in bed, she marveled over the fact that she was living in the same house with the woman who'd written that book. It was simply amazing. And she was getting a whole new picture of who Eva was. Because nobody coldhearted could make up such wonderful characters and give them such true feelings. She couldn't wait to finish the book so she could tell Eva how much she'd loved it. Plus there were five more of her novels upstairs in the living room, and those two paperbacks, too.

She was tremendously impressed, and excited in a way. Eva was special, and she, Bobby, actually knew her and saw her every single day. And now that she was reading something Eva had written, Eva's activities up in the office over the garage seemed very important. From now on, she knew she'd be seeing Eva in a completely new way.

She fell asleep quite quickly, and dreamed she and Eva were sitting in the living room talking like friends. She was asking Eva how she came up with the ideas for her books and Eva was explaining that she got a lot of her ideas from reading the newspapers.

"I'll have to start reading the papers," Bobby said, a bit ashamed to admit that she'd never been one to follow the news. Sometimes she'd watch on TV if Joe was late getting home and she was keeping supper hot, but mostly what news she heard was on the car radio, driving to and from work, or taking Pen to the dentist, or like that.

"It's important to be aware of what's going on in the world," Eva was saying, and Bobby had to agree. "After all, even indirectly, these things affect us."

"I know," Bobby concurred, recalling how, after he'd retired, her grandpa used to read three newspapers every day. He'd never remembered to wash his hands, so there'd always been black fingerprints around the light switches and on the kitchen countertops.

"That's how I get many of my ideas," Eva went on, and Bobby felt very privileged to be having this conversation. "Sometimes you reach a point where you know something has to be done, like your deciding to take Pen and run away. A day comes when we realize we have resources we didn't know about, and we take action. It isn't consciously planned. It simply happens. The time is right. I get ideas for books just the same way."

"That's it," Bobby agreed vigorously. "That's exactly it." She smiled and Eva smiled back at her, and Bobby felt wonderful because they had an understanding, and could talk to each other.

"I didn't recognize you there for a minute," Dennis said when he came on Thursday.

"I got my hair done," Bobby said, complimented that he'd noticed.

"It looks great," Dennis said.

Flustered, she latched on to another subject. "We've been doing the exercises," she told him. "But only about fifteen minutes' worth a day. She won't do any more."

"Listen," he said. "That's fifteen minutes more than any of the others managed to get her to do." With a frankly approving smile, he said, "Good going, Bobby."

She left him with Alma and went downstairs, hearing Ruby running the vacuum cleaner in Eva's bedroom. Remembering what he'd said the previous week, she got a pot of coffee made, then, taking a chance on getting in trouble, went up to knock at the office door.

"What?" Eva asked from inside.

Timidly, fearful of interrupting, Bobby said through the door, "I was wondering if you wanted some coffee. I just made fresh."

"Come in!" Eva said.

Bobby cracked open the door saying, "I don't mean to interrupt. But I'll fetch you a cup, if you want some."

Eva looked over her shoulder, her eyes a bit blank, and said, "I'd love some. Thanks."

Relieved, Bobby smiled and said, "Be right back." She ran to the kitchen, found the mug Eva used most often, and fixed her coffee, cream no sugar, the way she liked it.

On tiptoe, Bobby carried the coffee over to the desk and set it down. Eva murmured, "Thanks," and Bobby crept away, feeling good, as if she were actually contributing to the work that was being done.

For the rest of the hour Dennis was upstairs with Alma, she lost herself in Eva's book.

"Those fifteen minutes a day are making a difference," Dennis said, coming into the kitchen and going directly to the cabinet to get a cup. "Keep up the good work."

Bobby marked her place in the book with a bit of paper and drank some of her now-cold coffee as he came to sit down opposite her at the table.

"So," he said, "how're you making out?"

"Oh, real . . . really good. My girl Pen loves the school. She's already made a whole bunch of new friends. And I'm starting to find my way around. You live in town?"

"Yup. I've got an apartment over in Glenbrook."

"You come from around here?" she asked, hoping he wouldn't think she was being too nosy.

"Mamaroneck," he said. "That's just down the pike, in New York."

"Oh!"

"Your eye's almost back to normal," he observed.

"Uh-hunh." Automatically she put a hand to her face, then returned it to her lap. "I heal fast," she said, then wondered if saying that was a dead giveaway that she'd been beaten up regularly.

"That's a good thing," he said.

"Yeah," she agreed, right out of things to say.

"So, are you divorced or separated or what?" he asked.

"Separated, I guess. What about you?"

He laughed, showing his teeth. "Never been married," he said. "I figure I've got plenty of time. I'm only twenty-nine."

"You don't look more than twenty-two or three."

"I've been getting that all my life. Up until a year or so ago, I was still getting carded at the local bars. That was a pain. You, too?"

"Get carded? I haven't been to a bar in a real... really long time." Joe hadn't taken her out in years.

"No kidding," he said. "What d'you do in your time off?"

"I don't know," she said, thrown by the question. "Mostly, I look after Pen."

"And read," he said, indicating the book.

"I love to read."

He studied the jacket for a moment, then said, "Maybe you'd like to come out for a drink one night."

"Oh, I don't know," she said, nervous at the prospect. "I work every night."

"Come on," he said coaxingly. "Alma would let you off one evening for a couple of hours. Come out. We'll go dancing. You like to dance?"

That was something else she hadn't done since before Pen was born. "Yeah," she said. "I used to love to dance."

"Okay," he said. "I'll tell you what. Check with Alma and see what night's good for her, and I'll give you a call tomorrow. We'll set a date."

"I don't know," she said again, flustered.

"I'll even buy you dinner," he said, as if sweetening the offer.

"I'll ask," she said, then chewed on her lower lip.

"Good. I'll call you tomorrow and we'll set it up." He finished his coffee and got up to put the mug in the sink. "I've gotta head on up to Norwalk now. Thanks for the coffee."

"You're welcome," she said, following him to the front hall, where she watched from the doorway as he got into an old VW Beetle and drove off. Her hands were shaking as she closed the door.

When Pen got home from school, Bobby went downstairs to give her a glass of cranapple juice and some cookies. And before Pen sat down to watch *Happy Days*, Bobby asked, "How would you feel if I went out one night for a couple of hours with a friend?"

This was such an unprecedented situation that Penny directed her deep blue gaze at her mother, asking, "Where you gonna go?"

"Just out for a little while."

"What friend?" Penny wanted to know.

"He's a new friend, Dennis. He comes once a week to give Alma her physical therapy. Exercises," Bobby elaborated.

"Is he nice?"

"Uh-hunh. Would that be okay with you, Pen?"

"Can Emma come over on Saturday to play?"

"Sure she can. That'd be fine."

"Okay," Penny said, as if having decided fair was fair. "When you goin'?"

"I don't know yet. I have to ask Alma first. Maybe Monday or Tuesday."

"Okay," Penny said again. "C'n I watch TV now?"

"First a hug," Bobby said, and felt the love catch her by the throat as Penny's arms wound tightly around her neck and her small body vibrated with the force of energy she put into the embrace. "I love you, Pen."

"Love you, too, Mom," Penny said, already easing away to turn on the TV set.

Bobby sat for a moment, watching her, forever astonished by the fact of Pen's separateness. Pen was somebody else, a complete person all to herself. She had thoughts, ideas, emotions; everything that went into creating an individual. I made her, Bobby thought. I made her, and I love her more than anything else in the world, but we're separate. Penny would grow up and stop being a child, but Bobby would be a mother forever. The concept staggered her. Penny's reality had awed her from the moment when, in her fifth month of pregnancy, she'd felt the inner nudging that proved a small being was actually alive and growing inside her. Penny was the only thing in her life that she knew she'd done absolutely right. Joe could say she was stupid and slow, that she was dumber than shit and could never get anything right, but he was wrong. And he'd never understand that. It was something no one could ever take away from her: She'd made Penny. It was, to Bobby's mind, an incredible accomplishment. Without Penny, she'd probably have stayed with Joe until she died. Penny was her life.

Alma said, "Well, well, well. Now isn't this interesting," and gave Bobby a penetrating look.

Bobby wilted, folded her hands in her lap, and looked down at the carpet, thinking she should've told Dennis no right off. She didn't really want to go out to some bar anyway. And she hadn't danced in so long she probably didn't even remember how.

Taking in Bobby's reaction, Alma felt both angry and sorry for her. It irked her that a pretty young woman obviously didn't believe she had the right to a social life. She had to remind herself that this wasn't Bobby's fault. But she was nevertheless annoyed by Bobby's almost complete lack of self-esteem. She'd have liked to see the young woman hold her head up and declare her intention of taking a few hours to herself. Impossible, of course. And terribly sad.

"You know what you need?" Alma said, all at once able to see what was missing.

"What?"

"You need to get angry."

"Pardon?"

"What's the *matter* with you?" Alma railed. "Aren't you furious at having been treated the way you have by that man you married?"

Bobby shook her head, feeling deficient.

"Well, you should be," Alma stated. "You should be positively outraged."

"I just feel scared," Bobby said in a small voice. "When people get mad it always scares me."

"I'm not mad at you," Alma clarified, "so stop being scared. I'm trying to tell you something for your own good. You've got to get angry. You've got to look at your life, at what's been done to you, at what's been taken away from you, and get damned good and mad. I want you to think about it, Barbara," she said in her firmest head mistress's voice. "I want you to think long and hard about it, because you can't become your own person until you decide you're angry, that you have the *right* to be angry. Once you've located your anger, you can work your way through to selfhood. Do you understand?"

"I think so." Bobby met her eyes. "But I don't know as I can get mad just because somebody tells me that's the way I ought to feel."

"I'm suggesting you think about it," Alma insisted. "You've got a good brain. Use it! And of course you may take some time to yourself. Whenever you like. Just let me and Eva know when, so we can be sure someone's home to see to Penny."

Bobby said, "Long as you're sure it's no trouble."

"I've been looking after children my entire adult life," Alma said with indignation. "I think I can cope with one small girl."

"Yes, ma'am." Bobby gave her a smile. "Thank you."

"Listen, my dear," Alma said more quietly. "You have certain rights. Don't be so fearful of claiming them. Dennis is a very decent young man. Go out for a few hours and enjoy yourself. You deserve a little pleasure."

"Yes, ma'am."

"And stop calling me *ma'am!*" Alma near-shouted. "I *loathe* it!"

"Okay." Bobby's smile widened.

When Dennis called the next afternoon, Bobby could scarcely speak.

"When's a good night for you?" he asked.

She thought she should tell him to forget it, but remembered what Alma had told her, and said, "Monday?"

"Great. Pick you up at seven?"

"I can't go that early," she said with near panic. "I've got to get Pen to bed."

"Okay. How's eight?"

"All right," she agreed, feeling weak with dread. This was a mistake.

"Fine. See you then," he said, and hung up.

Eva was watching, half-smiling, from the other side of the kitchen.

Bobby felt so scared and so stupid she didn't know what to do. "You're sure it's okay?" she asked Eva.

"Of course," Eva said. "We'll leave the kitchen door open. If there's any problem Alma and I will be right here."

"I've never gone off and left her before," Bobby confessed.

"Don't be silly," Eva chided gently. "You're apart every day while Penny's at school."

"It's not the same thing."

"What're you going to wear?" Eva changed the subject.

"I don't know," Bobby said, more and more wishing she'd said no.

"I have a few things I thought you might like," Eva said. "Come on up and I'll show you."

Bemused, Bobby followed her up to her bedroom.

"You're not offended, are you?" Eva asked, getting a stack of clothes from the slipper chair by the window.

"Oh, no," Bobby said, astounded that Eva wanted to give her what looked like perfectly good sweaters and blouses.

"The blouses might be a bit too big, but I thought you'd be able to use the sweaters. It's really a pity my other things would be too big for you."

"This is wonderful," Bobby said, accepting the clothes.

Eva thought she looked like a child at a surprise party, dazed and elated. "Take whatever you like. We'll give the rest to the Good Will."

"Thank you," Bobby said, carrying off the clothing.

"Bobby?"

"What?" Bobby stopped at the top of the stairs and turned back.

"Go and have fun. Don't worry about a thing."

Bobby nodded and continued on her way down the stairs. She could never in a million years have explained how much she was dreading this date.

Thirteen

As arranged, Mrs. Whitton delivered Emma to the front door at ten o'clock Saturday morning. The child was carrying a large box, and Bobby at once relieved her of its weight.

"I'll be back to pick her up at five," Emma's mother told Bobby.

"I'm really sorry about the inconvenience," Bobby said. "I'm working, otherwise I'd bring Emma home."

"No problem," said Mrs. Whitton. To Emma she said, "Be good, dumpling," then kissed her and went off to her station wagon.

Bobby took the bespectacled child downstairs where Penny was waiting.

"Hi!" Penny sang, racing over. "Mom says we can watch cartoons."

Bobby set Emma's box down on the coffee table while she got the child out of her coat.

"I brought stuff," Emma announced, and the two girls at once began removing items from the box: a pair of Barbie dolls with several changes of clothing, a 64-pack of Crayolas and a pad of drawing paper, some games, and a box of junk jewelry.

"Where's your room?" Emma asked, looking around.

"Over there," Penny pointed. "Wanna watch cartoons?"

"Yeah, okay."

The two girls flopped down in front of the TV set and Bobby hung up Emma's coat, then came back to say, "I'll be upstairs, Pen, if you need me."

Engrossed in the cartoon, Penny murmured, "Uh-hunh."

Bobby left the kitchen door open so she'd be able to hear if the girls started making too much noise. Eva was already at work in her office, and Alma was in the living room going section by section through the *Times*. Bobby took her book from the kitchen table and went to join Alma in the living room.

She tried to get back into the story, but she was so agitated by the prospect of having to go out with Dennis that she couldn't concentrate, and wished for something to keep her hands busy. Maybe next time she went out she'd pick up a pattern and some wool, start a sweater for Pen. She hadn't done any knitting in years, not since she'd nursed Grandpa, when she'd sat for hours at a stretch at his bedside.

Why had she agreed to go out with Dennis? After half an hour in her company he'd be bored. He'd think she was stupid. Then he'd fall into brooding silence as he stared into his glass of beer, and she'd sit agonized, waiting for the blowup that would come the minute they got in his car. He'd assault her with insults, flinging hurtful words and threats, until she was cringing in her seat, knowing he'd go on ranting until they arrived home, when he'd take his anger out on her with his fists.

It didn't help telling herself it wasn't Joe she was going to see. Somehow Joe had become a part of every man; she'd keep on encountering him in one form or another for the rest of her life. If there was one thing Joe had taught her, it was that anger and violence lived right beneath the surface of most people—not just men. Eva was an example, the way she could be so nice and then all of a sudden turn mean.

"What's bothering you?" Alma rasped, startling her.

"Nothing," Bobby said guiltily, wondering for a moment if she'd been talking out loud to herself. Sometimes, at home, she'd done that: She'd gone through the house doing her chores, the whole time talking things out with herself, trying to understand why her life was the way it was.

"What is it?" Alma asked again, her tone softer. "You've got that same look in your eyes you had the first day you came here."

She did? Bobby wondered what that look might be. She had no idea her face could be so easily read. Was that one of the reasons why Joe had always been so mad at her? Or was it a matter of Alma's being someone who had a special gift for reading people's faces?

"I was just thinking," Bobby said. "If I had that Dennis's number, I'd call him and tell him I've changed my mind about Monday night."

"Why?"

"I shouldn't've said I'd go."

"Why not?" Alma persisted, the business section of the paper resting open on her lap.

"I don't know. Maybe he thinks I'm more interesting than I am. I don't know. I feel like it's a mistake."

"And what if it is?" Alma asked, puzzled by her thinking. "Are you not allowed to make mistakes?"

Almost inaudibly, Bobby replied, "No." Looking down at the cover of Eva's book, she wet her lips, then said, "That's how come I was always in trouble with Joe."

"That's why," Alma corrected her.

"That's why," Bobby said. "Because I could never do anything right, the way he wanted."

"I see. And you imagine Dennis will find fault with you?"

"Uh-hunh."

"Is it possible you might find fault with Dennis?" Alma asked shrewdly.

Bobby was stymied by the question.

"Is it?" Alma asked.

"I never thought of that," Bobby admitted. "I'm used to being told how stupid I am."

"You're *not* stupid," Alma said. "We've got to break you of the habit of believing that you are. That's number one. And number two, you need to discover for yourself that all men are different. I can't conceive of Dennis being remotely like your husband. But even on the off chance Dennis has some hidden similarities you dislike, you can simply refuse future invitations from him. You've merely agreed to spend an evening with him, not the rest of your life."

"That's true."

"Bear in mind that you have choices, Bobby. You're a free agent, with the right to say no, if you so choose."

"It's okay for you to say that," Bobby said, with a faint flutter of anger in her chest, "but you've never had anybody holding you down, telling you you don't have choices."

"No, I haven't," Alma agreed. "But that doesn't alter the fact that whether you're prepared to accept it or not, you *do* have choices. You do not have to obey simply because in the past that's what was expected. My understanding is that you ran away from an abusive situation because it had become intolerable, and you wanted things to change. It's up to you to make those changes, and you begin by refining your attitude. Dennis may only be the first of any number of men who find you attractive. Learn from the experience. If he suggests something that displeases you, say so. It's been my experience that the majority of men will respect that."

"I think maybe I'd be just as happy not to have to go through it."

"That, of course, is your decision. But since you've already consented to spending a few hours with the man, go along and see what's to be learned, if anything, from the experience."

"Okay," Bobby said, no less doubt-filled than before, and wishing they could drop the subject.

"How are you getting on with Eva's book?" Alma asked, as if having read Bobby's mind.

"Oh, I love it," Bobby said enthusiastically.

"Yes," Alma said contentedly. "She's good, isn't she?"

"Wonderful," Bobby declared.

"Writing that trash is eating her up," Alma said, looking over toward the windows. "It's a prime example of what we've been discussing: someone exercising her choices mistakenly. What a shameful waste!" She sat in silence for a time, then finally returned to the newspaper.

Bobby opened the book and tried to read, but was still unable to concentrate. She doubted she'd be able to read another line until this date with Dennis was out of the way.

Alma stared at the newspaper, able, on one level, to sympathize with Bobby's nervousness. For more than a year after her breakup with Randy Wheeler, she'd made her job the focus of her life. She took extra care marking the girls' essays and compositions, and spent hours reviewing the curriculum, revising the recommended reading lists to include books she believed would be of interest to her classes. Whenever the school required someone to accompany a group on a field trip or to chaperone a dance, Alma volunteered. She was willing to do absolutely anything so long as she didn't have to sit home alone evenings or weekends, when the temptation to feel sorry for herself was overwhelming. In very short order it became automatic to ask Alma first if something came up that required supervision.

She was chaperoning a senior class dance when she met Joel Whittaker, a phys-ed teacher at the boys' school where the dance was being held. After being introduced, he offered to get her some punch. She declined, thinking he'd go away. He didn't. He remained by her side, and a short while later he asked if she'd care to dance. She'd turned to take a good look at him then, wondering if he was too thick to read her signals or if he'd read them and decided to make a pitch anyway.

He was reasonably attractive, solidly built, and had an innocent-looking smile. She said, "Thank you, but no." And he said, "Fair enough." But instead of going away, he continued to stand there smiling at her. "You're a good height," he said approvingly, as if there'd been some contest and he'd been the adjudicator.

"*I* think so," she'd said, wishing he'd go. Couldn't he tell she wanted to be left alone?

"Not too many women I can talk with eye to eye. It can be a problem."

"Why?" she'd asked, disinterested.

"Lower back pain, for one thing," he'd said, straightfaced.

She'd laughed, and her laughter had taken her by surprise. She'd thought she might never again find anything amusing. It was his ability to make her laugh that prompted her to accept his subsequent invitation to go out to dinner the following weekend.

As soon as she'd agreed to go she'd wanted to back out. But she couldn't find any legitimate way to do that. So she spent the intervening days angry with herself for accepting, and angry with him for upsetting her precious equilibrium.

During their dinner she kept trying to find faults in him, and failing. He was pleasant and witty and even more attractive than she'd thought initially. She found herself studying his large, broad hands, taking note of the way he used his utensils, the way his fingers wrapped themselves around a water or wine glass. He had a certain grace that she hadn't expected to find in someone who'd gone through college playing football. Joel was altogether unexpected, and she liked him. She never relaxed her guard for an instant, but she had a far better time than she'd thought she might. So she agreed to see him again. And, just like that, there was another man in her life. Her parents were visibly relieved. Cora took to asking outrageously personal questions to which Alma didn't bother to respond. As a teenager her sister had spent hours giggling with her girlfriends about the boys they knew. Even when she'd been engaged to Randy, Alma had never been tempted to discuss him with her sister. She couldn't abide giggly, confessional conversations.

She knew her family thought she was finally picking up the threads of her life. She could almost hear them heaving sighs of relief, imagining that in the not too distant future she'd be announcing her engagement to this new young man they found so pleasant, and so very suitable. She found her family touchingly transparent. But she had no intention of becoming emotionally involved with Joel Whittaker.

She did become sexually involved with him, though. They went to his small apartment after their third Friday night date, and before his startled eyes she took off her clothes and climbed into his bed, deriving great pleasure and relief from the encounter. Unfortunately, Joel assumed that allowing him access to her body signified a depth of feeling. She tried to set him straight without coming across as cold and calculating, but it was difficult. He was essentially a simple man, who believed that sex equated with love, and since she'd made herself sexually accessible, it was only logical she must therefore love him. At the moment of his climax, he professed to love her, and she thought that was very sweet, but she couldn't make him see that what he really felt was gratitude.

"Let's enjoy it for what it is," she told him many many times.

But that concept was a violation of everything he'd been taught about women. He believed that sex without marriage basically dishonored a woman. Nothing she said would convince him that she preferred to be what he considered dishonored rather than committed to a relationship she knew had no future. He wanted to marry her. She wanted to go on making love with him. He simply couldn't comprehend her attitude, and something began to alter in his eyes when he looked at her. They managed to get through seven months before she knew she had to end it. The expression in his eyes was turning hard; he was beginning to think of her in unpleasant terms. She thought it was a pity. If he'd been satisfied with things the way they were, she'd have been content to continue the relationship, possibly for years. She liked having a male companion; she liked their lovemaking. She liked men in general. She just didn't want to play out the role most men were so anxious to assign to women. She didn't want—at least not then—to be anyone's property.

And so, during dinner one evening, she set him free. At the time it felt to her as if she'd landed a large game fish that put up a tremendous fight while she tried to free the hook from its mouth. She had to let it go because she had no interest in trophies, and in purely practical terms the flesh would go bad long before she could possibly consume it all.

Joel Whittaker was intelligent and kind. She tried to tell him he deserved someone who would cherish these qualities. He insisted she was that person, and was clearly distraught at her calm, quiet declaration otherwise. He took it, however, like the athlete he was, squarely and without flinching. He saw her home and said if she changed her mind he'd be waiting. Not six months later, he married someone else. Alma wasn't in the least surprised.

In retrospect, though, she could see she'd been unkind. And she regretted the fairly coldhearted way she'd stated her position. For some months after the affair ended she wished she'd handled matters differently. In future, she decided, she'd pick more wisely and deal more gently. It was not her intention to give pain. She simply wished to spare herself any. The affair with Joel established a pattern from which she'd never deviated since. She took up with slightly older men who had an experienced air, even

a somewhat wearied one. They were invariably free of de-
lusions, and almost always grateful.

What was truly ironic—and she'd long since savored
life's ironies—was the fact that her attempt to lose herself
in her work proved to be the foundation of her later success. The head of the school took note of her willingness
to be available for any and all duties. It was interpreted,
not necessarily incorrectly, as dedication. Despite her
comparative youth and lack of seniority, she was nomi-
nated as a viable candidate to replace the retiring head of
the English department. And two years later, at the age of
twenty-eight, Alma became the youngest department head
in the school's long history. Two years after that, having
completely revised the curriculum and revitalized the department, the retiring head mistress named Alma her suc-
cessor, and the board went along with the recommenda-
tion. Alma accepted the post, but only on the condition
that she be allowed to continue teaching senior English.
Since, in essence, she was offering to do two jobs, the
board was more than happy to acquiesce.

In time, as the administrative demands on her prolifer-
ated, she was forced to concede she could no longer teach
and attend to the nuts and bolts of running the school, as
well as being mother to a teenaged girl. So, at the age of
thirty-eight, she gave up teaching. Relinquishing her
classes meant she had more energy as well as more time for
Eva, who, at fourteen, was actively testing the boundaries
Alma had established for her. Eva was going through a
phase of lip-curled contempt for adults. She was demanding more freedom, and the right to set her own curfews.
Her bedroom walls were covered with posters of pop stars
and college pennants; the top of her dresser was filled with
an assortment of cosmetics and colognes; and she seemed
bent on trying every hair product that had ever been mar-
keted. Alma had her hands full, both at school and at
home.

But now and then, when a teacher was taken ill or was for some reason unable to make it to school on a given day, she would let the secretary take charge while Alma, secretly pleased, took over the class. In a way, it was Randy Wheeler who was responsible for her success.

Throughout the remainder of the weekend, Bobby mulled over Alma's remarks, trying to find some comfort in them. She couldn't. Regardless of her supposed rights and freedoms, she was dreading Monday evening. The part of her that had agreed to the date was a younger Bobby, from the time before Joe. That other Bobby had been full of optimism, envisioning a happy future. She'd believed, as her friends did, that the future held only good things. Eight years later she was another woman altogether, one who believed that the future was all for Penny. She'd run from Joe more for Penny's sake than her own. Whatever future she herself might have left was directed toward Penny. For her own part, she wanted only to be allowed to live in peace, without some man shouting orders. She'd never once thought about another man, even though Joe was forever accusing her of seeing other men on the sly.

She had to wonder about his brain when he made those accusations. Why would he think any other man would be interested in a woman who was all banged up half the time, and scared to breathe the other half? She'd thought for a long time that there was something wrong with the inside of Joe's head. There had to be. So often the things he said and did made no sense. Like the way he talked about his mother. He hated her. But they had to spend every Christmas with her, and Joe spent good money buying her presents she never seemed to like. It was the same every year, with Joe making out like the proud family man, the responsible hardworking breadwinner, and his mother looking at him like he was dirt.

They'd exchange presents, then they'd eat, then Bobby would help Ruth clean up the kitchen while Joe pretended

to play with Pen in the living room. Then they'd pack up
and go home. And the minute they came through the door,
Joe would start in about what a bitch his mother was. The
one time Bobby asked—very reasonably, she'd thought—
why they bothered to see her if he hated her so much, Joe
had screamed, "She's my fucking mother, isn't she?" as
if that explained everything, and then he'd backhanded
Bobby so hard he broke her nose. She'd ended up spending what was left of Christmas Day in the emergency room
at the hospital while Aunt Helen babysat Pen and Joe was
out somewhere. He didn't come home until late the next
morning.

She'd believed in all kinds of things once upon a time,
before she met Joe. Now she wasn't sure what she believed in. She only knew she was always nervous when she
happened to find herself alone with a man, any man, even
nice Mr. Grainger, the manager of the Burger King back
in Jamestown. She didn't understand men, didn't understand what they wanted. And it didn't matter how many
people told her that Joe was an exception, she couldn't
quite believe that. So why had she agreed to go out with
Dennis Forster? She was setting herself up for more of
everything she'd run away from.

She scarcely slept Sunday night. Each time she descended into sleep she had such frightful nightmares that
she forced herself to wake up. Three times she got up and
went into the kitchen, heart racing and hands trembling,
to smoke a cigarette and try to shake off the dreams. They
weren't so much dreams as re-creations of scenes of tor-
ment, nighttime variations on the horrors she'd experienced in reality with Joe. She sat at the kitchen table
thinking that if someone had told her at the age of nineteen what would happen to her in the subsequent years,
she'd have run for her life there and then. It amazed her to
realize how much pain the human body could withstand
and still continue to live, even when, in the midst of the
pain, she'd been convinced that this time he'd succeed in

killing her. She'd confronted the prospect of her death dozens of times, and it was in large measure her fear for Penny's well-being and her determination to protect the child that had ensured her own survival. Never again would she allow Penny to be put at risk.

There was no check for her on the refrigerator door on Monday. Throughout the day she kept popping in to look, but it wasn't there. Her two weeks were up, and by the time Penny got home from school she was convinced Alma and Eva were going to let her go. Somehow, in some way, she'd failed; they were dissatisfied with her. She was so upset by the prospect of having to leave that she was on the verge of tears throughout dinner, automatically cutting Penny's food and Alma's, then carefully avoiding looking at either of the women.

Dennis arrived at five to eight. A bitter taste in her mouth, Bobby said, "I'm all ready to go. I can't be out too late. Pen's not used to being left alone."

"That's fine," he said, walking with her to his Beetle and holding the passenger door open for her. "I start work pretty early in the morning myself."

Shivering, she got her seat belt fastened and waited for him to climb behind the wheel.

"Hungry?" he asked with a smile as he fitted his key into the ignition.

"A little." Her teeth were chattering and she couldn't get warm.

"Good. You like Indian food?"

"I've never had it."

"Want to try?" he asked, reversing out of the driveway.

"What's it like?"

"A little spicy, but good."

"Okay," she said, keeping her eyes on the road, wishing she'd brought her gloves. She could feel him looking at her.

"Don't worry," he said. "I'm a careful driver."

She glanced over at him. "I guess I'm kind of a nervous passenger. You can tell, hunh?"

He laughed, and said, "Oh, hell no. Everybody sits in that seat and keeps slamming an imaginary brake pedal. I'm used to it."

"You're joking, right?"

"Right. Your husband a lousy driver?"

"Terrible," she said, feeling disloyal, yet relieved to have an opportunity to talk about it. "Joe drives too fast and too close to the car ahead. He's always honking and cursing out the other drivers."

"One of those, hunh. I know the type," Dennis said. "What's he drive, something hot?"

She smiled, surprised. "A Firebird."

"It figures. It's usually that or a Trans Am." He chuckled and said, "You can tell I'm not into speed. I just love this car." He patted the steering wheel. "I'm only sorry Volkswagen stopped making the bugs. Far as I'm concerned, they're the greatest cars ever."

"I read in this magazine where they still make them in Mexico," she said, her teeth no longer chattering.

"That's right," he said approvingly. "I'd love to get my hands on a brand-new one. So, how's it going? Think you'll be staying?"

"I don't know. I hope so."

"I don't think you've got anything to worry about," he said, picking up the edge in her voice. "Alma's pretty high on you. More than any of the others, that's for sure. A couple of those women, I don't know *how* Alma put up with them."

"Is that right?" she said politely.

"No kidding. This one, Shirley, was hopeless, couldn't get anything right. I mean, the woman was a *registered nurse*, and she had the worst attitude I've ever encountered. Seriously. Everything was too much trouble for her. She'd get Alma downstairs in the morning then go sit in the apartment until it was time for lunch. After lunch, she'd get Alma back upstairs and off she'd go again until it was time for Alma to get up. Alma said she wouldn't do the exercises, that was fine with Shirley. Alma put up with a week of that, then kicked her out. From what I hear, you're spending all kinds of time with her, and you're the first one to get her to do the exercises.''

"I like her," Bobby said. "We talk a lot."

"That's great," he said, smiling over at her. "It's what she needs. You, too, I guess."

"How d'you mean?" Bobby asked warily.

"I get the impression you've had kind of a rough time."

She stared straight ahead, trying to think what to say.

"You don't have to talk about it," he said, "if you don't want to."

"I don't want to," she said nervously.

"Sure. I understand. Oh, beautiful!" he exclaimed. "A parking spot right in front of the restaurant." He directed the small car into the curb, then switched off the engine. "You like Mexican food?"

"I thought we were having Indian," she said, ducking her head to look over at the restaurant across the street.

"We are. I figure if you like Mexican you'll like Indian."

"I don't know," she said. "All I've ever tasted were tacos."

"Well, let's find out. Okay?"

She busied herself unbuckling her seat belt, then reached for the door handle, but he'd already come around to open the door for her. Unaccustomed to such treatment, she carefully avoided the hand he extended to assist her out of the car.

It was a pretty restaurant with pink and pale gray decor and white tablecloths and real cloth napkins. They were given a table by the window and Bobby sat down with her coat on, still feeling chilled.

"How about if I order for both of us?" Dennis offered. "I promise not to get anything weird." He smiled, and she nodded. He asked the waiter for two lassis, explaining, "They're yogurt drinks. Delicious, you'll see. You want to take your coat off?"

"I'm kind of cold," she said.

"Got any pictures of your little girl?" he asked, taking her completely by surprise.

"Yeah, I do," she said. "You want to see them?"

"Why so surprised? I thought everybody carried pictures of their kids so they could show them off."

"Is that why? I carry them so I can look at Pen when I'm not with her."

"Let's see," he asked.

Opening her bag, she got out the two color photos she kept with her all the time and handed them across the table to him. "Do you like children?" she asked.

"Some children," he answered. "She's a real sweetie, isn't she?" he said, smiling. "She looks a bit like you."

"She's got my chin and my forehead, I think."

He looked over at her, eyebrows lifted. "Why those parts?" he asked. "Usually people say she's got my eyes or my nose. Chin and forehead's a first."

She shrugged, waiting for him to return the pictures.

He handed them back. "Maybe one weekend I could take the two of you to the zoo or something."

"Why?"

"So I can feed you both to the lions," he joked. "Don't be so suspicious. I'm harmless. Ask anybody. I'll give you my parents' number; you can ask my mom, or my sister. My brother might not be such a good idea. We have major differences of opinion on almost everything. You have any brothers or sisters?"

She shook her head. "Not that I know of."

"You mean you might and not know it?" He sat with his chin in his hand, looking interested.

"Maybe," she said. "My mother had me at seventeen and ran off. For all I know she got married and had a bunch more kids."

"So who raised you?" he asked as the waiter brought their lassis.

"My grandpa and my aunt Helen."

"What about your grandmother?"

"She died when my mother and aunt were real . . . really young."

"Oh, that's too bad. Try the lassi," he urged.

She did and was pleased to find the drink sweetly cool. "It's good," she told him.

"I knew you'd like it," he said happily. "Wait'll you try the food. You'll want to come here all the time."

He seemed so nice, she thought, so unguarded. She took another sip of the yogurt drink, wondering what he was like when something made him mad. He didn't look like someone who'd start using his fists, but you could never tell. Still, she was beginning to relax a little, and she'd finally stopped shivering. Maybe it wasn't going to be so bad after all.

Fourteen

Eva went downstairs to check on Penny and to her surprise found the child sitting up in bed reading one of Mellie's old books.

"Aren't you supposed to be sleeping?" an amused Eva asked, sitting down on the side of the bed.

"Uh-hunh," Penny answered, her eyes remaining on the book as if unable to tear herself away.

"It's almost eight-thirty," Eva said. "I think maybe you've read enough for one night."

At last looking up, Penny said, "It's a very good story."

With a smile and a shake of her head, Eva said, "You're an amazing little girl. Are you actually reading that?"

"Sure. Want me to read you some?"

"No, I believe you." Eva gently removed the book from the girl's hands, asking, "Have you got a bookmark?"

"Uh-hunh." Penny reached over and grabbed a piece of paper from the bedside table. "My mom says you musn't ever fold the corners of a book or write anything in it but maybe your name, to show it's yours."

"That's absolutely right," Eva said, marking Penny's place and setting the book aside. "Why don't you slide down now, and I'll tuck you in."

Penny obeyed, then held her arms out—a gesture Eva perceived to be automatic but which touched her nonetheless, like a subtle stabbing in her chest. She bent to kiss the child's soft cheek, remembering the hundreds of times she'd bid Mellie good night in this fashion, inhaling the incomparable purity of her little-girl flesh. "Sleep well," she murmured, momentarily caught up in a time warp, her own daughter and this child briefly becoming one.

Penny turned onto her side, tucked her hands under her cheek, and closed her eyes, then opened them again, saying, "My mom leaves the bathroom light on for me."

"Okay," Eva said, and returned upstairs to the living room, still feeling the yielding warmth of Penny's cheek beneath her lips, that subtle stabbing gradually fading to a kind of distant ache. Putting another log on the fire, she stood for a few moments watching the flames, thinking.

"Was she sleeping?" Alma asked.

"No," Eva answered, eyes still on the fire. "She was sitting up, reading. I persuaded her it was time to go to sleep."

Alma gave a soft laugh. "She's wonderfully bright."

"Did you have girls like that at school?"

"Perhaps a handful over the years. I was like her, as a child. With books, that is," Alma clarified.

"Were you?" A hand on the mantel, Eva looked over at her aunt.

"I used to read under the covers with a flashlight. My mother was forever telling me I'd go blind. Obviously, I didn't."

Eva suddenly remembered riding a tricycle up and down the driveway of the house where they'd lived before her parents died. She could recall the moment perfectly, even to the feel of the pedals under her feet and the bumpy surface of the paved driveway. A few seconds, then it was gone, replaced by the equally clear memory of herself at six years old, being left to stay for two weeks with Aunt Alma while her mother and father flew off for a skiing vacation out west. As a child she'd adored her visits with her aunt, finding her exotic and elegant. Unlike her mother who fussed and fretted if Eva got dirty or disarranged anything in the living room, Aunt Alma said, "Children are supposed to get dirty," and allowed Eva to play anywhere she liked. It was understood that Eva was to put things back where she'd found them and to try her best not to break anything, but it was also understood that Aunt Alma wouldn't punish her for the occasional accident. The only not so good part about visiting was the food. Her aunt didn't make regular meals the way her mother did. Sometimes they had sandwiches for dinner, or odd combinations of things her aunt liked to eat—fresh asparagus and toasted English muffins with jelly, sliced tomatoes and bowls of cornflakes with raisins. Eva actually came to enjoy these peculiar combinations. The odd dinners merely added to her aunt's appeal.

Her parents' plane crashed; they'd never returned home, and she'd simply stayed on with her aunt.

"You seem a tad distracted," Alma said.

"Do I?" Again Eva looked over at her. "Bobby's two weeks are up tomorrow. How do you feel about keeping her on?"

"Surely you're asking me as a formality," Alma said. "Of course we'll keep her on. Already, I see improvements in her."

Eva laughed. "You're the one who's supposed to be showing improvement."

"I am what I am, and evermore shall be so. But that young woman has potential."

"For what?" Eva asked, at last going over to sit on the sofa.

"Among other things, for becoming her own person."

"Someone who doesn't allow herself to get beaten again."

"That's one thing," Alma said. "One very big thing. She's been brainwashed, programmed to believe she's useless and stupid; it's been beaten into her. That infuriates me."

"So you're going to oversee her emancipation," Eva said somewhat caustically.

"I may just do that." Alma's chin lifted stubbornly. "You're being bitchy. Perhaps it's time to go visit Charlie."

Eva gave in with a smile. "Perhaps it is. As it happens, we're having dinner tomorrow night." Her eyes going back to the fire, she asked, "What kind of potential do you imagine for her?"

"Purely personal," Alma said. "A great part of the joy of teaching was seeing young minds blossom. Bobby has a young mind. Great areas of it are still untapped. And," she added, as if it were of no consequence, "I'm growing quite fond of her."

"I never dreamed she'd last a week," Eva said. "But she does have a knack for making herself fairly indispensable. The thing is, her willingness tends to set my teeth on edge."

"That's because you're a control junkie."

"A *what?*"

"You need to be in control," Alma elaborated. "I used to. And I savored it. Now I haven't all that much choice; circumstances have rendered me dependent. But you, Eva, hate to concede an inch, if you don't have to."

"What's wrong with that?" Eva asked defensively.

"I didn't say there was anything wrong with it. I'm merely stating a salient fact."

"Well, I don't happen to agree with you. We're all subject to externalized powers, for God's sake. I simply try to stay on top of what I *can* control."

"That's fine," her aunt said indulgently. "No one's criticizing you."

"It certainly sounded that way. Calling me a control junkie. God! Where do you come up with these things?"

"From limited television viewing and reading the daily newspapers," Alma said blithely.

Penny came padding barefoot into the room, complaining, "I'm not sleepy." Going directly to Alma, she leaned on the arm of the wheelchair, asking, "Whatcha doin'?"

"We are conversing," Alma said, lifting her right hand to stroke the girl's hair. "It's long past your bedtime, miss."

"I know, but I'm not one bit sleepy. When's my mom comin' home?"

"In another hour or so," Alma told her.

"I'll tell you what," Eva said. "I'll make you some hot chocolate. And after you drink it, you'll go back to bed. Okay?"

"Okay." Penny took the hand Eva offered and went along with her, twisting around when she was halfway out of the room to wave good-bye to her granny.

Eva lifted her onto the counter saying, "Sit there while I make it," and Penny placidly said, "Okay. You gonna make it with water or milk?"

"Milk."

"Good. Milk's better." She watched Eva pour milk into a pan, then asked, "When's your little girl comin' home?"

"In a week or so, for Thanksgiving."

"Are you gonna have a turkey party?"

With a laugh, Eva said, "Yup."

"Can me and mom come too?"

"Yup."

"Oh, good!" Penny said. "I love stuffin' best."

Eva stirred the hot chocolate mix into the warm milk and handed the glass to Penny saying, "Drink this, then straight to bed."

"You not havin' any?"

"No. I don't care much for sweet things."

Penny looked scandalized. "You don't like *candy?*"

"Not much, no."

"Chocolate?"

"No."

"Boy!" Penny was impressed. "Not even gummy bears?"

"Especially not gummy bears."

"Granny does," Penny said. "I gived her some of mine and she liked 'em real good."

"You gave her some of yours and she liked them very much."

"That's right!" Penny smiled widely, then drank more of the hot chocolate. "This is good, not too hot. I don't like it when it's too hot."

"Finish it up, Penny," Eva said warningly. "You've got to go back to bed. I think your mother would be upset to come home and find you still up."

Penny thought about that, her dainty features firming. Then she drained the glass and put it down on the counter. "Okay," she announced, holding out her arms to be lifted off. "I'm ready."

Eva picked her up, experiencing another memory jolt, more subtle interior stabbing, as Penny's legs wrapped around her waist and her arms fastened around her neck. For a few seconds Eva considered setting the child down, getting her to walk downstairs under her own steam. Then, succumbing to the pleasure of Penny's weight and binding limbs, she gave in and carried the girl back to bed.

Upon returning to the living room, still feeling Penny's phantom grip on her, she looked over at her aunt who, eyes closed, was listening to a soaring passage of a Mozart piano concerto emanating from the stereo speakers.

The day after her parents had been due to return, her aunt had sat down with her in the living room and in the simplest possible terms explained that the airplane carrying her parents and a lot of other people had crashed, which meant that they wouldn't be coming home, ever, and from now on Eva would be staying for good.

She recalled the great care and concern her aunt had displayed that day, the patient manner in which she'd answered all of Eva's questions. They'd sat together for quite some time and then, evidently satisfied that Eva understood, her aunt had gone off to make a number of telephone calls that had to do, Eva had gathered, with her mother and father not ever coming back from their holiday.

For Eva their deaths had been too abstract. She'd been unable to take in the full meaning and so had interpreted her aunt's words to mean that she'd simply be staying somewhere longer than originally intended. And even though she attended the funeral, sitting between her aunt and her grandfather, both of them holding her hands, she'd clung to the idea that she'd soon be going home. In the meantime, she'd been put into a class at Auntie Alma's school and had to wear a uniform every day. She didn't get to see any of her old friends, and she missed her old house. She also began to miss the way her mom did things, which wasn't at all the way Auntie Alma did them. The strange meals started to bother her. So did the continuation of her freedom to lose hair ribbons and to come into the house after exploring down on the beach with sand and grit under her fingernails.

And so one evening, five or six weeks after she'd been told she'd be living with Auntie Alma for good, she got out of bed and went downstairs to the living room, where her aunt was sitting at the desk, and said, "I want to go home now, please, Auntie Alma. Okay?"

Her aunt looked up at her and started to say something, stopped, started again to speak, then dropped her head into her hands and began to cry. Eva felt terrible then because she loved her aunt and didn't want to make her unhappy, but she really wanted to go home. She went around the desk and patted her aunt on the back the way grown-ups always patted her when she was upset, and waited for her aunt to stop crying. And that was when Alma took her on her knee and explained in more graphic terms why she couldn't go home. Then Eva cried, still not really able to understand what dead meant, but convinced finally that she was going to be staying with her aunt forever.

The only other time she saw her aunt cry had been, for all kinds of reasons, far more devastating. At fourteen, Eva had grown accustomed to Alma's unemotional way of dealing with most situations and was at a stage when she was determined to provoke her into what she believed to be more honest reactions. She'd come to view Alma's self-control as a pose, an attitude that masked her true feelings. In point of fact, she was suspicious at that stage in her personal history of the behavior of the majority of adults, as were her friends. And it was particularly stressful having to attend a school where her aunt was the head mistress, not to mention coming home every day to find little or no difference between the head mistress and her guardian. Alma's consistency was something Eva depended upon on the one hand and found suspect on the other. So she'd taken to saying and doing things intended to push her aunt over the edge.

They were in the midst of a fairly heated argument about Eva's right to date on school nights when the telephone rang. Fuming, but secretly enjoying this contest of wills, Eva sat slumped in the armchair by the fireplace, arms folded across her chest, waiting while her aunt went to answer the telephone.

But when, a few minutes later, her aunt came back to the living room, she looked so distressed that Eva completely forgot the argument. Alma walked over to the fireplace and stood with one hand on the mantel, gazing down at the fire, her demeanor so altered that Eva was immediately frightened.

"What's wrong?" she asked.

"Your grandfather died," her aunt said, and then, without making a sound, began to cry.

Initially, Eva couldn't absorb it. She was so unnerved at seeing Alma this way—even though it was what she'd been angling to accomplish—and so guilty for having behaved badly, that she didn't know what to do. With anyone else, Eva's automatic response would have been to offer an embrace. But this was her aunt, and the usual rules of behavior didn't apply. Not that Alma wasn't affectionate, because she was. All her life she'd run to her aunt for hugs and kisses, for approval. Yet this time Eva was uncertain. They'd been battling for weeks. What if she went to put her arms around her and her aunt pushed her away because Eva had been such a bitch lately? But if she didn't do what her every instinct told her was right she knew she'd regret it. So, cowed by this view of her aunt's basic humanity—which, in her heart of hearts, she'd known all along was there—Eva got up and embraced her. And then she became so upset that Alma ended up consoling her, thereby reestablishing the balance in their relationship. It marked the end of Eva's brief-lived rebellion. It seemed pointless after that to pursue it when she'd known from the outset that she was provoking her aunt purely for the sake of proving she could.

If Alma had wept over the stroke, she'd done it in private. All she'd shown Eva was her anger, and that had subsided considerably over the months. Until Bobby and Penny became part of the household, Alma had been disinterested in almost everything. She still kept abreast of world news and had spent most of the summer watching the Yankees on television and groaning over their losses. She'd been rough on the nurses, quick to criticize, and had managed to discourage her friends from coming to visit. She didn't, she insisted, want anyone to see her looking like a gargoyle. She'd retreated deep inside herself, only occasionally revealing her old personality. Perhaps that Alma was gone for all time and never would return. The idea worried Eva.

But Alma was responding to Penny, and to Bobby, too. As a result, regardless of Eva's own conflicting responses to Bobby, it felt as if the air in the house was daily growing lighter.

She wondered suddenly if the house seemed as enormous to Penny as it had to her as a six-year-old, and felt a pang, remembering how Alma had read her to sleep every night, endless wonderful stories. When she had bad dreams she'd climb into bed with her aunt. And when she'd been sick, Alma had always let her stay in the big bed. Her aunt had never left her to go on vacation but had always taken her along. Alma didn't start traveling until after Eva was married. She'd stayed close by, in case Eva needed her. It was an incredible thing to have done for someone else's child. Now, Eva knew—she'd heard Penny knocking at Alma's door in the early morning—her aunt was once again playing a special role for another child. And, setting aside her own mixed feelings about the child's mother, Eva was glad.

They had paratha—heated soft chewy flatbread, and raita—a cucumber and yogurt salad, a biryani, which was rice with vegetables and raisins, and a mild chicken curry. Bobby loved the food and ate hugely.

"I knew you'd like it," Dennis said when, with a small groan, she put down her knife and fork and leaned back in her chair.

"It's the best food I've ever had." She gave him a smile so he'd know she wasn't just being polite.

"Now I know for sure you'll like Mexican, too."

"Probably," she said. "You mind if I smoke?"

"Nope. Go right ahead."

She got a Marlboro from her bag and lit it, then, over-come by curiosity, had to ask, "Why'd you ask me out?"

"Why not?"

"No, really. Why?"

"I don't know," he said, looking uncomfortable, as if she'd pushed him into a corner. "It seemed like a good idea."

"That's it?" she asked. "That's why?"

He thought for a time, then said, "Well, I'm kind of impressed by the progress you've made with Alma, and I was curious to know what sort of person you are. And now that your face is healed up and you had your hair done, you look really good. You've got great eyes. I would've thought you'd say your girl had your eyes, not your chin or your forehead.''

"Pen's got great big eyes," she said, her inflection indicating that she, by comparison, had much smaller ones.

"So do you."

"They don't look so big to me," she said, made uneasy by his compliments.

"You and your girl both have great big deep blue eyes," he insisted. "I guess most of all I was curious."

"What about?"

"About who you were and how you came to be working for Alma. What's the story kind of thing, is what I mean."

"Oh!" She looked around. No one was paying them the least attention. "I took Pen and ran away," she said, all at once aware of the pulse beating in her throat. For some reason, perhaps to scare him off or perhaps to test the depth of his interest, she wanted to tell him about Joe. "Joe, my husband, he's real mean."

"I figured that much out."

"He hit Pen real hard a few weeks back. I couldn't allow that."

"No," Dennis said quietly.

"It didn't matter about me," she explained. "But it mattered about Pen." Her throat was starting to choke closed. She coughed to clear it, then took a puff of her cigarette. "There's nothing to know about me. I was just a housewife, worked part-time at the Burger King. I'm nobody."

"Of course you're somebody," he said, echoing Alma so that she had to smile a little.

"No," she disagreed. "I'm nobody. I'm happy to be left alone. It's all I want.'

"You must've been married pretty young."

"Nineteen."

"That's pretty young."

"Yeah," she sighed. "It seems like a hundred years ago now."

"I'll bet."

"I'm not too good at this," she said apologetically.

"At what? Eating, talking?"

"Talking to men," she elaborated. "It kind of sets me on edge."

The waiter came to remove their plates and Dennis asked her if she'd like coffee. She said she would and he ordered two cups. The waiter left, and Dennis said, "It's just talking. What's your name anyhow, Roberta?"

"Barbara."

"Barbara," he repeated. "It suits you better than Bobby."

"That's what Alma said. I don't see what difference it makes. I'm the same, whatever you call me."

"Now, see, that's where you're wrong. A name *establishes* you, in a way. For example, I'm Dennis. That sets you up for the Irish red hair, the pasty skin, and orange freckles." He smiled at her. "Bobby had a whole lot of wild blond hair and a black eye, a lip out to there. Barbara has nice brown hair and two big blue eyes."

"Are you a Catholic?"

He laughed and shook his head. "Protestant. You?"

"My grandpa used to take us to the Episcopalian church. But since he died, I'm not anything anymore. I guess I wasn't anything then, but I liked going. It was kind of peaceful. I liked the church air. It was . . . bigger sort of than regular air. And I liked the music, the hymns. I'd get kind of swollen in the heart when they'd sing 'Jerusalem.'"

"That's nice," he said. "Myself, I like Christmas carols."

"Yeah," she agreed. "Me too."

"That's a nice sweater," he said. "I meant to tell you that before."

She looked down at herself, at the royal blue cashmere pullover that was softer than anything she'd ever felt, and said, "Eva gave it to me. She gave me a whole bunch of things."

"Good deal."

"She's real…really complicated. One minute I think she can't stand me. The very sight of me seems to get her riled. And the next minute she's giving me a load of expensive clothes that're like new." Again she wondered if Eva was planning to get rid of her. She hoped with all her heart that wasn't going to happen. She wanted, more than she'd ever wanted anything, to be able to stay. The thought of moving on, trying for another job, made her feel a bit sick.

"I know what you mean. She's tricky," he agreed. "But I think it's because most of the time her mind's somewhere else, on her work, I guess."

"I'm reading one of her books. She's a *wonderful* writer."

"Yeah?"

"Wonderful," she repeated. "Maybe writers are like that."

"Maybe. So, what d'you think? Want to go to the zoo or something one weekend? We could even take Penny into the city to see a show."

"I don't know," she said, at once nervous again. "I'm working seven days a week."

"Alma will let you have the time off. Wouldn't you like to see New York?"

"I never thought about it. I don't know. Maybe."

"Why did you say you'd come out tonight?" he asked.

She shrugged, knowing she couldn't tell the truth, which was that she'd been afraid to say no. He was a man. When a man said to do something, you did it. It's what scared her more than anything else: the helpless knowledge that she couldn't say no. "I don't know," she answered, thinking she sounded every bit as stupid as Joe had always said she was. "You seemed real nice." That, at least, was true. "You like to have a good time. I mean, you like to laugh."

"That's true. Don't you?"

"I don't know what I like," she admitted. "I'm going to have to find out."

"Maybe I can help you do that."

"I don't know," she said plaintively. "I'll have to see."

"Don't make any hasty decisions," he teased.

"I told you, I'm not good at this."

"There's nothing to be good at," he said reasonably. "You get used to people, spend some time with them. It's called socializing."

"I've never done any of that."

"So I gather. Maybe it's time to start."

"We'll see."

"Sure," he said, backing down. "We'll see how it goes."

She scrambled out of the car before he had a chance to get halfway around to the passenger side.

"Hey, slow down a minute," he said, hurrying to catch up as she all but ran toward the door.

"What?" She was scared he'd try to do something, touch her or kiss her or something. And that was the second scariest thing she could think of: someone wanting to fold her body into painful positions in order to make himself feel good.

"I just wanted to say good night," he said, keeping his distance.

"Oh. Yeah. Thanks for the dinner, Dennis." She managed a quick smile. "It was really good."

"You're welcome. I'll see you Thursday."

"Yeah, okay," she said, desperate to get inside the safety of the house.

He looked as if he wanted to say something more, but didn't speak, and after a moment he said, "Well, good night, then," and headed back to his car.

With the door open at her back, she waved as he went down the driveway. The horn gave a brief toot, and then he was gone. She was exhausted, and it was only twenty after ten.

Alma and Eva both looked up as she came into the living room.

"Have a nice time?" Eva asked.

"Very nice," Bobby said, like a polite child, Eva thought. "Pen wasn't any trouble, was she?"

"Not a bit," Alma said.

"Good. I'll go check on her, then come help you upstairs."

"Take your time," Alma told her. "I'm not going anywhere."

Penny had kicked off the blankets. Bobby covered her, then went to sit in the apartment living room for a few minutes, reviewing the evening. It hadn't been anywhere near as awful as she'd imagined it might be. And the food had been fabulous. But what she didn't understand was why this man was so eager to spend time with her. Couldn't he see she had nothing to offer? Or did men only see what they wanted to see, and not things the way they really were? Women weren't like that. Women saw things pretty much the way they were. But a lot of the time they had to pretend they didn't, because men said they didn't know what the hell they were talking about.

I'm not going to be that way anymore, she decided, getting to her feet with a sigh. It was time to help Alma up to bed. Maybe, she thought, climbing the stairs, Alma knew the truth and said it straight out because she'd never been married, had never had to keep it in a secret place in the back of her head in order to keep some man from getting riled. As she walked through the kitchen, she was all at once filled with admiration for Alma, impressed by the fact that she'd made the choice to live alone and be able to talk about true things. It seemed like an incredibly smart and brave thing to have done.

Fifteen

Bobby was so worried about what Eva's failure to pay her might signify that she couldn't even think about going to bed. On top of that, she kept going over her dinner with Dennis, fretting that she'd been poor company and probably hadn't thanked him properly. It shamed her to think she was so ignorant, that she knew so little about how to deal with people. Well, he'd probably back away now, and maybe that would be for the best. To take her mind off everything, she decided to sit down and finish reading Eva's book. It was so good she didn't want it to end; but she was also dying to know how things wound up. So she went on reading even though she was so tired the words were blurry.

When she got to the bottom of the last page she sighed, tremendously satisfied. She stayed on the sofa for a time, reluctant to put the book down and be parted from people she'd cared so much about. She wondered how Eva knew the things she did, and if she'd written about people she'd actually known, or if she'd just imagined everything.

It must be wonderful to be a writer, Bobby thought, at last setting the book aside, to be able to use words to create such fascinating characters, to have them say and do the things they did. Sometimes books were so much better than life, made so much more sense of things. She looked at the two paperback novels, tempted to start one of them right away. But it was after one, and she really was too tired.

Wait till she told Aunt Helen she was living in a house with a famous writer. Her aunt would be impressed, although Eva didn't act at all the way Bobby had always imagined famous people did. She wasn't especially glamorous, didn't drive a big expensive car, or wear a lot of jewelry. Her clothes were good, and she always looked nice enough, but to see her, say, in a supermarket, you'd never go thinking she was a famous author.

It was pretty incredible, she thought, already sinking into sleep. Evangeline Chaney and Eva Rule. Somehow, they were different people. And while she really liked the author, she was fearful of the changes the day-to-day woman might bring about in her own life.

Dennis lay in bed in the dark with his arms folded behind his head and asked himself what he thought he was proving. Inviting Bobby out had been a spur-of-the-moment impulse prompted primarily by curiosity. He'd never encountered a woman quite like her; certainly he'd never met a woman who'd been beaten, and something about her aroused his sympathy as well as a surprising, fairly primal, instinct to protect her. Which was, to a degree, not only sort of presumptuous of him but maybe kind of arrogant, too. After all, he didn't know a thing about her, so how was he going to protect her? She probably didn't want some gangling dope offering to look out for her.

But maybe she didn't know what she wanted or needed. Everything seemed to scare her; she treated the simplest question like a possible land mine, visibly worrying about what it was or wasn't safe to say. In a way, though, that added to her appeal. She was pretty and really had no idea, and that made her more appealing, too. She was the only pretty woman he'd ever encountered who didn't, privately, know she was good-looking and use it, in some way, to her advantage. He found that fascinating.

Then there was the progress she was making with Alma. That was really something. Half a busload of women of all shapes and sizes had come and gone in that household and the only one of them who'd done Alma any good at all was the last one on earth he'd have picked to do the job. Which went to prove what a gigantic mistake it was to go judging people strictly on appearances.

Thinking back to their dinner, he wondered if he hadn't been pushing maybe a bit too hard. But on reconsideration he decided he'd been reasonable. If you didn't ask questions, you didn't get answers. Without the answers you didn't have a hope of getting to know the other person. And the thing of it was, he wanted to get to know Bobby and there was nothing logical about that. He could analyze it all he liked, but no amount of analysis would alter the simple fact that he was drawn to the woman and couldn't give any single, specific reason why. Every time he'd managed to get a smile out of her, he'd felt as if he'd really accomplished something.

Maybe it was a kind of a challenge, but he tended not to see people in those terms. He wasn't interested in conquests. Oh, sure, maybe at seventeen or eighteen, he'd gone through a phase when, like every other guy he'd known, he'd been looking to score. But it hadn't made him especially happy at the time, and he'd grown out of it in a pretty big hurry. Locker room conversations had always bothered the hell out of him, made him feel a raging need to defend the girls being talked about. Naturally, he'd stayed quiet. He'd never seen the sense of making waves. But it had turned him off, and for a while there he'd wondered if maybe there was something wrong with him for feeling so out of it. There were all these guys smirking about their prowess and it'd made him feel embarrassed for them and ashamed of himself for even listening. It was a tremendous relief to leave high school and go off to college where he didn't feel obligated to hang out with guys he basically didn't like but couldn't brush off because he'd known them most of his life.

The headlights of a passing car arced across the ceiling as he wondered if he should cool it, just leave Bobby alone. The woman had a lot of problems and he certainly didn't want to be the one to add to them. But he couldn't get past the idea that he could help. He really wanted to. He liked her. He liked the fact that she hadn't been everywhere and done everything, liked her husky voice and the way she talked about her little girl. He liked what she'd said about carrying her daughter's photographs around so she could look at them when she wasn't with her. That had touched him. Altogether, she touched him. The bottom line was, he'd go ahead and ask her out again. The worst that could happen was she'd say no.

Eva was sitting by her bedroom window in the dark, looking out at the moonlit Sound thinking about the night in Montaverde after that first time she'd seen Ian with the gun.

Dinner on the veranda with Deborah and Ian had been particularly strained. Ian had been drinking since late afternoon and consumed the better part of a bottle of wine with his meal. Although she didn't say a word about it, Deborah was plainly bothered by his drinking. Eva wanted to say something to lighten the atmosphere but couldn't think of a thing. At a loss, she praised the stew Deborah had prepared.

"Thank you, darling," Deborah said from her perch on the railing without looking up.

As if inspired by Eva's compliment to remember his manners, Ian said, "Yes, very good actually."

Deborah didn't acknowledge him and the silence again closed around them.

Finally, determined to have a few minutes alone with Deborah, Eva said, "I'll do the dishes tonight."

"That's good of you, darling," Deborah said. And then, instead of coming out to the kitchen, as Eva had hoped she would, Deborah announced, "I'll go to bed now, if you don't mind."

Eva had wanted to scream that she *did* mind, that the two of them had to talk; she wanted some sort of explanation for what was going on, needed some clue how to handle it.

"Good of you," Ian echoed, and then he'd strolled off after his wife to the master suite, leaving Eva to clean up.

Frustrated, isolated, defeated, she washed the dishes, then went to check on the children. Mellie and Derek were asleep side by side on their cots in the third bedroom. She stood for a time watching them and finally tiptoed out. In her own room, she read for half an hour, then turned out the light and lay in bed listening to the strange rustlings and stirrings in the underbrush. All four of the bedrooms had louvered windows on the front and rear walls, to provide cross-ventilation, and, being so high up the mountainside, there was always a breeze at night. The palm fronds clattered dryly, animals and lizards scurried about, and Ian lurched drunkenly past her window, muttering to himself, startling her so that she was instantly, completely alert. From the sound of his irregular footsteps, she guessed he went to the end of the walkway, turned, and came back. But this time he stopped to look in Eva's uncurtained window. She closed her eyes to slits and remained very still, fear like a hand at her throat. A few moments and his shambling footsteps indicated he'd moved on. She opened her eyes and drew a tremulous breath, suddenly perspiring despite the breeze.

A minute or two later the light went on in the kitchen and she watched Ian stagger into the middle of the room, then stop and look around. It was like a film. She sat up to watch, filled with antipathy and fear of this hatefully pretentious man Deborah had married. His view of himself as an aristocratic colonizer was so firmly entrenched that the Montaverdeans clearly disliked him on sight. Eva had seen their eyes narrow when Ian spoke to them, had seen their bodies straighten as if in preparation for attack. He had no idea. He called them "old chap" and "my good fellow" and the natives despised him. It was one of the primary reasons why, Eva now knew, construction on the house was proceeding so slowly. No one wanted to work for Ian. He was insufferably arrogant. They were willing to work for Deborah—she was a Montaverdean, after all—but Ian's interference irritated them, and so they invented problems that caused delays. And Deborah's outrage was building daily, visibly, pervasively, like a slow, steady leak of some potentially lethal gas.

Eva couldn't tell what Ian was doing in the kitchen, but she guessed he was getting himself another drink. A few minutes later the light went out, and a minute or so after that she heard the door to the master suite close. Exhaling shakily she lay back and tried to sleep.

The next morning Deborah was so angry Eva didn't dare speak to her. She fed the children breakfast, then tried to keep them out of the way while it was determined whether or not they'd be going to the site. Deborah sat on the veranda railing and sipped a cup of tea, waiting for Ian to get out of bed, all the while berating him under her breath. Tea in one hand, a cigarette in the other, she frowned at the mountainside, muttering, "Useless bloody bastard. Drinks half the night, then sleeps half the day. No wonder they're laughing at us. Pissing all our bloody money away."

"Why did you come back?" Eva ventured to ask, the children busy for the moment with some game of Derek's devising.

Deborah shrugged, then looked over, saw Derek doing something of which she didn't approve and went flying through the room to grab him by the upper arm, saying, "Play properly or you'll spend the day locked in your room, alone!"

Horrified, Eva approached, automatically taking a frightened Melissa's hand, saying, "It's all right. He didn't mean anything." She actually had no idea what he'd done to anger his mother, but she didn't care for Deborah's threat to lock him up.

Deborah regarded her coolly for a moment, as if on the verge of telling Eva to mind her own business, then abruptly she swung about and went marching toward the master bedroom, shouting as she neared the door, "Get out of that bloody bed! There's work to be done. *Get up!*"

Once satisfied that Ian was awake, she came marching back through the empty rooms, her strong, beautifully-shaped bare feet shaking the floor boards, on her way to the kitchen to fix him a cup of tea.

"Will we be going to the site today?" Eva asked.

Deborah paused and looked at her with an expression at once infinitely sad and utterly livid. "I'm sorry, darling. This is a complete cock-up." A pause, a sigh, then, "Yes, I expect we will."

"I'll make some lunch for the children," Eva said, knowing Deborah didn't eat at all in the middle of the day; she herself had lost her appetite; and Ian each day brought along a large English cucumber which he ate in slices throughout their time at the bay. The native workers caught fish and cooked them in buckets of boiling water over small brush fires. So Eva daily fixed sandwiches and brought fruit along for the children.

Deborah stood gazing at her. "I'm sorry," she said again. "I know none of this is quite what you had in mind when you agreed to come."

Here was the opening she'd been seeking, and Eva wanted to ask her friend dozens of questions: Why had she married Ian, why had she agreed to sell her lovely home in London to return to a place she hadn't known since childhood, why were they fighting impossible odds to build a house that, in the end, would cost them everything they had? She wanted to ask what Deborah imagined she'd live on, since Ian had been granted only a visitor's visa that prohibited him from working on the island; wanted to know why she didn't leave the man, take her son and start her life again somewhere else. Did she know that her husband kept a gun hidden in the car? And most of all, she wanted to know why Deborah had asked her to come. Was Deborah expecting something Eva was failing to provide? She longed to say, "Tell me what you want and I'll help you. Just, please, tell me what you want." She had so many questions that she couldn't speak at all. Helplessly, she simply gave her friend a sympathetic smile, and for a few seconds Deborah laid her hand on Eva's arm. Then Ian came reeling out of the bedroom, complaining under his breath, and Deborah was off, ranting at him as she stormed up to the kitchen to get his tea.

It was one of the few times during her stay on the island that Deborah expressed any sort of fondness for or awareness of Eva. From that point on, Deborah's anger spread to include Eva and Mellie, too. It began to appear as if Deborah wanted them gone as badly as Eva herself did. But she couldn't leave. She was convinced she'd be letting Deborah down, abandoning her. They were friends. Friends were understanding, they helped each other. Yet Deborah didn't want her help. Or did she? Eva felt, finally, like a child, unable to take decisive action in any direction.

Studying the way the moonlight dappled the relatively calm waters of the Sound, Eva pulled her thoughts back to the present, asking herself if there was anything she might have done to alter the course of events on the island. She didn't think so. But that didn't ease her deep-seated feeling that she'd somehow failed her friend. There had to have been something she could have done. The problem was that even now, years after the fact, she simply could not see what.

She yawned, then got up and made her way down to the kitchen for a cup of tea.

* * *

It was raining hard Tuesday morning. Bobby got Penny into her rubber boots and slicker, made sure she had her lunch, then, with an umbrella shielding them both from the downpour, went to the top of the driveway to await the school bus.

When she returned, Eva was sitting at the kitchen table with her checkbook. "Come sit down for a minute," she said without looking up, and Bobby was terrified that the moment had come when Eva was going to pay her off and tell her she'd have to go. Her apprehension was made even deeper by the set of Eva's features, by her very business-like manner.

Mouth dry, her stomach jumpy, Bobby sat down and waited while Eva finished writing a check, then tore it from the book and pushed it across the table. "The two weeks are up today. Alma's very happy with you," she said, "so we'd like you to stay on."

Bobby's relief was so immense it made her dizzy. Her eyes filling with tears she quickly blinked away, she said, "Thank you," and looked down at the check on the table.

Eva watched Bobby's eyes alter, growing liquid before she lowered her gaze, and wondered what the tiny woman was thinking. There was something almost childlike about Bobby, something vulnerable and maddeningly defenseless. It showed in the slight inward curve of her narrow shoulders and in the habit she had of ducking her head, dropping her eyes when unsure of a situation. "At some point soon you really should go over to Motor Vehicles and reregister your car, get a Connecticut driver's license. And you'll have to notify your insurance company, too."

"Yes," Bobby said. "I'll do it this week."

"It's Thanksgiving the end of next week," Eva said. "My daughter will be home from school for a few days. There'll be six of us for Thanksgiving dinner, counting you and Penny."

"We wouldn't want to intrude..." Bobby began, never able to anticipate the things Eva might say or do. Suddenly, she missed her friend Lor, and her uncomplicated ways; she reminded herself to phone first chance she got, let her know she and Pen were all right. Lor would be worried.

"Nonsense," Eva cut her off. "You'll join us. You and Penny are part of the household."

"That'd be real...really nice," Bobby said, thinking of the wonderful party dress she'd seen in the children's store. A pity it was so much money, but maybe she could find something less expensive. "I could help out with the cooking, if you like."

"I'll probably take you up on that," Eva said, then on a whim inspired partly by curiosity and partly by generosity, added, "If you like, we could invite Dennis to join us."

"That's up to you," Bobby said, wondering if they thought she and this man had a romance going after one meal together. "You know him better than I do." She hoped she wasn't coming across rude, but she really had no idea how to handle this.

"I'll check with him Thursday, see what his plans are. Unless, of course, you'd prefer I didn't."

"I hardly know him," Bobby said, not sure one way or the other how she felt about the possibility of Dennis spending Thanksgiving with them. He seemed nice enough. But Eva and Alma knew him way better than she did. It almost felt as if Eva was pushing him at her.

"Do you think you'll go out with him again?" Eva asked, thinking it might do Bobby a world of good to spend time with someone as open and patently gentle as Dennis.

"I don't know," Bobby said. For all she knew, after last night, Dennis might not want to be bothered with her. And she wasn't sure if she was relieved by that prospect, or saddened.

"But you had a good time, didn't you?" Eva persisted, despite Bobby's obvious discomfort.

"It was nice," Bobby told her, wanting Eva to get off the topic. "I'm not looking to get involved with anybody, though." She looked over at the clock on the stove, then said, "I guess maybe I'd better go on up now."

Eva smiled and said, "I'm naturally curious. Don't get upset."

"I'm not upset," Bobby lied, getting up from the table. "I'm just no good at . . . this kind of thing." What kind of thing? she wondered—making friends with another woman, or socializing, as Dennis called it, with a man?

"Don't forget your check," Eva said, wishing she hadn't mentioned Dennis. Obviously the date hadn't been a great success.

"Thanks." Bobby took the check and folded it into her pocket, moved to go, then turned back, anxious that they be on good terms. "I make real good pastry. I could make some pies."

"That'd be great," Eva said, smiling again. "My pastry always sticks to the board and the rolling pin. I usually wind up buying pies."

"Okay, then. I'll make 'em," Bobby said, trying for a smile that didn't quite come off. "I, uhm, just wanted to say I really liked your book."

"Which one?" Eva asked expressionlessly.

"*The Summer House,*" Bobby said. "I liked it a whole lot."

Eva looked neither pleased nor displeased. "I'm glad," she said, tapping the checkbook with her pen.

"Yeah," Bobby said. "It was really good." She took a breath, waiting to see if Eva would say anything more, then decided maybe Eva didn't care one way or another whether or not Bobby—who was nobody after all—liked her book or not. She turned and went on her way.

Annoyed by her inability to respond appropriately to Bobby's praise of her work, Eva went to her office. Sitting down at the desk, she stared at the computer, fatigued in advance at the prospect of writing another chapter. She was coming to despise these category novels, and wished she'd never contracted to do them. Between this work and her obsessive reliving of the events that had taken place on the island, she was beginning to feel beleaguered. Maybe Alma was right, maybe she was betraying her gifts by taking the easy money, and when in the future she attempted to write something that really mattered to her she might find the ability gone. The idea of spending the rest of her professional life writing commercial fiction depressed her. She was writing strictly for money, and the reasons she'd had at the outset no longer seemed valid.

Taking a deep breath, she switched on the machine.

"How was it really?" Alma asked as Bobby drew the brush through her hair.

"I was so nervous I couldn't hardly speak," Bobby admitted, finding it easier every day to talk to this woman. Alma was critical, all right, but she didn't seem to sit in judgment the way Eva did.

"I suppose that's to be expected," Alma said, looking out at the driving rain. "I hope you're not discouraged."

"How about if I do you a French braid?" Bobby suggested.

"Do whatever you like," Alma said. "It's not as if anyone's going to see or care."

"Don't be like that. Sure they do. I see and I care. I think you'll look real . . . really nice," she said, separating the top layer of Alma's hair into three parts, then beginning the braid.

Lulled by the motions, Alma looked at the sodden garden, the grass bent flat under the rain. "Sometimes," she said, "you have to take the chance, Bobby, even if it doesn't work out."

"What chance? Why?"

"We need to confront the things that scare us," Alma said, wondering how she could say this to Bobby when she couldn't manage it herself. Her own present reality confounded and alarmed her, but rather than meet it head on she merely glared at it angrily, from a distance. Still, it was the truth. "By confronting them we defuse them of their ability to scare us."

Bobby pictured Joe racing across the rain-soaked lawn with a shotgun under his arm, and thought Alma couldn't possibly mean what she was saying. The woman simply had no idea. She threaded another strand of hair into the braid, considering the things that scared her, and decided that no matter what anyone said she had good cause to be afraid. As long as Joe was alive in the world, she'd keep on being afraid, maybe not so much as she had been living in the house with him, but afraid all the same. "When you've been scared for a long time," she said, "you don't just suddenly stop."

"No," Alma agreed thoughtfully, "you don't." Fear was a damned insidious thing, the ultimate human common denominator. "Still," she said, "you should give Dennis a chance."

To do what? Bobby wondered. To find some new and different way to hurt her? "Why?" she asked, gathering in another strand.

"To prove to yourself that there are some men worthy of your trust."

"Maybe," Bobby said cautiously. "We'll see." It was only talk, she thought. Dennis probably wouldn't even ask her out again.

Sixteen

Tuesday evening after getting Alma settled for the night, Bobby asked if she could use the telephone.

"It's long distance but I'll pay you when the bill comes in."

"Don't be silly. Go ahead and use the telephone."

Bobby thanked her, said good night, then went downstairs to use the extension in her apartment.

Lor said, "I was starting to get real worried about you, so I finally called your aunt the other night and she told me you got yourself some kind of live-in job there."

"That's right," Bobby said, reassured by the sound of her old friend's familiar voice. "It's a really good job and we've even got our own apartment downstairs here. How's everything with you and the kids?"

"Oh, same as ever, you know. Nothing ever changes around here. So where the heck are you, anyhow? Your aunt was all mysterious, wouldn't tell me a thing except that the two of you're all right."

"It'd be better if you don't know where we are, Lor, in case Joe comes around and starts making trouble. But I'll give you the phone number, in case you feel like calling me sometime."

"Better than nothing," Lor said. "Hang on a sec while I find something to write with. Okay, what is it?"

Bobby told her and Lor got the number written down.

"Hide it somewhere. Okay, Lor?"

"Listen, hon. I don't take crap from any guy, including my ex. Even if Joe stuck one of his goddamned guns in my face I wouldn't give him the time of day, and you know it. I'm just glad as can be you're finally away from that man. You should've taken Penny and gone a long time ago."

"I know that. Well, I'd better go. I don't want to run up the bill."

"I'm glad you called. Like I said, I was getting real worried. You stay in touch, okay?"

"I will," Bobby promised. "Take care, Lor."

"You too, hon."

Feeling better now that she'd talked both to her aunt and to Lor, Bobby curled up on the sofa with the first of Eva's paperbacks. Thirty pages into the book she'd already lost interest, and couldn't figure out how the woman who'd written *The Summer House* could've written this one. She could understand now why Alma was so anxious to get Eva to quit writing them.

Carrying the pair of paperbacks, she went upstairs to the living room, returned the books to the shelf, selected an Evangeline Chaney novel, and hurried back downstairs.

Lighting a Marlboro, she positioned an ashtray on the coffee table, and opened the book. Two paragraphs and she was engrossed. This was more like it. Sinking deeper into the sofa, the cigarette forgotten in the ashtray, she read on.

In the course of the next two days Bobby was able to change the car registration, obtain a new license, and, through Eva's insurance agent, get the appropriate coverage for the Honda. She also took the car into a Midas shop where in no time flat they put on a new muffler and changed the front brake pads. The nearest gas station did an oil change and a lube job in under an hour while Bobby sat in the office and waited. The car ran like a dream and, pleased with herself, she returned to the house on Sound-view Drive to assist Alma downstairs after her nap. She knew it was foolish to feel so good about accomplishing such mundane tasks, but she was, for the first time, beginning to feel in charge of her life and Pen's.

Joe had never allowed her to do a thing, accusing her of being too dumb to deal with matters concerning the house and the cars. He'd refused to drive with her, claiming she was the worst driver in the world and saying he didn't know how in hell she'd ever passed the driving test. The truth was, she was a far better driver than he, more careful and more considerate of the other drivers on the road. Joe got in the Firebird every time like he was going off to a war, and drove as if the streets were a battleground. He laughed at her for buckling herself and Pen into the seat belts.

"Think that's gonna save your asses if we're in an accident? It'll probably wind up getting you killed," he'd scoff, and then cite statistics he said he'd read in some magazine about how seat belts cost more lives than they saved. She'd tune him out while pretending to listen, convinced the only reason she and Pen were still alive after countless near-misses was because of the belts. He was forever stomping on the brake to avoid a car that had suddenly stopped, or flooring the accelerator to shoot around vehicles that were moving too slowly to suit him. "Fucking asshole!" he'd shout, giving people the finger as he shot past.

With each day spent away from him, she seemed able to see him more clearly, and to see, as well, that she *had* been stupid. She'd put up with his many forms of abuse because he'd convinced her that without him she wouldn't be able to manage on her own. That had been stupid. She didn't need him, or anyone, to support her. She was capable of managing by herself. And that was a stunning revelation, as was the fact that now, from a safe distance, she could admit—if only to herself—how much she hated him. The two of them had played a kind of game, and in a lot of ways she was guilty of encouraging his terrible behavior. Instead of standing up for herself and saying she wouldn't take any more, she'd kept trying to figure out what she'd done wrong and how not to repeat her mistakes. The truth, she was beginning to understand, was that she'd played her part in the marriage as the victim. He'd scared her into it. And she was still scared, with good reason. She might have left him, but Joe wouldn't just let her get away. Not for the first time, she wished he were dead.

When she thought about her evening with Dennis, and compared him to Joe, Dennis came off as a real gentleman. He hadn't pushed at her when she'd said she didn't want to talk about something, and he hadn't tried to make her feel like a moron because she'd never had Indian food and didn't understand the menu. He seemed to enjoy introducing her to something new, and said he wanted to introduce her to even more new things.

Maybe Alma was right. She probably should give Dennis a chance. It would, if nothing else, help her learn more about herself. If he asked her again, she'd go out with him. She couldn't spend the rest of her life being afraid of all men because of Joe. And thinking this, she finally understood what Alma had meant about confronting the things that scared you. It wasn't actually Dennis who scared her, but her own past experiences. This amazed her. She considered it at random hours, marveling at Alma's wisdom. She felt as if she were back in school again, studying a fascinating new subject: her own life.

On Thursday afternoon Dennis came to the front door, smiled, and held out a long-stemmed yellow rose. "This is for you."

Bobby accepted the rose shyly. No one had ever given her flowers. She smiled back and said, "It's beautiful. Thank you."

"I thought maybe you'd think it was kind of corny but I decided to go for it anyway," he said hanging up his coat.

"It isn't corny," she said softly, breathing in the flower's scent and wanting to cry. It was the nicest thing anyone had ever done for her.

"So how goes it?" he asked, rubbing the chill from his hands, still smiling at her.

"I'm going to be staying on," she said, thinking she sounded like a child, but so pleased she had to share it.

"I figured you would. That's great." He looked up the stairs, then said, "We'll talk when I finish up. Okay?"

"Sure. I'll make some coffee."

"Good deal. Did you get her to do the exercises?"

"Uh-hunh. She complains the whole way through, but she does them."

"Good, good," Dennis approved, and went off, taking the stairs two at a time.

She found a tall water glass in the apartment cupboard and sat down at the kitchen table to admire the rose and have a cigarette before going up to make a fresh pot of coffee. She had plenty of time, so she fixed a cup for Eva and took it to the office above the garage, knocking quietly, then carrying the cup over to the desk when Eva called, "Come in."

"Here's some coffee," Bobby said, prepared to back right off.

"You're sweet," Eva said. "I could use a cup." She turned away from the screen, asking, "Is Dennis with my aunt?"

"Uh-hunh."

"You want to ask him about Thanksgiving, or do you want me to do it?"

"I don't want to interrupt your work," Bobby said. "I guess I can ask him."

Eva studied her appraisingly. "Changed your mind, have you?" she said with a half smile.

"I don't mind asking him, if you want," Bobby equivocated, afraid to confide in this woman the way she did in her aunt. Like Joe, Eva had the ability to make Bobby feel stupid, but in different ways.

"Well, if you're sure you don't mind," Eva said, turning back to the screen. "Let me know what he says."

"Do you write about real people?" Bobby asked impulsively. "I mean, like the people in *The Summer House*. They seemed so real to me, I thought maybe you wrote about people you know."

Eva actually looked pleased by the question. "They're entirely fictional," she said. "But I'm glad they seemed so real to you. I try very hard to make my characters come alive."

"Oh, they do," Bobby assured her. "I hated for it to end."

"That was my first book," Eva said, feeling an ache in her midriff thinking about all the rewriting she'd done after Ken's death. "I think the others are better, but some people, my aunt for one, don't agree."

"I'm going to read them all. I just started *Family Friends*," Bobby said, and moved toward the door. "You're a really good writer."

"Thank you," Eva said, then sat listening to the small woman go quietly on her way. "Damn!" she said, staring blankly at the screen. Now she very definitely wasn't in the mood to work. Why didn't she call it quits and get back to writing what she really wanted? There was nothing stopping her. Nothing at all.

"Come out with me on Sunday afternoon," Dennis was saying. "I'll take you and Penny to the Maritime Center in Norwalk."

"I'll have to ask Alma," Bobby replied, both gratified and slightly unnerved by this second invitation.

"I already did," he told her. "She said it was fine with her."

"She did?"

"Yes, ma'am, she did. So, are we on?"

"Okay. I guess that'll be all right."

"Great," he said, and gulped down the last of his coffee. "I've got to run."

"Your client up in Norwalk," she said with a smile.

"Right. I'll pick you and Penny up at, say, one-thirty. That way you'll be back in time to get Alma squared away for her nap."

"Okay," Bobby said, impressed by his consideration. She walked with him to the front hall and waited while he got his coat on. "Oh!" she said, remembering, "I'm supposed to ask if you want to come to Thanksgiving dinner next week."

He paused with his hand on the doorknob and looked at her.

"It was Eva's idea," she added, to keep things clear.

"That's really nice of her," he said. "I wish I could, but I've promised my folks I'd spend the day with them."

"Sure," she said, disappointed but relieved, too. She'd have enough to cope with meeting Eva's daughter and her friend Charlie. "I told her I'd ask."

"Thank her for me," he said. "I'd have liked that. Too bad." He got the door open, said, "See you Sunday," then hurried to his car. He tooted the horn before driving off.

"Who's Dennis and where're we goin'?" Penny wanted to know.

"I told you. He's Alma's physical therapist," Bobby said. "He comes every week to give her exercises. He's a nice man, Pen."

"You gonna marry him?"

Bobby laughed and gave Pen's ponytail a tug. "Don't be silly. I'm already married to your dad."

"I thought that was all over now."

"It is, but legally we're still married."

"Do you *want* to marry Dennis?"

"He's a friend, that's all. He's taking us to the Maritime Center."

"What's that?"

"I think it's a place where they've got fish, stuff like that."

"Big fish?"

"Maybe."

"I wanna see a *whale*," Penny said. "A great big whale."

"Maybe you'll see one. D'you need to go to the bathroom?"

"I already went."

"Are you sure?"

"Yup."

"Are you positive?"

"Yup."

Bobby admired the way Dennis handled Penny. He didn't try to charm her, and he didn't talk down to her. He shook her hand and said, "Hi, I'm Dennis. Would you like to go see all kinds of fish?"

"Uh-hunh." Penny looked up at him assessingly. "They got any whales?"

"I doubt it," he said. "But there are sharks and blues, and lots of other fish. And we can see a movie on a great big screen."

"Yeah? What kind of movie?"

"One that takes you up in the air in a plane called a glider that doesn't have any engine but just floats on the air."

"Way high up?"

"Pretty high," Dennis said. "Think you'll like that?"

"Uh-hunh."

He stood aside to let Bobby buckle Pen in the back of the Beetle. He didn't act impatient, didn't mock her for making a fuss. He just went along with what she wanted. And when they got to the Maritime Center, he was willing to look at whatever Penny wanted to see and answered her questions as if he actually liked talking to a small child.

Bobby watched him, fascinated. He liked Penny, didn't get impatient with her, and talked to her the same way he talked to everybody. Within half an hour, Penny was reaching to hold his hand as they moved through the place. Bobby saw this and was moved. Joe had never touched Penny, except in anger, and had always referred to her as "your kid."

In the Imax theater, they sat with Penny between them, but Penny complained she couldn't see, so Dennis lifted her onto his lap. He appeared to be perfectly at ease with the situation, and Bobby scarcely noticed the film, so taken was she with the sight of Penny with this man. Something so ordinary, but Penny had never had a father's lap to climb into. Bobby had had that. Her grandpa had cuddled her before bedtime; he'd mussed her hair and tickled her behind her ears and called her "dearie." Her grandfather and her aunt had loved her; she'd had a happy childhood. But all Penny had experienced was rejection and, at the end, abuse, with Joe saying, "Get out of my face," any time Pen approached him.

Who was this tall muscular man with the carroty hair and warm brown eyes, and why was he being so nice to them? Maybe he was simply a nice person, someone who liked small children and not very smart women. She could see how he'd like Pen. But she really couldn't figure out why he was wasting his time on her.

"You're awfully quiet," he observed as they were on the way out of the theater, with Pen holding his hand and skipping along at his side. "Did you enjoy the film?"

"It was very good," Bobby said, recalling only a sinking sensation in her stomach as the glider swooped low over a river, then soared again.

"I liked it a whole whole lot," Penny sang, extending her free arm like an airplane wing, ducking her body, pretending to be a glider. "I wish I could fly."

"When I was a kid," Dennis told her, "I used to dream all the time that I could fly. I flew over my school and the kids would look up in the air and point. I flew over the treetops and houses, way up in the air.''

"Yeah?" Penny was entranced. "I never dreamed that. You're really lucky."

"Sometimes I still dream of flying," he said, "but not as much as I used to. How about some ice cream?" he asked, looking at Bobby. "We've got time."

"You want some ice cream, Pen?"

"Yeah! Chocolate chocolate chip in a sugar cone."

"That's her favorite," Bobby said with a somewhat abashed smile.

"Mine's French vanilla," Dennis said. "What's yours, Bobby?"

"Mom loves jamocha almond fudge," Penny said. "That's what she always has."

"Is that right?" He grinned at Bobby.

She was able to smile back at him, but her face felt stiff.

When he dropped them home, Penny insisted on giving him a big hug good-bye, asking, "You gonna come see me again?"

"I'd like to," he told her, swinging her around in a circle before setting her down on the driveway. "Maybe next weekend. Your mom and I will talk during the week and see what we can work out."

"Okay," Penny said, already running toward the door. "Bye, Dennis!"

Bobby thanked him, then stood awkwardly, saying, "Thank you for taking us. It was real . . . really nice."

"She's a great girl," he said, his eyes on Penny, who was letting herself in the back door. "So," he turned to her, "want to eat out one night this week? I thought we'd try Mexican this time."

"Okay," she said. "That'd be nice."

He held out a hand and she stared at it a moment before realizing he was offering to shake hands with her. Uncertainly, she put out her hand and he leaned forward and kissed her cheek. Her heart seemed to jump forward in her chest, and she was so scared she could hardly breathe.

"Take it easy," he said, letting her go. "I'll talk to you in a day or two."

"Okay," she managed to say, her heart beating so fast it was hard to speak. His hand had been smooth and warm; his lips had merely grazed her cheek, yet she felt scalded. She told herself he was only being friendly, but it didn't slow down her heart or ease the panic that had her scanning the property, fearful of spotting Joe lurking in the shrubberies.

Dennis drove off with a toot of his horn and she stood in the driveway, trying to catch her breath and telling herself it was okay, she and Pen were safe, nothing bad was going to happen. Becoming aware of the cold, able to smell snow in the air, she turned and ran to the back door. She shouldn't have said she'd go out with him again. She was just begging for trouble. Joe would find out; he'd know somehow, and then he'd come after her and kill her.

She stood inside the kitchen door, her face stinging from the heat and from Dennis's kiss, and wished her memory could be cleaned, erased like a blackboard. She had a chance at something here, and she wanted it. But every time she took a step forward, the past wrapped itself around her like a black blanket, reminding her of what could happen when you let your guard down.

It was eating him up, trying to figure out where Bobby'd gone. In the evenings he cruised by Lor's place, by her Aunt Helen's, expecting to spot her. He saw Lor coming out one time and tailed her but she was just going to the supermarket. He waited where he could keep an eye on her car in case the market was a cover but twenty minutes later she came out with a couple bags of groceries, dumped them into the back of her Chevette, and headed home. He followed. She pulled into the driveway, carried the bags of groceries into the house, closed the door, and that was it. He gave up, drove on over to check out that bitch Helen's place.

Her crummy Ford Escort was in the driveway. Lights were on in the living room. He parked a block or so away, then walked back up the street. No one around. Ducking down, he crept along the side of the house, checking the windows. The TV was going in the living room, Entertainment Tonight, *but the room was empty. Staying tight to the wall, he eased around back of the house, grabbed a look through the kitchen window. She was cooking, standing by the stove stirring some shit in a pot. He studied the room looking for something, he didn't know what, didn't see fuck-all. But he knew there was something in the house that'd tell him where Bobby was. And he was going to get it.*

Creeping back, he made it to the street, and headed to the Firebird. He had to think it through, come up with a way to check out the house. Once in the car with the motor running and the heater on full, he tried to pin it down.

Helen was out every day at work. He figured she left the house by eight-fifteen, eight-thirty. No good. He clocked on at eight. His lunch break didn't give him enough time to get out here, to go through the house, and get back. She got home by five-thirty, six the latest. He clocked off at four-thirty. Again no good.

Finally warmed up, he took off. It was starting to snow. He hated the stuff, hated coming out in the morning to

*find the Firebird covered with ice and shit and the drive-
way blocked off by a big mound left by the snowplows. As
he headed home he wondered if maybe Bobby had called
his fucking mother. Doubtful. Bobby couldn't stand the
old bitch. Nobody could. In the twelve years since his dad
died she'd stopped pretending, let her true colors show.
She didn't give a shit anymore. If he went asking her did
she know where Bobby was, she'd laugh right in his face.
He wouldn't give her the goddamned satisfaction.*

*He was hungry. All this sneaking around, he hadn't had
anything to eat since lunch. But he didn't feel like going to
Garvey's. He was sick of goddamned hamburgers, limp
half-cooked frozen fries.*

*Pulling into the driveway he took the key from the ig-
nition and sat looking at the house. Pitch dark. Snow already covering the walk and front steps. He'd have to get
up early in the morning to shovel the goddamned snow. He
felt like burning the fucking place down.*

*He'd spend a few more nights checking out Helen's
house, then if nothing happened he'd call in sick. Having
made up his mind, he locked the car, then headed for the
back door. That Helen knew where Bobby was, and one
way or another he was going to find it out from her.
Slamming the door shut he stood looking at the sinkful of
dirty dishes, outraged. He opened the fridge. No beer left.
Nothing to eat. He'd either have to go to the goddamned
market or hit Garvey's again. The thought of wheeling a
fucking cart up and down the aisles at the market made
him crazy. That was a damned woman's job, not his.
When he found her, he'd fix her ass once and for all.*

Seventeen

Bobby dreamed she and Dennis were walking through a snowfall, leaving a trail of footprints. Looking back over her shoulder, she could see they'd come a long way. The trail followed a bend in the road and disappeared out of sight. Thick flakes caught in her eyelashes and coated her clothing. There was no color; everything was glaringly white. An occasional clump of snow would slip from the branch of a tree and fall noiselessly to the ground.

She was holding Dennis's hand. It felt right. She turned inward to search for signs of anxiety but there were none. Everything was okay. She looked at his profile, which had an almost childlike sweetness. There was nothing to fear in the high rounded forehead, the small tidy nose, the squared chin. He turned to smile at her and she saw more of his sweetness, his face containing the only color in the landscape: brown eyes, pink mouth.

"Why was I so afraid of you?" she asked him, astounded by how calm she was.

He laughed, snowflakes caught in his eyebrows, and said, "Everybody's afraid, but of different things. See how beautiful this is?" His mittened hand lifted and indicated the snowscape before them. White smoke drifted from the chimneys of the houses on either side of the road.

"It's wonderful," she said, her gloved hand warm inside his.

"We have good winters," he said with satisfaction. "It's why I live here."

"Very good," she agreed, feeling better than she ever had; feeling young and healthy and free. She couldn't wait to get home to tell Pen how happy she was. From now on everything was going to be fine. She had wonderful new friends and she wasn't afraid anymore. There were people who cared about her, who were teaching her important things about herself.

"Anybody ever tell you you've got a great speaking voice?" he asked. "It's pretty funny. On the telephone you sound as if you'd be about five-ten, maybe one-fifty." He laughed again. "But here you are, big as a minute."

"That's what my grandpa used to say."

"I know. He told me."

"He did?" She blinked snow out of her eyes to look at him. She could tell it was true. He'd talked to her grandpa, and it made her feel even happier. She looked ahead, up the road. Something dark was coming. It seemed to be growing to fill the horizon as it approached. Dennis's hand tightened around hers.

"We'll have to run for it," he said, urging her toward the side of the road where the snow was deep and thick.

She squinted, trying to see, instant fear spreading like heat inside her chest. It was Joe, in the Firebird, barreling down the road at a tremendous speed. Dennis was pulling at her hand but the heaviness rooted her in place. "It's no good," she told him, her throat thick with despair. "I should've known he'd never let me get away. You go," she said, her hand slipping free of his.

"Come on!" he insisted, trying to take hold of her.

She pushed him and, with an expression of disbelief, he fell into a snowbank. The car was closing in on her, so close she could see Joe's face through the windshield. She started walking forward to meet the car, thinking, let's get it over with. I'm tired of being afraid of you. She stopped in the middle of the road and waited, wanting to close her eyes but keeping them open so he'd see and know what he'd done.

The car kept coming. She braced herself for the impact, and at the last moment her eyes closed of their own volition. She waited, teeth clenched. Nothing happened. When she opened her eyes the car was gone and Joe was standing naked in the snow, the rifle under his arm. *"See what you made me do!"* he screamed. *"It's all your goddamned fault!"*

"I didn't make you do anything," she said, her voice muffled by the snow, tears hot on her cold cheeks. "If you're dying, it's your own fault, not mine."

"You're going to come over here and help me!" he said, lifting the rifle.

"No, I'm not," she said, and turned her back on him. Dennis was nowhere in sight. Good, she thought, and started running, following the trail of footsteps back up the road. Keep on going, she told herself. He can't get far without any shoes or clothes. She lifted one booted foot in front of the other, taking care to keep to the trail. Behind her Joe was screaming, but she ran on and after a few more steps his voice got swallowed up in the wind. It was okay. He wasn't going to come after her. Keep going, she told herself. He's already starting to freeze.

A stitch in her side, the cold air cutting into her lungs, her booted feet growing heavier, and sweat coating her torso under the bulky jacket, she ran forward, her eyes on the trail she and Dennis had made in the snow. Not too much farther and she'd be safe.

When Dennis called on Monday afternoon, Bobby smiled at the sound of his voice.

"How about Friday night?" he asked. "We could do Mexican and maybe take in a movie."

"I'll ask, but I guess it'll be all right," she said, unable to think of any reason to say no. "We had a nice time yesterday. Thank you."

"My pleasure. Penny's a great little girl."

"She liked you, too," she said. It was true. Penny had spent an hour telling her "granny" all about Dennis and their trip to the Maritime Center.

"I'm between calls," he explained, "so I've got to run. But I'll see you Wednesday."

"Wednesday?"

"Thursday's Thanksgiving," he reminded her, "so this week I'm seeing Alma on Wednesday."

"Oh! Okay."

"Catch you later," he said, and hung up.

She put down the receiver and looked around the kitchen, hearing Ruby running the vacuum cleaner in the living room. She wished she could actually see Lor, talk to her about what was happening. She and Lor had discussed everything from the time they were in the sixth grade together. Lor was the only one of her friends Joe hadn't scared off. For years she'd been telling Bobby to take Pen and get away. Now she'd done it, and for the most part she was feeling better about herself every day. But this business with Dennis was confusing. And while she could talk to Alma, Alma didn't know the way Lor did about the things Joe had done to her.

Even Lor didn't know all of it. No one did. There were things she doubted she'd ever be able to tell anybody, things she wished she could forget, that came back at her in the dark as nightmares that would probably have her up two or three times a night for the rest of her life.

She got herself some coffee, deliberating whether or not to take a cup up to Eva in the office. Better not. Eva had been a bit grouchy at lunch, and had snapped at Alma when she'd observed that Eva was wasting precious time these days. She'd left most of her lunch and gone back to the office obviously upset.

Best to leave her alone, Bobby decided, staring at the wall phone. Lor would be at work now and an incoming call could get her in trouble. But Helen's boss at the dealership never made a fuss about her getting personal calls.

On impulse she picked up the receiver and punched out her aunt's work number from memory, smiling when Helen came on the line.

"It's me, Aunt Helen. I just wanted to say hi, see how things're going."

"Things're fine. Everything okay with you?"

"Really good," Bobby answered, then paused. "Any word on Joe?"

"I'm pretty sure he's driven by the house a time or two," Helen told her. "I could tell from the way he peels rubber when he takes off. Nobody around here drives like that."

"But he hasn't been bothering you or anything?"

"Not a peep out of him."

"Good." Bobby breathed deeply with relief.

"How's my Pen?" her aunt asked warmly.

"She's great, loves her new school, has a bunch of new friends. I know she misses you, though."

"I miss her, too; I miss the both of you. But you're better off where you are. You did the right thing, Bobby. I know it's probably hard on the two of you, but it's for the best and you know it."

"Yeah, I do."

"One of these times we'll get together, have us a visit."

"Yeah," Bobby said softly. "One of these times."

"Oops. I've got another call coming in, dearie. Gotta go."

"Okay, sure. Oh! And have a happy Thanksgiving. You going somewhere?"

"Uh-hunh. To the boss's annual turkey party. Call me again soon," Helen said. "Love you, babe."

After a moment Bobby hung up, retrieved her coffee from the counter, and went to sit down at the table with her book.

Eva sat with her fingers resting on the keyboard, unseeing eyes fixed on the screen, where a sentence hung unfinished. It had been hanging there, dangling, for nearly a week. She couldn't make herself complete it. Slowly she removed her hands from the keyboard and let them fall to her lap.

Why was she going on with this? What was she trying to prove? She'd demonstrated that she could write commercial fiction and had been paid top dollar for her efforts. The contract had been satisfied and now she was working on an option book. If the publisher liked this one, they'd go to a new contract, which would mean another book, then another, on and on. But what was the point? They didn't really need the money. Alma had a lifetime's savings and investment income, as well as a pension. Melissa's college fees were covered, and then some, by the insurance Ken had left. Eva had her own savings and the money from the sale of her New York co-op. She had to admit that the reasons she'd had at the outset for writing these books had never been valid. Her aunt's stroke had frightened her, the fear of losing Alma prompting her to sell the co-op and move back here in an attempt to repay her aunt for seeing her safely into adulthood. Taking on the new writing had been a noble gesture, but, she now saw, an unnecessary one. It wasn't something Alma had wanted or needed, nor had she approved.

Leaving the desk, Eva crossed the room, threw herself into the old armchair, and turned to look out the window. Random snowflakes drifted in the air. She couldn't keep on with this. It was turning her into a low-level monster, growling at Alma every time her aunt raised the subject, taking an adversarial position to defend something she no longer believed in. The truth was, if Alma hadn't started raising objections, she'd probably have quit of her own volition after the second book.

Letting her head fall back, tired, she thought of Deborah as she'd known her at the beginning in London. Young and so beautiful that people had gaped at her on the streets; slim and elegant Deborah who stood behind a microphone in clubs and sang in a low smoky voice, who performed supporting roles in West End shows, and appeared in full-color layouts in upscale women's magazines, modeling sequined evening dresses and minuscule bikinis that revealed her enviably long perfect body. "The first black woman, darling, in a British fashion magazine." She could still hear her friend's jubilant laughter.

What happened? Why did it end the way it did? She looked over at the desk, at the computer screen where the cursor blinked like a pulse, awaiting her. She was tempted to cross the room and erase the disks, wipe out every word of the nine chapters she'd done so far. But, she thought, her heartbeat quickening, she couldn't just stop and erase it all. Could she?

Melissa called after dinner that evening. Bobby was downstairs putting Penny to bed, and Eva and Alma had just moved into the living room. At the sound of her daughter's voice, Eva felt herself lifting, a smile automatically reshaping her mouth.

"Hi, Mom. How's everything?"

"Fine. How are you, Mel?"

"I'm really dead. I've been up every night till two or three, working on this philosophy paper in the library. I've got to hand it in by Wednesday morning."

"Is it almost done?" Eva asked, knowing full well that Melissa put everything off until the last possible moment. During her freshman year, Eva had advised her repeatedly to get a little work done every day and her papers would be ready on time. But Melissa couldn't function that way, just as she couldn't be bothered taking the time to do her laundry and could never manage to balance her checkbook. By Melissa's second semester Eva had stopped trying to change her and now hoped that time and experience would bring her daughter around to a less chaotic way of doing things.

"I'm staying up tonight to work on the computer," Melissa said. "I wanted to let you know I'm not going to make it home until Thursday morning. I've got too much to do. And I'm only going to be able to stay until Saturday. I've got an economics paper due next Monday."

Let down but not entirely unprepared for this eventuality, Eva said, "All right. I understand."

"I've got to run," Mellie said tiredly. "I'll see you Thursday. Okay?"

"Okay. Have you got time to say hello to Aunt Alma?"

"I really don't. Just give her my love. Okay?"

"Okay. I love you, Mel."

"Love you too, Mom. See you Thursday."

Alma was waiting.

"She can't come until Thursday morning, and she has to go back on Saturday. She sends you her love."

"Too bad," Alma said, reading the disappointment all over her niece's face. "We scarcely see her anymore."

Eva sighed and rubbed her forehead. When Melissa graduated from high school, Eva had all at once realized that the life they'd had together was ending. And even though she'd been preparing herself for the separation for years, the reality had been hard to take. Not that she didn't enjoy the time to herself, and not that Melissa hadn't the right to her own life, but it was hard to stop being a full-time parent. Even with her child three hundred-odd miles away, she was still a mother and would be one forever. A segment of her brain was permanently directed toward Melissa. She could go for days without consciously thinking of her, but Melissa was always inside her head, the stages of her life playing endlessly on a mental loop. And there were moments when Eva got lost in time and felt the small girl's arms wound tightly around her neck, in the same way Penny had enclosed Eva with her limbs. It was a mild shock every time she was confronted by Melissa's reality, by the woman her daughter had grown to be. Melissa represented twenty years of Eva's life, and that hardly seemed possible. But of course it was. Time was such an odd concept, so elastic a dimension in so many ways. It carried your body forward, changing and distorting it, while it layered itself over your brain like sheets of gauze.

"I'm going to have a drink," Eva announced. "Would you like anything?"

"Are you going to marry Charlie?" Alma asked, out of the blue.

Taken aback, Eva said, "What makes you think he'd want to marry me?"

"Men are marrying creatures," Alma said sagaciously.

Eva had to laugh. "Why on earth do you say that?"

"Personal experience," Alma said somewhat airily. "The majority of men I've known wanted to be married. They think life'll be easier if they have someone to do their laundry."

"That's a riot," Eva said laughing. "Charlie certainly doesn't need me, or anyone, to do his laundry."

"A euphemism," Alma said patiently. "Cooking, cleaning, general maintenance. You know what I'm saying."

Sobering, Eva considered it. "You might be right," she allowed. "But the issue for me, since Ken died, has always been: What do I need a man for? And the answer every time has been: entertainment. I don't have to be married to have that. And as far as Charlie's concerned, I think he feels the same way."

"So you entertain each other," Alma said. "Wouldn't you like to have that full-time?"

"I'd never get anything done," Eva argued. "Besides, I like things the way they are."

"I think you dislike intensely the way things are. You're fed up and it's plain as day. I hate to be contentious, but at the risk of setting you off again, I'll say it one more time: You need to get back to work that matters to you, Eva." She sat prepared for an argument but, to her surprise, Eva sank back onto the sofa and again rubbed her forehead.

"Could I get anybody anything?" Bobby asked from the doorway.

Both somewhat irritated by the interruption, the women said no thank you.

Sensing her timing was all wrong, Bobby said, "I'll be doing the laundry if you want me," and hastily removed herself.

When she was gone, Alma asked, "What were you going to say?" her eyes boring into Eva's.

"Nothing," Eva answered, asking herself if she wanted to marry Charlie. She didn't know. It certainly wasn't an unappealing idea.

"Yes, you were. Are you going to deny you're unhappy with the way things are?"

"No," Eva said quietly. "But I'm not ready to discuss it, either. Let me get to this in my own time, please. I need to think things through."

Feeling a small satisfaction in having moved Eva to this point, Alma opted to let the matter drop for the time being and fell silent.

Eva continued to sit rubbing her forehead, thinking that Melissa had inherited her stubbornness. Neither one of them could admit to being wrong without first putting up a good fight. In this case, though, it was ridiculous. She hadn't done any real work on the latest manuscript in days, and it was unlikely she'd do any in the near future. Yet somehow she couldn't cope with the loss of face the admission of defeat would cost her at this point. Sighing again, she got up to fix herself a drink. Maybe tomorrow she'd talk matters over with her agent. Carrying her glass of neat Glenlivet back to the sofa, she wondered again if she wanted to marry Charlie. When she looked up, it was to find her aunt smiling at her. "What?"

"Oh, nothing," Alma said wryly, and busied herself with the newspaper, placing a mental wager on how long it would take Eva to own up to everything Alma could see so plainly. Not long, she thought. Not long at all.

Eighteen

Tuesday afternoon while Alma was having her nap, Bobby drove to the children's clothing store in the shopping center and, after careful deliberation, picked out a royal blue pinafore dress and a long-sleeved white blouse with red and blue embroidered trim on the collar and cuffs.

The snotty saleswoman who'd refused to take her check the last time was at the counter as Bobby, suddenly nervous, approached to pay for Penny's new outfit. She dreaded having another scene with this woman but she was determined to pay by check and to use her new Connecticut license as ID.

"How would you like to pay for this?" the woman asked.

"A check," Bobby answered, her throat tight.

"Fine. I'll need a driver's license and a credit card."

"I don't have a credit card," Bobby said, her stomach knotting.

The woman looked at her, her eyes narrowing slightly, then said, "Everybody's got a credit card."

"Not in my family," Bobby said, prepared to do battle but somewhat sickened by the idea nonetheless. "We don't buy what we can't pay for."

To her surprise, the woman nodded and said, "That's damned sensible."

"I've got a Connecticut license," Bobby told her.

"Okay. That'll be fine. You want this gift-wrapped?"

"No, thanks."

Her hand a little shaky, Bobby wrote out the check, tore it from the book and gave it and her license to the woman, who copied the number onto the back of the check and returned the license, saying, "Decided to stay in the area, huh?"

Her tone was friendly; she even smiled.

Bobby said, "We like it here."

"Good. Come again. We'll be having a sale after Thanksgiving."

"Okay, I will," Bobby said, feeling as if she'd just passed some crucial test. "Thanks a lot."

Reassured of her own competence, she went next door and bought herself a smart pair of black slacks.

At the shoe store she got Penny new loafers like the ones she herself had worn in high school. In the handicrafts shop she purchased a pattern and some pale blue wool to knit Pen a sweater. Finally, at the supermarket she collected the ingredients for pumpkin and mincemeat pies.

Penny was very excited about her new clothes and insisted on trying everything on, then raced upstairs to show Alma.

"I got brand-new clothes for the turkey party," she said, whirling in a circle in her slippery new shoes.

"You look very fetching," Alma told her.

"What's fetchin'?"

"It means attractive, pretty."

Penny grinned and came closer, saying, "Know what, Granny? I've got a loose tooth." She put two fingers in her mouth and wiggled one of her front teeth. "See!"

"That's splendid," Alma said. "You'll be having a visit soon from the tooth fairy. Won't that be exciting?"

"Yeah. That's what Mom said."

"Why don't you go change out of your new clothes," Alma said, "then come back and read to me."

"Okay. I got a new book. It's called *Stuart Little*. I'll go get it. Okay?"

"Okay," Alma said.

Her shoes were so slippery Penny had to hold on to the banister going down the stairs. "I gotta change," she told Bobby. "I'm goin' up to read to Granny."

"Take your time, Pen," Bobby told her. "She'll wait for you."

After Penny had gone back upstairs, Bobby got out the knitting pattern and sat down to read it through, wanting to be sure she understood all the directions before she started.

"I'm having trouble," Eva told Beverly Bloom, her agent. "I don't know if I'm going to be able to finish this one."

"Then don't," Beverly said. "Throw it out and do something else. The third book's in production. You've satisfied the contract. You're tired of doing them, quit."

"You make it sound awfully simple." She'd been expecting Beverly to give her an argument, and had geared herself up to state her case.

"It is simple, Eva. Don't do the book if you don't want to. Junk it and get to work on one of your own. Give me an outline and six chapters and we'll start offering it."

"I haven't an idea to my name."

"You'll come up with something," Beverly said confidently. "You always do."

"What if nobody wants it?"

"Look, you're acting as if this is the end of the world. I can assure you it isn't. You've got a decent track record. Get something down I can show around and we'll worry about it then."

"I'll have to think about it."

"Fine. Let me know what you decide."

The call concluded. Eva got up from the desk and went over to the window. More flurries but no real snow yet. It was as if winter were holding its breath, preparing itself for one good blow. The water was choppy and gray, the sky heavily overcast. All she had to do was erase the disks and the whole thing would be over; she'd be free to start something that mattered to her. Except that there was nothing she wanted to write. It had been almost two years since she'd completed the last Evangeline Chaney novel, a year since its publication. Even if she started writing tomorrow and managed to finish in six months, it could take up to another year after that before it was published. Maybe people would have forgotten her by then. Or maybe they'd be primed for a new book. It was pointless speculating. She walked over to the desk and tapped out Charlie's office number.

Luckily he was between patients and came on the line right away.

"Have you got plans for this evening?" she asked him.

"Leftover meat loaf and *The MacNeil/Lehrer News-Hour*," he said, his voice amused. "I take it I can anticipate a visit from you?"

"Around eight?"

"Fine," he said. "I'll break out something strong but not incapacitating."

She laughed and said, "See you later."

"Looking forward, cupcake."

She put the receiver down and looked at the computer screen, her heart racing. All she had to do was depress a couple of keys and it would be gone. So why couldn't she do it? She stored the partial chapter, then went down to the kitchen to start a pot roast, needing to lose herself in the relatively mindless process of cooking. Maybe it would quell some measure of the low-level anxiety churning away inside her.

Eva watched as Bobby first cut Penny's meat, then Alma's, her small hands working quickly and efficiently. She scarcely resembled the creature who'd appeared at her front door a few weeks earlier. Her face was completely healed, and her hair now shone with health. She'd lost a substantial measure of the haunted look she'd had at the outset. She ate and between bites spoke softly in her husky voice to Pen, telling the child to sit up properly and stop playing with her green beans. Then she took the napkin from her lap and, with a smile, blotted Alma's chin. Alma rasped out a thank you then took another bite of her food.

What was it about this woman? Eva wondered. There was something in this routine domestic scene that was unique, and Eva watched the interchange between her aunt and the child and Bobby, trying to pin it down.

It wasn't until after Penny had been put to bed and the three of them were in the living-room—Eva killing time until she could leave to see Charlie, Alma occupied with a book, and Bobby with her knitting—that it came to her. Mendelssohn's violin concerto in E minor was playing on the stereo. Eva jabbed at the logs in the fireplace, then looked over at Bobby, small hands busy with her knitting, head bent over her work, and she understood all at once that Bobby was a species of woman Eva hadn't encountered since her own childhood. The mothers of her friends had been like Bobby—nurturing, domesticated women for whom the duties of home and family had represented complete satisfaction. Bobby actually liked fixing people cups of coffee and doing the laundry; she liked caretaking, tending to Alma and to Penny. It gave her visible pleasure; she didn't consider it work. Which was why, Eva concluded, she accepted her weekly check with such delight and surprise. She was doing things that pleased her, and being paid for it.

Eva was momentarily filled with envy. She was doing work that held no meaning for her, and felt guilty at being paid for it. Before the commercial fiction, she'd daily approached her writing with anticipation, looking forward to being reunited with her characters. It had been like an ongoing party with her dearest friends. What she'd been doing for the past nine months or so felt like the world's worst cocktail party, attended by numbskulls and ninnies with whom she was obliged to make small talk while her legs ached from standing too long in high heels.

Returning to the sofa, she looked at her aunt. Alma was completely engrossed in the latest P. D. James novel. She loved complex plots and finely delineated characters, books that had, as she liked to say, plenty of meat on their bones. And she loved rich lyrical music that had intricately woven counterthemes. Alma loved the Evangeline Chaney novels. She defended them as if they were high-spirited but gifted students for whom she had a special affection. She'd read the first paperback, then tossed it across the room and looked at Eva as if she'd committed a crime. "You've made a mistake," she'd said. "You've debased your talent. Please don't do this for my sake, Eva, because it makes me very unhappy."

"I'm going out for a couple of hours," Eva announced finally, having checked the time.

Both Bobby and Alma looked up at her. She felt guilty and obvious, then angry. What a mess. She went over to kiss her aunt's cheek, saying, "I won't be late."

Alma read her eyes, deciphered her mood as only she had ever been able to do, and said knowingly, "Take all the time you need. We'll be here."

Eva went for her coat, and climbed into the Volvo feeling as if she were fleeing from a pack of wolves. Alma alone had the ability to make her feel guilty simply with a look. It was a mother's talent. Well, she'd been Eva's mother, after all.

Cora Ogilvie had married Willard Chaney and they'd had a daughter, Evangeline. But her mother was Alma. And Alma could see into her as if she were made of glass. She couldn't hide successfully from her aunt. They could argue; they could lob words at one another, but Alma had parental radar, and it hadn't been affected in any way by the stroke. She could peer into Eva's eyes and point with precision to what was wrong, or out of alignment. Until the stroke, when Eva came back to live with her aunt, she'd forgotten Alma's ability to penetrate her mind. But for the past year she'd been presented regularly with Alma's perceptions. And it was like living with the personification of one's conscience, being made to feel in too many ways like a child again. She could only hide out from it for brief periods when in Charlie's company.

He came to the door in his old gray sweatsuit, wearing socks but no shoes, cupped her chin to give her a kiss and said, "I've got a nice new bottle of Heaven Hill that'll mellow you out in two swallows."

He hung away her coat, then took her hand and led her to the living room. Two glasses with ice sat on the coffee table next to the bourbon and a bowl of cashews. He poured a measure into each glass, gave one to her, then sat back propping his feet on the coffee table. "So tell me all about it," he invited, extending an arm across her shoulders.

She let her head fall back on his arm and said, "Do you ever think about getting married again, Charlie?"

"Are you proposing?"

"No, I am not. It's merely a question. Do you?"

"Now and again, now that I'm over the worst of my guilt. Why?"

"How do you think of it?" she asked. "I mean, why would you want to?"

"Oh, for the companionship primarily, I think."

"Not for the sake of being looked after?"

"I look after myself quite nicely. I'm a grown-up fellow. I can manage the appliances without the manuals. Why?"

"Just wondering," she said. "Alma and I were discussing it. She's of the opinion that men want to be married in order to be looked after."

"Depends on your interpretation, I suppose."

"I suppose," she said, and took a swallow of the bourbon. It burned going down, then created a radiant heat in her stomach. "I don't think I'm going to be able to finish this latest book. I can't get myself to work on it."

"Then chuck it," he said, in a near echo of Beverly's advice.

"I'm afraid to. What if it's all I'm able to write anymore?"

"I doubt that, cupcake."

"For a year before I started these things I was completely dry. Maybe there's nothing left."

"You'll have to try and find out."

"It's not that easy."

"Sure it is," he disagreed. "You get an idea, then you sit down and start writing. I guarantee you'll come up with something."

"You guarantee it?" She shifted to look at him. "You *guarantee* it?" She was smiling.

"I don't happen to think the well's gone dry," he said. "If all else fails, what about reliving ancient history? Why not write about that?"

She stared at him, jolted. Was her preoccupation with Deborah merely a prelude to writing about her? Did she dare novelize an incident from her past? She'd never raided her own life for material; she'd never had to. Ideas had simply come to her, like gifts from a benevolent, unknown relative. But maybe writing about Deborah was something she had to do; maybe that was why she couldn't stop thinking about her. Could she? Should she? God, it was a tantalizing idea. She'd have an opportunity, within the framework of a novel, to examine why she'd acted as she had, to list the many fears that had prevented her from taking any action. She'd had good reasons; they still seemed valid even now: She'd sought to protect the children and she'd done it by remaining an observer rather than a participant. It wasn't what she'd have imagined herself doing in some hypothetical situation, but reality had a way of tempering one's acts. She was now, and had been back then, more than capable of confronting head-on all kinds of things, but she'd discovered the truth of the old adage that one never knew how one would behave until the situation presented itself.

"What?" He gave her a smile both benevolent and inviting.

"I'm thinking about what you said." In fact, her mind was suddenly busy pulling narrative lines together, probing the possibilities of interweaving fact and fiction. It felt so right she couldn't imagine why she hadn't thought of it herself. It was so *obvious*. Despite its having been one of the most horrific experiences of her life, what happened on the island was first-rate material—if she chose to view it in that light. And if she did decide to write about it, her constant recollections would be for a purpose. It would no longer be a form of very painful self-indulgence, but bona fide research. She could legitimately inspect every detail of her stay on the island without feeling guilty and oddly beleaguered, as she did now. Her regular, concentrated trips into the past would be completely justified. And she'd also be able to document all that had been so wonderful and unique about her friend. She was overcome by a feeling of rightness, and had to wonder why she'd been unable to see any of this for herself.

She looked at Charlie, slowly realizing that what she missed most about marriage was the exchange of ideas, the freedom to bounce thoughts off your partner. Charlie gave her that. He was the only man she'd known since Ken who derived pleasure from thought.

"I might do that," she said, still staring at him, feeling the creative wheels beginning to turn. "You may just be a genius, Charlie."

He beamed at her. "Shucks," he said, "T'weren't nothing."

"No, seriously. I think you may have hit on an answer."

"We aim to please, cupcake."

She swung her legs up across his lap and smiled at him, holding the glass to her mouth.

"So," he said, "did you propose to me, or what?"

"Sorry, I did not."

"Too bad. For a minute there, I got pretty excited. I wouldn't mind seeing you on a daily basis."

"Are you saying you'd *want* to?"

"Maybe. Would you want to?"

"I don't know. I don't think so. It'd be impossible. There's Alma to consider, a million details. Let's forget it. I didn't mean to start anything."

"Well," he said, "let's think about it."

"Charlie! Are *you* proposing?"

"I'm suggesting we think about it."

She leaned forward and kissed him, then sat away again, saying, "That makes me feel a lot better. I've been a mess for the last little while."

"You're fine, Eva. You've just needed to rearrange your priorities, get your life back in order. It's been a rough year."

"It's been horrendous," she said. "Sometimes I hate being competent. I really do. Every so often I have the arbitrary notion that if I weren't, someone else would have to take over and do it all for me."

"Never happen."

"I know. I wish to God this had never happened to her. Alma was so on top of everything. She was exactly the way I wanted to be when I got to her age. She loved her life. Now she's just getting through it day by day. Although I must admit Bobby's making a difference, and Penny, too. I was watching the three of them at dinner this evening, Bobby in particular, and I realized it actually makes Bobby *happy* taking care of Alma."

"Some people are natural care-givers," he said. "It's a talent in its own right. I take it you're not finding her as annoying as you did."

"Not as much," she said. "I'll tell you something. Every so often when I watch her with Alma she seems more Alma's child than I do. She's less inhibited, less constrained with her in many ways than I am."

"You got lucky," he said. "You've finally found the right person to look after your aunt."

"It's more than that, Charlie," she said, running her fingers around the rim of her glass. "The three of them seem to be . . . adopting each other, creating a unit."

"And you feel excluded?"

"No, not at all. I think primarily I feel relieved. And that makes me feel guilty. Alma is my responsibility, after all."

"I think maybe," he said carefully, "you've got to stop thinking in those terms. Alma loathes being thought of as a responsibility. Surely you know that."

"I know that," she said. "I know."

"So now, cupcake,"—he grinned impishly—"about that proposal you made . . ."

Bobby got up and changed the record, putting on the Maria Callas Alma said she wanted to hear. Arias from Puccini. Returning to the armchair, she picked up her knitting, then lowered it to her lap at the sound of the woman's voice.

"Wonderful, isn't it?" Alma said, watching her.

Bobby nodded. "She's got a really sad voice."

"Brimming with emotion," Alma said. "An incredible gift."

"Eva's writing's like that," Bobby said.

"That's true," Alma said, deeply gratified. "It is. She doesn't hold anything back. She has a profound capacity for truthfulness. Her work is deeply felt. It's why the books are so good. And it's why those things she's been writing lately are so bad. There's no depth to them. But she's close to stopping. Any day now she'll announce she's starting something new, something of her own."

"How do you know that?"

"I can tell. When you spend a dozen years living with someone, you come to know them in ways no one else ever could."

"I don't know about that," Bobby said. "I definitely know Pen. But I lived with Joe eight years and I don't understand him. All I know is how he'll act when he's mad about something, when he's thinking of ways to hurt me. He smiles, as if it gives him a good feeling." She looked off into space, wishing she could unburden herself once and for all, say out loud every single one of the things he'd done to her.

"The man sounds psychopathic. There's no knowing someone like that."

"What does that mean?"

"It means he has a mental disorder."

"You mean he's crazy?"

"Well, what do you think?" Alma said impatiently. "You're the one who lived with him. Based on your experiences with this man, would you say he was in his right mind?"

In a small voice, Bobby said, "No."

"There you are, then," Alma said.

"Are you ever afraid?" Bobby asked her.

"I never used to be," Alma admitted with some bitterness, "until my body betrayed me. Now it's the only thing I *am* afraid of: that it will betray me again, put me into some physically vegetative state where my mind's trapped inside a body that won't function. I'd prefer to die."

"That's not gonna happen."

"Going to," Alma corrected her. "And when did you get your medical degree?"

Bobby laughed, set aside her knitting, and crossed the room to give the woman a kiss on her cheek. Then, squatting down in front of her, she placed one hand over Alma's and said, "It's not going to happen. You're going to be fine."

Alma shook her head, daunted by this young woman's instinctive kindness. "Go sit down," she said, "and listen to the music."

"You'll keep doing your exercises and getting stronger, and you'll be fine. You'll see."

"Go do your knitting and listen to the music," Alma told her, wishing she had Bobby's faith.

"You'll see," Bobby said again, then returned to her chair.

Alma closed her eyes and listened to the repressed sob in Maria Callas's voice as it soared into the upper registers. Pain made into music. Exquisite sorrow. Fear made tangible, transmuted into beauty.

Nineteen

As usual, Eva had fallen asleep soon after she turned out the light. And less than two hours later she was awake again, having suffered through a dream she had, in one form or another, too often for comfort. In this dream, the telephone rang and Eva picked up the receiver to hear Melissa, in a broken voice, begging her mother to come get her. Instantly alarmed, Eva asked, "Where are you?" But then they were disconnected, and Eva, frantic, knew that someone had taken her daughter, had harmed her. In the dream she went mad with grief and fear. She had no idea where Melissa was, had no means of finding her. The fear was like a plastic bag tied over her head, suffocating her. She had to fight to escape the gruesome details the dream wanted to provide, claw her way out of sleep.

Filled with residual anxiety, she sat up in bed telling herself yet again that she was powerless to protect Melissa. She'd done everything she could as a parent to make her aware of the dangers that lurked everywhere for women and small children. She could only sit back now and offer up a silent prayer for Melissa's continued well-being.

Her heartbeat steadying, her breathing having slowed, she rested against the pillows and let her mind go back.

Although mightily hung-over, Ian had dropped the women and children on the beach before taking off for an undisclosed destination in the car. Eva and Deborah and the children were in the boat with Deborah's uncle at the tiller, on their way to the construction site on Crescent Bay. The uncle, a robust, placid man in his early fifties, concentrated on steering the boat through the choppy swells. Eva sat in the middle, the children on either side of her, watching Deborah, who sat facing her. Deborah was gazing somewhat fearfully into the water and Eva knew she was frightened of the boat's capsizing. Not only had she never learned to swim, but she was also terrified of the water.

It was a fairly gray day, the sky hazy with intermittent low-hanging clouds. The sun stabbed through here and there sending angled beams downward like spotlights. As they rounded a rocky outcropping before entering the bay, the boat lurched on the crosscurrents and Eva put an arm around each of the children, her sneaker-clad feet braced against one of the ribs. Deborah continued to stare, mouth slightly open, at the roiling waters.

Once in the lee of the bay, the water was calmer and they made it quite quickly to shore. Deborah's uncle offered a large hand to help Eva and the children out of the boat. Eva lifted Derek forward and the man lost much of his usual stony reserve, breaking into a beautiful smile as he took the boy in his arms and, in one smooth motion, swung him through the air and set him down on the sand. His smile held as he repeated the motions, accepting Melissa and lifting her to the ground. His hand around Eva's was strong and warm and surprisingly gentle, and she gave him a smile, thanking him as he directed her down onto the beach. He nodded, his eyes connecting with hers for a second or two. She had an impression of sadness and apology. Bemused, Eva led the children up to the dry sand and knelt to remove their life vests.

Deborah, looking faintly green around the mouth and nose, watched her uncle beach the boat, then stood talking to him in low urgent tones. Eva concentrated on the children, wondering how she'd entertain them. It was too cold to swim. The clouds were pulling together, the beams of light farther out now over the bay, highlighting patches of rough sea.

Mellie complained of being cold and Eva got a sweater for her out of her large canvas bag. "Are you cold, Derek?" she asked the boy, but he was watching his mother, his sturdy body turned in Deborah's direction. Eva had his sweater too, and reached to put it on him, but he shrugged her off and went running along the sand after his mother and her uncle, who were headed toward the far end of the bay where a small group of workers sat on their haunches beneath the scrubby trees.

Eva turned to look behind her at the house. She couldn't see that any work had been done. The site looked exactly as it had two and a half weeks earlier. A mound of concrete blocks sat under a tarpaulin to one side of the foundation, the tarp anchored by spades and shovels. Eva sank down on the sand and Melissa sat between her legs, her hands on Eva's knees, asking, "When're we going home?"

"Home to New York?" Eva asked, wondering if Mellie was feeling it too, the ominous weight of each additional day they spent on this island. "Soon," she said. "Just a few more days."

"I don't like it here anymore," Melissa said, her tiny hands surprisingly cool on Eva's bare knees.

"Soon," Eva promised, determined to talk to Deborah, to ask straight out if there was anything she could do. If Deborah said there wasn't, Eva would take Melissa home.

Deborah was returning, scowling with displeasure. Her uncle finished speaking to the group of workers, who began getting to their feet, then he turned and, head down, followed after Deborah. Derek ran along at Deborah's side, trying to catch hold of his mother's hand, but she was moving too quickly. He tried several times, his chunky arm reaching out to her, but she seemed oblivious.

"I will *kill* that bloody man," Deborah seethed, her anger and frustration having clearly reached a peak of desperation.

"What's wrong?" Eva asked, her arms automatically closing around Melissa.

"He hasn't paid them," Deborah said, her mouth downturned with disgust. "He hasn't bloody *paid* them. We're going back." She swatted at Derek's hand, saying, "Leave Mummy be just now," as she watched her uncle approaching.

"There's something you should know," Eva said quickly, latching onto the moment. Deborah looked at her, her expression one of utter impatience, and Eva said in a low voice, "Ian has a gun."

Deborah emitted a bark of derisive laughter. "He's had that bloody thing forever. Next to his precious Dunhill, it's his favorite toy." She looked away, over at her approaching uncle, saying, "Ian's a *child*, darling. A fucked-up child who's very likely pissed away the crew's wages. I *swear* I will *kill* him."

Nonplussed, feeling somehow small, Eva reached for one of the vests she'd left stacked on the sand and began fitting Melissa's arms into it, saying as she did, "Come here, Derek, and let me put your vest on."

His frustration as great as his mother's, Derek shouted, "*No!*" and ran across the beach toward the construction.

Deborah flew after him, caught him by one arm, and delivered a resounding whack to his backside. At once the boy began to howl. She ignored it as she dragged him by the arm back to the shore. "Be quiet," she warned. "Behave yourself!"

Pulling on her own vest, Eva got to her feet, feeling a dreadful sympathy for Derek. Every day he was going a bit more out of control, his behavior deteriorating in direct proportion, it seemed, to his mother's discontent.

The uncle pushed the boat back into the water, then assisted the women and children back on board. They sat bobbing in the shallows while he tried to get the engine started. It took several times before the Evinrude roared to life. Deborah sat alone facing Eva and the children, her eyes on the construction. Eva watched her, wishing now that she'd never mentioned the damned gun. She should've said something about the fights but she hadn't wanted to discuss any of that in front of the children. They were upset enough as it was.

They had rounded the treacherous rocks and were perhaps a hundred feet from shore when Derek suddenly stood up, evidently with the idea in mind of going to his mother. The boat lifted in the chop, lurched, and the boy toppled over the side. Melissa screamed. Deborah half-stood, terrified, a cry breaking from her throat.

The uncle cut the engine, commanded, "Sit, Deborah!" and dived from the back of the boat. Mouth agape, prepared to go in too if necessary, Eva held Melissa, held her breath. Two strokes, three, then the uncle had hold of Derek, turned, and was towing him back to the boat. Just below the surface Eva could see the elongated bodies of barracudas. A few more seconds and the uncle had one arm over the side, lifting Derek by the back of his life vest with the other. Deborah seemed frozen. Releasing Melissa, wondering why the hell Deborah wasn't helping, Eva braced herself and hauled the now sobbing boy into the boat. Then she held out her hand to the uncle, glancing briefly over her shoulder, telling Melissa to hold on tight.

The boat tilted almost into the water as the uncle pulled himself in. With a murmured thank you to Eva, he pressed her shoulder as he climbed past her to seat himself again at the tiller. "Keep a hand on your boy, Deborah," he said angrily, then proceeded to direct them toward the shore.

Deborah held Derek between her knees, his back pressed to her chest. He continued sobbing until they hit the sand. Then, abruptly, his crying ceased. He pulled away from his mother and shoved Melissa aside to get to the uncle and be lifted ashore. He seemed suddenly to have a very definite destination, and when Eva looked up and saw Ian leaning against the car, the silver Dunhill lighter turning, turning in his hands, that perpetual sneer on his face.

Deborah climbed down from the boat and went marching across the sand, fists swinging at her sides.

Eva sat Melissa on the beach, told her not to move, then went back to help the uncle pull the boat up onto the sand. They worked together in silence. The uncle said softly, "It's bad. Take the child and go home, girl."

Wanting to weep, she whispered, "I'm trying to help, but I don't know what to do. She doesn't seem to want to talk to me."

"Take the child," he said again, "and *go home.* Don't be waitin'." He then raised his large liquid eyes to look over at the car where Deborah, holding Derek's hand, was talking to Ian, her upper body leaning into him, the actual words inaudible, her tone deadly. Derek turned suddenly and waved, all smiles.

"But she's my *friend,*" Eva murmured. "I can't go off and leave her, not with the way things are."

The uncle gazed down at her for a long moment, then gave a slow shake of his head. "She not the girl you knew from England. She not the girl anybody knew." His eyes moving to Melissa, he gave the child a dazzling smile so reminiscent of Deborah's smiles once upon a time, that Eva's eyes were suddenly full of tears.

Melissa returned his smile and leaned against his knee, staring up at him adoringly. With a hearty laugh, he threw her up into the air, beaming as she squealed with pleasure. He caught her, set her gently down, and turned back to Eva. "Take your baby home, Mistress Eva," he counseled sympathetically, then started away.

Eva knelt on the damp sand to remove Melissa's life vest as the uncle marched resolutely down the beach. Deborah's voice was rising. Ian continued to lean against the car, his expression unchanged, the lighter turning, turning in his fingers. She'd give it two or three more days, then do as Deborah's uncle advised.

Wednesday after lunch Eva turned the kitchen over to Bobby, saying, "There's no sense in your working down-stairs when everything you need is here." She got out the pastry board and the rolling pin, pointing out where the measuring cup and wooden spoons were, then left to go to the office.

Alma sat in her wheelchair at the table enjoying the sight of Bobby assembling her ingredients on the countertop. Unlike Eva, for whom cooking was an escape, Bobby ob-viously found it pure pleasure. She sang softly in a tune-ful voice as she measured out cupfuls of flour; she wore a smile as she greased pie and tart pans; she practically danced as she adjusted the racks and started the oven heating.

"Want to help?" Bobby asked.

"What on earth could I possibly do?"

"Mix this," Bobby said, and set a bowl in Alma's lap.

Using her deadened left arm to brace the bowl, Alma took hold of the wooden spoon in her right hand and stirred the mincemeat, inhaling the spicy scent with a mix-ture of pleasure and amusement. "I loathe cooking," she said, sent time-traveling by the activity; remembering sit-ting on her knees on a chair at the kitchen table, licking clean the frosting bowl while her mother slipped a cake into the oven.

"So does my aunt Helen," Bobby said, coating the rolling pin with flour. "I did most of the cooking at home from the time I was eleven."

"Tell me about your aunt," Alma invited.

"She's tough, but she's kind," Bobby said. "After my grandmother died she stayed home to take care of Grandpa and then me. She's a bookkeeper," she explained, "been working for years for this Ford dealer back home."

"I had the impression she's elderly."

Bobby laughed. "Aunt Helen must be about Eva's age."

"And she never married?"

"She got engaged a time or two but always changed her mind and gave the rings back. How come you never got married?" she asked, so at home in the kitchen that her usual inhibitions were temporarily set aside.

"I changed my mind and gave the ring back."

Bobby looked over, eyebrows raised. "That true?"

"Not entirely, but close enough."

"Did you want to be married?"

"When I was very young," Alma said. "I grew out of it."

"You make it sound like measles or something." Bobby smiled at her, then looked back at the dough she was rolling.

"Given your experiences, would you want to marry again?"

"Not the way I feel right now, no, ma'am," Bobby said with a firm shake of her head.

"Take this damned thing out of my lap! It's getting on my nerves."

Bobby came and took the bowl, then stood holding it with both hands, saying, "I hope you don't think I was being nosy."

"I don't think that," Alma said, waiting for Bobby to meet her eyes. When she did, Alma said, "It's all right to be curious, my dear. It's human nature, after all."

Turning away to put the bowl down on the counter, Bobby expertly lifted the pie crust, rolled it onto the pin, then unrolled it into one of the waiting pans. "I don't know anymore what's all right and what's not."

"I understand that. It'll come to you with time."

"Are you happy with me?" Bobby asked, feeling very close to the old woman at this moment.

"Yes, I'm happy with you," Alma answered, moved by Bobby's constant uncertainty. "Just go about your business and don't worry so. You'll know when I'm not happy."

Dennis arrived as Bobby slid the last of the pies into the oven. She went to the door and he smiled at the sight of her, leaned in and kissed her cheek before she had any chance to move. It didn't seem so bad this time, although her heart started hammering apprehensively.

"Something smells wonderful," he said, closing the door.

"I'm making pies for tomorrow. Alma's out here with me in the kitchen." She started down the hallway, very aware of his presence behind her.

"My favorite customer," Dennis said, and patted Alma on the top of the head.

She swatted him with her good hand, but she was smiling.

"I'll take her up," Dennis said, turning the wheelchair toward the door.

"The agony hour," Alma grumbled.

"You love it," Dennis teased as they went down the hall.

Bobby rinsed the mixing bowls and utensils, put them in the dishwasher, then got a pot of coffee going. When it was done, she poured some with cream into a cup and carried it through the garage up to the office.

Eva called to come in and Bobby opened the door to see her sitting, not at the desk but in the armchair over by the window. Her long, trouser-clad legs were stretched out straight in front of her and crossed at the ankles, her elbows resting on the arms of the chair. She looked worried.

"Brought you some coffee," Bobby said, carrying it over and setting it down on the windowsill.

"Thanks," Eva said, eyeing her. "Dennis with my aunt?"

"Uh-hunh."

"Pull up a chair and talk to me for a minute," Eva said.

"Okay." Taken aback, Bobby got the old wooden kitchen chair from over by the wall and sat down.

"I want to ask you something," Eva said, reaching for the coffee.

"Okay."

"It's about your husband."

"Okay."

Eva looked at her, struck again by Bobby's childlike vulnerability. "Why did you let it happen to you?" she asked, fascinated by Bobby's youthfulness. She didn't look more than twenty, not a line on her face. But her eyes were perpetually cautious. The eyes belonged in a much older face.

"Let what happen?"

"The beatings."

Feeling suddenly angry and humiliated, Bobby said, "I didn't *let* anything happen. It was done *to* me." Who *was* this woman? Bobby wondered. Where did she get off saying the things she did?

"I'm sorry. I phrased that badly." She came forward and placed a hand on Bobby's knee. "What I want to understand is why you stayed, why it went on for so long."

"Why?" Bobby asked. She couldn't read Eva's face, couldn't think what she was after. She felt hurt and wanted to get away.

"It's something I've been trying to understand for a very long time," Eva said, sitting back and looking out the window. "I had a friend," she said. "She got beaten." She was quiet for a moment, then asked, "How did you *feel* about it?"

"I didn't just let it happen to me," Bobby insisted, the anger a new and threatening emotion. She felt as if it could take her over, have her doing and saying almost anything. "I've got pies in the oven," she said, standing, breathing fast. "I don't want to talk about it."

"God, don't take umbrage!" Eva said, returning the cup to the windowsill and rising from the armchair to take hold of Bobby's arm—small and thin as a twelve-year-old's. Bobby cringed, trying to shrink away from her, and she thought, Jesus! She was making everything worse, but she wanted to salvage the situation, and was trying the only way she knew how. "I'm not trying to hurt you. I want very much to understand. It's important."

Bobby looked at the woman's hand on her arm, and battled down her fear. "Let go of me, please," she said breathlessly. "I don't like people grabbing hold of me."

At once Eva released her. "You think I don't like you," she said, "but that's not the case. Not at all. I'm sorry if I put it badly. If it's any consolation to you, I have much the same problem with Melissa. I can't seem to speak with the clarity I manage to put into my writing. Maybe it's because I have more time when I'm writing, time to phrase everything precisely. I want to understand, Bobby. I want to know how it happens. Please don't think I'm attempting to blame you. It's nothing like that. I can see I'm upsetting you and that's the last thing I wanted."

"I can't tell you why," Bobby said, trying to calm down. "I don't *know* why. It's about being afraid and trying to do everything right but never being able to because there isn't any right way." The words came tumbling out of her mouth in a rush. While she could see plainly enough that Eva meant what she said it didn't stop the hurt, and she wished she knew how to defend herself. "Nobody sets out wanting to get hit," she said. "It's not what you think's gonna happen when you marry someone. You think everything's gonna be settled. But then one time he gets mad, you don't even know what at, and the hitting starts and you think it must've been your fault, you must've messed up, it's your fault, you deserve to get hit. And later on he's sorry and you think it'll never happen again, but it does. And pretty soon it's happening all the time and there's nowhere to hide and nobody to help you, and that's your whole life—getting hit and trying to figure out why." She paused and dragged air into her heaving lungs. "I've gotta get back," she said, looking over at the door, then again at Eva whose eyes were wide, mouth a little open, appearing stunned. "The pies'll burn," Bobby explained, feeling naked, and scared. This woman and her aunt, they didn't know *anything*, asking how could she let that happen to her as if she'd said to Joe, okay you can hit me, I'll take it.

"Could we sit down and talk about this?" Eva asked. "Maybe later? It's *very* important."

"I don't like talking about it," Bobby said shakily. She took one step toward the door, then another. Eva remained standing where she was, grappling with what she wanted to say. She looked so distraught that Bobby wanted suddenly to help her. It was as if the two of them spoke different languages. She stopped and waited, able to see Eva struggling. After a moment, Bobby said, "You scared me," and Eva lifted her hands, then let them drop in a gesture of impotence.

"Everything frightens you," Eva said quietly. "It must be hell. The last thing I intended was to make it worse."

"I want us to be friends," Bobby said.

"So do I. I *do* like you," Eva said. It was the truth. She thought that in so many ways Bobby was a much better person than she, more forgiving, gentler, far more patient.

"What happened to your friend?" Bobby asked softly.

Eva looked at her, gray-green eyes revealing old pain. "She died."

"Oh, damn!" Bobby shivered and wrapped her arms around herself. "I'm real sorry."

Eva nodded slowly. After a moment, Bobby went to the door and left.

"I made you a couple of tarts," Bobby said, putting them and a mug of coffee on the table in front of Dennis. She was still a little shaky from her run-in with Eva.

"That's so nice of you," he said, pushing up the sleeves of his white uniform so that she could see the fine golden-red hair on his arms. "You're nice altogether."

"No, I'm not," she disagreed, thinking of the way she'd spewed words at Eva; they'd positively gushed out of her.

"You just can't take a compliment," he said.

"I don't believe them. Mostly when people give compliments it's 'cause they want something."

"And what is it you think I want?"

"I don't know," she said.

"I like you," he told her. "Don't you like me?"

"I like you well enough," she said. "But I don't know you."

"That's what we're working on," he said sensibly, "getting to know one another. That's what people do when they like each other. It's not complicated."

"Seems to me as if it is." She took a sip of her coffee and watched him devour one of the mincemeat tarts in three bites.

"Mmnn, good," he said, washing the tart down with a gulp of coffee. "So, are we on for Friday night?"

"Okay."

"We could take Penny with us, if you want, go a little earlier."

That pleased her and she smiled. "She'd like that."

"Okay, good. I'll pick the two of you up at six-thirty. Mind if I take another one of these along with me?"

"I don't mind. I'll wrap it for you." She found a Baggie in one of the drawers and put the tart in it.

He got his coat and put the Baggie in the pocket. She stood well away in case he tried to kiss her again. But he didn't. He said, "Have a good Thanksgiving. See you Friday," and headed across the driveway to the Beetle. He tooted the horn before driving off, and she closed the door feeling rather dizzy. All of a sudden it felt as if there was an awful lot going on.

When she went back to the kitchen, Eva was standing there halfway between the table and the sink. She looked so unhappy, so sad and sorry and confused, that Bobby set aside all the harsh words and misunderstandings and walked straight over to give her a quick hug. "It's okay," Bobby told her. "It's okay."

When she went back to the kitchen, Eva was standing

their hallway between the hang and the sofa. She looked

so unhappy so sad and sexy, well contained, that both sat

sides all the harsh words and intimate touchings and

we'd straight over on all waves and over him. "It's okay,"

below told her writes.

Twenty

Eva was awake before six on Thursday morning and had been in the kitchen for close to an hour when Penny came up.

"Whatcha makin'?" Penny came to stand close to Eva and on tiptoe tried to see into the oversized mixing bowl.

"Your favorite," Eva smiled.

"Stuffin'!"

"Yup. How come you're up so early?"

Penny shrugged. "I wasn't sleepy no more."

"Anymore," Eva corrected her.

"Well, I wasn't," Penny said. "C'n I help?"

"Not now, but maybe in a little while you could help me fix Alma's breakfast tray."

"Okay," Penny said excitedly. "I know where the tray is. I could get it."

"It's too early," Eva told her. "In a little while."

"Oh!" Penny looked around the kitchen for something to do. "My mom's still sleepin'," she said, bouncing her bottom back and forth against the lower cabinet. "I know how to make the coffee machine."

"Do you?" Eva looked down at her.

"I watched my mom do it. Want me to make the coffee machine for you?"

"All right." Amused, Eva watched Penny drag a chair over to the counter, climb on it to get the empty carafe, then climb down again. Setting the carafe beside the sink, she relocated the chair to the sink, stood on it to fill the carafe with water, used both hands to put the carafe on the counter, moved the chair again, returned for the carafe, put it down on the far counter, climbed back on the chair, lifted the lid of the coffee maker, and poured in the water. Then she hoisted herself up onto the counter, opened the upper cabinet, found the package of filters and the coffee canister.

"How much coffee?" Penny asked, back standing on the chair, fitting the filter paper into place.

"Use the scoop inside and keep going until I tell you to stop."

"Okay." Sucking on her lower lip, Penny began scooping out the coffee, every other second glancing over at Eva. "Is that enough?" she asked, holding the filter out for Eva to see.

"A bit more."

Penny added several more scoops. Eva said, "That's fine," and Penny put the lid back on the canister, pushed the filter home, positioned the empty carafe on the base, then reached around the base and switched the machine on, declaring, "There! Told you I could do it."

"You certainly can." Washing her hands, Eva checked the time. It was nearly seven.

"What else c'n I do?" Penny asked, sitting on the edge of the counter, legs dangling over the chair.

"You can come up and help me make Melissa's bed."

"Okay." Penny slipped down to the chair, then to the floor.

"Put the chair back, Penny."

"I was gonna," Penny said, and did as she'd been asked.

"We'll have to be very quiet so we don't wake Aunt Alma."

"Okay," Penny whispered, taking Eva's hand and going with her up the stairs.

On the landing, Eva stopped to get sheets and towels from the linen closet, then led Penny into the bedroom next to Alma's.

"Your little girl comin' home?" Penny asked, as Eva removed the spread from the bed.

"Yup. Today."

"This her room?" Penny looked around. It didn't look like a kid's room.

"It is when she comes to visit." Eva began putting pillow slips on the pillows.

"Where's all her toys an' everythin'?"

"Melissa's grown-up. She doesn't have toys anymore."

"What happened to 'em?"

"They got given away before we came to live here."

"Who to?"

"To the Good Will." Eva shook open a fitted sheet. Penny scooted to the far side of the bed and began pulling the sheet over the corner. "You know how to make beds too, hunh?"

"My mom taught me."

"Taught you."

"That's right. I got a loose tooth. Wanna see?"

Eva laughed, took hold of Penny, and sat on the side of the bed with the girl in her lap. "Let's see it."

Penny pulled back her lip and wiggled the tooth. "See! Mom and Granny said the tooth fairy's gonna come visit me when I'm sleepin', leave me a big surprise."

"Do you ever miss your daddy, Penny?" Eva asked, hoping she wasn't overstepping an invisible boundary.

Without hesitation, Penny shook her head, saying, "Uh-uh. He's bad. We're never seein' him ever ever again, and I'm *glad.*"

"Why?"

"'Cause he's always hurtin' my mom. He's very bad."

"Did he hurt you, too?"

"Two times. He hitted me."

Eva hugged her close, wondering if Melissa ever returned to the island in her dreams. She claimed to have no memory whatever of that summer, but Eva couldn't help believing it was buried somewhere in her subconscious and might one day resurface.

"You smell nice," Penny said, looping her arms around Eva's neck.

"So do you." Eva pressed a kiss into the fragrant, impossibly soft flesh at the point where Penny's neck met her shoulder. "Let's finish here and go make breakfast. Okay?"

"Okay."

Eva set her down, quickly straightened the bed covers, then took Penny's hand, tiptoeing with her past Alma's door. Penny grinned at her conspiratorially and held one small finger to her lips. Eva wished she had as much ease with Bobby as she did with this child.

Bobby awoke, saw Pen's bed was empty, and had a moment of complete terror. She looked around wildly, throat dry, heart pounding, then heard footsteps overhead and exhaled shakily. Pen was upstairs in the kitchen with Eva. For a moment she'd thought somehow Joe had found them, had sneaked in and taken Penny. It was the kind of thing he'd do to punish her, because he knew Pen was her world. Every day while she waited for the school bus, she feared Penny wouldn't be on it.

Weak in the legs, she got up and went into the bathroom. When she came out she pulled on jeans and a T-shirt. In the kitchen Penny was using a whisk to beat eggs in a bowl and Eva was making bacon.

"You shouldn't be up here disturbing Eva," Bobby told Pen, greatly eased merely by the sight of her. She glanced at Eva, trying to gauge her mood.

"I'm helpin', aren't I, Auntie Eva?"

"That's right. Have some coffee," Eva invited. "It's fresh. Penny made it."

"You did?" Bobby smiled at her daughter.

"All by myself," Penny said proudly.

"Yes, she did," Eva confirmed. "And later on, she's going to help me with the cooking."

So everything was all right, Bobby thought, pouring herself some coffee, saying, "I could give you a hand, if you like."

"I'll put both of you to work," Eva said, with a pair of tongs dropping cooked strips of bacon on several folded paper towels.

"What time's your girl due home?" Bobby asked.

"Knowing Melissa, she'll probably arrive as we're about to sit down to eat. The car will be crammed with bags of dirty laundry, and for the next two days the machines'll be going nonstop." She squirted liquid detergent on the broiler pan, ran some water over it, then put four slices of bread into the toaster. Moving to take the bowl of eggs from Penny, she smiled and said, "These are perfect, Pen. One day you'll be a good cook."

"Yeah." Penny grinned. "C'n I have some coffee, too?"

"A little bit," Bobby said, "if that's okay with Eva."

"It's okay," Eva said.

Bobby fixed a cup that was half milk and half coffee, added a small amount of sugar, and told Pen to sit down properly at the table to drink it.

"Coffee's *good,*" Penny said appreciatively.

Eva finished scrambling the eggs, then arranged a plate for Alma. "Help yourself to some breakfast," she told Bobby, lifting the tray.

"You hungry?" Bobby asked Pen after Eva had gone.

"C'n I have some bacon?"

"Sure." Bobby got a plate, put two strips of bacon and a piece of toast on it and set it in front of Penny. She'd just resumed her seat and lifted her mug of coffee when the doorbell rang. She started, eyes going wide.

"Somebody's at the door," Pen said, wriggling off her chair. "I'll go see." Before Bobby could say a word, she was racing down the hall.

Getting up to follow her, her mind filled with an image of Joe, Bobby was right behind her as Penny unlocked the door. There on the doorstep was a young woman who had to be Eva's daughter, an immense backpack weighing her down, half a dozen assorted straw and canvas bags at her feet.

"Couldn't find the key," she said as if to herself. Then, "Hi! Who're you?" she asked Penny.

"I'm Penny Salton. I'm six. Who're you?"

With a laugh, the young woman said, "I'm Melissa Rule. I'm twenty. You going to let me in?"

"Yup! Want me to carry some of those?"

"That'd be great." Swinging the heavy pack down off her back, Melissa looked over and said, "Hi. You're the nurse, right?"

"That's right. I'm Bobby."

Penny dragged one of the bags into the hall, then darted back for another. "She's cute," Melissa told Bobby, going to the door to collect more of the bags.

Bobby thought Melissa was one of the most beautiful girls she'd ever seen. Tall and well-built with thick dark brown hair falling almost to her waist, a creamy complexion, with round eyes so dark they were almost black, a strong nose, wide smile, and slightly squared cleft chin. She was dressed like a hippy, in a long Indian cotton skirt, a white turtleneck under a black shirt and a rough-woven Guatemalan vest. On her feet she wore heavy gray woolen socks and ugly double-strapped sandals. On anyone else the outfit would have been dreadful. But on Melissa it looked good.

"Where's Mom?" she asked Bobby, dropping the last of the bags in the front hall.

"Upstairs, giving Alma her breakfast. Are you hungry? There's food already fixed."

"Fantastic! I could eat a truck."

"You c'n come eat with me," Penny said, taking hold of her hand and swinging it back and forth.

"Great!" Melissa let Penny tow her to the kitchen.

"There's fresh coffee," Bobby said, "if you'd like some."

"I'll get it." Melissa poured a mug of coffee, added cream and several spoonfuls of sugar, then sat down at the table, dropping her head to smile close-to at Penny. "You're a real sweetie, aren't you? What grade're you in?"

"First," Penny said, munching on a strip of bacon. "What grade're you in?"

"I'm a sophomore in college." Melissa drank some of the coffee. "I need this," she told Bobby. "I stayed up till almost three working on this paper and then it seemed pretty pointless to go to bed for two hours, so I loaded the car and took off. I made fantastic time. The roads were empty."

"You must be tired," Bobby said.

"Completely whacked," Melissa said. "I figure I'll grab a nap before dinner. Mom's going to freak when she comes down and finds me here. She *hates* surprises. And she'll have fits over the laundry." She smiled as if speaking of a difficult but lovable child. "How's Aunt Alma doing?"

"Oh, really well," Bobby said, finding Melissa immediately and enormously likeable.

"*I* made the coffee," Penny announced, wiping toast crumbs from her face with the back of her hand.

"Use your napkin, Pen."

"You did?" Melissa said. "It's excellent."

"Yeah," Penny said, "I know. I made your bed, too."

"Wow!" Melissa said. "You're something, hunh?"

"Yeah." Penny beamed with satisfaction.

Eva came down the stairs with the tray, saw the bags in the hallway, and felt instantly annoyed and elated. Melissa was home.

Bobby got a whole new perspective on Eva when she came in with the tray and saw Melissa. Her face lit up and she smiled so hard it looked as if she might cry. She put the tray down. Melissa got up saying, "Hi, Mom," and Eva hugged her, asking, "Did you stay up all night?"

"Yup."

"Well, you look all right in spite of it."

"Thanks. You look all right, too. I'll just run up and see Auntie Alma for a minute."

Eva let her go, appearing somewhat dazed. Then she laughed, ran a hand through her hair, and said to Bobby, "Didn't I tell you she'd bring home a carful of laundry?" She felt like screaming. On top of all the preparations for dinner, she'd be up to her ears in laundry. Why the hell did Melissa do this every time? It wasn't as if there weren't laundry facilities at the school.

Bobby smiled. "She's real nice," she said. "Looks a lot like you."

"She looks like her father," Eva said, clearing the tray, putting dishes in the sink. She told herself to forget it, but those bags in the front hall infuriated her.

"He must've been a real . . . really good-looking man."

"Yes," Eva said. "He was."

Sensing it was time to get out of the way, Bobby said, "Come on, Pen. You can watch TV while I get Alma up and dressed."

"Auntie Eva said I can help her with the cookin'."

"Later," Bobby said firmly.

"Melissa's a glorious girl, isn't she?" Alma said as Bobby brushed her hair.

"She's beautiful," Bobby agreed.

"Beautiful and intelligent and wonderfully good-natured. She's the only one who can actually handle Eva. She simply laughs and teases her when Eva starts carrying on about something or other. Calms her right down. It's difficult to stay angry when someone's standing there laughing at you."

"I guess so," Bobby said, drawing the brush through the thick silver hair.

"College has opened her mind," Alma said. "She's positively blossomed."

"Sometimes I wish I'd gone," Bobby said, imagining ivy-colored buildings and students rushing through echoey corridors.

"You could take some evening courses," Alma said, "study something that interests you."

"I don't know about that." Bobby could almost hear Joe laughing at the idea of her taking courses, learning new things.

"Think about it," Alma counseled. "It would be good for you."

"I always wished I'd learned typing."

"Then take a course," Alma said. "You can do anything, you know. Anything at all. You simply have to decide to try."

"What would I have to do?" Bobby asked, imagining there'd be tests to pass before they'd even let her in the door.

"You get a catalogue and decide what interests you, then you sign up for the course. There's nothing to it."

"Really? You don't have to pass exams or anything to get in?"

"You enroll for a course and you go. It's that simple. You like the idea of that, don't you?" Alma turned her head to look at her.

"I never knew you could do that," Bobby said, gathering the mass of hair in her hands and shaping it into a coil. "It's something to think about, all right."

"You could acquire new skills," Alma said, "become more independent. After all," she reasoned, "you don't want to spend the rest of your life looking after some cantankerous old woman."

"I wouldn't mind," Bobby said, pinning the hair into place. "I like it here."

"It's not enough," Alma said sternly. "You could do more. It's important to work to your full potential."

"I'm already doing that."

"You are not!" Alma barked. "You must consider the future, consider Penny's future. Are you done with that yet?"

"Uh-hunh. All set."

"Then, let's get downstairs. And think about what I've told you."

"I will," Bobby promised, imagining herself going to work in some office, maybe being a secretary to an important executive. She couldn't quite see it. But she did like the idea of learning new things.

The bags had all been emptied and an immense pile of dirty clothes sat on the floor in front of the washing machine. Melissa poured detergent over the first load, closed the lid, then started the machine. She got herself some more coffee, sat down at the table, and picked up the toast Penny had left, eyes on her mother as she pushed stuffing into the turkey.

She could tell her mother was pissed off again, probably because she'd stayed up all night and come home with a carful of laundry. No biggie, but her mother let dumb little things make her crazy. She was dying for a cigarette but knew if she lit up her mother would freak altogether. So she ate the cold toast, sipped the coffee, and watched her mother, pinpointing every last sign that indicated how pissed off she was: the eyebrows pulled together, mouth clamped shut, chin jutting, concentrating totally on cramming the bird full of damp stuffing.

"What's up?" she asked finally, wanting to get it out in the open so her whole visit wouldn't be wrecked. There were times when her mother could stay mad for an entire week. Sometimes her mother's moods made her want to crawl into bed and sleep for days on end. Admittedly, she'd been way better since she'd started seeing Charlie Willis. But she still had her moods. Partly it was because of her work, sitting up in the office every day and hardly ever seeing people, living inside her head. But the rest of it remained fairly much a mystery. It was hard to get her mother to talk about the things that really bothered her.

"Nothing's up," her mother said with that wide-eyed expression of innocence that was a dead giveaway.

"Come on," Melissa coaxed, smiling. "What is it, the laundry?"

"I was expecting that," her mother said, starting now on the neck cavity, brows drawing together again.

"What then?"

"Nothing, Melissa."

"Nothing, Melissa," Melissa mimicked her. "I know this routine. It's the mother-from-hell number."

Eva sighed and said, "I pay for laundry service at the school. *Why* can't you use it?"

"Oh, wow," Melissa said. "This *is* about laundry. I can't believe it. You're pissed because I brought my stuff home."

"It's inconvenient, especially today."

"Lighten up, Eva," Melissa said, and gave her a wide smile. "I'll get a couple of loads done now and finish the rest tomorrow. It's no biggie."

"It's very inconsiderate of you."

"Mother from hell murders daughter over laundry," Melissa said, as if reading a headline. "What're you really pissed about?"

"I loathe that expression."

"Okay. What is responsible for your puckered brow, Mommie dearest?"

Eva laughed giddily, and went to the sink to rinse her hands. Why did she always do this? Every time Melissa came home she started fault-finding. It had something to do with caring too much, with wanting to let go but being unable to relinquish the last flimsy strands of parental control. It also had to do with Melissa's youth and freedom, and Eva despised herself for feeling faintly jealous and resentful. Drying her hands, she looked over and said,

"I'm sorry. I really don't give a damn about the laundry. Forget I said anything. I'm glad to see you."

Storm passes by, no damage done, Melissa thought. "Me too," she said.

"Mother from hell," Eva laughed, shamed by her daughter's forgiving nature.

"I'm going to grab a nap for a couple of hours. Okay?" Melissa got up and put her mug in the sink.

"Good idea. You look tired."

"What time's dinner?"

"Three."

"Don't look at my feet," Melissa said. "I know you hate my Birkenstocks, but they're very comfortable." She moved closer and said, "Gimme a hug, Eva."

Again Eva had to laugh, and hugged her, running her hand over Melissa's luxuriant hair, jolted every time by her daughter's size and height, her adulthood, her astonishing reasonableness. "Go take your nap," she said, easing Melissa away, seeing the amusement shining in her eyes.

"You've really got to learn to lighten up, Eva," Melissa said, heading for the stairs. "Wake me in a couple of hours. Okay?"

"Okay," Eva said, watching her go, furious with herself for making a fuss over the laundry. What the *hell* was the matter with her?

Twenty-One

Everyone gathered in the living room to have a drink before the meal, and Bobby was able to stay in the background, sipping at a glass of red wine, and watching. Alma was having a white wine spritzer and Penny offered around a crystal dish with carrots and celery and olives. Then she went to squeeze in beside Melissa in one of the armchairs. Melissa didn't mind and sat with an arm around Pen, asking her about school. Eva was back and forth to the kitchen, pausing in between times to perch on the arm of Charlie's chair and drink some of her red wine. Bobby covertly studied them with interest, fascinated by this new view of Eva, and intrigued to see Melissa observing her mother as if their roles had been reversed and Melissa was the doting mother.

Once they moved to the dining room, Bobby cut up Alma's food the same as every other day, and would have cut Pen's too but Pen insisted that Melissa do it. Melissa laughed and did it. She was very good-natured, lively and full of fun, somehow exotic with her beautiful features and long flowing hair. She changed the atmosphere, made everything lighter, more amusing. Pen was captivated by her, didn't want to let Melissa out of her sight. With anyone else, Bobby would have worried that Pen was making a nuisance of herself, but Melissa obviously liked her so Bobby didn't say anything.

Eva's friend Charlie was a nice man, friendly and relaxed. He was slim and not too tall, and looked really good in gray slacks with a white shirt, a striped tie and a navy blazer with gold buttons. He had beautiful hands, immaculate, with long tapering fingers. Bobby liked him. He was someone who listened with his eyes, who gave approval in his very manner. She could easily imagine going to him for medical help. He would, she thought, be sympathetic and understanding. He didn't seem the least bit uncomfortable being the only man present, but actually appeared to enjoy it. He teased Alma but Bobby could tell she didn't mind. And Eva was altogether different with him and Melissa around. The wine changed her, too. She moved more slowly and laughed often, getting flushed in the face when Melissa talked about her laundry and how her mother had fits every time she came home with another carful.

At Alma's urging, Bobby kept the music going, getting up to go to the stereo in the living room and change the records or cassettes. Penny ate two helpings of stuffing but very little of anything else, even though Bobby whispered to her to eat some of the white meat she'd asked for.

"Never mind, Bobby," Eva said. Then to Penny, "The stuffing's a lot more interesting than the turkey, isn't it?"

"I love stuffin'," Penny declared. "It's better even than ice cream." To Melissa she explained, "Dennis bought us ice cream at Baskin-Robbins."

"He did, hunh?" Melissa smiled over at Bobby.

"Yeah, after he took us to see the fish. And we saw a great big movie way high, higher than this whole house."

"You went to the Maritime Center, right?" Melissa said.

"That's *right*. You been there? It's really good."

"No, I haven't," Melissa said, "but I'd like to."

"I could go with you sometime," Penny said excitedly.

"Maybe we'll do that when I'm home for Christmas."

"Okay! And you know what else? Tomorrow Dennis is gettin' us *tacos!* I love tacos. You ever have them?"

"Yup. They're great," Melissa said.

Bobby kept her eyes on her plate, expecting somebody to comment on her and Pen's going out with Dennis, but no one did. Charlie asked Alma if she was doing her exercises, and Alma said, "This diminutive martinet has me laboring every afternoon."

"That's wonderful," Charlie said, and Bobby glanced up to see him smiling at her.

"She argues every time," Bobby said, then looked to see if Alma got mad, but she seemed pleased that Bobby was contributing to the conversation.

"Damned right I do," Alma concurred. "They're a colossal waste of time."

"You're just lazy," Charlie accused fondly.

Alma sniffed and speared some peas, forked them into her mouth.

"She could eventually get around with a walker," Charlie said, "if she keeps on with the exercises."

"That's great, Aunt Alma," Melissa began.

"I have no interest in a walker, thank you," Alma cut her off.

"Don't be silly," Melissa told her. "You wouldn't be stuck in that chair all the time. You'd be able to get around by yourself."

"I'm bored with the subject," Alma said gruffly. "I hope you brought your papers home for me to read, Melissa."

"I forgot. I'll bring them at Christmas. You'll have three weeks to go over them and argue with the grades the professors've given me. My aunt," she told Bobby and Charlie, "never agrees with my grades. She thinks my professors are all morons. And Mom," she went on with a laugh, "starts editing them, pointing out my run-on sentences and dangling participles. It's bad enough getting it at school without coming home to the resident critics." She shook her head and helped herself to the candied yams, saying, "Good grub, Mom."

Bobby swallowed some of the savory stuffing and said, "It's very good," and was rewarded with a smile from Eva. Their eyes held for a moment, then Bobby looked away, wondering where Joe was and what he was doing. He'd probably be at his mother's place, the two of them eating in silence, hating each other. She was intensely grateful not to have to be there, not to have to breathe in the thick risky air. Eight years of Thanksgiving and Christmas meals she'd choked down with Joe and his mother, making a tremendous effort to be pleasant, pretending nothing was wrong. Two days of suffering every year, on top of the ordinary days of anticipating blame and blows. It hadn't been a month yet but she felt as if she'd been away from Joe for a very long time. For the first time in years there were no bruises on her body, no aching tender spots that jabbed her into wakefulness when she tried to turn over in her sleep. She didn't have to be constantly on her guard, fearful of saying or doing something that would trigger an explosion. She was in the midst of clever, friendly people, being treated like part of the family. She was anxious to demonstrate her gratitude and once the meal was ended she immediately rose to begin clearing the dishes.

Eva said, "Don't bother," but Melissa got up, too, saying, "You sit and relax, Mom. You did the cooking. Bobby and I will clean up."

"Me too," Penny chimed in, climbing off her chair, insisting Melissa give her something to carry.

Eva reached for her wine and watched the three of them push through the swing door into the kitchen. She was intrigued by Melissa's reaction to Penny. For some reason she hadn't expected her to be as taken as she was with the child. It was a new aspect to her daughter, another in an endless series of revelations. Melissa was no longer a predictable child but an autonomous woman. Her views had been widening, deepening since her first week of college. Their time apart had been very good for Melissa; she had

acquired her own set of values, had honed her perceptions, and somehow turned the tables so that she now had
more of a fix on her mother than Eva had on her. Eva had
to admit Melissa had also acquired an impressive skill in
handling her, and she wondered if all children eventually
came to know their parents better than the parents knew
them. Certainly as a child, Eva's every move had been
predictable to Alma; she'd exercised an almost mystical
comprehension of the inner workings of Eva's mind. And
now Eva felt much of the time as if she could transcribe her
aunt's thoughts merely by watching her facial expres-
sions. Granted, since the stroke, it had become more difficult, transcribing as it were only half of her face. It had
to do with familiarity, Eva thought, and with long-term
exposure to all of someone's moods. And that only occurred within a family environment. In every other situation, people were performing to a lesser or greater extent,
usually in the hope of ingratiating themselves. Under the
table Charlie's hand stroked her knee, breaking her train
of thought, and she turned to look at him. She loved his
face, and tried for a moment to recall precisely when he'd
become so important to her.

"Delicious meal, cupcake."

"Thank you," she said, relishing the weight of his hand
and its gentle motion. There hadn't been a specific time,
she thought. Very gradually he'd become an emotional
focal point, as important to her in his own way as Melissa
and Alma were in theirs. It was intriguing the way one's
emotions could expand. They were pliant, adaptable, per-
plexing, and often ungovernable.

"First rate, Eva," her aunt said, with knowing eyes, so
that Eva had to wonder if she knew what Charlie was doing.

"Bobby made the dessert," Eva said, made languid by
the wine. Let her aunt enjoy her vicarious thrill, she
thought. There was little enough she enjoyed these days.
Eva wished she knew what she could say or do to bring

back the Aunt Alma who'd been her mother, the rather glamorous, always active Alma who'd had to keep track of her commitments in a large diary. The woman who sat facing her now at the far end of the table had Alma's intelligence but none of her energy or direction. It grieved her to witness her aunt's ongoing frustration and anger. The only relief in a year had come through Penny, and through Bobby. Eva could see that Bobby offered the same sort of challenge that Alma's students once had, and in small ways she was rising to the challenge. In cultivating what she viewed as Bobby's potential, Alma was finding a reason for surviving each day. Eva felt suddenly very glad of Bobby, and wondered if she hadn't had too much to drink. A glass or two of something alcoholic and she had a tendency to become very emotional. And very amorous, too. She wanted to bury her face in Charlie's neck and breathe in the warm fragrance of his cologne.

"I take it she and Dennis are dating," Charlie said quietly.

"I don't know that I'd call it dating," Eva said. "She's afraid of her own shadow. But he's harmless. They've gone out a couple of times."

"It's doing her good," Alma put in. "She needs to learn to trust people, and Dennis is certainly trustworthy."

"The little girl's adorable," Charlie said. "Smart as a whip. And Mel seems to be thriving at school."

"She loves it," Eva said. "She's already talking about graduate school, although she has no idea what she wants to do."

"Mark my words," Alma said. "She'll wind up a writer."

Eva laughed. "She thinks it's a dismal occupation. She's convinced I'm socially retarded because I spend my working days alone. She claims she'd rather do anything else."

"You *are* socially retarded," Alma said. "And she will wind up writing. It's all there. She has an indisputable gift."

"Don't say that in front of her," Eva cautioned. "You'll set her off. She'll go on for an hour about my pointless optimism and my perennial disappointment; she'll recite from memory every negative thing I've ever said about being a writer."

Penny came skipping in, asking, "What else?"

Eva gave her one of the smaller serving dishes and said, "Walk with it, Pen."

Penny turned sedately and walked very slowly to the door.

Charlie laughed and squeezed Eva's knee. Eva smiled at him, feeling pleasantly warm and slightly aroused. She moved her leg so that it was touching his. Her limbs felt wonderfully heavy and she looked at Charlie's mouth, feeling a jab of lust in the base of her belly. She wanted to slide under the table and pull him down after her. Picturing it, she smiled to herself. She was able to imagine herself performing all sorts of lewd acts but in reality was incapable of more than a bit of innocent, clandestine knee-touching. Why was there such a dichotomy between one's fantasies and one's actual capabilities?

Alma watched the two of them, suddenly terribly envious, missing her own life. A year ago she'd been someone else, active and on the go, still seeing men; she'd even slept with Bill Fitzgerald the week before the stroke. She hadn't felt or looked her age, and had believed it was her God-given right to go on being a fully functioning female, perhaps even into her eighties. She'd been seeing Bill on a fairly regular basis for close to two years, and she'd been more than fond of him. Then she'd awakened one morning as someone else, someone impaired and irrevocably altered. She'd awakened thinking she must've slept on her arm, and she'd tried to lift it, to shake the blood back into circulation. The horror had overcome her as the minutes had passed and the arm refused to move at her command; it had been compounded by her inability to leave her bed, and had been doubled and doubled again in the aftermath. But the ultimate horror had been the sight of her own face.

Bill had come once to see her in the hospital and had never returned. She didn't blame him; she was, in fact, glad. The horror he couldn't quite conceal had merely confirmed her own feelings. She'd become grotesque, a gargoyle on wheels. Now she couldn't see the point to life. She was merely biding her time, getting through the hours until another stroke or heart attack put an end to her. She wished she had the courage to do away with the monstrosity she'd become. But she didn't. Something—a lingering curiosity, perhaps, or an intrinsic tenacity—kept her holding on to a useless existence. Right then she wanted to shout at Eva and Charlie, to order them to behave in a more seemly fashion. And yet, what were they doing after all? They were simply physically aware of each other. But now that she herself was considerably less of a woman, she found herself irritated and faintly sickened by Eva's still healthy sexuality. It took some effort to contain her disdain, to relocate the mother love she'd had for so long for this woman who'd been her child. And then, having managed to contain herself, she was appalled by her meanness of spirit. Eva was still young. She deserved to have someone to love. She hadn't had an easy life.

In the kitchen, Bobby was making the coffee and organizing the dessert while Melissa rinsed the dishes and Penny put them into the dishwasher.

"You've very sweet to my aunt," Melissa told Bobby. "The others all treated her... professionally, kind of. But you're so patient and natural with her. I can tell how much she likes you."

"I like her," Bobby said quietly.

"I can see that," Melissa said. "You been a nurse long?"

"I'm not a real nurse."

"No kidding! You seem more like one than the rest of them. They all acted as if looking after my aunt was too much trouble. It was interfering with their lives."

"That's what Dennis said."

"So?" Melissa grinned. "Are you two an item, or what?"

Abashed, Bobby said, "We're just friends."

"Well, that's cool. He's a sweetie, Dennis." Seeing that the subject was making the woman uncomfortable, Melissa said, "You make the pies?"

"Uh-hunh."

"I thought so. Mom can't make pastry. She used to make quiche and she had to put the dough right in the pan and push it into shape with her hands. It tasted all right but it was always thick and lumpy. So, how're you making out with her anyway?"

"Oh, okay," Bobby said carefully.

"She can be tough," Melissa said objectively, trying to see her mother through Bobby's eyes. "But don't let her scare you. Half the time she's wandering around in a daze, her mind on the latest book. You can talk to her and it seems as if she's listening, but she's not really there. She's off in space, fitting things together. Sometimes it's as if the writing's more real to her than we are. Then, all of a sudden, she'll click back in, and she's completely different. You can actually see it happen. The thing is, she's okay, really, and basically very fair. She can just be kind of schizzy sometimes. What's amazing about her is, if you ask her something, she'll be totally, one hundred percent truthful, doesn't hold anything back. My friends were always hanging around our place when we lived in the city, having coffee and talking with my mom, because she was one of the few parents who'd give you straight answers to whatever you wanted to know. When I was about thirteen, it embarrassed the hell out of me. But now I can see how cool she really was. Hey, Pen! Good girl. We're all done." She bent down, grabbed Penny under the arms and swung her around. Penny giggled happily.

"It's hard to know how she's going to be from one day to the next," Bobby said, admiring Melissa's easy way with Pen.

"Tell me about it!" Melissa said, setting Penny down. "I never know what'll set her off. She's been a lot more mellow since she started seeing Charlie, though. Isn't he a *honey?* I'd kill to meet a guy like that. Most of the guys at school are so *young.* They make me feel positively middle-aged."

Bobby laughed at this.

"No, I'm serious," Melissa said. "There are a couple who're pretty cool but most of them are...*adolescent.* I don't know. At the rate I'm going I'll never get married."

"Would you like to?"

"Uh-hunh. I'd like to have a bunch of kids."

Bobby picked up the tray of cups and saucers, saying, "I'm sure you will."

"I don't know," Melissa said, handing Penny the sugar bowl. "I'm almost too discriminating. And intelligent women scare the crap out of men. Have you noticed that?"

"I wouldn't know," Bobby said.

"Oh, you must," Melissa insisted. "After all, you're intelligent. Haven't you found that men run for the hills?"

"I wouldn't know," Bobby said again softly.

Melissa gazed at her for a moment, then, realizing she'd just unwittingly stepped into uncertain territory, let the matter drop. "Well, anyway," she said, consciously moving onto safer ground, "I'm glad at least Mom's got herself someone like Charlie, who doesn't scare easily." She reached for the coffeepot, saying, "Let's get in there and have some of that pie. It looks fantastic."

When it came time, Penny didn't want to go to bed. "It's a holiday," she said. "I wanna stay up."

"It's already past your bedtime, Pen," Bobby said quietly.

"Tell you what!" Melissa said. "How about if I put you to bed?"

"*Yes!*" Penny cried. "You put me to bed."

"Okay with you?" Melissa asked Bobby.

"Sure, if you don't mind."

"It'll be good practice," Melissa said, scooping Penny up and carrying her off over her shoulder.

"You gotta give me a bath," Penny was saying as they went.

"She's gone positively wild over Melissa," Alma observed, looking up from the game of chess she was playing with Charlie.

"Seems like it," Bobby agreed.

"I think you've got me in a trap here," Charlie said, having studied the board for several minutes.

"Admit defeat," Alma said with a gruff chuckle. "I want to go up now. I'm tired."

"You didn't get your nap today," Eva said from the fireplace where she was lazily poking at the burning wood.

"I'm well aware of that," Alma snapped.

"I concede," Charlie said.

"It's as well that you do," Alma said. "A move in any direction and I'd have had you."

"Would you like anything before you go up?" Eva asked as Charlie began clearing the board and returning the pieces to their box.

"Not a thing," Alma said. "Come give me a kiss."

Eva crossed the room and embraced her aunt, murmuring, "You know you love me."

"Yes, I do," Alma admitted. "I'm just tired."

Bobby had put aside her knitting and stood at the ready by the wheelchair as Charlie thanked Alma for the game and bent to kiss her good night. "Thank you for including me today."

"It's always a pleasure to see you outside that damned office," Alma told him, then signaled to Bobby that she was ready to go.

When Bobby came downstairs half an hour or so later, Melissa was alone in the living room, smoking a cigarette.

"Mom and Charlie went for a walk," she said. "I hope you don't mind. I pinched one of your Marlboros."

"I don't mind." Bobby put away her knitting. "Thanks for putting Pen to bed. She give you any trouble?"

"Nope. She read me a story," Melissa said, grinning, "then I tucked her in and that was that. She's a sweetheart. I'm going to finish my smoke and head on up myself. I'm wiped."

"I'll go down, then," Bobby said. "Thanks again for looking after Pen."

In the apartment kitchen, Bobby sat down at the table and lit a cigarette, feeling rarely contented. It had been the best Thanksgiving since her childhood.

Twenty-Two

Melissa dreamed she was small again and she and her mom were on their way from the city to spend a weekend with Aunt Alma. It was spring and the Connecticut countryside was brilliant with color—blossoming dogwood trees in pink and white, azaleas of hot pink and orange and red, wisteria and lilac, tulips. Melissa looked out the car window, entranced. She always forgot how nice it was outside the city, how the air smelled better and people were friendlier.

Her mom had a small typewriter on her lap and was typing with one hand and steering the car with the other. Melissa wondered how she could do that and for a few moments watched her mother's fingers moving over the keyboard. Her mom wrote books and sometimes when her friends came over for dinner she would read them something she'd just written and her friends would sit quietly and listen. Melissa would hear her from her bedroom and think it was like being in school with the teacher reading out loud to the class. But her mom's friends got excited and they all started talking over each other the minute her mom finished reading.

Melissa thought writing books was a strange thing to do, not really work like other grown-ups did; it was just typing, but her mom did it all the time, even when they were driving somewhere in the car. "How come you're doing that now?" Melissa asked, annoyed, and her mother looked over and said, "I have to get this finished." Melissa turned to gaze out the window, thinking that writing was dumb and boring. You couldn't even talk to someone when they were doing it. They were getting near to Aunt Alma's house; she saw houses, streets she recognized.

Her aunt was in the back garden when they arrived, talking to some man who was building a high wall around the house. Melissa ran to give her a hug, asking, "How come you're building a wall?" and her aunt said, "There's too much light."

"But we won't be able to get to the beach," Melissa said, very bothered by the bricks and bags of cement on the lawn.

"There'll be a door," her aunt said.

Melissa's mother came across the grass carrying her typewriter in one hand and a big stack of papers in the other. She looked very angry, and said, "Where am I supposed to work if you do this?" And Aunt Alma said, "There's more to life than writing. Don't you ever put that damned machine down?"

They were going to argue and Melissa didn't want to hear, so she went into the house and saw that there were dolls sitting all along the counter. Excited, hoping this was a surprise intended for her, she went to pick one up. Behind her, her aunt bellowed, "Don't do that! They're being punished for unruly behavior."

Melissa said, "I'm sorry," and backed away, staring at the dolls and trying to imagine what they could have done wrong.

Then it was dark and she was in her nightgown, cuddling up in bed with Aunt Alma the way she always did when she and her mom came to visit. Aunt Alma was sitting on top of the covers wearing a low-cut red evening gown, and when Melissa asked where she was going, her aunt said, "You'll have to look after the baby while I'm gone."

What baby? Melissa wondered, and her aunt reached down and lifted a basket onto the bed to show Melissa the baby. "But where're you going?" Melissa asked her. "And how come Mom can't look after the baby?"

"I want *you* to do this," her aunt told her. "I know I can trust you."

"But you can trust my mom."

"This is our secret, Melissa. I don't want your mother to know."

That made sense. Melissa lay down on her aunt's bed with one hand on the basket and closed her eyes. When she opened them again she was standing on top of the new high brick wall at the back of the house, shading her eyes from the sun as she looked out at the Sound. There was a ladder close by and she climbed down it to the sand. She walked to the water's edge, testing the temperature with her foot. It was warm, very clear, and almost turquoise in color. She waded in and slid beneath the surface, then came up and floated on her back, looking at the wall. The ladder was gone, which meant she couldn't get back inside. But she realized she didn't have to worry. She knew where the secret door was.

Eva was thinking about that afternoon when they'd returned to the plantation after the brief trip to Crescent Bay. In the car on their way back, Eva said, "I have to go into town. There are a few things I need."

Deborah had looked over her shoulder to say, "Ian will take you. I've got to get Derek home and into some dry clothes." Then she'd stared pointedly at Ian until his eyes met Eva's in the rearview mirror and he gave her one of his sneering smiles, saying, "Happy to oblige."

But before they could go, she had to wait for Ian to change clothes. Deborah had promised to look after the children.

She stood by the open front door, wondering why it took Ian so long to do everything. She'd never encountered anyone who was as chronically late as this man. He was never on time. Except today, when he'd been waiting for them on the beach. How had he known they'd be coming right back? She could only guess it was because he'd realized that once Deborah discovered the crew hadn't been paid and wouldn't work until they had been, she'd have no choice but to turn around and come back. But why would he do something that was bound to be found out so quickly? Could it have just been a misunderstanding? She'd probably never know. Once the five of them got into the car, Ian and Deborah fell grimly silent.

Shading her eyes from the sun, Eva looked around. The weather had cleared and everything glowed now in brilliant shades of green. Turning, she could see Mellie and Derek playing on the grassy enclosure, kicking a ball back and forth and running, whooping, in circles. Deborah was sitting on the side of the concrete walk with a cigarette, arms folded on her knees, eyes following Mellie and Derek.

Had Eva realized it was going to take Ian so long, she'd have leaped at the chance to sit out there with Deborah. Maybe, while the children were occupied playing, she'd have been able to talk to her old friend. It was too late now, and Eva was grieved by yet another lost opportunity to make contact.

Ian came sauntering from the bedroom and, without a word, went out the door to the car, expecting Eva to follow. She slid into the passenger seat and barely had time to close the door before he was reversing wildly out of the driveway. He started down the steep road at a speed that alarmed and sickened Eva, barely slowing down as he made the turn onto the main road at the base of the mountain. They'd gone perhaps a mile when she asked if he'd mind not driving quite so fast. "I'm sorry," she said, "but I get carsick."

He didn't say anything but he did reduce his speed somewhat. Feeling queasy, she put her face close to the open window and breathed deeply, concentrating on not being sick.

As they approached the outskirts of town, he said, "I've got to make a quick stop, if you don't mind."

She said she didn't mind and he pulled up in front of a row of shops. As she watched, he went into the travel agency and, thinking that was odd, she sat back to wait. As the minutes passed she looked around the car, noticing something sticking out from under the floor mat on the driver's side. Curious, she ducked down, lifted the mat, and saw two passports. Checking to make sure Ian wasn't coming, she opened the passports. One was Ian's, the other was Derek's. She let the mat drop and sat up again, wondering what it meant. Passports and a travel agency. She was certain Deborah knew nothing about this; she hadn't said anything about their going anywhere.

At the chemist's shop, she bought tampons, aspirin, several rolls of toilet paper—she'd noticed there was none in the children's bathroom—a box of tissues, and a package of fruit-flavored hard candies for Derek and Melissa. Then they were back in the car and Ian was asking, "When is your book being published?"

"October," she answered, deciding she'd give it one more day, try one last time to talk to Deborah. If it didn't work out, she'd take Melissa and get off the island.

"Hmmn," Ian said. "Has it been sold outside America?"

"Actually, we've sold British, French, German, and Italian rights."

"Jolly good," he said, impressed. "Well done! One looks forward to reading it."

"I'll send you both a copy when it comes out."

"Hmmn, super."

Studying his Punch-like profile, trying but failing to suppress her dislike of this man, it came to her with sudden and unavoidable clarity that nothing she could say or do would have any effect on him or on Deborah. They'd embarked on a bizarre game with ugly rules and if her role was supposed to be as witness, she no longer cared to play.

She'd call BWIA when they got back to the plantation and make reservations.

Upon her return, Mellie greeted her as if she'd been gone for days. "Derek hit me!" she cried, seeking consolation. "He had to go to his room 'cause he was being bad."

"They rather got on each other's nerves," Deborah said. "Get everything you needed?"

"Stocked up on some toilet paper." Eva showed her, feeling foolish. Here she was, concerning herself with things like toilet paper in an effort to illustrate her caring. It was pathetic.

Deborah said, "Thank you, darling," and looked amused, as if she considered Eva's domesticity sweet but essentially stupid.

Eva debated whether or not to tell Deborah about the passports and Ian's trip to the travel agency. She felt like a tattletale child at the prospect. But Deborah deserved to know what was going on. Christ! What an impossible situation. "I'll just put my things away and get lunch for the children."

"That would be lovely," Deborah said vaguely. "What's he doing in the garage?" she wondered aloud, and went through to the kitchen. She was calling down the steps as Eva took Melissa with her to the bedroom.

"I wanna go home," Melissa said, sitting on the side of the bed while Eva put away her purchases. She'd save the candy for later.

"We'll be going in two days," Eva told her. "Come here and let me wash your hands and face."

Should she say something or not? It nagged at her as she fed the children. Friends again, Mellie and Derek ran to ride the tricycle and Eva sat out on the veranda and considered the possible repercussions of telling. It might be nothing at all in Deborah's eyes, like that business with the gun, and Deborah would be annoyed with her for making something of it. Or it might be very important, and she'd be grateful.

Deborah came out with a cup of tea and sat on the railing. "Another wasted bloody day," she said, gazing into the distance.

"Look," Eva said very quietly, "it probably doesn't mean anything, but I thought I'd mention..." Quickly she told Deborah about finding the passports and Ian's stop at the travel agency. Deborah listened closely, her eyes riveted to Eva's.

"That bastard," she said in an infuriated whisper. "Thank you, darling." Leaving her tea on the floor, she ran barefoot through the kitchen and down the stairs to the garage. She was gone for several minutes. When she returned, she lit a cigarette, retrieved her cup, and whispered, "I know what he's up to. He'll have to kill me first."

Eva could feel her body tense and knew she couldn't go any further with this. Anxiety made her innards twist. She got out of bed and stood in the dark sweating, the bones in her neck creaking as she reached for her robe.

In the kitchen she went to the refrigerator and poured a glass of orange juice, then stood leaning against the counter as she drank it, her eyes on the apartment door, which stood open an inch or two. She could smell cigarette smoke and knew Bobby was sitting down there in the dark. The glass cool in her hand, she tried to think how she could get Bobby to confide in her. She badly wanted to hear the details of Bobby's life as a battered wife.

Alma lay in the dark thinking about Eva and Charlie, feeling in her bones that the two of them were bound to get married. She only hoped Eva didn't allow inconsequential considerations to get in the way of something that would be good for her. Eva had a tendency to get derailed by issues that had no real bearing on what was going on. Like getting annoyed at Melissa's bringing her laundry home, allowing a minor irritation to spoil her pleasure in seeing her daughter again. It would be an enormous mistake to let Charlie go. And she wondered once again if she herself hadn't made the greatest mistake of her life in turning down Howard Kramer's proposal of marriage. Simply thinking of him now made her smile to herself. Of all the men she'd known in the years after Randy Wheeler went on his way, Howard was the one she'd liked best.

They'd met when Howard brought his twin daughters to the school for the requisite interview prior to admission. It was immediately plain to her that the man had an extraordinarily close and loving relationship with his children. He'd sat back, allowing the girls to speak for themselves, quietly confident that they would be able to represent themselves. Alma had found him a refreshing contrast to the majority of parents who too often spoke for their children, as if fearful the girls would say the wrong things, thereby reducing their chances for acceptance.

Not Howard. A widower who with the help of a housekeeper had raised his girls since their mother's death when they were four-year-olds, he'd demonstrated rare tolerance and understanding. Alma had been very taken with the girls and had, in due course, accepted them into the ninth grade class. During their four years at the school Alma encountered Howard Kramer on parents' nights and sundry other functions. And each time she was impressed anew by his radiant pride and deep affection for his children. He harbored no unreasonable expectations for them, never resorted either to bribery or threats to force them to achieve higher grades, but professed that as long as they were doing their best he couldn't ask for more. He said he wanted his girls to be happy, and he meant it.

A week after the twins graduated, he telephoned Alma at the school and asked her out. Surprised and pleased, she accepted. Over dinner he admitted that he'd considered asking her out soon after their initial meeting but confessed with a self-deprecating laugh that he'd imagined she was bound by professional ethics not to socialize with the parents of her students. "I had the idea," he'd told her, "that it was tantamount to a doctor dating one of his patients."

He hadn't been entirely wrong, she'd told him. "But it's a personal ethic, not necessarily a professional one. I've always thought it wise not to mix business with pleasure."

"So I was right," he said, gratified. "And now that the girls are no longer at the school, I can finally get to know you."

She liked his integrity, his sense of humor, his looks, and his understated elegance. Howard was a wealthy man, having inherited a great deal of money in his early twenties along with a furniture company he'd built into an even bigger success than his father and grandfather before him. At the time of their first date he'd agreed to become chief executive officer and leave the day-to-day running of the company to a nephew he'd been grooming for the presidency.

"Now," he told Alma that evening. "I've got the time to do the things I want." He wanted to travel and play golf and tennis; he wanted to read all the classics and go to concerts at Lincoln Center; he wanted to take a cooking course and to learn Spanish; and he wanted someone in his life whose interests coincided with his.

"I don't think you'll have a problem finding someone," she'd said, imagining that women would line up to have a crack at this man.

"Well, now, you see," he'd said, "I do have a problem. And I have a hunch it's the same problem you have. I'm just not happy having another body handy. I want the body to have a brain, too."

She'd had to smile because he wasn't far wrong. She was forty-two at the time. Eva was away at college. And she, too, had been thinking about traveling.

She always thought that if he'd asked her sooner she might very well have said yes. But they were together for eight years before Howard raised the subject of marriage for the first time. And by then, although she was tempted, she couldn't help feeling it was too late. It would be best, she decided, to continue on as they were. Why change something that was close to perfect? She did give it a great deal of thought, but in the end she simply said, "I don't see the point."

Howard, astonishingly, was crushed. He took it as a personal rejection. She was flabbergasted by his reaction. Instead of being content to continue on, Howard framed his response in the form of an ultimatum. Either they married, or they called it a day. It was the first and only indication in eight years of that ludicrous emotional chasm she'd come to think of as male pride. Saddened, seeing the situation as nonsensical, she'd had to hold her ground. She really didn't see the point. Why, after so many years, did he suddenly feel the need to be married? And why was he willing to toss aside a relationship that was successful on every level? It made no sense to her, but he was inflexible. He got a look on his handsome face that she'd never seen him wear before. His chin outthrust, brows drawn slightly together, eyes dark with disappointment, he reiterated his position. She tried to jolly him out of it, pointing out all they'd both be losing. He found her attempts at concilia-tion somewhat insulting. Suddenly, after eight years of harmonious interchange, she couldn't get through to him. She'd said no. Therefore it was over. Howard refused even to contemplate the middle ground. They parted with her saying they'd talk further once they'd both had a chance to sleep on it. But when she called the next afternoon, he was chilly and distant. She'd rejected him. It was over.

Had she been as inflexible as he? she asked herself now, reviewing that final absurd conversation. Perhaps. But in the long view, she'd probably been right. That damnable male pride would have revealed itself at some stage, and she thought it far better to have met it head on when she did rather than a year or two into a marriage. There was no question that she'd have found its appearance later on every bit as ridiculous and unacceptable as she did then, and she'd have removed herself from the situation later rather than sooner. Still, it had been splendid while it lasted. And every now and then she did miss him. But it was a toss-up as to what she found more irritating: silly females or pride-bound males.

Penny announced she wanted to stay home with Melissa.

"But Dennis'll be disappointed," Bobby said, although the truth was she herself would feel safer with Penny along. She looked at Melissa to see how she was responding to all this.

"I've got reading to do for school, sweetie," Melissa said. "You go with your mom and Dennis. I'll still be here when you get back. I'm not leaving till tomorrow morning."

"Will you put me to bed again?" Penny asked her.

"Now, Pen," Bobby said, "don't go making a pest of yourself."

"Sure I will," Melissa said.

"You promise?"

"Promise."

"And a bath too," Penny reminded her.

Melissa laughed and said, "A bath too."

"Okay," Penny said and, turning to her mother, announced, "I wanna wear my new clothes."

"Okay, but we're going to have to hurry. Dennis'll be here in a few minutes."

"I'll hurry," Penny said, and flew toward the apartment door. "Come on, Mom!"

When Dennis arrived, Penny insisted he admire her new clothes, turning in a circle for him.

"Fabulous," he said. "You hungry, kiddo?"

"Yup."

"What about Mom?" he said to Bobby. "All set to try more new food?"

Busy getting Penny into her coat, Bobby smiled up at him.

As they were waiting to cross the street from the parking lot to the restaurant, Dennis said, "Hey! I forgot to say hello properly," and kissed Bobby on the cheek.

Embarrassed, she glanced at Penny, but Penny seemed to think nothing of it. On edge now, her uneasiness was compounded when he took her arm as they crossed the street. He let go once they reached the other side, and she forced herself not to look around. Joe was hundreds of miles away. No one else would care. She imagined that to the other people on the street they looked like a couple taking their little girl out for Mexican food. Joe had refused to take Penny out to a restaurant even when Bobby had said she'd pay. "I'm not having no kid making a fuss in public," he'd said. So Bobby had taken Penny out a few times when she'd known for sure Joe would be out for the evening. And Penny had loved it; she'd behaved perfectly.

Once they were seated with menus, Dennis said, "Try a margarita. They're terrific here."

"C'n I have one too?" Penny asked him.

"They're for grown-ups. But we'll get you a Shirley Temple. How's that?"

"Okay." Penny sat back and began reading the menu, sounding out the Spanish words under her breath. "Tor-ti-lah, en-chil-a-dah, taco, chicken mole." Her brow furrowing, she asked, "What kind of animal is a chicken mole?"

Dennis laughed. "It's mole-ay," he explained, reaching across the table to pinch Penny's cheek.

"Well, it *says* mole," Penny insisted indignantly.

"I know, hon," Bobby told her. "But it's Spanish and the words are said differently."

"I want tacos," Penny declared.

"What should I have?" Bobby asked Dennis, for the first time feeling a closeness to him. He'd yet to show any sign of a darker side to his nature. And he was so kind and patient with Pen.

"How about if I order for you?" he suggested.

"That'll be fine." Bobby opened her bag for a Marlboro and Penny made a face at her, saying, "Smokin's bad." She waved her hand at the smoke. "It's stinky, too."

"It's not as if I smoke that much," Bobby defended herself. "I only have a few a day."

"Don't pick on your mom, Pen," Dennis said gently. "That's not nice."

Penny looked at him, then at her mother, then back at him, trying to decide how to respond. At last, she said, "Okay. But don't blow the smoke at me. It's stinky."

"I don't mind it," Dennis said, resting his arm on the back of Bobby's chair. "Now, cigars are stinky," he said to Pen. "Ever smell one of those?"

She shook her head.

"Believe me, cigars are bad."

The waitress came, and he ordered their drinks and a platter of nachos, then turned to Bobby to say, "Nachos are my weakness. And hot salsa." Pointing to the two containers on the table, he explained, "This green stuff'll dissolve your tongue, but the red's not too bad. It'll just temporarily paralyze your vocal cords."

Bobby laughed again. "Really?"

"No kidding." He put a dab of the green salsa on his spoon and held it out to her, saying, "Taste."

Fairly staggered by the intimacy of the gesture but determined to behave in front of Pen as if everything were normal, she touched her tongue to the spoon. At once her mouth burned and she quickly drank some water. "You weren't kidding," she said. "That's wicked."

"I stick with the red," he said, offering Penny a tortilla chip from the basket on the table.

Penny took one and bit into it, turning in her seat to look around the restaurant. A woman at a table across the way smiled at her and Penny waggled her fingers, then looked again at Dennis and her mother. "How come that lady smiled at me?"

"Because you're so cute," Dennis said, "and because you look so nice in your new clothes."

"Oh!" Pleased, Penny took another bite of her tortilla chip. "I like it here."

"Good, I'm glad," Dennis said. "What about you, Mom?"

"It's very nice," Bobby said softly, taking another puff of her cigarette, thinking that ordinary families did things like this every day of the world. They took their kids out to restaurants, and talked and laughed together. It felt good. She was conscious of Dennis's arm on the back of her chair but she didn't really mind.

"I can make chocolate chip cookies," Penny said.

"You can? Are you going to make me some?" Dennis asked.

"Uh-hunh. I'll make 'em on Sunday. You gonna come on Sunday?"

"I don't know. I'll have to ask your mom."

Bobby said, "I guess that'd be okay. But only for a couple of hours. I have to work, you know," she addressed Penny.

"Maybe I'll swing by for coffee," he said. "I don't want to wear out my welcome."

"That'll be okay," Bobby said, able to tell that he wanted to come. She was getting used to him, and he was good for Penny.

"Tell you what, kiddo. I'll bring over my VCR and we'll watch a movie. You do have a TV, don't you?"

"Uh-hunh. What movie?"

"Ever see *E. T.?*"

Penny said, "No."

"All right. We'll watch *E. T.* You'll like it." To Bobby he said, "I know it's dumb, but I love that movie. Did you see it?"

"I haven't been to a movie in a long time."

"Okay," he said. "Sunday, two o'clock. Chocolate chip cookies and a movie. Great."

When they arrived back at the house, Penny gave Dennis a big hug, then said, "I gotta go now. Melissa's puttin' me to bed." She ran to the door, calling out to Melissa before she even got it open.

Dennis laughed. "Looks like she's really taken with Melissa."

"She sure is," Bobby agreed. "Well," she said, awkward again now that she was alone with him, "thanks for the dinner. It was great." He moved closer, casting his shadow over her. It was like drowning. All at once she couldn't get enough air, and there was nowhere to go.

"I'm glad you had a good time," he said, and put his hand under her chin, tipping her face up so that she had to look at him. "I like being with the two of you."

"Penny likes you real well," she said, trapped with him in front of her and the car at her back.

He dropped his head—she watched it happening as if in slow motion—and he kissed her on the mouth. His lips were very soft and he didn't push himself at her but kissed her lightly, then ran his hand over her hair. She didn't know what to do, and hoped he'd let her go now. She wanted to get away.

"Do I interest you at all?" he asked, so close she could smell the soap he'd washed with.

"You're very nice," she said, not knowing what he wanted her to say.

"Just as a friend?" he asked. "Or maybe as something more?"

"What does that mean, something more?"

He smiled. "You know," he said. "Sparks, chemistry. All that good stuff."

"Sex, you mean?" Her mouth was too dry.

"Sure. I find you very attractive."

"I don't like it much," she said, wishing he'd drop this and leave.

"Maybe you've just had bad experiences. Not that I claim to be all that great or anything." He laughed softly and again ran his hand over her hair.

"I got beat up and hurt all the time," she said. "I guess that's a bad experience."

"That's terrible," he said, letting his hands fall to his sides and taking a step back so that she had more breathing room. "I don't understand guys who get off on that. It's sick."

"I better go in now."

"You're scared," he said, "but I'm not someone who'd ever hurt you."

"No, I know that."

"You want me to back off?" he asked. "I can do that, although I really do like spending time with you and Pen. It's up to you," he said. "This kind of situation's new to me. I don't want to go scaring anybody."

He was saying he'd leave her alone, he'd stop taking her and Pen out, and she asked herself if that was what she wanted. It didn't seem to be. It felt as if she'd miss him. "I need to get to know you," she said. "I only ever went with Joe, and that turned out to be really bad. He liked to...to *do* things, you know? Things that hurt. Knives and guns, treating me like an animal." She saw herself on her hands and knees and felt shame, thick as glue, wash over her. "But I like you," she admitted with a pain in her throat. "It's just hard for me. You know?"

"I think I understand," he said quietly. "I won't rush you into anything."

"No," she said. "You can't do that. I do get scared. I've never talked about any of this, not to anybody, not even when I took Pen and went to the shelter. I was too ashamed." She wanted to lower her eyes but forced herself to keep on looking at him. He looked sad and sorry.

"We'll take it slowly," he said. "Okay? And see how it goes."

"Okay," she said, shaky with relief. "I really have to go in now."

"Are we still on for Sunday?"

"If you want to," she said.

He smiled and said, "I've never done anything the easy way in my entire life. Let me give you a hug." He waited and when she didn't object, he put his arms around her and, with his mouth close to her ear, said, "I won't hurt you." Then he released her, smiled, and went over to the Beetle.

She waited at the door until he drove off, then went inside feeling somewhat stunned. His hug had been very comforting, unexpectedly reassuring. It had made her feel protected and cared for—something she hadn't felt since before her grandfather was taken ill. As she hung up her coat, she couldn't help thinking that things were going to turn out better than she'd ever dared hope.

Unwilling to take any time off from work yet—the last thing he needed was the fucking foreman chewing out his ass—he'd been sitting night after night watching the house, waiting for an opportunity to get inside. He'd already checked around and found a basement window that'd give with one good push. Now he wanted goddamned Helen to go out so he could whip in and find something that'd tell him where Bobby was. He didn't doubt for a moment that there was something. It was just a matter of finding it.

But the bitch never went anywhere and he was freezing his balls off sitting in the car every night, watching, waiting. The more time he spent on this, the more determined he was to get into the house. And if she didn't go out sometime soon he was going to have to march up to the door and force her to tell him. He'd just ring the bell and when she came to the door he'd show her the gun, put an end to all this bullshit.

Thanksgiving Day he was supposed to go to his goddamned mother's place. It was the last thing he wanted to do, but the house was so damned depressing these days that he didn't want to sit there all day and eat a lousy frozen pizza for dinner, so when his mother called him at work demanding to know was he coming or not, he told her he'd come eat turkey with her as usual. "You might've taken five minutes to call and let me know," she'd complained, "instead of making me have to call you." The foreman was giving him a look and he'd felt like telling both of them, the foreman and his goddamned mother, to go fuck themselves, but he didn't. And now the old lady was expecting him. Why the hell couldn't he ever say no to her? He always meant to, but as soon as he heard her voice on the telephone asking was he coming or not, or would he put up the storm windows or shovel the stinking snow off her front walk, he said okay, as if this time she might actually thank him or say something halfway pleasant to him. Which made him a total asshole, because no way would she ever have two good words to say. So he was go-

ing to have to spend Thanksgiving with her. But first he'd cruise past Helen's house, park for a while to see if she'd maybe finally be going out.

He got there around eleven in the morning and settled in to wait, cleaning his fingernails with his pocketknife, checking the house every couple of minutes. The street was dead, nothing happening. This thing was driving him nuts. If he didn't get in there today he'd have to get in after the holiday when the bitch was home. He'd had enough of this, every goddamned night. He was wasting half his life on this shit.

Just before one o'clock, Helen's Escort backed out of the driveway. This was it! Excited, he slid down low in the seat so she wouldn't see him, and waited till the car had driven off. This was it. No way was she going to the market or anything like that because everything was closed. She had to be going to her boss's place like she did every year, which meant she'd be gone for hours. This was his chance.

He got out of the Firebird, checked the street, crossed over, ducked along the side of the house, dropped down, gave the basement window one good shove and pushed it in. Open. Another quick look around. Then he crawled inside, landed feet first on the cement floor, took the time to push the window shut. He was so excited he almost laughed out loud. This was easy. There was enough light for him to see and he crossed over, climbed the stairs, stood at the top listening, his heart hammering so hard he could hear it in his ears like footsteps. Annoyed with himself—what the hell was this nervous-type crap?—he listened for one minute, two. Nothing. Hands sweaty, he turned the knob and stepped into the kitchen. He was in. Again he wanted to laugh out loud.

He started in her bedroom, checked the drawer of the night table, the top of the dresser. Nothing. He went through each drawer, being careful to leave everything the way he found it, then the closet, looking in pockets, in the *purses on the shelf above, all the time those damned foot-steps hammering away in his ears. If she suddenly came home for some reason he'd be fucked, because he'd left the gun home. Which was so goddamned dumb he could hardly believe it. The last thing he needed was to have her turn up and catch him there. She'd have him arrested again.*

Moving fast, he looked through the living room, then the kitchen, around the phone, the wall calendar, checked out a bunch of bills, her address book, went through it cover to cover. Nothing under Bobby or Salton. Just the old address and phone number. He opened every drawer in the kitchen, even looked on top of the refrigerator. Not a fucking thing. If she'd written anything down she had to be carrying it around, probably in her purse. He'd gone through all this for zip, wasted hours, days. Jesus! Maybe Bobby had gone off without telling anybody where she was. But he didn't believe that. He knew her. No way she'd go without letting her goddamned aunt know she was okay.

He let himself out the back door, slipped along the side of the house, made it back to the car, where he pounded his fists on the steering wheel, incensed. He started the engine and sat glaring at the house, tempted to go back in, get a fire going in the cellar and burn the fucking place down. Instead, he forced himself to drive away slowly, so as not to call any attention to himself—the last thing he needed was some nosy fucking neighbor telling the old bitch some guy in a Firebird had come nosing around the house—kept his speed down until he hit the main drag, then let his foot down on the accelerator and headed home. He had to get cleaned up to go eat with his mother. The thought of spending hours in that house with her made his stomach knot. He should've told her to go fuck herself, he wasn't coming—ever again. He didn't owe her jack shit.

While he was in the shower, he tried to think of what else he could possibly do. Not a goddamned thing. Either he

*found out from Helen where Bobby was, or he gave up.
Brought down by his wasted search of the house, he told
himself to give up, forget it. With Bobby gone he had a
shitload more money; he didn't have to put up with that
pain-in-the-ass kid of hers; he could do whatever he
damned well wanted. He sure as shit didn't need her. She
couldn't do anything right, wasn't even a decent lay. But
it bugged the hell out of him. He just couldn't let it go.*

*He got to his old lady's place by four and waited for her
to say something, make some crack about how Bobby had
taken off on him. But she didn't. She sat in the fusty-
smelling living room with the TV going and didn't say
squat. He sat there with her, depressed, thinking he was
going to have to force Helen to tell him what he wanted to
know. And then, when she'd told him, he'd take her out.
Otherwise she'd have the cops on his ass, and she'd warn
Bobby he was coming for her. No two ways about it, he
thought, firing up a smoke to get the crummy smell of the
house out of his nose. He was going to have to whack
Helen. The more he thought about it, the more logical it
seemed. But he'd take his time. He'd plan it down to the
last detail. He'd let Bobby think she was getting away with
it, then he'd catch her when she least expected it.*

Twenty-Three

Everyone was taken aback by Penny's reaction to Melissa's departure. The little girl sobbed and clung to Melissa's long skirt, begging her not to go.

Melissa knelt down to hold Penny, telling her with a smile, "I'll be back in a few weeks for the Christmas break, sweetie."

"I don't want you to *go!*" Penny wailed, grinding small fists into her eyes, her body rigid.

"I've got to," Melissa told her. "But it's not for long. You'll see. I'll be back before you know it."

"Come on, Pen," Bobby said. "Melissa's got to leave now. She's got a long drive back to school. Come on, hon."

With great reluctance, her chest still heaving with sobs, Penny allowed herself to be lifted into her mother's arms, and she laid her head on Bobby's shoulder, refusing now to look at Melissa.

"I'll see you very soon," Melissa said, offering Bobby an apologetic smile as she patted Penny's back.

Penny kept her head down, her face hot on Bobby's shoulder, as Melissa said good-bye to her aunt and her mother.

Alma, mightily impressed by Penny's misery, looked deep into her great-niece's eyes with increased respect for Melissa's maternal instincts, then kissed her good-bye, saying, "You've made a conquest."

"I feel awful," Melissa admitted. "Will she be all right?"

"She'll be fine," Alma assured her, intrigued by Penny's anguish and by Bobby's equanimity. She displayed no jealousy of Melissa, nor was she upset by her daughter's passion for someone else. Rather, she behaved as if it were Pen's right to form attachments and all she could do as the girl's mother was attempt to console her. It was an intriguing new aspect to Bobby's personality, one of which Alma approved.

Wondering if perhaps Penny was feeling abandoned, Eva walked out with Melissa to the Toyota and watched her load the last of her bags into the trunk, saying, "Drive carefully, and call to let me know you've arrived safely."

As if still humoring Penny, Melissa said, "Yes, Mother. I will, Mother. Don't worry, Mother." She smiled at Eva with amusement.

Eva hugged her, saying, "What did you do to that child? She's positively bereft."

"I don't know," Melissa said somewhat doubtfully. "That was really something, wasn't it?"

"I imagine she's seen a lot of unpleasant things in her short life," Eva said. Then, aware of Melissa's confusion, told her, "I'll fill you in when you get home again. Penny'll be all right. Don't worry about her. Be careful," Eva said again.

"Lighten up, Eva," Melissa teased, climbing behind the wheel and fastening her seat belt. "I'll call you tonight." She started the engine, then said, "Why don't you take Penny with you to the pool this afternoon? I'll bet she'd love that."

Eva's immediate reaction was annoyance. She had enough to do on these Saturday afternoon outings, what with getting her aunt dressed and undressed, and in and out of the pool, without the additional burden of supervising a six-year-old. But then, considering it, she thought Melissa was probably right. It would take Penny's mind off her upset. Shivering with the cold, she waved until the Toyota was out of sight, then returned inside to see how Bobby would feel about Penny's going with them to the Y.

At once Penny declared, "I wanna go!" and it seemed her sorrow at Melissa's departure had been forgotten. "C'n I go, Mom?"

"Are you sure it's not going to be too much trouble?" Bobby asked Eva.

"We'll manage," Eva said curtly, anxious to have the matter settled. She loathed belaboring points, and Bobby seemed congenitally unable to take certain things at face value.

"Well, okay," Bobby said. "But I'm going to have to run out and get her a bathing suit. It won't take me long."

"That'll be fine," Eva said. "You go ahead and do that."

As excited now as she'd been forlorn minutes before, Penny was already running to get her coat, urging Bobby to hurry up. Thrown as always by the contradictory aspects of Eva's nature, Bobby went for her purse, not at all certain Eva actually wanted to do this.

But when they returned from the shopping center and Bobby ventured to ask Eva again, "Are you sure it'll be okay?" Eva quite sharply said, "I *told* you I didn't mind. I wouldn't have suggested it otherwise."

"If it's okay," Bobby said very quietly, "why're you getting so mad?"

"When I say I'll do something," Eva answered, "I very much dislike being asked if I'm sure about it. I don't say things simply for the sake of hearing myself talk. You really must learn to take me at my word."

"That's hard to do," Bobby said, "when you act so mad."

"I'm not mad," Eva declared firmly but with a smile. "I wish you could accept things as they are. I am not in the habit of saying things I don't mean. And by the way, before I forget, I've got a health insurance application for

you to fill out.'' She got the file from the top of the refrigerator and placed it on the table. ''The sooner we get this
in, the sooner you and Penny will have coverage.''

''Okay,'' Bobby said, eyes on the application.

''As I told you at the outset, I'll pay half the premiums.''

''Okay.''

''I'm *not* mad,'' Eva insisted, wishing Bobby would stop
behaving like a whipped dog. ''Don't you think if I were
I'd tell you?''

''I don't know if you would,'' Bobby said, meeting her
eyes.

''Well, I would,'' Eva told her. ''I know I'm not like
anyone else you're used to, and I know I often give the
impression of being angry when I'm not, but I think
you've been here long enough now to know that I mean
what I say. Penny needs a little distraction, so I'll take her
with us this afternoon. If I thought it was too much trouble, I wouldn't have suggested it. Tell me something,'' she
said, pausing to catch her breath. ''Have you always been
like this?''

''Like what?''

''So in need of reassurance,'' Eva said.

''Mostly I'm like that with you,'' Bobby admitted.
''And with Dennis, a bit. But that's different.''

''I'm sure it is.'' Eva laughed, and at once regretted it.
''Don't take that the wrong way,'' she said quickly. ''I
didn't mean anything by it. It's just that dealing with men
is always different. Look, I'm going up to the office for a
couple of hours. Don't forget to fill out that application.
All right?''

''All right.''

''By the way, does Penny know how to swim?''

''Uh-hunh.''

''Well, good. Fine.''

''It's really nice of you to take her,'' Bobby said.

"It's nothing," Eva said dismissively. "It'll give you some time to yourself. We all need that."

"I guess so," Bobby said.

Eva took some chicken breasts from the freezer and set them on a plate on the counter to defrost, then left. Bobby stood for a few minutes listening to the silence of the house. Alma was in the living room reading the *Times*. Penny was downstairs in her new bathing suit watching cartoons on TV. The house felt all at once lifeless without Melissa. It seemed that Eva was as distressed in her own way as Penny was in hers by Melissa's leaving. That's what it was, she decided, heading downstairs to the apartment. That's how come Eva got so sharp with her.

That afternoon while they were gone, Bobby drove over to the supermarket to get the ingredients for chocolate chip cookies. And then, giving in to an impulse she didn't stop to analyze, she bought Eva a bouquet of yellow daisies.

As she drove home, she thought about Eva and decided they were, one way or another, working things out between them. She was no longer quite so crushed by Eva's mood-swings; she was beginning to make sense of the woman.

Eva knew now she wasn't going to go back to the book, but she couldn't bring herself to take the final step and erase the disks. Five minutes would do it, and the whole thing would be over. She stood for some time staring at the computer, then at the disks. Turn on the machine, depress a couple of keys, and that would be that. But she couldn't seem to take that final step. Giving up, she went over to slouch in the armchair and gaze out the window.

Alma hated leaving the house. In public, she felt as if everyone were staring at her, pitying her for her too-visible disabilities. And so, except for her visits to Charlie's office, she refused to go out. The weekly trip to the pool, however, was tolerable because for an hour she was returned to a satisfying state of renewed mobility and independence.

Once in the water, she was capable of functioning unaided. With Eva sitting in her swimsuit on the side of the pool keeping watch, and with Penny eagerly dog-paddling next to her, Alma side-stroked her way from one end of the long pool to the other. Usually, for the time it took her to do ten lengths, she allowed her mind to drift, but today she kept her pace slow and watched Penny.

The child chugged along grinning, as visibly happy in the water as Alma was, her small limbs churning beneath the surface, utterly unafraid. When they arrived at the deep end, Alma said, "We'll have a little rest, then swim back."

One hand clinging to the pool's edge, Penny stayed afloat by slowly scissor-kicking her legs. "I *love* swimmin', don't you Granny?"

"Yes, I do," Alma agreed. "You swim very well."

"Yeah." Penny beamed. "I was the best of the tadpoles. The teacher said so. My mom used to take me every Sunday morning. C'n I come all the time with you?"

"I don't see why not." Alma allowed herself to float motionlessly, anchored by her hand to the pool's side.

"I can do three whole lengths," Penny said proudly. "I got a junior badge and I was the littlest one in the entire class."

"That's wonderful."

"Yeah. I c'n do *life*savin' and everything."

Alma chuckled, charmed by the child's enthusiasm. "Shall we head back to the other end now?"

"Uh-hunh." Penny pushed off, and after a moment Alma followed.

After completing a third length, Penny was tired and said, "I'm gonna watch for a while. Okay?"

Alma watched the child pull herself out of the pool, then said, "Why don't you go keep Eva company?"

Her chest heaving, Penny huffed, "Okay," and got to her feet.

Alma watched until Penny was safely seated next to Eva, then she turned onto her back and began kicking her way down the length of the pool.

Comfortable in the water, pleased by her buoyant power, she gazed at the ceiling and indulged as she did each week, in the fantasy that she'd been restored to herself and was no longer someone whose physical appearance distressed strangers and prompted them to offer assistance she didn't want or need. In this pool she was once more her own person. She could ignore the sympathetic eyes of the women in the changing room, who saw her being dressed and undressed by her niece. Don't waste your pity, she wanted to rage at them. Once I'm in that damned pool I'll be every bit as good as you are, possibly better.

Completing one lap and commencing another she wondered, as she did every week, why the general population was so intimidated by the visible disabilities of others, why they so often reacted as if proximity to her handicap might prove contagious. Only very young children, and occasionally someone elderly, addressed her as if cognizant of the human being warehoused behind the altered edifice. She too had been guilty in the past of seeing flawed surfaces first and the essential humanity second. But at last she'd recognized the common denominators. Now she was on the receiving end of those curious and apprehensive stares, and she wanted every time to shout, as the Elephant Man had done, that she was not an animal. Rather than risk succumbing to the temptation, she stayed out of sight.

By the time she'd finished her ten lengths she was contentedly tired and grateful for Eva's help getting out of the pool.

"You're a real good swimmer, Granny," Penny said, taking hold of her hand as they headed for the changing room. "I was watchin'."

Winded, Alma gave her hand a squeeze and geared her-self for the ignominious business of being dried and dressed and bundled off home.

"Auntie Eva says I c'n come next week too," Penny told her.

"Good," Alma said, and glanced at Eva to see that she appeared distracted again.

Penny hopped into a stall to shower and, relieved that she didn't have to oversee the child as well as her aunt, Eva quickly and efficiently got herself and Alma showered. She knew her aunt strongly disliked this aspect of their weekly outing and wasted no time in getting her through it. She was as matter-of-fact as she was able to be, having learned that undue solicitousness enraged Alma. She wanted as little attention as possible paid to her within the viewing range of others.

As they were heading home, Penny spotted a Mc-Donald's and asked, "C'n I have a milkshake?"

"I'm afraid not," Eva said.

"I've got money," Penny told her, fishing in her pocket for her plastic change purse.

"Aunt Alma likes to go directly home after her swim," Eva explained, looking into the rearview mirror at her aunt.

"But we could go in the drive-thru," Penny said, squirming to look back between the seats at her granny.

"I'll survive it," Alma said to Eva's surprise. "Let Penny get a milkshake."

Knowing better than to question her, Eva signaled for the turn.

"Thanks, Granny," Penny crowed.

"Maybe I'll have one too," Alma said.

Amazing, Eva thought, but kept silent. Penny had ac-tually managed to get Alma to venture, however periph-erally, back into public.

* * *

Upon returning from the Y, Eva put the wet towels and suits in the washing machine while Bobby got Alma upstairs for her nap. Setting the controls, she told herself it was time to erase the disks. She was merely procrastinating now, delaying the inevitable. No one would care, and she might begin feeling more like herself.

She went along the hall to her aunt's room and tapped lightly on the door. As always, Alma was weary from her time in the pool. Eva sat on the side of the bed and said, "I've decided not to finish the book."

"Congratulations. It's about time."

"I know you think they were garbage, but those three books have brought in good money."

"Money we didn't need in the first place," Alma scoffed.

"I got scared," Eva admitted, not without difficulty. She hated admitting to emotions like fear; they seemed to reduce her, make her less of the person she believed herself to be. "Especially when the insurance company said they weren't going to pay for the nurse or for Dennis. I had a vision of our losing everything."

"I saved throughout my entire working life," Alma said. "There's more than enough, as you well know."

"I was scared," Eva said again, finding as she always did that once she'd confessed to a failing, however minimal, there was something cathartic in repetition.

"There was not then, nor is there now, any need to be."

"No, I'm beginning to see that." Eva looked over at the door, then back at her aunt. "I'll let you sleep now. I just wanted to let you know."

Alma smiled at her. "It's the right thing to do," she said drowsily.

Eva left, closing the door quietly behind her. With a sense of purpose she descended the stairs, made her way through the kitchen to the garage and up the stairs to the office, where she switched on the computer and began erasing the disks. Only minutes and it was done, but she was trembling and had to go sit in the armchair. She'd destroyed weeks of work and it felt criminal, particularly when she didn't have a firm fix on how she wanted to write about Deborah.

How far back should she go? Should she start on the island and following events sequentially? Or should she create a chronological narrative and fabricate the parts she didn't and couldn't know?

She was certain of only one thing: She not only wanted to write about Deborah, she had to. And maybe, once she'd started, she'd be able to get back to dreaming in color.

Penny was still a bit blue, and Bobby decided it might cheer her up to talk to Aunt Helen. They chatted for a minute or two, then Bobby said, "Want to say hi to Pen?"

"I sure do." Her aunt laughed. "Put her on."

Penny got on the phone and started telling Helen about Melissa and about swimming at the Y. "I swimmed with my granny and Auntie Eva," she said. "I'm goin' again next week. Auntie Eva said."

Bobby let Penny talk for another minute or so, then got back on to tell her aunt she'd call again in a week's time. "Don't worry about us," she told her. "We're doing fine."

"I'm happy for you, babe," her aunt said, her voice going thick. "Look out for my girl and take care of yourself."

"I will. I love you."

"Love you too, babe."

At dinner, she mentioned the telephone call and said to Eva, "If you let me know how much my share is when the bill comes in, I'll pay you for it."

"Don't worry about it," Eva said.

"Okay," Bobby said, determined to take the woman at her word as she wanted. "Thanks a lot."

"Dennis is comin' tomorrow," Penny announced. "I'm makin' chocolate chip cookies and he's gonna show us a movie."

"That's okay, isn't it?" Bobby asked, looking first at Alma, then at Eva.

"Of course it is," Alma preempted any comment her niece might make. "The apartment is your own place, after all."

"He'll be coming when you're up for your nap," Bobby explained, not wanting them to think she was taking advantage.

"I don't like mushrooms," Penny said, making a face as she pushed them to the side of her plate.

"Don't make a fuss, Pen."

"They touched my chicken."

"Then just eat your vegetables."

Penny frowned at her plate.

Alma emitted one of her gruff laughs and said to Bobby, "You fail to understand, my dear. The vegetables have touched the chicken. Isn't that right, Penny?"

"That's right," Penny said.

"Bobby, get Penny another plate and we'll give her fresh servings of the rice and vegetables," Alma said.

"What a waste," Eva muttered under her breath.

"You used to do the same thing as a child, Eva," her aunt said as Bobby removed Penny's plate and went off to get a clean one. "In fact, you were worse." She stared at Eva for a long moment, then said, "You're decidedly on edge. What is it?"

"Nothing. I erased the disks."

"Well, good."

"I've never thrown out a manuscript. It feels odd. I feel guilty."

"You'll recover," Alma said blithely.

"I'm sure I will," Eva shot back. "You could be a bit more sympathetic."

"I refuse to indulge your self-pity."

Eva glared at her but said nothing more.

Bobby returned and put some food on Penny's plate, then, with a warning look, set the plate down in front of her. "No more fussing now, Pen. Sit quietly and eat."

"Eva's about to begin work on a new book," Alma told Bobby. "She's going to get started on something worthy of her abilities."

"That's good," Bobby said, looking across the table at Eva. "I like your books a lot."

Eva was about to speak, but the telephone rang and she got up saying, "I'll get it."

It was Charlie, asking, "What're you doing this evening, cupcake?"

"I'm coming over to see you in about an hour," she answered, so glad he'd called she could've wept.

He chuckled and said, "I'll be looking forward."

She went back to the table, saying, "I'll be going out after dinner."

"Charlie beckons," Alma said, one eyebrow lifted.

"Tell me, Bobby," Eva said. "Does your aunt behave anything like mine?"

Bobby laughed and said, "She used to, when I still lived at home. It's only 'cause she cares."

"Ah!" Eva said. "Is that what it is? I've been wondering about that for years. So let me see if I've got this right." She looked over at her aunt. "You treat me like a ten-year-old because you care."

"I treat you like a ten-year-old," Alma said, "because too often you behave like one."

Amused by their bickering, Bobby continued eating. She was excited about Eva's starting a new book, and wondered what it would be about. She wished it was already written so she could read it right away. She was getting to the end of the second book and had already decided which one she planned to read next.

"Do you know what the new one's going to be about?" she asked Eva.

Eva appeared pleased by the question. "Actually," she said, "I do. Right now I'm trying to sort out the logistics."

"She'll walk around for weeks in a fog," Alma said, "putting the pieces in place. She'll stand in the kitchen for an hour staring into space, and she'll go out to do errands and come home having forgotten why she went out."

Eva smiled, as if in anticipation.

Bobby smiled too, thrilled by the prospect of actually being there in the house while Eva wrote another wonderful book. It seemed like a great honor.

Twenty-Four

Eva sat holding Charlie's hand, listening to the music for a moment, finding it familiar but unable to remember what it was. Something by Bach. She closed her eyes and suddenly had an image of a jug of yellow daisies on the kitchen counter. "My God," she said, "Bobby gave me flowers."

"That was very nice of her," Charlie said, content to follow where she led. He was fascinated by her mental peregrinations, always intrigued to see where she'd go.

"They were just there on the counter and I really didn't take any notice of them," she said. "She must think I'm awful."

"Somehow I doubt that," he said.

"But I didn't thank her," she explained, shifting to look into his calm hazel eyes.

"So you'll thank her when you get home."

"You don't understand," she said, running her thumb over his knuckles. The skin on his hands was always silken, supple, while her own hands were often rough, ignored. She invariably intended to use the hand cream that sat on the bedside table but rarely got around to it.

"Enlighten me," he invited with a slight smile.

"We keep colliding, Bobby and I," she said. "We come to terms; then, an hour or a day later, we're smashing into each other. I say or do something. She misinterprets it. Then I turn myself inside out trying to correct it."

"You'll thank her when you get home," he repeated.

"She didn't seem hurt," she said, reviewing their dinner. Bobby had actually laughed at one point, she recalled. Had she ever heard Bobby laugh before? She didn't think so. During those weeks on the island Deborah had never laughed, not once.

Charlie watched her eyes lose their focus. She was off again, mind-traveling. He waited, wondering if all artists were similarly distracted, and wishing it were possible to follow along after her. She seemed to go to astonishing places, visiting briefly, then moving on. He knew himself to be firmly rooted in the present, with only occasional trips into the past, and admired her mental flexibility. He'd never known anyone remotely like her, and was never bored in her company as he was with so many others, both male and female. And it seemed to him altogether fortuitous that she was physically appealing, too.

"Why are you looking at me that way?" she asked, fixing her gaze on him.

"What way?"

"With intense interest," she said, laughing, "as if I were a tissue sample."

"Well, you are," he said, "in a certain sense."

"What did you think of Bobby, anyway?"

"What did I think?" He looked away, fine-tuning his perspective. "First of all," he said, "I didn't expect her to be quite so pretty. She is, don't you agree?"

"Very," she said.

"And secondly," he went on, "I got the impression that, despite her size, she's very strong. Not just physically," he added. "She has a certain...I guess I'd call it stoicism. Of course, she's almost pathologically shy. But I found that touching."

"Yes," Eva said thoughtfully, "so did I."

"All in all," he said, "I liked her. I was very impressed with the way she handles Alma. No nonsense, no looking to curry favor. She just gets on with it. She doesn't do things in order to be thanked. She simply does what needs to be done. There aren't a lot of people like that."

"I'm impressed," she said, looking at him squarely.

"Why, because I'm such a fine judge of human nature?" He grinned.

"You're pretty damned good, Charlie. I'm better at understanding the characters I create than I am at dealing with the real people in my life."

"I wouldn't say that," he disagreed. "You probably just spend more time on your characters."

"I've spent a lot of time on Bobby," she said, her eyes drifting away from him. "I *want* to understand her. I need to, for the new book." Looking at him again, she said, "I erased the disks, trashed the manuscript. It was one of the scariest things I've ever done."

"But you did it. Which means you're going to start something of your own, I take it."

"It was your idea," she said. "I mean, you gave me the idea of writing about Deborah."

"Deborah?" He looked puzzled.

"Reliving ancient history," she elaborated.

"Oh! And who is Deborah?"

"She was my friend. We met in England when I was twenty-one. Remember I told you I spent a semester in London?" He nodded, and she went on. "We were very close. Then Ken was transferred back to New York and we didn't see each other for four and a half years. In the meanwhile, she and her husband sold everything and moved back to Montaverde where she was born. I took Melissa and spent three weeks with her on the island. It was roughly eight months after Ken died. Anyway, she and her husband were fighting horribly, almost from the moment we got there. I wanted to go but I also wanted to stay and help. I felt incredibly stupid, sitting there waiting day after day for an opening that never came. In a way, I've always blamed myself for what happened. I was convinced there had to have been something I could've done to stop it."

"I had no idea," he said, "that you were so anal retentive."

She stared at him for a few seconds, laughed loudly, leaned over and kissed him hard on the mouth, then sat back and laughed some more.

"Was it that funny?" he asked, half-smiling.

"Hilarious," she said, brimming with fondness for him. "I do love you," she told him. "You're so good at keeping me grounded."

"Is that what I do?" he said. "And here I thought I was an inspiration."

"Everything inspires me," she said, giving the matter some thought. "Not that I want to play fast and loose with your male pride or anything, but it's the truth. I get ideas from everyone I know, from every conversation, even from things I notice through the car window when I'm driving somewhere. Sooner or later, it all gets used." As she spoke she returned gradually to her introspection, thinking that she'd always known she'd one day write about Deborah. She'd just never dreamed it would be more than fifteen years before she got to it.

He moved, his hand slipping out of hers, and she asked, "Where are you going?"

"To put on another disc," he said. "Don't worry. I'll be back."

"I thought perhaps you were offended."

"Nope," he said cheerfully. "I'm not wounded that easily."

"Thank God for that," she said fervently, thinking how easily Bobby was wounded. Did that come as a result of anticipating pain? If that was the case, it invalidated all her theories about Deborah. Because Deborah had become coarsened, tougher in her anticipation. She'd evolved into Ian's counterpart in almost every way, so that at the end she'd been as demented in her own way as Ian in his.

A Beethoven symphony began emerging from the speakers as Charlie returned and sat back down beside her. "So tell me," he said, "what happened on the island."

Reaching for his hand, she said. "I really do love you, you know, Charlie."

"I know you do, and I really love you too. Tell me what happened."

With a sigh, she began to tell him.

Bobby set her book aside and went to the bedroom, intending to get ready for bed, but instead she found herself watching Penny sleep, admiring the spill of her hair over the pillow, her dainty sleeping features. Bobby was permanently awed by her daughter's passionate nature and the ready attachments she was able to form to other people— to Melissa, for example.

She'd felt so sad for Penny that morning when she'd sobbed so brokenheartedly over Melissa's leaving. She understood that to Penny Melissa appeared magical, like a princess in one of her storybooks. With her long flowing hair and long flowing skirts, Melissa had taken Penny into her beauty, had cuddled and bathed her and tucked her into bed. Bobby had known exactly how Penny felt; she'd felt some of it herself. There was something about Melissa, a goodness that was tremendously compelling. And Bobby knew that from now until the Christmas break began, Penny would be talking about Melissa, asking regularly when she'd be coming home, and planning fantasy adventures the two of them would have.

She knew what it was like because once upon a time she'd been a little girl very like Penny, spinning tales around the visitors who'd come to their home, imagining her own fairy-princess mother one day appearing to claim her and take her away to live in a magical castle. Those things never happened, of course; they never could. But little girls did dream of the possibilities, especially ones like Penny and the child Bobby herself once had been, with their eyes and minds gobbling up words on the pages of books, being transported to splendid, far-off places by the stories they read.

She respected Penny's attachments, and waited on the sidelines to comfort her when her fairy-tale-inspired imaginings failed to become real. It was right that Penny should dream, that she should care immediately and deeply for people like Dennis and Melissa, like Alma and Eva, too. Penny went around adopting people, and most of the people wanted to be adopted. Look at Dennis, for example, she thought, adjusting the bedclothes over her sleeping child. She'd turned Dennis into a father, climbing willingly into his lap, placing her self and her trust in his hands with fairly unerring instinct.

She thought of Dennis's mouth touching hers, and of his hug, and wished she still had the ability to trust, to place herself in a man's hands, secure in the belief that no harm would come to her. But she could no longer be sure, even when everything *seemed* all right. It was dangerous to trust her own reactions, let alone someone else's actions. Dennis didn't behave or talk like a man who secretly longed to inflict pain, but it would take time for her to stop watching his every move, expecting him to throw off his outer skin like a snake to reveal the dangerous impulses underneath.

Yet when she lay down, and as she hovered on the edge of sleep, she imagined herself naked with Dennis and there was no pain. He touched her with respectful hands and her flesh responded in ways she hadn't known it could, with a tingling and a gladness and a yielding openness. Her body knew about sensations she'd never experienced, and she didn't understand how that was possible. She wondered if everyone was born into the world equipped with a set of responses that lived hidden inside until someone came along or something happened to draw them out. And if that was true, if everything was still intact inside her, then maybe she could experience pleasure after all; maybe all contact didn't have to be brutal, painful, something merely to be endured.

It was an intriguing concept, she thought, turning onto her side as she slid down into sleep. Maybe there was a part of her that had never been touched, never been violated. And maybe Dennis would introduce her to that unsuspected region of her own self. If she could learn to trust him.

Eva was going back over that final evening on the island, filling in all the details she'd omitted telling Charlie. She lay curled into herself, hands fisted against her chest, knees drawn up tightly, prepared to confront the complete picture.

It was the evening of that same day Eva had found and told Deborah about the passports. By dinnertime Derek had developed sniffles and insisted on being allowed to sleep with his mother and father. Deborah impatiently took him off to get ready for bed and Eva told Melissa, "You'll sleep with me tonight. We'll move your cot into my room. Okay?"

"Okay," Melissa said, then asked again, "When're we goin' home?"

"Tomorrow afternoon," Eva told her, having telephoned BWIA before dinner and booked seats. "We'll spend a couple of nights in Antigua, then we'll go home."

"I wanna go see Auntie Alma," Melissa said, as if expecting an argument.

"So do I," Eva agreed, longing for the sanity and security her aunt represented.

She set up the cot in her bedroom, then got Melissa undressed and into the shower. By eight o'clock both children were asleep, and Eva was sitting out on the veranda, watching the mountainside go gray as the light waned. Ian had gone off somewhere in the car—off yet again on another of his mysterious errands—and Deborah was in the kitchen fixing herself a cup of tea. Eva hadn't yet told her they were leaving. In a way she felt like a dreadful coward, going off and abandoning her old friend. But things had deteriorated to such an extent that the air seemed electric with hostility. Certainly the children felt it; they'd fought off and on ever since returning from Crescent Bay. At one point Derek had lashed out and hit Melissa hard, squarely in the chest. Eva had longed to take the boy on her knee and try to explain things to him—it was what he needed badly—but she didn't dare. All she'd been able to do was reprimand him quietly while he stood blinking at her—exquisitely beautiful even in his defiance—then turned and went to ride the tricycle.

Deborah came out and perched on the veranda railing with her tea and a cigarette and Eva knew the time had finally come for them to talk.

"We'll be leaving tomorrow morning," she said. "I'm sorry but I really think it's better that we go."

Deborah sighed and, without looking at her, said, "I expect it is. I'll tell Ian so he can drive you to the airport."

"That's all right," Eva said. "I've arranged for a taxi."

At this, Deborah turned to look at her. "I don't blame you," she said. "He's a shocking driver, frightful. Remember your first day when he nearly sent us over the cliff?" She spoke of the event as if fondly recalling the exploits of a naughty but lovable child.

Unable to fathom this odd fondness, Eva said, "I remember."

Deborah turned away again, her eyes on the horizon. "It hasn't been a very pleasant time for you, I'm afraid. All in all, it's a fucking disaster." She spoke without inflection, as if too tired to put any emphasis in her words. "We've wasted thousands of pounds, and all we have to show for it is a foundation. I can't think how we'll finish it."

"Deborah," Eva said, leaning forward over her knees, "why don't you take Derek and leave, go back to London?"

"I can't. I've no access to whatever money's left."

"But it's your money. How did that happen?"

"It's too complicated." Deborah sighed and drank some of the tea, then took a drag on her cigarette. "I wasn't aware, actually, that it *was* happening. And by the time I was, it was too late. It was Ian's idea, you know, to come back here. I was quite content to stay as we were. But he fancied himself a plantation owner or somesuch. I don't know." She put her cigarette out in the large, chipped, glass ashtray, then set the ashtray on the floor.

"I'll lend you the money to go," Eva said.

"That's very good of you, darling," Deborah said, "but where would we go? Everything's gone."

"You could go back, stay with friends until you started working."

"Afraid not," Deborah said dully, reaching into her shirt pocket for her pack of cigarettes. "But thank you for offering. You've always been very generous."

"I could lend you enough to get the two of you back to England and see you through for a few weeks. Surely you can't want to stay here, not with the way things are."

Looking slightly surprised, Deborah said, "Things are the way they've always been. I'm sorry if it's been unpleasant for you." She presented Eva with her profile. "I'd expected the house to be further along. I hadn't imagined we'd be so... so on top of each other."

"It's not just that... It's Ian, and the fights..."

"It's really none of your business, darling," Deborah cut her off crisply.

Stung, Eva said, "I'd like to help you."

"Actually, to be perfectly truthful, it'll be a help that you're going." Deborah took a fierce drag on her cigarette, her eyes on the darkening sky. Hurt, Eva didn't know what to say.

Ian returned a minute or two later and, defeated, Eva said she was going to bed. Feeling shut out and wounded, she left the two of them sitting on the veranda. Melissa was deeply asleep. Eva washed and got into the shorts and T-shirt in which she slept, then settled on the bed to read. Deborah's and Ian's voices drifted through the house like the low drone of insects. She tried to ignore them, to ignore the tension that knotted her neck and shoulder muscles. Tomorrow, she and Melissa would be gone from this desolate place. There'd be no more treacherous boat trips through barracuda-infested waters, no more waiting for a heart-to-heart conversation that wasn't ever going to take place. She and Melissa would spend two nights at Half Moon Bay in Antigua, eating food that was prepared for them, sightseeing, enjoying the amenities of the island, while she tried to put these three dreadful weeks behind her.

It was Derek's howling screams that awakened her. She shot into wakefulness with her heart drumming and knew something terrible was happening. In the dark, she flew barefoot down the walkway to listen for a moment outside the door of the master bedroom. Inside, Ian was saying, "I want you to stay in the bathroom until Daddy says you can come out. No arguing now. *Don't you move one bloody muscle!*" This last was obviously directed to Deborah who, with a sob, cried, "Leave us be!"

What to do? Panting, Eva raised her hand to knock at the door just as Ian's voice rose to a shout. Now she could hear that the two inside the room were physically grappling. There was nothing she could do, and if she tried to intervene she might wind up one of Ian's victims. In a panic, she tore back to her room convinced that she and Melissa had to get out of there. With Deborah's and Ian's shouting voices intercut with Derek's muted howls from the bathroom, she began pulling the louvers from the window at the back of the room.

Melissa woke up, asking, "What's happening?" and Eva shushed her, whispering, "Get dressed as fast as you can! Hurry!"

"What'cha doin'?"

"Get dressed!" Eva got the last of the louvers out, put it on the floor, then pushed at the screen. It fell backward out of the window, toppling into the brush as the gunshots came. One. Two. She stood rigid for a moment, hearing the echoing waves of the shots riding on the current of the night breezes, certain Ian was about to come for them. He couldn't leave any witnesses. She looked at the deep closet, then at the window. In an instant, she'd decided. Snatching Melissa into her arms, grabbing her purse with their passports and money, she climbed into the deepest corner of the closet, leaving the sliding door open. Warning Melissa not to make a sound, she piled their luggage into a concealing barricade and squatted on the floor with Melissa in her arms, one hand over her daughter's mouth.

Not two minutes later, Ian's footsteps came pounding along the cement walkway. The door was flung open. Then a few moments of silence as he took in the empty room. The overhead light went on. Eva hunched lower, her hand tightly clamped over Melissa's mouth. His footsteps moved to the window. "Bloody hell!" he muttered, and bolted from the room. Eva heard him running along the walkway, then he was tearing his way through the brush at the rear of the house, going first this way, then that. Another few minutes and his footsteps returned. And Derek started howling again. Ian ran toward the master suite. Derek's cries subsided instantly.

Melissa squirmed in her arms, but Eva continued to hold her tightly, her hand still covering Melissa's mouth. With her lips right against Melissa's ear, she whispered, "We mustn't make a sound. Something very bad is happening." Melissa nodded and relaxed somewhat, her body heavy against Eva's chest.

She could hear Ian's voice, could hear him talking to his son, felt his urgency as the minutes ticked past. Sweat trickled down her sides, her whole body sheltering Melissa. Then, distinctly, she heard the slam of the car door.

The engine roared, the car reversed with screaming tires and went shooting off down the mountainside. She didn't move. Minute after minute went past as she crouched at the back of the closet, Melissa now asleep in her arms. She looked at the luminous face of her watch. Ten past ten. Where was he going? Was there a flight off the island at this time of night? What had he done to Deborah?

She waited another fifteen minutes, then, her muscles protesting, she stood up with Melissa, kicked the suitcases out of the way, and emerged from the closet. Her entire body was quaking, hips and thighs aching as she stepped back into the room. The door stood open. The overhead light was still on. Moths fluttered around the light fixture. Her arms ached to put Melissa down but she didn't dare. She moved to the doorway and looked out. The door to the master suite was wide open. Cupping the back of Melissa's head, she went along the walkway, barely able to breathe for fear of what she might see.

Approaching the threshold of the master suite she was so afraid she thought she might throw up. Her stomach heaved. She took a deep breath, another step, and looked into the room. One glance and she inched away, even more afraid. Tears streaming down her cheeks, she carried Melissa to the bedroom and laid her on the bed while she pulled on jeans, a sweatshirt, socks, and sneakers. Then she dressed the sleeping Melissa. Finally she got her purse from the closet, looped the strap over her shoulder, picked Melissa up from the bed and carried her on tiptoe through the house to the telephone. Ian had cut the line. Fear made her want to scream. She couldn't stay there.

She got the flashlight from the kitchen, then started down the long narrow road, Melissa unbelievably heavy in her arms as she kept to one side, certain Ian would return at any moment to complete what he'd begun. Her arms feeling as if they were being pulled from their sockets, she followed the beam of the flashlight the two miles down the plantation drive, praying the whole time that there would be a car going past on the main road.

She longed to put Melissa down but couldn't. Upon arriving at the intersection of the drive and the road, she stopped and looked in both directions, lips moving as she prayed for a car to come along. She stood, chilled now as the sweat on her body dried in the cool night air, looking first one way, then the other, waiting, straining to hear the sound of an approaching car, terrified that if one came it might be Ian, but what choice did she have? She couldn't carry Melissa any farther and the nearest house was better than a mile away.

Finally headlights appeared. She switched on the flashlight and waved it back and forth. And the car, containing two Montaverdean men, stopped. Sobbing now, she ran to the car, saying, "We've got to get the police. My friend's been killed."

Once in the back of the car, speeding toward the nearest telephone, she was able to let go of Melissa. Her tears abating, she held her trembling hands together in her lap, unable to respond to the men's questions, unable to speak at all, her eyes filled with the image of Deborah's lifeless, contorted body, the blood—so much of it—splattered over the wall, the floor, the bedclothes....

In tears, she sat on the side of the bed drying her eyes on the sleeve of her nightgown. After a time, she got up and went downstairs to the kitchen. While the kettle was boiling, she sat at the table looking at the slightly open door to the apartment. Once again, she could smell cigarette smoke and knew Bobby, too, was awake. Why couldn't she bring herself to say or do something, to make some contact during these early morning sojourns?

Twenty-Five

"I didn't thank you for the flowers." Eva delivered this as an apology.

"Oh, that's okay," Bobby said, with a little dismissing lift of her hand.

"The thing is, I didn't really notice them. Otherwise, of course, I'd have said something earlier."

"I understand," Bobby said, smiling. "I know you've got a lot on your mind."

"Why did you do it?" Eva asked, perpetually curious about this woman and seeking links between her and Deborah. So far, she'd found none. The two couldn't have been more different. All they had in common was that they'd both been married to abusive men.

"I wanted to thank you for the special day, for including us." Anxious to get off that topic, she said, "Your Melissa's a beautiful girl, really nice."

Eva leaned against the counter and said, "She *is* beautiful, isn't she? Every time I look at her I see her father. She has his good nature and his sense of humor, his extraordinary ease with people. And," she added with a self-deprecating smile, "my stubbornness."

"Are you stubborn?" Bobby asked, finding Eva very accessible this morning.

"Don't tell me you haven't noticed," Eva said playfully.

"I've noticed you get a lot of moods," Bobby said. "But I haven't seen you being stubborn."

"Stick around," Eva said, laughing. "We'll get to it." Sobering, she said, "I get up in the middle of the night and come down here, have some juice or a cup of tea and sit for a while until it's safe to go back to sleep."

"I know," Bobby said softly. "I hear your footsteps."

"We should keep each other company," Eva said. "It seems ridiculous that we're both awake, sitting in separate places."

"I kind of thought that too," Bobby said, wanting to look down—at her hands or the floor—but keeping her eyes lifted to Eva's. "I usually have a cigarette," she said apologetically, as if her smoking were a breach of household etiquette.

"Next time, come up and have your cigarette with me," Eva invited. "Maybe we'll discuss our dreams." She kept her tone light, but she couldn't have been more serious. She wanted badly to get inside Bobby's experiences, to comprehend them in order that her book about Deborah would have more verisimilitude.

Bobby pictured the two of them sitting at the table in the dead of night and had to smile at the idea of their trading nightmare tales. It reminded her of how she and Lor used to discuss every last thing that happened at school. Invariably they'd ended up giggling over their speculations.

"Do you find the idea funny?" Eva asked, mildly dismayed.

"In a way," Bobby said. "But it'd be kind of a nice change, talking about the things I dream." She doubted she'd ever be able to tell anyone her dreams, because that would be telling about the things Joe had done to her. But maybe she could, and maybe it would make her feel better.

"Do you dream in color?" Eva asked.

"I guess so. I never really thought about it. Do you?"

"Not recently," Eva said, and stood away from the counter to get on with the preparation of Alma's breakfast. She wondered again, as she had dozens of times before, where Ian was now. As it turned out, there had been several flights off the island that night—one to St. Kitts and Nevis, one to Barbuda, and one to Antigua. From Antigua he might have gone anywhere. By the time the Montaverdean police got around to checking, he and Derek were long gone.

She invariably pictured the two of them in London. Perhaps Derek was a college student now, like Melissa; a young man with only the haziest memories of his mother; or possibly he was tormented by nightmares of his mother's death. But maybe Ian had killed him too, and somewhere hidden in the brush on the island was a small skeleton. She preferred to think Derek was alive. Since she still had difficulty dealing with the facts of Deborah's death, she simply refused to believe Derek might also be dead. Perhaps Ian had married another woman, who'd willingly played mother to the boy while Ian slowly, steadily beat her into mental shape. Or maybe he'd found someone who wouldn't be beaten, and he spent his evenings listening to her complain while he sat turning his silver Dunhill lighter over and over in his hands.

Bobby felt Eva drift away and respectfully left her to herself, returning downstairs with the cookie sheets she'd come up to borrow. As she plaited Penny's hair into a pair of French braids, she tried to recall if her dreams were in color. She had the impression that they were, but she couldn't be sure.

She imagined climbing the stairs to the kitchen, to have her cigarette and keep Eva company in the middle of the night. The idea appealed to her and she thought maybe she'd do it. Having someone to be with might make the nights less frightening. Somehow, at night, horrible things were more likely to happen. Fear seemed to be a nighttime emotion, something that lived in the deepest corners and fed on darkness.

* * *

After Alma was settled in the living room with the Sunday papers and a Mozart violin concerto on the stereo, Bobby slipped away to help Penny make the chocolate chip cookies.

When they were done and sat cooling on the counter, she and Penny went back up to the living room. Penny went at once to lean on the arm of Alma's wheelchair, asking, "Granny, when's Melissa comin' back?"

"In eighteen days," Alma told her, daily more taken with this child. She'd never have admitted it, but she was secretly delighted every time Penny called her Granny. For a few moments, here and there, she was able to reconstruct history, viewing herself as a woman who had shared her life and, as a result, would leave behind a living legacy. More and more of late she was coming to view the life she'd led as narrow and arid. Sundry lovers notwithstanding, she'd given nothing of herself in any significant fashion—except, of course, to Eva. She knew it was ridiculous, but she couldn't help thinking that if she'd used her body for something other than pleasure it might not have betrayed her so terribly. "You could mark off the days on the calendar in the kitchen, if you like."

"I could do that," Penny said, as if rising to a challenge.

"That way," Alma said, "you'll know exactly how many more days you have to wait."

"I'm gonna do that," Penny said again, decisively. "We made the cookies. Mom says I can bring you some when they're cooled."

"I'll look forward to it," Alma said, unable to suppress a chuckle. "Are you enjoying *The Secret Garden?*"

"I *love* it! It's the bestest book I ever read."

"It's the best book you've ever read," Alma corrected her.

Penny's brow furrowed slightly and she asked, "How come you always say over again what I just said?"

"I'm trying to teach you good grammar."

"What's grammar?"

"It's the correct way of speaking and writing."

"Oh! I thought that was for school."

"No," Alma said. "It's for every day, in your life and at school. When you're older and out in the world, you'll find that people have a tendency to judge you by the way you speak. If you speak correctly, you will be judged more favorably—particularly when you enter the working world."

"I'm gonna be a school bus driver when I grow up," Penny said, "and drive all the little children to school. I'll sit up front and tell everyone to sit down or they can't ride on the bus. And I won't let nobody fight on my bus or throw trash on the floor."

"Very admirable," Alma said. "I'm sure you'll have the finest bus in the fleet."

"Yes, I will," Penny said, reaching to touch her finger to Alma's left hand, asking, "Can you feel this?"

"Not really."

Penny touched her finger next to the downturned side of Alma's face, asking, "Can you feel this?"

"Pen, stop that," Bobby said quietly but firmly. "That's not nice."

"Was that bad?" Penny asked, looking first at Alma, then at her mother.

"Yes," said Bobby.

"No," said Alma. "I'm not bothered," she told Bobby. It was true. Somehow the openness with which Penny approached her disabilities robbed them of much of their horror. It had to do with the purity of the child's motives, with the lack of anything but simple curiosity in her questions. Penny accepted her as she was, which was more than she was capable of doing herself. She would live out the rest of her life in a state of denial because her memories and her image of herself were at war with her current reality. Only with Penny was she able, to some degree, to forget that she was no longer all of a piece. With everyone else she was like a misplaced steamer trunk that had to be shifted from one location to another, doomed never to arrive at its proper destination. And she was aware during every waking moment of just how cumbersome she'd become. Penny enabled her to forget for long minutes at a stretch, enabled her to live up to her old, outdated mental image of herself. With Penny she was still the Alma Ogilvie who went out for social occasions dressed in high heels and good-looking clothes, still the Alma who'd refused to be dictated to by her age, still a complete human being. And for that, as well as for all Penny's other attributes, she was coming to cherish the child. "I don't mind your asking," she told Penny. "I want you always to feel free to say whatever you're thinking." Tomorrow, she decided, she'd put in a call to her lawyer, arrange to make provision for Penny in her will. It was the least she could do in return for the valuable moments of brightness Penny brought into her life.

"See, Mom!" Penny said. "Granny says it's okay."

Bobby simply smiled.

Dennis arrived while Bobby was still upstairs getting Alma settled for her nap. On hearing the doorbell, Penny came racing up from the apartment and was right behind Eva as she opened the door.

Singing out, *"Dennis!"* Penny threw open her arms, and Dennis caught her up and held her, grinning.

"How're you doing, Pen?"

"Did you bring the movie machine?"

"I sure did," he said. "It's in the car." Leaning around Penny he greeted Eva, asking how she was.

"Fine, thank you. Bobby's still up with Alma. Come on into the kitchen. There's fresh coffee."

"I made your cookies," Penny said as he set her down to remove his jacket.

"I was counting on that. You promised, after all."

Taking him by the hand, Penny led him to the kitchen, saying, "Granny's lettin' me mark off the days on the calendar 'til Melissa comes home. I'll show you." She let go of his hand to run across the kitchen and indicate the big X she'd put through that day's date.

"How many more days to go?" he asked her, sitting as Eva indicated he should, at the table.

"Seventeen, after today." Penny came over and indicated she wanted to be lifted onto his lap.

Watching, taken by his naturalness with Penny, Eva wondered what he hoped for from Bobby. He seemed very relaxed, and she took a good long look at him, deciding he was an attractive man. In jeans and a brown Shetland crew-neck over a white shirt, with heavy white socks and boating shoes, he appeared very young and very alert, with healthy color riding his high, freckled cheekbones. In many ways, she thought he was quite perfect for Bobby: a gentle, well-bred young man, uncomplicated and undemanding. "Coffee?" she asked, deciding in one moment that she approved of him, and in the next wondering why she was, in however abstract a fashion, involving herself in Bobby's life. It was none of her business.

"That'd be great," he said. "How's the writing going?"

Why did people always ask that? It was one of two questions she was asked constantly. The other was: Still writing? The question seemed to imply her writing was a frivolity, something she did instead of real work. But she answered politely, as always, saying, "I'm getting ready to start a new book," and busied herself pouring his coffee. She was placing it on the table when Bobby came in, and she was intrigued to see Bobby brighten, smiling at the sight of him with Penny on his knee.

Eva felt a sudden leap of protectiveness toward her, and found herself thinking, If you hurt her, I'll kill you. Surprised at the intensity of these feelings, she poured coffee for Bobby while Penny slipped away to bring the cookies up from downstairs.

Almost every day Eva read in the newspapers some story about a demented husband going after his estranged wife with a gun, killing her—often in front of witnesses—then turning the gun on himself. The psychology of these men bewildered her, just as Ian, even after all these years, continued to defy her comprehension. The Joe Salton that Bobby talked about didn't seem quite real to her. Her eyes on Bobby, she wondered why that was. Obviously the man was real. Bobby had turned up at the door bearing the physical evidence of his reality.

"Have you seen *E.T.*, Eva?" Dennis was asking, and she said she had, thinking she really should spend a couple of hours in the office working on a story outline. But she didn't feel like it; the need wasn't there. She'd probably walk around preoccupied with Deborah and Ian and Derek for a week or two or three, then one morning the story would start pouring out in such a rush that she'd spend up to ten hours a day attempting to keep up with the flow. It was exciting when that happened. She could sit by and follow, fascinated, the evolution of the tale, using her skills to give it shape and momentum, but as intrigued to know the ending as any reader would be.

"Why don't you watch it with us?" Dennis said.

"Perhaps I will," Eva said, looking to see if Bobby harbored any objections. She obviously didn't. She smiled encouragingly, and Eva said, "Why not use the VCR in the den?"

"Okay, we'll do that," Dennis said as Penny offered around the cookies. "It'll save me the hassle of hooking mine up."

"We have to keep some for Granny," Penny warned everyone.

Bobby stole surreptitious glances at Dennis, thinking that he, like Charlie at Thanksgiving, didn't seem to mind being surrounded by females. He acted as if he felt right at home, and took Penny back on his lap after she finished passing around the cookies, holding her as if it was something he did every day, something that made him feel good.

She got a little shock whenever she stole another look at him, wondering anew why he was interested in her. He could've had all kinds of women, but he kept on coming back to her. It made her feel honored in a way, even though she expected he'd be disappointed in her and give up soon. And yet he seemed glad to go along with things, unlike Joe, who was always insisting everything had to be different from what it was. The entire eight years with Joe, he'd been at her to be different, to be someone other than the person she was. He wanted her hair blond, wanted her to walk around naked when the very idea made her cringe with mortification; he wanted her to be exactly the opposite of what she was. Dennis hadn't once acted as if he expected anything at all; he behaved as if he was satisfied with her the way she was. But he couldn't be. Could he?

Penny sat on Dennis's lap and exclaimed aloud, distraught over E.T.'s misadventures and wildly elated by the ending.

"That's the *best* movie I ever saw!" she declared when it was over, flushed in the face, eyelids reddened, cheeks tear-stained.

"It's one of my favorites," Dennis said, hugging her. "I knew you'd like it. How about you, Bobby?"

Bobby was afraid to speak for fear she'd start crying again. Convinced by Joe that it was a sign of weakness, she disliked having people see her cry. All she could do was nod and give him a wobbly smile.

He smiled back at her, saying, "I know. It gets me the same way."

"I wish Granny could've seed it too," Penny said, looking toward the door.

"Perhaps another time," Eva said, checking her watch before getting up. "I have a couple of things to do before

I start dinner." She paused, taking in the trio on the sofa. "Would you care to stay to dinner, Dennis?"

"Oh, that's really nice of you," he said, "but I'm going down to my folks' place."

"Well," Eva said, "I'll be in the office," and left them.

In the office she looked at the row of her books on the shelf, feeling both proud of her accomplishments and daunted by them. Her ambition was to make each book better than the last, and every time she was about to embark upon something new, she went through a period of worrying that she no longer had anything worthwhile to say. Going to the armchair by the window, she sat and looked out at the Sound, fearful that she didn't know enough to write about Montaverde and Deborah. Yes, she had the facts. But did she have the understanding? She would have, she thought, if she could only convince Bobby to confide in her, if she could hear firsthand what it was like to be abused.

Penny kissed Dennis good-bye, then ran upstairs to tell Alma about the movie.

Bobby walked him to the door, finally able to say how much she'd liked the movie and to thank him for bringing it.

"How about Friday?" he asked, while he pulled on his jacket. "We could grab something to eat, take in a movie."

"All right," she said. "But this time it's my treat."

"Okay. You're on," he said. He kissed her lightly, quickly on the lips, then went out to his car, saying, "See you Thursday."

The air was cold and sharp; the sky was already beginning to go dark. She stood in the doorway with her arms wrapped around herself and watched him get into his car. After he'd gone, she turned and looked up the stairs, hearing Penny excitedly telling Alma all about E.T. She felt oddly full, as if she'd just consumed a delicious meal. Smiling to herself, she started up the stairs.

Twenty-Six

Eva was remembering a particular afternoon early in her stay on the island. She was sitting on the sand at the very apex of Crescent Bay with the children beside her. The sun shone blinding white overhead as the three of them watched about fifteen Montaverdeans at the water's edge prepare to haul in the immense seine net they'd cast by boat over the water. The natives stood in two lines, each grasping one end of the net, and slowly, hand over hand, brought it in to shore.

Inside the net hundreds of fish surged, silvering the water. The air was heavy with the reek of the roiling fish as they were pushed closer and closer together by the tightening net. On the sand, the Montaverdeans chanted, counting or singing—Eva couldn't quite interpret their patois—as they drew in the net and it fell in wet folds to the sand.

The closer to shore the net came, the stronger the stink grew, of fish and blood. The fish thrashed, trying to free themselves, but the net continued to shrink in size, cutting off their escape. Above the chanting of the natives was the ungodly sound of the fish as they churned up the water, their fins cutting the surface like knives.

Eva put her arms around the children, finding the scene alarming. Melissa and Derek sat openmouthed, scarcely blinking.

As the net closed tighter and tighter, blood darkened the surface of the water, and half a dozen more natives materialized, waded in, and began flinging fish onto the shore, where they leaped and quivered, their scales catching the sunlight, the noise growing louder, an unearthly din. Eva had never witnessed anything remotely like this. The scene was primitive and frightening. The fish flopped about on the sand. People with mallets swung at them, killing them, spilling more blood; scales littered the beach like hundreds of mirror fragments.

At last the net was a bulging, pulsing mass that was being slowly dragged up onto the sand. And once the fish were beached and bludgeoned, the natives began apportioning them, carrying them off in buckets or with their fingers looped through the gills; several filled their boats. Very quickly, all that remained was the massive net and a wide area of churned-up, bloodied sand. The pungent fishy blood-smell continued to hang in the air. Eva's stomach churned. She breathed through her mouth, concentrating on not being sick. The children appeared dazed. They both sat very still, as if in a state of shock.

Returning to the present, she lifted the damp hair from the back of her neck and let her head rest on her bent knees. After a time, cooler, she got up and went downstairs.

Bobby went to the closet in the living room, opened the door, and there was Joe. Smiling, with a shotgun in his hands. He lifted the shotgun, aimed it straight at her. Terrified, her heart in a seizure, she turned to run, but he reached out and grabbed a handful of her nightgown. She wanted to scream, opened her mouth, but all that came out was a whisper, "No."

His smile scared her almost as much as the gun. If she could only scream, Eva and Alma would hear, they'd get help. But if she screamed, Penny would wake up, and she didn't want to remind him of Penny.

Why couldn't she make any sound? Frustration had her fighting, even though she knew perfectly well it was always worse when she struggled. It seemed to incite him to greater acts of sadism and bestiality.

She began telling herself this was a dream, she could wake up. But her eyes felt glued shut on the sleeping level, gaping wide on the dream level.

With a massive effort, she clawed her way to the surface, lungs heaving, body wet with perspiration, eyes and nose streaming. She sat up, hoping she hadn't made any noises in her sleep, hadn't done anything to frighten Penny. She turned to look over at the other bed. Penny slept peacefully.

After a minute or two she got out of bed and pulled on the cardigan she used in lieu of a bathrobe. Her robe, so far as she knew, was still hanging on the back of the bathroom door of the house in Jamestown.

She got her pack of cigarettes, then turned to look up the stairs at the slightly open door to the kitchen. She always left the door open a few inches, couldn't stand to close it, let alone lock it. That would've made her feel too trapped somehow. There was no light on upstairs, but she knew Eva never bothered turning it on.

Without stopping to think about it, she started up the stairs. She could see Eva sitting at the table. Mopping her eyes on the sleeve of her sweater, Bobby stepped barefoot into the room.

Eva said, "I got an ashtray for you, in case you decided to come up."

Bobby slid into the chair across from her and lit a Marlboro with trembling hands. In the murky light she felt for the ashtray and pulled it toward herself, feeling eight years' worth of experiences compressed into a chestful of words that suddenly had to be spoken. All she needed was the least little encouragement and she'd be off and running.

"What did you dream?" Eva asked.

"I dream most every night he's hurting me again," Bobby whispered.

"It must be awful."

"Yeah. He had so many ways of hurting me. Toward the end there, I'd kind of wait for him to get it over with, go ahead and finally kill me. And that's when I got really scared, 'cause I knew if I didn't get away I'd wind up dead. It was like he was working up to it all those years, practicing, sort of." She glanced at Eva but couldn't make out her expression. It didn't matter. That was the one good thing about night: You didn't care about things the way you did in daylight because so much got hidden by the dark.

Eva was very still. Bobby could feel her listening. It was an extraordinary moment, one unparalleled in her experience, this opportunity to talk openly while safely concealed by the darkness. Eva was merely a presence that would absorb the details.

"You must have been very frightened," Eva said, encouraging her to go on.

"At the beginning," Bobby said, "he'd always be sorry. He'd slap me around some, then the next day he'd be nice as pie. But that was only at the very beginning, maybe the first six months. After that he didn't bother pretending anymore he was sorry. Because he wasn't. He *liked* it. He was happy when he was hurting me. He'd always smile. And every time I saw that smile I got a sick feeling in the pit of my stomach because I knew how good it made him feel to break my bones, to draw blood. And the whole time it was happening, there was a part of me standing back watching, asking how did I come to be married to this man. I never knew exactly what it was I said or did that sent him crazy, but I was forever waiting, nervous about every word that came out of my mouth, every step I took."

Eva listened, feeling faintly nauseated. She'd instigated this. Now she was beginning to regret it. She hadn't expected Bobby to be quite so forthcoming, or so graphic; she'd imagined herself dragging the information out of her in slow degrees.

Bobby took a last drag on the Marlboro, put it out, then went on, the words coming fast now. "When I got pregnant, he wanted me to get rid of the baby. I wouldn't, and he pretty much left me alone until after Pen was born. But I was home three days from the hospital with the baby when he started in. And that's when things turned really bad, when he got really serious about the beatings. The stuff that had happened before, that was nothing compared to the things he did after I had Pen. I wanted to get away, but now I had a baby and there was nowhere to go. My friend Lor and my aunt, they were sorry but they couldn't take me in because Joe would make so much trouble for them. So I kept real quiet and cooked nice meals every day and pretended I liked the way he jumped on me in bed. I made the kind of moans he wanted to hear and didn't let on he was hurting me, even though he knew he was."

Eva wanted to shut her eyes, to close this out. She was being told far more than she'd ever wanted to know, and there was no way now to stem the flow. Her damned curiosity had opened the floodgates.

"He always said I was the stupidest person in the world," Bobby went on, "and he was right because if I'd been one bit smart, I'd never have married him. He was right. I was stupid, and I deserved to get my nose broken and my ribs broken; I deserved to have my breasts burned with cigarettes, or have him rip out whole handfuls of my hair; I deserved to have my little finger twisted back until the bone broke, and get raped with a curling iron that was still hot, or with the shotgun while he held a knife to my throat telling me not to make one sound or he'd cut my throat. I deserved every last thing he ever did to me. Because I was so *stupid*." She was crying again. It affected her breathing and her ability to get the words out. She fumbled with the pack of cigarettes, got another one lit, steadied her breathing.

Eva remained silent, embarrassed for this woman and appalled by the form of vampirism that had prompted her to encourage Bobby to reveal so much. She was in no way qualified to deal with what she was being told, hadn't a single thing to say that might alleviate Bobby's suffering. All she'd been thinking of was the new book, of being sufficiently informed to write it accurately. Having to hear this horror story was making her dislike herself.

"He convinced me that everything that happened to me was my own fault," Bobby hurried on. "I couldn't do anything right, even when I pretended. In bed I was supposed to move certain ways, make certain sounds, but all I could do was try to copy the things he did because I didn't know what he *wanted*. There were all these things that made him feel good and made me feel like filth . . . pulling my hair and forcing me to open my mouth, then laughing when I gagged; making my backside bleed . . ."

God! Eva thought. Don't tell me any more! I don't want to know. She wished she could cover her ears with her hands. But she couldn't do a thing. She had to sit there and absorb the information she'd thought she'd wanted.

"The whole time he was doing it to me I'd think about going away somewhere and living alone with Pen someplace where nobody ever made me feel scummy because I was female. And along with hating him I hated me too, hated *being* female because men did disgusting things to females, made them get down on their hands and knees and pretend to like being *hurt*, pretend to like it when they made your backside bleed." Impatiently, she wiped her eyes with the back of her hand, seeing the scenes brightly lit in her mind, one after another. "I kept on taking my birth control pills because I knew if I got pregnant again he'd kick me and burn me and pound me until I died." She gave a gasping, rueful laugh, took another puff on the cigarette, then said, "When I went for my checkup six months ago, I asked the doctor for another prescription and he said what for. There was no point to taking the pills because I couldn't have any more babies. There was too much internal damage, he said. I'm twenty-seven years old and I'm ruined inside. I don't feel sorry for myself, though. It was my own fault."

"No, it wasn't," Eva finally spoke, knowing she had to, knowing this was the price to be paid for soliciting the ugly intimate details of Bobby's life. "It wasn't your fault."

"Yeah, it was," Bobby said, feeling sleepy now after releasing so much that had been pent up inside for so long. "It's funny," she sighed, fatigue making her eyelids heavy. "I thought when and if I ever got away from Joe, it'd all be over. But it isn't. It keeps happening over and over inside my head and in my dreams."

"It'll get better in time."

"How do you know that?" Bobby challenged.

"Because it will," Eva said, with absolutely no grounds upon which to base this declaration. She simply wanted to put an end to this encounter she'd so foolishly instigated. Her head was filled with ugly images, pornographic pictures. She hated feeling as she did, even felt angry with Bobby for her capitulation.

"How do you *know* that?" Bobby asked again.

"Because for months after Deborah was killed, every night when I lay down to sleep, I saw her body and the blood everywhere and I was terrified all over again."

"This was your friend?"

"That's right," Eva said. "I was in the house when her husband killed her."

"God! That's awful!"

"Now it's fifteen years later and it's still horrible, but it's not the same. It's *of the past.* You understand?" Was it possible she could exert some positive influence here? She hoped so. It would go a long way toward tempering the harrowing guilt she now felt.

"Sort of. Yeah, I guess I do. But I'm never going to forget any of what Joe did."

"No," Eva agreed. "You never will. But it'll get better. And nobody will ever hurt you that way again." What an absurd thing to say! She couldn't guarantee that. This conversation had become more hateful than any of her worst nightmares. She was spouting platitudes, saying whatever she could think of in order to bring this to an end.

"You shouldn't ever say never," Bobby said, superstitiously believing that if you put your thoughts into words you might make them come true.

"You're through playing out your role as a victim," Eva said, trying desperately to be upbeat. "You've started a new life with Pen. And there's Dennis."

"I'm scared to death of what Dennis might want," Bobby confessed. "I don't know why he keeps on wanting to see me. I told him a little bit of what I told you and he was really good about it. I mean, he acted like he wanted to understand. But that doesn't stop me from being scared."

"I know," Eva said, striving to sound sympathetic. "But try not to be. He's not a dangerous man."

"They're all dangerous," Bobby said.

"Not all of them," Eva corrected her. "Charlie isn't, and neither is Dennis."

"They're dangerous," Bobby explained, "because they hope for things some of us can't give them."

"I'm sorry," Eva said, feeling lost and promising herself she'd never again as long as she lived invite anyone to confide to her in this fashion.

"Why're you sorry?" Bobby asked, perplexed.

"I'm sorry such dreadful things have happened to you. You didn't deserve any of it. No one deserves to be treated the way you've been treated." That much was true, and she could state it with conviction. But, God, she felt like an appalling hypocrite.

Bobby's eyes flooded again, the tears scalding her cheeks. She couldn't speak for a time, and took another puff of her cigarette, working at regaining her self-control. At last her throat eased some and she said, "You're a nice person."

"I'm a lot of things," Eva said, anxious to keep the record straight, "but nice isn't one of them. I'm intolerant and impatient. I'm temperamental and sometimes very judgmental. But I do try to be fair," she said critically. "I know it's very difficult for you to talk about...the things that happened." She wished she could admit how dreadful it had been to have to hear it. And she didn't know what she'd do if Bobby decided to reveal anything more.

"Are you going to use it in a book?" Bobby asked.

Eva was stopped cold. It wasn't an illegitimate question, or even a naive one. Bobby had managed to glean a fundamental truth about her: that in one way or another everything she saw or heard was source material. There were times, like now, when Eva strongly disliked that part of herself that hungered for information. Her curiosity was a greedy, powerful entity that often dominated her instincts with its rapacious appetite. "No, not specifically," she answered truthfully, "but I'll use the understanding you've helped me gain. That I will use."

"Give it a happy ending," Bobby said strongly.

"But it didn't end happily," Eva said, nettled. How dare anyone tell her what to write?

"Find a way," Bobby insisted, feeling that she knew something Eva didn't; that she had, in her own way, a better fix on reality than Eva ever would. Granted, it was a different reality and not an especially good one, but it pertained for an awful lot of women. "It's one of the best things about your books: You leave people feeling good. And that's important. People need an ending that leaves them feeling better, gives them some hope."

It was Eva's turn to sit silently for several moments, considering this. "You have a point," she said, wondering if vanity hadn't blinded her to an awful lot of things.

She seemed to have less of a fix on this woman now than she'd had before. "I'll think about it."

Bobby put out her cigarette, saying, "I'm going to go to bed now. I'm really tired."

"Me too," Eva lied. Her brain was racing, ideas jumping around wildly. She'd probably be awake most of the night.

Bobby stood up, holding her cigarettes and matches. "I haven't ever told anybody those things," she said meaningfully.

"I know," Eva said, getting up. "I understand." She knew the truth when she heard it. The problem was, she hadn't enjoyed hearing it.

"I was too ashamed. You know?"

"I understand," Eva repeated, looking at Bobby's diminutive shape in the darkness. "Sleep well," she said helplessly, feeling she'd defrauded this little woman.

"You may not think so," Bobby said, starting toward the door, "but you really are a nice person. G'night."

"Good night," Eva said, reaching for the half-full glass of orange juice on the table.

Bobby left the door open a few inches, and Eva continued to stand there, feeling like a monster. She'd grown up following Alma's lead, and Alma didn't espouse niceness. Niceness was a namby-pamby code of behavior for dishonest people to hide behind. You were nice instead of truthful; it was kinder. Alma had always stated she preferred truthfulness; she insisted on knowing where she stood with people and mistrusted those who were nice.

Nice, Eva whispered to herself, very ashamed. She was anything but, she thought, taking a swallow of juice. She felt like a psychological con artist who'd just pulled off a major scam. And hard as she tried, she couldn't shake the revulsion she felt at the thought of getting raped with a hot curling iron, nor could she shut down the mental image of Bobby on her hands and knees, being sodomized. Thoroughly shaken, she went back upstairs, wishing fervently

that she'd kept her distance, that she'd had more respect
for Bobby's privacy.

He dreamed he was a little kid again, and he was sick. He had a fever so he had to stay home from school, and spent most of the day sleeping. He wasn't hungry and didn't eat the peanut butter and jelly sandwich his mother brought him in the afternoon. She looked mad but didn't say anything, just went back to her soap opera.

When his dad came home he sat on the side of the bed for a few minutes, touching the back of his hand to Joe's forehead, saying, "You're running a pretty high fever, son. Best thing for you is sleep." His dad went away.

He slept, then woke up again when his mother brought him a mashed-up aspirin in a spoon and a glass of milk. He tasted the milk and said, "It tastes funny." He didn't want to drink it. The smell made his stomach heave.

His mother sad, "That's just the aspirin. Drink the goddamned milk."

So he had to drink the whole glass because his mother was standing there waiting. He got it down but right away, before his mother even got halfway to the door, he was vomiting, the spoiled milk spewing from his mouth.

She went to the kitchen, came back with some rags and a bucket and said, "Clean up your stinking mess!"

Shivering, he got down on his hands and knees and did as he'd been told. He was so woozy he kept wanting to curl up on the floor and go to sleep. But he got the job finished, and climbed back into bed.

Then he was out in the back yard with his dad, playing catch. He went chasing after a ball that went way over his head when his dad seemed to fly up into the air, then fall to the ground, his head hitting the cement path—hard. Joe could hear the hard hollow sound it made and was scared. He came running over the grass, got down on his knees and held his dad's hand, saying, "It's gonna be okay, Dad. Just don't move."

His dad's eyes were closed and Joe yelled at his mother to call an ambulance but she kept on standing there. Joe screamed at her and finally she went inside. Joe stroked his dad's hand, more scared than he'd ever been. He saw blood starting to spread under his dad's head, and Joe knew he'd cracked his head wide open, but he still couldn't understand why his dad had fallen.

"It'll be all right," he kept repeating, wanting someone to come help, but knowing no one would. The blood was spreading, thick and very dark, and his dad wasn't moving at all. Joe sensed his mother at the back door looking out. He was scared she hadn't called anybody, scared his dad was going to die.

He awakened feeling murderously angry. He fired up a smoke and went into the kitchen to fix a cup of instant coffee, adding extra crystals to make it strong. He drank it sitting at the kitchen table, his head propped on one hand.

The house was cold but he didn't hike up the thermostat. No way was he paying out his good money to heat this dump. Sitting there sipping the coffee, he decided this was it. Tonight after work he was going over to Helen's place to find out where Bobby was at.

He stowed the rifle and the handgun and a couple of boxes of bullets in the trunk. Then, while he waited for the Firebird to warm up, he flashed again on that dream of his father. Was that the way it had actually been? He couldn't remember. But it sure as shit felt as if it had been.

Twenty-Seven

Penny came bouncing off the school bus and flew to her mother with her lips pulled back to show the gap in her front teeth.

"My tooth came out!" she crowed. "The tooth fairy's gonna come tonight."

Bobby said, "That's great, Pen," but for a few seconds she was stricken, realizing her daughter had taken another step forward, that she was less of a child than she'd been even that morning.

"Yeah," Penny said, enormously gratified. "It's great. I'm gonna go tell Granny." She threw down her backpack, pulled off her coat, and went running up the stairs.

Bobby carried the backpack down to their apartment, making a mental note to leave a little surprise under Pen's pillow. She could remember finding a pair of quarters under her own pillow years ago, and being ecstatic at the discovery. These things meant so much to little kids.

She sat down for a minute, wanting to give Pen some time with Alma, and considered what a momentous day this was. Most likely it wouldn't have seemed anything special to a lot of people, but to her it was highly significant. Pen was going to lose all her baby teeth now. She'd begin changing every day in small but important ways. Before she turned around, Pen would be a teenager, spending hours on the telephone and going out with boys. And where would the two of them be then?

She looked around the room. Probably not here, she thought, and felt saddened. She wanted them to be able to stay; she imagined herself taking courses and learning new skills, using them here, in this house, with these people. She wanted to go on reading Eva's books and doing up Alma's hair in different ways; wanted to maintain the routines they'd established. But she couldn't help feeling it wasn't going to be that way. Things never stayed the same, no matter how much you wanted them to.

Eva was sitting in the armchair in the office, looking out the window and wondering how to take what had been a tragedy and give it a happy ending. In order to do that, she'd have to make Deborah's story a secondary theme, shifting the focus. What initially had seemed a good idea had become, with Bobby's suggestion, very complicated.

The linear narrative she'd been considering was simple and straightforward. Shifting Deborah to a lesser role would entail much more plotting, not to mention the development of additional characters. All for the sake of a happy ending. Why was she letting herself get turned around by Bobby? Guilt, she thought tiredly. She was fussing over Bobby's suggestion in order to avoid the larger issue of her culpability.

She knew that for Bobby the night before had been a tremendous breakthrough. She'd confided the long-secret details of eight years of horror. Eva wanted her to feel secure, to believe that she hadn't placed her trust unwisely. It had been a great show of faith on Bobby's part, telling the things she had, and Eva felt an obligation to honor that. But she hated knowing as much about the woman as she now did, hated the too-graphic images that kept popping into her mind. So, in an effort to ease her guilty conscience, she was actually attempting to appease Bobby by planning an upbeat ending for the book. The effort was heightening both her self-disgust and her profound distaste for what she'd learned of Bobby's life. She found

herself wishing the woman would pack up and go away.
The thought of continuing to see her every day was driving Eva to despair. She was furious with herself for having willfully, intentionally encouraged Bobby to confide in
her, and furious with Bobby for having told her far too
much. For the first time in her life, she truly disliked herself.

After Pen had been put to bed that evening, Alma and
Eva each gave Bobby five dollars to put under her pillow.
"We'll use it to buy her a new book. She'll like that,"
Bobby said. Touched by their generosity, she went to each
woman in turn to give them a kiss. Eva hugged her rather
awkwardly, without the warmth and ease she'd demonstrated in the darkened kitchen the previous night, and
Bobby thought she was probably a little uncomfortable
with her own good instincts. Like Bobby, she was able to
do things in darkness that were difficult, if not impossible, in the light.

Alma said, "You're too sentimental," and shooed
Bobby away, saying, "Go find the Rachmaninoff second
piano concerto and put it on for me."

Bobby went to do as she asked, anticipating Pen's excitement when she awakened in the morning to find so
much money under her pillow. After adjusting the volume on the stereo, she sat down with her knitting, noticing that Eva seemed fidgety. When the telephone rang, Eva
jumped up to answer it and Bobby could tell from the
smile that came over her face that she'd been waiting and
hoping Charlie would call.

Sure enough, Eva announced, "I'm going out for an
hour or two."

"Now there's a surprise," Alma said, working her way
through the *Advocate*. "I'm sure our office visit this afternoon merely whet your appetite."

Eva laughed and said with mild sarcasm, "That's it exactly." She crossed the room, put a hand on either arm of

the wheelchair, bent until her nose was touching her aunt's, and said, "You're turning into a genuine curmudgeon." She kissed the tip of Alma's nose, ran a hand over her aunt's hair, then straightened, saying, "I'll see you both later," and went to get her coat. So great was her relief in being able to escape that she was actually able to smile at Bobby on her way out. "Hypocrite," she whispered to herself as she opened the hall closet.

When the front door had closed behind her, Alma said, "They're good for each other."

"They seem to get along really well." Bobby smiled over at her, then looked back at her knitting.

"They'll get married," Alma said with certainty. "It's time."

"Maybe they're fine as they are."

Alma sniffed and folded the newspaper in her lap. "Speaking of marriage, what are you going to do about that husband of yours?"

"In what way?"

"I assume you'd like to be rid of him," Alma said. "You might want to start thinking about consulting a lawyer."

"I'm kind of scared to do that. I mean, if I file papers or something, Joe will find out where I am." Her fear came rushing back, then, and she wondered if Eva had locked the front door on her way out; she also wanted to run downstairs and check on Penny.

Alma saw the way her expression changed, saw the fearful alertness darken her eyes, and tried to imagine what it must be like to be so afraid. It was alien territory. There'd never been anyone she'd feared, and she wondered if perhaps she hadn't been exceedingly lucky. "Sooner or later you're going to want to take legal steps to be rid of him," she said, wishing she hadn't raised a subject Bobby plainly found so distressing.

"I had this legal aid lawyer tell me I could get a restraining order," Bobby said, "but I couldn't see the point of bothering, because no piece of paper would ever stop Joe. Nothing would stop him." Her hands had turned damp and the wool wouldn't slide smoothly through her fingers. She put the knitting down, wondering if these past weeks had been nothing but an illusion, like an extended dream. Because it was true: Nothing would ever stop Joe. She could hide, but he'd find her. Someday, somehow, he'd find her.

"What about Dennis?" Alma asked.

"What about him?" Bobby responded, thinking she'd dragged everyone into this mess with her. She was filled with Joe's poison and was spreading it around, like a virus. "We're just friends. I'm not interested in getting seriously involved."

"Don't be dishonest, Barbara," Alma said in her schoolteacher's tone. "It's obvious you're fond of Dennis. Don't you want to be free?"

"You don't understand," Bobby said softly. "Even if I went to court and got divorced tomorrow, Joe wouldn't care. So far as he's concerned, I'm his property."

"Perhaps he's found someone else."

"Don't I *wish!*" Bobby said with energy. "But he doesn't want anyone else. He has to have me, like I'm his perfect wife or something, even though I couldn't do one thing right, where he was concerned."

"Perhaps," Alma suggested shrewdly, "you're his perfect victim."

The remark rang with truth inside Bobby's head, and she nodded slowly, saying, "Maybe so. Maybe that's it. I never thought of it that way."

"But you didn't enjoy the role. You ran away. You're no longer willing to play the victim."

"No, I'm not," Bobby agreed.

"Then it's time to take the legal steps to validate your emancipation. Granted, it is only a piece of paper. But it's also a declaration, my dear, of your refusal to play out the role he assigned you."

"I guess that's true," Bobby said, drawing strength from the older woman's dogged insistence on holding the truth up for her viewing.

"I spoke to my lawyer about you this morning," Alma said. "He'll be more than happy to discuss the situation with you at any time."

"You talked to your lawyer about me?"

"Primarily, we discussed Penny," Alma explained. "I'm making provision for her education."

"You'd do that for her?" The fear was displaced by loving gratitude. No matter what happened to her, Penny's future was secure.

"I will do that for her," Alma stated, "because she deserves it. She's a child with a fine mind. I want her to have the opportunity to grow to her full potential."

Bobby was temporarily speechless. She could only stare at the woman in the wheelchair, marveling at how fate had brought them all together. "You make me believe in God," Bobby said at last.

"Please don't make religion an issue here," Alma said impatiently. "I believe in doing what's right, at least when it's within my power to do so. And, naturally, Penny's education would be of concern to me. I was a teacher, remember."

"I remember," Bobby said, humbled.

"So, that's that," Alma said with finality. "End of discussion." She picked up the newspaper and pretended to read, anxious to avoid any further display of gratitude on Bobby's part. Making provision for Penny was purely a practicality. She had no interest in gratitude, didn't want or need it. Her fulfillment was derived from putting her wishes into effect.

Bobby got up and moved from the sofa to the armchair next to Alma. She worked at what she wanted to say, sorting through variations and discarding them one after another. There was really only one way to say what she wanted, and yet the words felt like lumpy little pellets in her mouth, so unaccustomed was she to airing her true emotions.

She studied Alma, able to see very clearly the tall, handsome woman she'd been not so very long ago; able to feel the power Alma had wielded then and now, picturing dozens of schoolgirls awed and intimidated by her height and authority; and able, too, to feel the underlying anger that shaped so much of what Alma had to say now.

"Pen loves you," Bobby said, her voice even huskier than usual.

Alma looked over.

Bobby wanted to add, I love you too, but knew this wasn't the time. Determined not to cry, because she also knew Alma would be angry if she did, she looked directly into the old woman's clear blue eyes and waited.

Alma gazed at her for what felt like a long time. Bobby smiled and said, "You hated me saying that, didn't you?"

"I *told* you," Alma said, trying and failing to sound irritated. "You're too sentimental." Then she smiled, and for Bobby it was like that moment in the middle of the night before, when she'd told her secrets to Eva. They'd connected in a very important way. "Go do your knitting," Alma said gruffly, slapping the newspaper down in her lap to refold it to another page.

Bobby nodded and went back to her knitting.

"So how's it going, cupcake?"

"I'm getting there," Eva said, propping her feet on the coffee table. "I'm revamping my original concept, expanding it, because Bobby said the book should have a happy ending." She wanted to tell Charlie the truth but couldn't. If she did, she'd be as guilty as Bobby of saying too much.

"I'm all for happy endings," he said, one arm extended across her shoulders.

"When she said it, I was unbelievably offended," she admitted, deciding this was a reasonably safe area.

"Why?"

"It struck me as so profoundly presumptuous. What does she know about writing, after all? Who is she to tell me what to write? But then, when I really thought about it, I decided perhaps she does know something. It has to do with making people feel better about the human condition, and she was right about that—much as I hate to admit it."

"I told you I'm all for happy endings," he said with a smile.

She punched him lightly on the upper arm. "Don't patronize me, Charlie." She was in an extraordinary state of mind, had never felt quite like this: madly anxious mentally, and physically highly agitated. She wanted desperately to make love, to engage in a lengthy sexual tussle that would engage all her senses and ease some of the pressure on her brain.

"Never," he said, making a show of rubbing his injured arm. "I mean it. I usually get to the end of your books and heave a contented sigh, very pleased with the way you've tied everything up. I take it you were thinking of going with something downbeat?"

"Well, it seemed to me I'd have to. Deborah did die."

"True. But you're not writing a biography, are you?"

"No. Which is why I'm no longer offended." That much was true. She was no longer bothered by Bobby's suggestion. Now she was simply bothered by Bobby. "To be honest, I think the idea made me mad because I was opting for the easy way out. It's infinitely easier to write a book with three characters than it is one with, say, eight. The thing of it is, Charlie, I'm basically lazy." I'm also a fraud, she thought, feeling another twinge of guilt. Why hadn't she left things alone? She'd manipulated Bobby, encouraged her to reveal her past, and then felt something akin to loathing for having been made to view scenarios that sickened her. Again she saw that image of Bobby on her hands and knees.

"You, cupcake?" He feigned surprise with lifted eyebrows and widened eyes.

"Don't mock me," she warned, on emotional thin ice. One small push and she might blurt out the sorry details of what she'd done. And she despaired of reducing herself in Charlie's estimation.

"I'm not," he said, letting his face relax. "I think we're all basically lazy, if the truth be known. The temptation is always to take the easiest route. But those of us with conscience usually choose to go plodding down the more convoluted trail because we know we won't be able to live with ourselves if we don't. It's like prescribing medication for the superficial symptoms instead of digging deeper to find the actual source of the problem. Digging deeper takes more time, more thought, more care. It's the responsible way to go, but that doesn't mean the instinct isn't there to throw it all off by writing out a scrip. A hell of a lot of doctors do. Personally, I can't. And neither can you. It's why you're a good writer."

"You amaze me," she said, sitting up to look directly at him. "You actually understand what I'm talking about." Was she expecting too much of herself? she wondered. How was someone supposed to react to horror stories? Why did she have the idea that she should, somehow, have been able to absorb the things Bobby told her without feeling any measure of revulsion?

"Sure," he said with a shrug. "It's part and parcel of the old work ethic. You and I have that in common. It's one of the reasons why I like you, cupcake. You're a plodder, like me."

"That's one way to put it, I suppose," she said, still looking at him closely. Alma was daily becoming more attached to Bobby and Penny. There was no likelihood of their leaving in the near future. How was she going to resolve this? What kind of person was she, anyway? Forty-three years old and she'd gone along thinking she knew herself well. Now she wasn't sure she knew herself at all.

"All right," he amended. "How about diligent?"

"Better," she said. "It sounds nicer than the other. The mental image of a plodder is someone acutely overweight waddling across the road on a yellow light." God! She was actually playing out the role of Eva Rule here, hoping to do a good-enough job so that Charlie wouldn't notice the understudy was on tonight. This was terrible.

He laughed and tightened his arm around her shoulders. "Definitely not you, Eva. Aside from everything else, you don't have an ounce of excess fat."

"What say we finish our drinks in the bedroom?" she said, leaning in to kiss the corner of his mouth. She'd take her clothes off and allow Charlie's body to close down her brain. Her flesh at least was still honest.

"That's one of the other things I like about you," he said, taking her by the hand.

"What did you do," she asked as they got up from the sofa, "make a list or something?"

"Or something," he said with a grin. "It's what we diligent types tend to do."

"You really do love me, don't you, Charlie?" she asked, wondering for the first time how he saw her. She was actually losing her confidence. Was this going to be the penalty for what she'd done to Bobby? But what *had* she done to the woman? Nothing, in fact. It was all in her head. In her head and crowding out rational thought.

"Uh-hunh."

She was very lucky, she decided, breathing in the enticing scent of his Obsession. He wasn't about to judge her the way she'd so harshly judged Bobby. If her luck held, perhaps he never would. And perhaps in another day or two she'd get past those appalling mental images. "I love you too," she said, and wrapped her arms around him, telling herself she wasn't a bad person. But she wasn't a nice person, either. Not nice at all.

Twenty-Eight

It was completely dark by the time Helen Chandler went out to her car, which was parked at the side of the Ford dealership. It was bitingly cold but the sky was very clear, although snow was forecast. She was thinking about Bobby and Pen as she pulled out into the traffic, on her way to the supermarket, trying to decide what to get them for Christmas. The previous two years she'd bought Pen books, but she was no longer up-to-date on what Pen was reading and hated the idea of duplicating something she might already have. If Bobby had given her a phone number, she could have called to ask. But all she had was the address. Before Bobby's last call, she'd tried to get the number from information and had been told it was unpublished. And she'd forgotten to ask for it, so pleased had she been to hear Pen's darling voice. Next time Bobby called, Helen intended to get the number. She wanted to be able to check in from time to time and not have to wait for Bobby to get in touch with her.

She decided she'd get Pen a cute little outfit to wear and maybe some coloring books and crayons. And there was a sweater she'd seen at the mall, pale pink with a lace Peter Pan collar, that'd look good on Bobby; pink had always been a good color for her. As a teenager, Helen had been responsible for buying Bobby's clothes, and she'd enjoyed it, sometimes pretending Bobby was her child and not Susan's. Getting pregnant and leaving the baby on their hands was so typical of Susan. Helen was only surprised she hadn't turned up again with another child for them to raise. But aside from a postcard from Arizona that arrived when Bobby was about six months old, they'd never heard from Susan again. For all anyone knew, she was long dead. Which, so far as Bobby's well-being as a child was concerned, was probably for the best. Susan had been far too self-centered ever to have made an even halfway decent parent. Still, now and then Helen couldn't help wondering what had become of her older sister.

She made the trip to the market a quick one, picking up a package of center-cut loin pork chops, potatoes, some frozen broccoli, and a Sara Lee cherry cheesecake. She'd do a real shop on the weekend, but right now she was anxious to get home after a long day's work, have something to eat, and curl up on the sofa in front of the TV.

The potatoes were on the boil, the broccoli was in the steamer, and the chops were baking in a pan with about a quarter inch of orange juice. The aroma of the spitting chops and the warmth of the oven gave her the same cozy sense of well-being she felt every evening as she prepared herself for a few hours of relaxation. She'd never cared much for cooking but had promised herself she wouldn't be one of those people who ate out of cans or took all their meals at restaurants. So she fixed herself a decent supper each night of the week. She thought of this time as her reward for the eight hours she put in Monday to Friday, and the four hours on Saturday, at the dealership. It wasn't the best job she'd ever had but it was far from the worst. And she did get a new car, free, every year and free servicing, to boot.

She was just setting the table in the kitchen when the cellar door burst open and there was Joe, inside the house, with a gun in his hand and a chilling smile on his face.

It happened so quickly she had no time to react. She was so shocked—her heart pounding frantically from the noise, the surprise—that for a few precious seconds she was frozen in place, trying to comprehend how he'd managed to get into the house. Had he been hiding in the cellar for hours waiting for her to get home? The front door had been properly locked. But she hadn't checked the back door, and was stupidly tempted now to turn and see if she'd left it off the latch. How did he get in? she kept asking herself, frightened but determined not to show it.

She turned automatically and put a hand out to the telephone, but he shot across the room, grabbed hold of the back of her sweater, and jammed the gun into her neck, saying, "Tell me where she is."

"Get your hands off me!" she demanded, trying to set free herself. "I don't know where she is, and even if I did, you'd be the last person I'd tell." Even as she spoke she was still trying to figure out how he'd gained entry to the house. Had she left the back door open? She didn't think she had. In fact, she now recalled taking out the garbage that morning and making sure the door was locked when she came back in. Which meant he'd found some other way to get in, maybe through one of the cellar windows. "How did you get in here?" she asked, knowing even as the words came out of her mouth that she was being stupid. It no longer mattered how he'd got in. He was in, and he had a gun to her neck.

He punched her between the shoulder blades, saying, "Don't give me any shit. I'm not in the mood. Tell me where she is!"

"I don't know, and I want you out of my house this instant!" she said, but her voice shook so the words emerged sounding feeble. Whatever authority she possessed had vanished. Strings of commands shunted around inside her head, but everything she tried to say to him came across as scarcely more than a whisper.

"Just what I figured you'd say," he barked, and shoved her in the chest with his free hand. "You're gonna tell me where she is," he insisted, eyes glittering with intent. "You *are* gonna tell me."

She looked at the pot of potatoes on the burner and thought if she could get close enough to reach it she'd throw it at him, but he backed her into the refrigerator, put his face close to hers, and smiled. "You're gonna tell me," he said again, so close she could see the tobacco stains on his teeth, could smell oil and some kind of solvent on his soiled work clothes. He put a hand over her throat, keeping her pinned to the refrigerator, and said, "I had this dream about you, Auntie Helen." He made the words Auntie Helen sound snide. "I dreamed I tied your hands good and tight behind your back. Then I took a big darning needle and some thread and I sewed your fucking lips shut." He made a pinching motion with his thumb and forefinger and she flinched, desperate to get away from him but there was nowhere to go. He had her right up against the refrigerator and was standing no more than six inches away. "Then," he went on, obviously enjoying himself, "I sewed your eyelids together." Again, he made the pinching gesture, this time directly in front of her eyes. "After that,"—he grinned—"I put the needle right through here"—he held the gun to her nose—"and sewed your fucking nostrils shut." His smile widened. "And you know what I did then?" He waited, as if expecting her to answer. When she didn't, he tapped her under the chin with the gun and said, "Then, Auntie Helen, I sat down and had a smoke while I watched you suffocate. You put up a damned good fight," he said, as if describing something that had actually happened. "I'll give you that," he said. "You fought like a bastard. I got off on it. I sat there and jacked off while I watched you croak, came so hard it felt like my spine cracked." He laughed at the look of disgust on her face. "I might even do it, just for the hell of it, if you don't tell me where she is." He pulled back the hammer, dropped his hand, and pressed the barrel into her thigh. "Give me the address," he said, "or the first bullet goes right in here."

She believed him. He was crazy. She'd always known it. But she'd never been able to get Bobby to see it. Time and again during the months Bobby was dating him after poor Dad died, she'd sat her down and tried to get her to see she was making a terrible mistake. But Bobby had been dazzled, and dazed, too, still grieving for her grandfather. She'd needed to be taking care of someone, and she believed Joe was that person. Nothing Helen could say would persuade Bobby that she was too young and too inexperienced to be getting married at all, let alone to a man as clearly disturbed as Joe Salton. There'd been no satisfaction for Helen in learning she'd been right. And Bobby, having given her word and committed herself to the marriage, couldn't or wouldn't admit she'd been wrong. "He needs me," she'd said dozens of times, but with an expression that indicated she was attempting to convince herself and not Helen. She'd come to the house with all manner of injuries—blackened eyes, puffy split lips, a broken nose, broken ribs, broken fingers, cuts and bruises, even a concussion—and Helen had begged her to leave him, but Bobby had wound up going back to Joe every time. The bastard had managed to convince poor Bobby that she was too inept, too defective in every way to cope on her own.

It had taken her far too long, but Bobby had finally escaped, and now this demented thug was going to go after her. Helen couldn't think of any way to get rid of him, or to gain a few seconds to call the police. All she could think to do was stall him. "The address is in my purse," she said. "In the bedroom." She thought she might somehow distract him, then she'd get to the extension upstairs and call 911.

"Okay," he said. "Let's go get it." He fastened his hand to her upper arm and marched her down the hall and up the stairs to her room. "So where is it?" he asked, looking around. "You jerking me around, Auntie Helen?"

"I forgot," she said, eyeing the extension on the bed-side table, knowing there was no way she could get to it. She felt foolish, incompetent, unable to outwit him despite her superior intelligence. It was because, she told herself, she lacked criminal instincts; because, with the exception of this despicable hoodlum, all the people she knew were decent, law-abiding citizens. No one was equipped to deal with a creature like Joe. He was an aberration, an abomination, the epitome of everything she abhorred.

"You *forgot?*" he repeated, eyes narrowing. "Don't play fucking games with me, bitch!" He backhanded her across the face, hard.

She wanted to kill him. It frightened her to feel such hatred. It was like bile rising into her throat. And it was compounded by outrage at her helplessness. She had no means of defending herself. She'd never conceived of a situation remotely like this, had never understood until this moment what it felt like to be utterly defenseless. And suddenly she knew how Bobby had felt being married to this man. It was an appalling sensation of being completely inconsequential, of no value or significance whatsoever, of being less than nothing.

"You think I'm playing some fucking *game* here?" he ranted, grabbing her by the hair and giving her head a fierce yank so that tears sprang to her eyes. "This is no fucking GAME!" He kicked her with his work-booted foot in the shin.

Pain shot up her leg and her stomach contracted. Instinctively, she reached down to rub her injured shin, but he shrieked, "Don't you move! You so much as twitch, and I'll get me a fucking needle and some thread and start sewing your goddamned face up. Now where's the purse?" he demanded, giving her hair another yank.

"In the kitchen," she whispered, trying not to be sick. This was what he'd done to Bobby. How had she survived eight years of this? Poor, foolish, nineteen-year-old Bobby, thinking this animal needed anyone.

"If it's not," he warned, "I'm gonna start shooting you. First one goes here"—again he rammed the gun into her thigh—" and the next one's going here." He stabbed the gun barrel into her upper arm. Another pain radiated upward into her shoulder, down to her fingers.

"It's there," she whispered, hating herself for being so afraid, for being so at his mercy. It was degrading, shameful. He made her feel defective for being smaller and weaker than he was. But he was crazy. How did you protect yourself from someone who was crazy?

He prodded her with the gun to get her moving back down the stairs. "It better be there," he warned, jabbing her again and again with the gun—minor jolts of additional fear, localized pain.

"It's there." She'd call the police the moment he left, get them to warn Bobby in Connecticut, get them to protect her and Pen. He'd be locked up; they'd never let him out. She wanted him put away somewhere for good.

In the kitchen he said, "Get me that fucking address *now!*" and punched her between the shoulder blades. "NOW!"

Defeated and terrified and angry, she got her purse from the back of the door, opened her wallet, and took out the folded piece of paper on which she'd written Bobby's address. "There!" she said, overcome by the sick sense that she was betraying the niece she'd so often pretended was her own child. "Take it and get the hell out of here." She'd never hated anyone, she realized. The animosity she'd felt upon occasion toward some salesgirl who'd been rude or one of the employees at the dealership who'd come into her office insisting she'd screwed up the deductions had been nothing compared to the twisting inner spasm of loathing she felt for this monster who'd somehow managed to get inside her home. She looked at the gun, wishing she could get hold of it. She'd kill him without hesitation. She wanted him dead.

He snatched up the paper, and, while he was looking at it, she took advantage of those few seconds when his attention was elsewhere to spring across the room and reach for the receiver on the wall phone. There was an ear-shattering roar of sound that bounced off the walls and ceiling of the small kitchen, and a searing bolt of pain as a bullet penetrated the back of her leg, spun her around, and threw her against the counter. The leg wouldn't support her and she slithered to the floor in disbelief, her upper body coming to rest against the cabinet under the sink.

This was what it felt like to be shot, she thought, watching him, knowing there was nothing she could do to stop him. He was going to kill her and she couldn't do a thing to prevent it. All she could do was pray one of the neighbors had heard the shot and was at that moment picking up the phone to call the police. Dear God, she was going to die and it wasn't supposed to be this way. She was supposed to have another thirty or even forty years before she died. She was only forty-four. She'd never suffered anything worse than the flu in her entire life, and now she was going to die. This couldn't be the way her life was going to end. It couldn't. She didn't want to believe it. But it was happening. This madman was going to take her life away.

"You're history, Auntie Helen," he said, lifting the gun and taking aim. "I always wanted to do this." He smiled again. Again there was an explosion of sound and pain. This time in her shoulder. She couldn't hear, and the whole left side of her body had gone dead. She couldn't take her eyes off him, although peripherally she could see blood on her sweater. She kept looking at him, arbitrarily convinced that he'd stop now because she could see him, and he could see that she saw him. They were staring at each other. But whatever it was he saw only seemed to fuel him. There wasn't the slightest hint of anything human in those eyes. The gun roared again, then again. Pain consumed her. Still she kept looking at him, watching him tuck the piece of paper into his pocket as he gazed back at her, smiling. He actually seemed happy. She couldn't make sense of it. How he could appear so happy? She studied him, looking for some sign of remorse, some small indication that he was human, that he cared even minimally about the effects of his actions. But he just kept on smiling, as if having the finest time of his life. And all she could think was that she was seeing the living incarnation of the devil. She'd never believed in graphic black-and-white distinctions, with God representing everything good and the devil representing everything evil. But she was seeing it, right there in the kitchen of the house she'd lived in all her life. And the devil wasn't a red-suited demon with horns and a tail. He was an ordinary-looking man, of average height and weight, with dark hair and demented eyes and a blood-chilling smile that revealed his tobacco-stained teeth.

"Thanks a lot, Auntie Helen." He blew her a kiss, then turned and walked down the hall toward the door. He didn't look back. He went out, closed the door.

She looked up at the wall phone, thinking she'd call the police now, but it was too far away, she felt too sleepy. All she wanted was to close her eyes and go to sleep. She had to warn Bobby somehow, told her body to move. It wouldn't. It didn't seem to belong to her anymore, didn't want to respond to her commands. Her ears were ringing, waves of sound washing in, then retreating. And the air reeked of gunpowder, making it hard to breathe. She'd just close her eyes for a minute. Then she'd get to the phone.

Her head impossibly heavy, she allowed her eyes to shut. She felt very cold and knew she'd have a stiff neck when she woke up. If she was going to take a nap, she really should go get the afghan from the sofa in the living room. But she was too tired even to think about moving. She'd sleep for a few minutes, and then she'd get to the telephone. She would. As soon as she woke up.

He was so high he wanted to start singing at the top of his lungs. He couldn't hear a goddamned thing, but he felt absolutely great as he climbed into the Firebird. Bobby was in Connecticut and he was gonna go get her. But first he had a few things to do. He'd go home and get cleaned up, then head over to Garvey's for something to eat.

There were a couple of people poking their heads out their front doors as he took off but he didn't give a shit. He'd blown goddamned Helen away. It'd been the greatest high of his life. He hadn't been sure he could do it, and that first shot had been kind of hard to squeeze off. But he'd done it, and she'd gone flying across the room like some huge invisible hand had whacked her one. Whacked. Yeah. He had to laugh. It was perfect. Blood all over the place, and the look on her fucking face, like she couldn't believe it. Beautiful. He'd seen his mother, made out to himself it was payback time for every stinking, rotten thing she'd ever done to him and to his dad, too. Rubbing shit in his face, locking him in the fucking closet for hours at a stretch, pounding on him when he hadn't done anything, dragging him around by his goddamned hair. And letting his dad die out there on the cement path, taking her time calling for an ambulance. All those rotten Thanksgiving and Christmas dinners when she'd said, "Yeah, thanks," for the presents he'd gone to the trouble to buy her even though what he really wanted was for her to keel over dead right in front of him. That one was for you, Dad, he thought, loving the feel of the car, the surge of power as he eased his foot down on the accelerator.

The gun smelled fantastic; he loved its smell, rubbed the gun over his cheek and lips, then sniffed the barrel, breathing in as deep as he could. He pushed the gun down between his thighs and got hard instantly. He'd never had such a rush, such a fantastic high. He tightened his thigh muscles, enjoying the ache in his groin.

The smell was on his hands, too. He held first one then the other under his nose, inhaling the smell of power. He was king of the fucking universe; he could do *anything*. His chest felt like it had swelled up to at least a forty-four. He felt huge, like the goddamned Hulk. Fantastic! And he was suddenly so hungry he could eat a fucking horse. He'd get a double cheeseburger with bacon and a plate of well-done fries, none of that uncooked pale shit, but well-done. He'd tell Garvey to make sure those fries were *golden*. He could practically taste them. His mouth was watering, and the gun was hot between his legs. He sniffed his hands again, then licked his fingers, tasting the bitter, metallic residue on his skin.

He couldn't wait to chow down. His stomach was growling. Jesus, but he'd loved it. He was halfway tempted to set off after Bobby there and then, forget going home, forget eating, just floor it and take off for the highway. Get to Connecticut, find the bitch, and take her out by inches, fuck her every way to Sunday, then shoot her in each arm, then the legs, then watch her flop around for a while before blasting her in the chest. But he had plenty of time and the advantage of surprise. He'd stick to his plan, go home and take a good hot shower, change into clean clothes, throw a few things in the car, then head to Garvey's. After that he'd play it by ear. He had all the time in the world, and he was going to enjoy this, prolong the high, keep it going until the very last minute.

Twenty-Nine

Penny dreamed the tooth fairy came and sat on the side of the bed. She looked just like Melissa but she had on a white sparkly dress and carried a magic wand with a star on the end. Penny thought she was beautiful, and the tooth fairy didn't even mind when Penny touched her sparkly dress.

"You get a wish with the first tooth you lose," the Melissa/fairy said. "Anything you want in the whole world."

"Anything?"

"That's right," the Melissa/fairy said. "Anything at all."

"I don't know what to wish for," Penny said, and sat looking at the flat white tooth in the palm of her hand. She poked her tongue through the gap in her teeth, then looked again at the tooth fairy, saying, "You look like my friend. Are you Melissa?"

The tooth fairy smiled and said, "No, I'm not, but we always choose a human form we like."

"You mean you can look like anybody you want?"

"That's right."

"I wish I could do that," Penny said, thinking with a giggle that she could be a Ninja Turtle, or one of the Jetsons, or even a giraffe. It was a good thing she didn't have to choose, because she couldn't decide who she'd be.

"You have to make a wish," the Melissa/fairy said very nicely.

"Right now?"

"Right now."

"But I don't know what to wish for," Penny said, worried. "I have to think about it."

"Oh, dear," the Melissa/fairy said. "You were supposed to have thought about it already."

"But I didn't know. Nobody told me."

The Melissa/fairy looked at her magic wristwatch, then gave a little shake of her head. "I'm afraid time's running out, Penny. You've got to make your wish now, or you'll lose it."

"Okay," Penny said anxiously, trying hard to think of what to wish for. "Wait just one minute. I'm thinking."

"Only one more minute," the Melissa/fairy said. "I have quite a few other children to visit tonight."

"Okay," Penny said, thinking as hard as she could. "Just another second." Should she wish to be the richest little girl in the whole wide world? That would be greedy, and her mom said it was wrong to be greedy. But maybe it would be okay to ask for a little money, and she'd give it to her mom. "I wish for..." Wait a minute. How much should she ask for? The seconds were ticking off the magic wristwatch. "I wish for eight, no, wait. I wish for twenty hundred dollars."

The Melissa/fairy waved her magic wand and the tooth disappeared from Penny's palm. A stack of money replaced it. She counted the bills. There were twenty of them. When she looked up, finished her counting, the Melissa/fairy was gone, and Penny felt bad at having wished for money. She should have used her wish to help other little children, or to save the rain forest the way Mrs. Corey told them about in school.

She got out of bed, being careful not to disturb her mom, and went to put the money on the night table beside her mom's bed. When she woke up, Mom would be surprised and happy, and she'd say now they could get the Honda fixed up or maybe they'd go to Disneyland. That'd be good. Her mom would be glad, Pen decided, getting

back into bed. And wait till she told Granny and Auntie
Eva that Melissa was the tooth fairy! They'd be so surprised.

Bobby gasped, "No!" and heaved herself into wakefulness, putting out a shaking hand to turn on the light.
She looked slowly around the room, mentally chasing Joe
back into the shadows, pushing the dream away. Penny
had kicked off her blankets. Bobby got up and drew them
back over her, then stood for a time watching Penny sleep.

After a minute or two she turned the light off and went
into the kitchen to get a cigarette. She took a deep drag,
then looked up the stairs. It would have been good to sit
and talk, but Eva wasn't up there. She'd phoned at around
ten to say she'd be home in the morning. She was spending the night with Charlie. She'd sounded kind of abrupt
on the telephone, but Bobby decided that was because it
embarrassed her to have to phone home like a teenager. It
had to be hard for her, Bobby thought sympathetically, a
grown woman obliged to let her aunt know where she was
almost every minute of the day.

She sat down and tried to think about beautiful things.
At first her mind, like a disobedient child, kept wanting to
go back to the nightmare. But gradually she was able to
focus on a magnificent garden, with carefully laid-out
flower beds and winding pathways leading down to the
ocean.

Penny threw her pillow aside, saw the three five-dollar
bills and whooped with excitement. Grabbing the money,
she said, "I'm gonna go show Granny!" and flew up the
stairs before Bobby had a chance to say a word.

Penny knocked at the door the way she was supposed to,
then ran inside and climbed up on the bed, exclaiming,
"Look what the tooth fairy gived me, Granny!"

"Aren't you the fortunate one," Alma said, enjoying Penny's excitement. What she loved about children was the completeness of their emotional reactions. They hadn't yet been tainted by exposure to the larger world and so displayed their joys and woes without inhibition, holding nothing back. Their eyes and their thoughts were clear, and they laughed or wept without restraint. She truly loved children, especially this child. Penny reminded her daily of the simple pleasures of her own childhood, of the many good moments she'd experienced in the course of her life. Penny was an unexpected gift. She could no longer sit for hours indulging in death dreams because at regular intervals Penny would come hurrying in to see her, bringing the bounty of her enthusiasm. "What are you going to do with all that money?"

Penny settled cross-legged atop the bedclothes and looked at the bills in her lap. "Maybe," she said, thinking, "I'll buy something nice for my mom."

"That's very generous of you," Alma said, "but I think the tooth fairy would expect you to buy something for yourself. And I think perhaps your mother would too."

"You think so?" Penny gazed wide-eyed at Alma.

"Oh, I think that's the intention."

"Weelll," Penny said, "maybe then I'll get some books and some crayons and some cut-out dolls. Or maybe I'll buy a new winter coat for Mr. Bear. I don't know. It's a big bunch of money, the most I ever had."

"You'll have to think about it." Alma smiled, fairly assaulted by fondness for this sprite-like child. It was the same battering at the heart she'd felt when she'd had to explain to a six-year-old Eva that she was going to be staying on in this house because that's what her mother and father had said they wanted. The first time she'd told her, Eva hadn't very much of a reaction. And Alma had been greatly relieved, having anticipated a wrenching emotional scene. Weeks went by, and then one evening the little girl had announced she wanted to go home now, and

Alma had crumbled inside at the prospect of having to explain, again and more clearly, that Cora and Willard Chaney were never coming back; translating death into practical terms a child could comprehend. One of the worst moments of her life. She herself had lost a sister she'd loved far more than she'd ever realized, and the pain had eaten away at her insides like acid as she'd held the child and introduced her to the facts of death. Over the years, she'd suffered that same sensation of dissolving inside whenever one of the particularly energetic little girls at school was sent to her office to be chastised for insubordination. She might never have carried a child of her own—except in certain remarkably real dreams she'd had from time to time, when she'd lain naked on a table in a sterile room and pushed an infant out of her swollen body—but she'd mothered dozens, even hundreds of girls. And she'd treasured certain moments—instances of minor revelation—when she'd seen a child's eyes brighten with comprehension, or with relief, or in response to an affectionate display. "You'd better run along now and get dressed or you'll miss the school bus."

Penny said, "Okay," and knee-walked across the blankets to give Alma a noisy kiss on the cheek before she climbed off the bed and, clutching her money, went hurrying off. "See you after school, Granny," she sang, closing the door with care before scampering off down the hall.

Alma sank back against the pillows, thinking about Eva, wondering how long it would be before she announced her intention to marry Charlie. Not long, she thought. Now that Bobby had proved herself capable of taking care of everything, Eva was essentially free. A month or two, and she'd move on. It was good. It was time. The greatest gift a mother gave to her child was its freedom. She wanted Eva to have hers once again.

* * *

Upon arriving home, Eva went directly to the kitchen to begin preparing breakfast for her aunt. She was putting bread into the toaster when Penny came running in, practically dancing with excitement.

"Lookit all the money the tooth fairy gived me," she said, showing Eva the bills.

"That's wonderful," Eva said, and bent to lift Penny into her arms, smiling as she swung the girl in a circle. "The tooth fairy came to visit you." Holding the child, she felt a sudden, wrenching sadness along with a heightening of her guilt. How could she wish that Bobby would pack up and leave when it meant removing Penny from the household? She loved this little girl. More importantly, so did Alma.

"Yeah!" Penny beamed, then her brows drew together as she tried to remember. There was something about the tooth fairy she'd wanted to tell Granny and Auntie Eva, but she couldn't think what it was. "I gotta hurry and get dressed. Granny said."

Eva put her down and Penny said, "Oh, I forgot," and went to put an X through that day's date on the calendar. Then she ran toward the apartment door, stopped and looked over. "How come you're wearing the same clothes from yesterday?"

Taken aback by the child's acute powers of observation, Eva said, "I slept over at a friend's house." She'd forgotten the way small children seemed to notice the things you thought they wouldn't and were fairly oblivious of the things you imagined they'd see. Penny had the ability to make Eva feel transparent, just as Melissa once had and, to a large extent, still did.

"Oh!" Penny nodded. "I'm gonna sleep over at Emma's, maybe, on Saturday if Mom says I can."

"That'll be fun."

"Yeah." Penny grinned, then hurried downstairs.

Eva shook her head and moved to pour herself some coffee. Penny constantly reminded her of those years, when she'd been engaged in full-time mothering. For a few moments, leaning against the counter sipping her coffee, she imagined what it would be like to have another child, to find herself pregnant at forty-three. One of her former editors had just had her first baby at the age of forty-two. Women were waiting later and later to start having families. Age was no longer the deterrent it once had been. She thought of the strenuous lovemaking of the previous night and felt a twinge in her thigh muscles. A few months off the pill and she might easily get pregnant. But she knew she wasn't going to begin all over again with another child. She enjoyed her freedom—or at least she had, prior to Alma's stroke—even if she did suffer the occasional pang, missing Melissa's need of her. She'd loved being Mel's mother; of course she still did, but it was very different now. She'd evolved into an adviser and a confidante. As the parent of an adult child, she was free primarily to worry about the plethora of misadventures that might befall Melissa. So Eva worried—both waking and sleeping—about car accidents, rapists, caustic cruelties inflicted by snotty students, madmen with guns opening fire in a crowded McDonald's, fire, swimming and boating mishaps, all sorts of sickening things. But she made a conscious effort never to burden Melissa with her fears, just as Alma had kept hers to herself during the years she'd mothered Eva.

Through the open apartment door she could hear Penny telling her mother to hurry, then the low husky murmur of Bobby's voice. Eva buttered her aunt's toast, thinking about the things Bobby had told her and her own overwhelming disgust at hearing those things. Under impossible circumstances, Bobby had managed to do a fine job of mothering. She was, as Charlie had said, a first-rate caregiver. She was unobtrusive, conscientious, generous, and gentle. At Eva's urging, she'd given voice to the alarming details of her marriage and now Eva could scarcely bear to

look at her. Bobby's past and present vulnerability infuriated and oppressed her, made her feel like screaming. But
it was wrong to feel the way she did. She'd solicited and
accepted the woman's trust and was now playing a game
of mental handball with it. God, but she wished Bobby
would go away! The anxiety was like heavy-grade sand-
paper, roughening all her surfaces. Contradictory emotions had her swinging first one way, then the other. She'd
sat at that table and told Bobby she didn't deserve to have
been treated the way she was. But a part of her didn't believe that. Just as a part of her insisted that Deborah had
somehow contributed to her own undoing. Her common
sense and compassion argued that none of this was true.
No one deserved to be beaten or to die because she had a
husband who was out of control. What she'd told Bobby
had been the truth. So why couldn't she put aside her
squeamishness and simply accord Bobby the respect she
deserved?

As she carried Alma's tray up the stairs, she tried to
reason through her negative feelings. She'd started out
viewing Bobby as a human resource, someone who'd help
her to understand what had happened on the island, perhaps give her insights that would strengthen the story she
planned to write. Well, Bobby was providing her with all
sorts of insights, many of them almost too grisly to bear,
and, at the same time, demonstrating an incisive home-
spun kind of wisdom. Eva had to admit she was impressed by the fact that, despite the ugliness of her
experiences, Bobby was capable of affectionate displays.
She was substantially deeper than Eva had imagined she
would be. What bothered her, Eva suddenly realized, was
Bobby's willingness to trust her. She should have been
more cautious, shouldn't have been so quick to reveal so
much. Because, had their positions been reversed, Eva
certainly would never have capitulated as readily and as
completely as Bobby had.

And there it was! she thought, at last getting to the root of her upset. She was angry with Bobby for not behaving as she, Eva, would have under the same circumstances. Which was insane, absolutely insane. You didn't go around condemning people because they weren't like you. How on earth was she going to resolve this? she asked herself as she reached to open the door to her aunt's room.

"I want you to drive me over to Len Morgan's office this afternoon," Alma told her as Eva set the tray on her lap. "I've got a one-thirty appointment."

"What for?"

"Just some papers to sign," Alma said offhandedly, picking up a triangle of toast.

"What papers?" Eva asked, sitting in the chair by the window with her coffee.

"Just papers," Alma said testily. "It won't take long."

"What're you up to?" Eva asked, mildly suspicious.

"If you must know, I've had Len prepare a codicil, making provision for Penny's future." She faced Eva down as if expecting an argument.

"That's wonderful of you," Eva said softly, and felt like weeping. How typical of her aunt, she thought, to put her caring to such practical effect. It made her present feelings about Bobby even more reprehensible. Her shame was growing deeper by the minute. Bobby wasn't going to be leaving this house in the immediate future. Somehow, Eva was going to have to come to terms with that fact. For a moment she longed to tell her aunt everything, to confess what she'd done and admit her terrible ambivalence. But just as she'd feared saying anything to lower herself in Charlie's estimation, she also feared appearing small-minded and harshly judgmental in her aunt's.

"It's simply good sense," Alma said gruffly. "Penny deserves every opportunity."

Eva got up and crossed the room to kiss her aunt on the forehead. "You're a good old stick. You know that?"

"Go sit down and let me eat!" Alma said, then had to smile because she was feeling particularly well. She'd always derived immense pleasure from seeing things through to completion.

Eva sat down again and reached for her coffee, thinking how close she'd been to turning Bobby away that first afternoon she'd come to the door. She hadn't done it because she hadn't had the heart to add to Bobby's visible suffering. She'd never been able to ignore pain, had never been able to walk past homeless people pretending not to see them. So she'd opened the door and allowed Bobby inside. And now she had no idea how she was going to be able to live with the consequences of her own actions. She'd never felt so ashamed.

Thirty

*T*he morning after whacking Helen, he got up as usual, showered, dressed, went out to the car, and drove to work. He was already walking through the plant door when he remembered he hadn't planned to come back. But since he was already there he figured what the hell and clocked in. One more day of this rotten job wouldn't kill him, and it'd give him some extra time to plan things out.

He spent the day working on automatic pilot, getting the job done without thinking about it. He was preoccupied with figuring out his moves, and he got through the eight hours without even noticing the time passing. By the end of his shift he'd made up his mind to set off the next morning. His plan was to go about halfway, then check into a motel for some sack time, sleep in late for a change, and get to Connecticut late Thursday or early Friday. There was no rush. He'd take his time, get a motel room in the area, then check out the address he'd taken off Helen, cruise the place and get some kind of fix on the setup, then revamp his moves if necessary. He wanted this to be perfect.

He saw the cruiser parked out front of the house as soon as he turned into his street, and couldn't believe they were on to him already. But they were, they had to be. Why the hell else would they be here? He got this nasty jolt in the chest and immediately started sweating, his mouth dry, hands wet. *Son of a bitch!* he muttered under his breath.

He couldn't fucking believe it! Stay cool, he told himself. Don't get thrown. Think!

He could pull in, park, and play it innocent, talk to the cops. They couldn't prove squat. But maybe they could. Maybe he'd left something personal, something incriminating in the house. What, though? He did a quick mental replay of everything that had gone down the night before and couldn't come up with a thing. But that didn't matter to these goons. They'd haul his ass in, maybe put him in a lineup, take up valuable time he couldn't afford to lose. He had a gut feeling he was only going to get one shot at Bobby and he intended to make good on it. Nothing was going to stop him. If they took him in they might keep him, and he'd never have another chance to finish what he'd started. He had to finish. It was all he wanted now, all he could think about. He didn't give a shit about anything else. It was like his whole life had been time he'd clocked on, just getting through it, until he could do this one thing.

There was only one smart way to go. He just cruised on by. As he passed the house, keeping his speed nice and steady at your basic residential-neighborhood twenty-five, he took a quick look and saw one cop at the front door and another going up the driveway to check out the back. He drove past, his mind racing.

Obviously he was going to have to take off now and hope every cop in the state wasn't out looking for him. It pissed him off royally because he'd wanted to take a shower, get into clean clothes, pack some stuff, go over everything in his mind at a nice, slow pace, then set off in the morning after a good night's sleep. Now he wasn't going to be able to do any of that. Luckily his munitions were in the trunk or he'd have really been fucked. Okay. That's the way things were. Fine. He'd just have to improvise from now on, he thought, heading out of town. His underarms were wet, his shirt sticking to him, and his goddamned mouth was dry as dust.

Passing a mall, he flashed on the K-Mart, wheeled into the lot, parked the Firebird, and strolled into the store. He'd been paid on Friday, so he had plenty of folding money. He used some of it to buy a pair of jeans, a couple of shirts, some socks and underwear, a package of disposable razors, a can of shaving cream, a toothbrush, and some Crest. If he needed anything else, he'd pick it up along the way. This was going to work out fine after all.

After stowing his purchases in the trunk, he climbed behind the wheel and took off for Route 17. It irritated the living shit out of him but he kept his speed down to sixty. No way was he going to get pulled over for speeding only to have some cop run his plate and find out he was wanted. So he kept it down even though his whole goddamned leg was shaking, and now that he was finally on the road and putting some distance between himself and the local cops, he was absolutely furious with the way things were going. Instead of starting out relaxed and fresh he was stuck in his stinking work clothes, smelling bad, and wiped out after working all day. He could smell himself and hated it. It reminded him of that time his goddamned mother had rubbed shit in his face. He couldn't get the scene out of his mind, and he felt like he was smothering, rage and panic squeezing at his lungs.

He cranked the window down a few inches and fired up a smoke, telling himself to chill out. Nobody knew where he was. And, even more beautiful, nobody—except maybe that goddamned Lor—knew where Bobby was. Lor was the wild card, the one person who might warn Bobby he was on his way. But he'd take that chance. He'd take care of Bobby, then disappear. Yeah. He loved the idea of that, and had an image of himself being the invisible man, vanishing like smoke. Get himself a new set of plates for the car and he could go anywhere, maybe cruise on up the east coast, even cross the border into Canada. All he had to do was keep his speed down, take his time, study his moves, and everything would work out.

"*Be cool, man,*" *he told himself, fiddling with the tuner knob on the radio. "Just be cool." He thought about the fantastic high he'd had the night before, and sniffed his fingers for the smell of cordite. But all he could smell was the goddamned gritty shit he'd used to clean his hands at the shop. He wiped each palm in turn on his pant legs, then took another drag on the smoke, feeling himself getting calmer. Imagining the look on Bobby's face when he caught up with her, he smiled, and felt even better. It was like all his life he'd been waiting for this. It felt right, one hundred percent right.*

"Getting her to do those exercises is starting to pay off," Dennis was saying. "She's a lot stronger, especially the left leg."

"She doesn't make such a fuss about doing them anymore," Bobby said, unwilling to take any credit for Alma's efforts.

Dennis drank some of his coffee and gave her a smile. "You really are pretty bad at accepting compliments," he said, "even backhanded ones."

"I know," she admitted, a bit more relaxed in his company each time she saw him. "I didn't used to be this way. My grandpa always used to tell me, 'Just say thank you and be done with it,' and I got pretty good at that for a while, although it seemed to me it was like saying thank you to people for noticing you had on a nice sweater, or blue eyes, or something. But if you said thank you, people sort of got past wanting to compliment you and went on to other things. So that was okay."

"But you still didn't like accepting compliments," Dennis persisted, his expression one of fond amusement.

"I guess not," she agreed, realizing that she and this man had become friends. It was a first in her life: friendship with a man. "Anyway, after being with Joe for so long, I got to believing there wasn't anything about me *worth* complimenting. You know?" She looked to see how he took this, not wanting him to think she used Joe as an excuse for every last little thing. She could remember in high school all the kids with the different excuses for why they weren't popular: They were too fat, or they had bad skin, or they were the wrong color. None of it had been true. Sometimes people just didn't like each other, for no reason at all. And that was the way Eva had been acting the past few days, as if for no good reason she'd stopped liking her. Things were almost back to the way they'd been at the beginning, when Bobby had first come, and she couldn't figure out why.

"I understand," Dennis said, meeting her eyes straight on, then looked at his watch.

"You've got to go."

"Afraid so."

"The client in Norwalk," she said, kind of relieved that he was going. She needed time to herself to think about the situation with Eva and what, if anything, she'd done to make her mad. "I've got to run out to the supermarket. I'm making the dinner tonight."

"Oh, yeah? What're you making?"

"Just spaghetti. Nothing special."

"That depends. Are you a good cook?"

She saw Joe heaving the plate of spaghetti at the wall, blinked away the image and said, "Not bad. One of these times I'll cook for you."

"That'd be nice."

"You like what you do, don't you, Dennis?" she asked, giving in to her curiosity about him. She wondered for a few seconds if maybe he could explain what was going on with Eva. But that was dumb. Even if she told him about it, the best he'd be able to do was guess at the reasons.

"A lot," he confirmed. "I'm my own boss and I get to see results most of the time. Sometimes it takes a while, but it's a real kick to see one of my people making progress. It makes me think I'm actually accomplishing something, and that's a good feeling."

"Not too many people like their work," she said, getting up to walk with him to the door. "Joe used to complain every single day about his job. He hated it, and he hated everyone he worked with." There was rarely a night when he hadn't come in raging about how he'd like to kill so-and-so, how he'd like to teach the son of a bitch a lesson he'd never forget.

"You and I are two of the lucky ones."

"That's true," she said, thinking maybe she and Pen wouldn't be around here much longer if Eva had anything to say about it. She wished she knew what was wrong. She hesitated for a moment, picturing herself loading their stuff into the Honda, driving off to God-only-knew-where. It made her chest ache. She wanted to stay here more than she'd ever wanted anything. "I hope you don't mind me talking about Joe."

"I don't mind. He used to be part of your life, after all."

Used to be, she thought. She imagined getting a telephone call and someone on the other end of the line saying Joe was no more, he'd simply ceased to exist. How wonderful that would be!

"I'll pick you up tomorrow night at seven-thirty. Okay?"

"That'll be fine."

He pulled on his coat, then took hold of her hand and bent to give her a quick kiss on the mouth. Without stopping to think about it, she hugged him, in need of comfort. Then, realizing the gesture might be misconstrued, she stepped away from him, sudden heat rising into her face. It was dangerous, what she'd done. She was getting used to him, letting down her guard, and that was when things could go wrong.

"Guess you surprised yourself, huh?" he said, smiling sympathetically, as if he actually understood.

"I wouldn't want you to think..." She trailed off, not sure what she wanted to say.

"Don't worry about it. I don't think anything. See you tomorrow," he said, reaching to open the door.

"I'll be waiting," she said.

He tooted the horn before driving off, the way he always did, and she closed the door wondering why she'd believed for eight long years that she deserved the treatment she'd had from Joe. Why had she thought that? Why had she allowed herself to be convinced? Somewhere along the line things had become completely turned around and she'd accepted Joe's version of the facts. Why? Now Eva was acting funny. She was polite and she smiled, but she'd stopped looking Bobby in the eye. Eva wouldn't tell her what she'd done wrong, and it was making her feel the exact same way Joe used to.

She returned to the kitchen and sat again at the table, reaching automatically for her mug. Drinking the coffee without tasting it, she thought of the countless times Joe had laughed nastily about something she'd said, the times he'd said she was "just a goddamned woman," as if women were inferior in every way. She'd believed him. Why? Well, one thing she knew for sure: It wasn't right. Not at all. And no matter what happened, nobody ever again was going to tell her she was no good and stupid just because she was female. And that included Eva, too. One way or another, she was going to find out what was wrong and try to fix it.

Having reached this conclusion and feeling marginally better, she put on her coat and went out to the car.

Eva could feel a buzzing beneath her skin, and every few minutes she experienced a kind of low-grade electric sizzling shock to her brain. It was the excitement she felt every time she was about to begin work on a new book, and it would build, daily, hourly, until the moment she sat down and actually commenced writing. It was her excitement that had been lacking for some time.

Now it was back, and she loved it. Not even making love had the same sort of giddy expectation. The only problem was that her mixed feelings about Bobby kept short-circuiting the excitement. She couldn't sustain that positive, creative mood. The pressure was building and she felt she might explode at any moment. She kept thinking about the Montaverdeans hauling in that net full of fish, and feeling she was as trapped and entangled as those frenzied, thrashing creatures.

While she watched Bobby prepare spaghetti sauce, her mind was operating on two distinct levels. On one level she was observing, noting the economy of the small woman's gestures, approving objectively of the organized way in which Bobby approached her cooking. On the other level she was fairly frazzled by anxiety, wanting Bobby gone. If she'd only go away, everything would be all right. It was appalling, but she could barely tolerate Bobby's presence in the kitchen. What the hell's the matter with you? she asked herself, hating her meanness of spirit, her lack of compassion. She'd never been particularly adept at hiding her feelings. Ken had always been able to read her accurately. Melissa could too. So could Charlie. And Alma had that uncanny parental radar. It was only a matter of hours or days before Alma demanded an explanation of her behavior, of her less-than-cordial treatment of Bobby. What could she possible tell her? She didn't dare admit that she was suffering from overexposure to the details of Bobby's life, that she kept seeing Bobby naked on her hands and knees. For God's sake, it was ridiculous! She herself had a hearty sexual appetite and had made love in any number of ways, any number of times, and the recollection had never bothered her. But of course no one had forced her; there'd been no pain involved; and she'd certainly never been sodomized. For Bobby, sex was merely another form of abuse. Which was why the images were so upsetting. They had nothing to do with lovemaking and everything to do with bestiality.

"I'll do the salad," she announced, automatically going to the refrigerator to remove the crisper drawer.

"I don't mind doing it," Bobby said, dropping several bay leaves into the pot of simmering sauce before turning to look over.

"I'll do it," Eva said, unable to keep the sharpness out of her tone.

"Is everything okay?" Bobby asked cautiously, determined if possible to clear the air.

"Everything's fine." Eva examined a tomato, saying, "Do you remember when tomatoes actually tasted like something? Now they're like red Styrofoam."

Bobby laughed, and Eva looked at her, aware again of how rarely Bobby laughed. "You're happy here, aren't you?" Eva asked, studying the contours of the younger woman's pretty features. She had no desire to hurt her; the last thing on earth she wanted was to destroy anyone's happiness, especially not this poor haunted woman's. How was she going to handle this?

It felt like a trick question, Bobby thought. If she admitted to being happy, maybe Eva would pull the rug out from under her and say, "Too bad, because you've got to go." *Why* wouldn't Eva say what was bothering her? If she'd only talk to me, Bobby thought, we could fix things. "I like it here," she admitted cautiously, fearful of losing the first security she'd known in too many years.

"Yes," Eva said distractedly, still holding the tomato. "I can tell."

Bobby waited to hear what else she'd say, but Eva didn't say anything more. She put the tomato down on the cutting board and reached for one of the knives in the rack.

Maybe it was okay, Bobby thought, letting her breath out slowly. Things would keep on the way they were going. She and Pen wouldn't have to pack up and go away. This was one of Eva's moods. That's all. Just a mood.

Thirty-One

❦

"**Y**ou can read ùntil seven-thirty, Pen, and then it's lights out. Okay?"

"Can I read upstairs in the living room with Granny and Auntie Eva?"

"I think that'll be okay." Bobby smiled and bent to lift Pen into her arms, hugging her close.

Penny wound her arms and legs tightly around her mother.

Bobby held her a moment longer then put her down, saying, "Don't make a pest of yourself. Sit quietly and read your book, then come on down and get straight to bed. I'm just going to eat with Dennis and I won't be out late."

"I wish I was comin' too. I like Dennis."

"I know you do. Next time. Okay?"

"Yeah, okay."

Upstairs in the kitchen, Eva told Bobby, "Don't worry. I'll get her into bed."

"She's all set to go. She's had her bath and brushed her teeth."

"It's all right," Eva said more firmly, determined to behave well because suddenly she wasn't so sure she wanted Bobby to go away. Her vacillating confounded her. All she knew was that Alma's opinion of her, finally, mattered more than anything else and she wasn't going to say or do anything that might affect that.

"Okay," Bobby said, aware that Eva had undergone a change of mood. She was looking her straight in the eye for the first time in days and that cranky edge had gone from her voice. "Thank you."

Penny came running up and went to greet Dennis, who was waiting with Alma in the living room. After giving him a hug and a kiss, she positioned herself on the end of the sofa nearest Alma, who was in her usual spot to one side of the fireplace. Bobby crossed the room and bent down to whisper, "Mind your manners, Pen. And don't overstay your welcome. Give me a kiss," she murmured, "and I'll see you in the morning."

Dennis was waiting. Bobby went to get her coat, feeling all at once dizzy with dread. She wished she weren't going. For no particular reason, she thought she should have been throwing things into boxes and getting herself and Pen out of there. She didn't know why. Half of her was convinced she'd found them a good home; the other half wanted to get going there and then. In part it had something to do with Eva's changes of mood. But it was more than that; it was as if an alarm bell had started ringing and she was the only one who could hear it.

Pushing aside the sudden, awful sense of apprehension, she forced herself to give Dennis a smile as she buttoned her coat, and she exclaimed involuntarily as they stepped outside. "It's really cold." She took in the street, looking, as always, for the Firebird. No sign of it.

"Winter is upon us," Dennis observed, holding the passenger door open for her. As he climbed in behind the wheel, he said, "I thought we'd do Italian tonight. How's that for you?"

"That's fine," she said mechanically, trying and failing to pinpoint some specific reason for her uneasiness.

"There's a place in Westport I thought you'd like," he said, getting his seat belt fastened.

"Okay," she said, settling in for the ride. She'd get over this feeling. It was nothing. She smiled again at Dennis.

* * *

At seven-forty the telephone rang. Hoping it was Charlie, Eva crossed the kitchen to pick up the receiver. Not Charlie, but a woman asking for Bobby.

"I'm sorry. She's out for the evening. Would you like to leave a message?"

"This is her friend, Lor, from Jamestown."

"Yes. Would you like to leave your number?"

"Has she heard yet?" The woman's voice was high and excited.

"Heard what?"

"Oh, damn! I was afraid of that."

"Of what?" Eva asked impatiently.

"I didn't know a thing about it until I read it in the paper not an hour ago. It was such a shock! I'm still shaking."

"Know what?" Eva's knees had gone wobbly.

"Her Aunt Helen," Lor said. "She was shot."

"My God!"

"According to the paper, she was killed a couple of days ago. The paper says they're looking for Joe, they want him for questioning. I can't hardly believe it. Me and the kids just got back from spending a few days with my folks in Buffalo, otherwise I'd've called her right away. See, I forgot to cancel the papers. So they were all over the porch, and the story about her aunt was right on the front page. It says they're holding the body pending notification of the next of kin, and that's Bobby. I called up the police and told them it's her, gave them your number. They said they'd be getting in touch."

"I'll tell her," Eva said, horrified.

"Tell her I'm real sorry. Okay? I guess she'll have to come back, take care of things. Will you tell her I said she and Pen can stay here? Lord, it's a terrible shock. I just can't believe it. I mean, I always knew Joe was bad, but I never thought he'd go killing people."

Eva was all at once very cold. "I'll have her phone you as soon as she gets in," she said, finding her throat had constricted.

"Okay. And will you tell her I said to let me know if there's anything I can do?"

"I will tell her. Thank you for calling." Eva hung up and stood staring at the wall. After a few moments she returned to the living room.

"What's wrong?" Alma asked.

"We'll discuss it later," Eva said, glancing over at Penny.

Understanding, Alma nodded, trying to imagine what she'd heard that had drained all the color from Eva's face.

Eva sat down in the wing chair by the fireplace, studying Penny. The child was seated cross-legged on the sofa with the book in her lap and she gazed down at the page, mouth slightly open. She was so engrossed that Eva hated to disturb her. But it was already twenty to eight and it felt especially important to keep to the child's regular schedule. She was also anxious to get Pen out of the way in order to tell Alma about the telephone call.

"Time for bed, Pen," Eva said, and watched her drag her eyes upward to look over.

"Five more minutes, okay?" Penny said, her eyes only briefly meeting Eva's before sliding back to the enticing block of print.

"Now, Pen," Eva said gently, keeping a lid on her fear for the child's sake. "It's already ten minutes past your bedtime."

"Okay," Penny sighed, reluctantly closed the book, then got up to approach Alma. "Time to say good night, Granny." She waited for Alma to lean forward so she could kiss her cheek.

Alma cupped Penny's chin for a moment, loving the sight of the child's face. "Sweet dreams," she said, and let Penny go.

As Eva took her hand and they went across the hall into the kitchen, Penny asked, "Are you mad at me?"

"Not at all. Do I seem mad?" Eva was somehow never prepared for Penny's awareness.

"A little, kind of."

"I promise you I'm not mad. In you go now." Eva folded back the blankets and Penny climbed onto the bed, sitting on her knees for a moment to put her book on the bedside table. Then she held out her arms expectantly.

As Eva kissed her good night, she all at once understood that Bobby and Penny had to stay here in this house. The two of them belonged with Alma. Easing Penny down, she moved to go. She had no idea how they were going to work things out, but she knew they would. They had to, for Alma's sake, and for Penny's.

"Don't forget to leave the bathroom light on for me," Penny reminded her.

Eva detoured to turn on the light, then went back upstairs. "Her aunt is dead," she told Alma. "The police want to question Bobby's husband. They're looking for him. He seems to have disappeared. I think he's on his way here."

"Who called, and what exactly were you told?"

Eva's mind was racing. Bobby's aunt had been killed. Her husband might very well show up here. Was history actually going to repeat itself? The thought terrified her. But surely there really wasn't anything to worry about. Was there?

"It was Bobby's friend Lor. She said it happened several days ago, but she was away until this evening. It was all over the local papers. The woman was shot. This Lor called the local police and gave them our number. She said they want to talk to Bobby. Maybe we should move the two of them into a motel for a few days, just in case."

"Before we start making decisions for Bobby and Pen, I think we should consider all the contingencies..." Alma began as the telephone rang. "Might as well answer that," she told her niece. "It's probably Charlie. If it is, I'm afraid you'll have to forego the pleasure of his company for this evening."

"I'd hardly be likely to go out at a time like this," Eva snapped, crossing to the telephone.

"Eva!"

"Sorry," she apologized to her aunt.

Alma sniffed.

It wasn't Charlie. It was a man identifying himself as sergeant Tim Connelly of the Jamestown police department, asking to speak to Barbara Salton.

"She's not available at the moment," Eva told him, her heart racing. "If you'll give me a number, I'll have her call you as soon as she gets in. I expect her back in about two hours."

The sergeant gave her the number and, in a wildly uncontrolled script, Eva jotted it down.

"That," she told her aunt, "was the Jamestown police." She was so rattled she had to sit down.

Coolly, Alma said, "Bobby will obviously have to go home for a few days. I think it would be best for all concerned if Penny stayed here."

Eva nodded woodenly, her heart still drumming.

"Once Bobby's had a chance to talk to the police, we'll have a better idea how to proceed."

Again Eva nodded.

"I wouldn't mind some coffee," Alma said.

Grateful for something to do, Eva said, "I'll make some," and hurried to the kitchen.

"Did you ever go with anyone besides Joe?" Dennis asked, serving himself from the plate of antipasto on the table between them. "Try some of this," he urged. "It's good stuff."

"Not really," Bobby answered, taking a roasted red pepper. "There were guys we hung around with in high school." She smiled. "You know how it is. Me and my best friend, Lor, and a couple of other girls went around to-gether. And there were the guys who went around to-gether. We'd wind up in the same places, kidding around. But I didn't date anyone, really. What about you?'' She hardly knew anything about him, now that she stopped to think of it. So much of her time with him had been spent in fearful anticipation of the things he might say or do that she'd never thought to ask him about his life. Now that she was beginning to feel comfortable with him, she found that she was curious.

"There was someone," he said quietly, speaking with unexpected sobriety, even pain, so that Bobby watched him closely, wondering if every single person alive had some kind of suffering to tell about. "We went together all through college. I always assumed we'd get married, but right after graduation Leslie decided it would be better if we put some distance between us for a while. She said she needed to find out who she was without me; she needed to find out if she was somebody different when I wasn't around." He looked at Bobby for a few seconds, the old injury plain to see in his eyes. "I said I understood, but I didn't. It seemed to me she was breaking us up for no good reason. But I had to go along. I mean, making a fuss wouldn't've done any good, so I figured I might as well be a good sport about it. Except that it killed me." He shook his head and gave Bobby a wry smile, as if still confused by this past experience. "On one level I did understand. I knew she wanted to find out if she behaved one way with me and another way with other people. But on another level I knew she was breaking us up forever, no matter what she said, and I couldn't get her to see that."

"So what happened?" Bobby asked.

He shrugged. "We never got back together. I knew we never would. Things were never the same between us. I still loved her and she still loved me but we couldn't get back to where we'd been. I couldn't seem to go from being completely involved to being just good friends. To this day

I don't know if she felt any different to herself. She didn't *seem* any different to me. Anyway, at first we hung out together pretty regularly. And then it got to be we'd see each other maybe once a week, then once every other week. Eventually we lost touch. The whole thing kind of dwindled away. I got worn out pretending, and in the end it was a relief not to see her anymore. Since then I've dated a few people, but not seriously."

"Did you get scared?"

His eyes widened and he said, "Maybe I did. I'd never thought of it in quite those terms, but maybe I did."

"Like me with Joe," she said, tasting a marinated artichoke. They were having a serious conversation, and she wasn't struggling to come up with things she thought he wanted to hear. She was simply telling the truth, and it felt right and good.

He nodded and carefully cut a slice of salami into four triangles. "We're all afraid of something," he said. "I hate the idea of getting dumped again. And you're scared of getting bashed around. It's a hell of a life, isn't it?"

"It's like we've all got secret thoughts nobody else can ever know."

"In a way that's true," he agreed. "But you get to a point where you can be fairly sure of the way another person's mind works. I mean, you know where they draw the lines, the things they would or wouldn't do. I'm getting a pretty good fix on you." He smiled again and she could see fondness in his eyes. She wondered what he saw in her eyes, if he could tell she was beginning to feel at ease with him.

"I'm a person who actually likes being understood," he said. "That's one of the reasons I was so thrown with Leslie. She never once *said* she was having an identity problem. If she had, I'd've tried to help her work it out."

"An identity problem," she repeated, testing the phrase in her mind, thinking it sounded right. "Maybe that's what I've got."

"I don't think so," Dennis disagreed. "I get the impression you know pretty well who you are. It's just that you can't figure out why such crummy things have happened to you."

"That's a fact," she said. "Sometimes I can't help wondering if the crummy stuff will ever end, or if I'm going to spend the rest of my life feeling safe for a little while, then getting scared all over again."

"It won't be that way," he assured her.

"You don't know that," she chided him gently. "It's hard to get past being scared, Dennis. It's kind of like smelling smoke when nobody else does," she tried to explain, wanting him to understand. "I can almost taste a fire that's burning somewhere, while everybody else goes on about their business, not smelling it and thinking maybe I'm crazy for saying I do."

"It must be awful," he sympathized. "I'd be a liar if I sat here and told you I understood, because I probably never could. I've never been through any of the things you have. But I can certainly see how a situation like that would turn you gun-shy. It sounds as if you're preconditioned, more than anything else. And that can be changed. You've started a new life and it'll take a while for you to get used to it, but you will because it's what you want."

"It's definitely what I want," she said with a smile, gratified by the progress they seemed to be making. They really were becoming friends.

"Then that's the way it'll be. There's no law that says people aren't allowed to get scared now and then. Everybody does. Maybe not for the same reasons, but scared is scared. Right?"

"I guess so," she agreed, comforted by his logic.

They'd arrived at an impasse. Alma flatly dismissed the possibility that Bobby's estranged husband was coming after her.

"I've never known you to go leaping to conclusions," she told her niece.

"It's simply logical," Eva defended herself. "Based on everything Bobby's told us about this man, it makes sense that he'd come looking for her."

"Even if he did, we're a telephone call away from the police. One call and the authorities will come and remove the man. You're allowing your imagination to run wild."

"You're right," Eva admitted. "I am. But not without justification. The man's a murderer."

"That's supposition."

Eva laughed darkly. "You sound like a lawyer."

"You sound hysterical."

"I'm hardly that. I'm simply, very sensibly, worried."

"It solves nothing. Once Bobby gets back, she'll find out precisely what the situation is, then we'll proceed accordingly."

Eva couldn't argue with that. She got up, intending to take the empty coffee cups to the kitchen, when the doorbell rang. Automatically she glanced at her watch as she started for the door. Eight thirty-five.

"Who could that be?" Alma wondered aloud.

"No idea," Eva said distractedly, on her way out of the room.

She looked out through the peephole to see a delivery man, holding a large floral arrangement. Automatically she assumed that Charlie had sent her flowers and smiled as she opened the door.

"Flowers for Bobby Salton," the delivery man said.

"I'll take them." Eva reached out with both hands. They were probably from Dennis, she thought. But wait a minute. Why would he send flowers when he could've brought them with him? She hesitated, her eyes still on the flowers.

"You do that," the delivery man said and thrust the arrangement into her hands. "Now back up a ways and let me in."

Eva looked up. The man was aiming a gun at her. She knew at once who he was, and thought what fools she and Alma had been. They should've called the local police at once, put them in touch with the sergeant in Jamestown. Instead, they'd wasted precious time debating the likelihood of this man's appearing at their door.

"Go on," he said, and gave her a smile that made her flesh crawl. Jerking the gun to one side, he indicated she should keep moving, and she continued to back up the length of the foyer, trying to think what to do. This was Bobby's husband, the previously faceless man looming over Bobby in that sickening late-night confession. Dead-flat eyes and a ghastly grin.

"What do you want?" she demanded, knowing perfectly well what he wanted. He'd come for Bobby, come to kill her. She felt incredibly foolish for having opened the door. Yet she knew it wouldn't have mattered if she hadn't. He'd have found some other way to get inside. For a moment she was stricken by a profound sense of déjà vu. All this had happened before in another time, another place. There was a sickening familiarity to every move, even to her every emotion. She wanted to be able to do something to avert disaster, to prevent what she knew was going to happen. She also felt a desperate need to protect Penny. She would not allow any harm to come to the child. That much was perfectly clear in her mind.

They arrived at the archway to the living room and Alma looked up, unable initially to believe what she was seeing. A delivery man in a peaked cap pointing a gun at Eva, who was holding a floral arrangement and looking positively thunderstruck. A moment, and then she understood. She shouldn't have been quite so cavalier, should have taken Eva more seriously. She decided instantly to pretend she had no idea who he was. "Take what you want and get out!" she said. "Eva, give him whatever cash we have."

"That's not why he's here," Eva said, impressed by her aunt's ingenuity but at a loss as to how to deal with the situation. She was unable to take her eyes off Bobby's husband, riveted by his glinting eyes and malevolent grin. He seemed to be in the grip of a barely controlled frenzy, energy radiating from him in almost visible waves. Without actually moving, he seemed to be dancing around inside his clothes.

"You got that right," Joe said, sizing up Alma in her wheelchair.

"What's going on?" Alma asked her niece, keeping up the pretense. Bobby had been right to fear this man, she thought. He was plainly evil; he exuded menace.

"I've come for Bobby," he said, taking a quick look around, getting his bearings, all the while keeping the gun directed at Eva.

"She's not here," Eva said.

"Where is she?"

"She's away for a few days."

He laughed and poked the end of her nose with the gun barrel. Shocked by the small jolt of pain, Eva put a hand to her face.

"Don't insult my goddamned intelligence, bitch. She's out with that long drink of water she's fucking, at this fancy-ass Eye-talian restaurant a couple of miles up the pike. You think I'm stupid?" he challenged Eva, jabbing her upper lip with the gun. "Put those fucking flowers down and get in there!"

She did as he asked, setting the arrangement on one of the end tables before going to stand beside Alma's wheelchair, her hand automatically coming to rest protectively on her aunt's jutting shoulder. She'd kill him before she allowed him to hurt anyone in this house.

He moved into the middle of the room, the gun now pointed at both of them, and took another look around saying, "We're gonna sit down now and wait for Bobby to get back. Fuck with me and I'll blow you away." Noticing the empty coffee cups, he said, "Get me some of that coffee."

"I'll have to make a fresh pot," Eva said, thinking he couldn't watch both of them. She'd have time alone, time enough to call the police.

"So make it," he said, spotting the telephone extension on the table near Alma. "Go on!"

Eva started slowly toward the door, fearful of taking her eyes off the man but determined to get to the kitchen phone.

He unplugged the extension, leaving the cord connected to the wall outlet, and tossed the handset behind the sofa. Approaching the wheelchair, he prodded Alma's left arm with the gun, then reached out, lifted her hand, and with a laugh watched it flop bonelessly back into her lap. Humiliated, Alma wanted to annihilate him.

Watching from the doorway, Eva clenched her fists but kept silent.

He smiled at Alma, said, "I guess you're not going anywhere," then followed Eva to the kitchen, where the first thing he did was disconnect the wall phone. "Hustle your buns," he told her, opening the refrigerator and tossing the phone into one of the crisper drawers.

He had a loud voice. Eva hoped to God he didn't awaken Penny. She also hoped he didn't notice the door to the apartment, which was standing ajar. Determined to keep her head, she filled the carafe with cold water and poured it into the well of the coffee maker. Behind her, she heard him pull out one of the chairs and sit down at the table. She could smell him. He emitted a powerful odor of cigarette smoke and sweat that had her breathing through her mouth. It staggered her to think she could function under these circumstances. But she could. Her hands automatically went about the business of making the coffee.

"Bobby's not going to go with you," she said, turning to look at him once she had the machine going.

"Bobby's not going anywhere with anybody," he said, taking his eyes slowly up the length of her body, making her feel naked; using his eyes to turn her into one of those vile mental images she'd been viewing for days. She understood now why Bobby felt as she did. She herself felt even worse for responding as she had to the things Bobby told her. She'd been wrong, judgmental and wrong. And she should have known better. She should have remembered the truth of that adage about not knowing how you'd behave in a given situation until you found yourself in it. She, more than most people, knew that from experience. Yet she'd failed consistently to give credence to the things Bobby had told her about this man. She'd insisted on viewing Bobby from the lofty vantage point of a woman with choices, and only now could she see that sometimes, in all innocence, some women were forced to surrender their right to choose.

"First," he went on, "I'm gonna take out that creep she's been fucking. Then I'm gonna fix her ass once and for all. You give me any grief while we're waiting, I'll whack your mother. Don't make a bit of difference to me."

Eva glanced at the rack of knives on the counter. She had a fleeting vision of herself stabbing the man. She knew it would feel right. God! Astonishing how quickly one could shed all one's notions of civilized behavior.

He laughed. "Go ahead and try," he said. "I'll shoot your fucking hand off. Think I give a shit?"

He meant it; he didn't care. And she understood that unless someone or something intervened, he intended to kill all of them. Deeply afraid, she was also arbitrarily convinced that she could outsmart him somehow. There'd be an opening. All she had to do was stay alert and seize the moment, when it came.

Thirty-Two

Bobby lit a cigarette, then took a sip of her coffee while Dennis went to work on a thickly frosted slab of chocolate cake.

"You sure you wouldn't like some?" Dennis asked, prepared to slide his dessert plate closer to her.

"I really couldn't," she said. "Thanks anyway."

"That's why you stay thin and I have to work out a couple of times a week to keep my weight down," he said with a smile.

"I got really thin being married to Joe," she confided, finding it progressively easier to tell him about her experiences. "I was too nervous to eat. Every time we sat down to the table I was waiting for him to go crazy, to jump up and start screaming." Unexpectedly, telling about it brought it all close to her again, made it very fresh in her mind, as if she'd only been away for a few hours.

Dennis had stopped eating and was looking straight at her. "It got you scared telling me that, didn't it? I'm starting to be able to tell when you're scared. I can see it in your eyes."

She nodded, impressed. "How old do you feel?" she asked him.

"How old? Interesting question." He took another bite of cake, chewed and swallowed. "It depends on the situation. My folks can make me feel about eight years old." He grinned and shook his head. "But most of the time I feel my age."

"I feel real old," she said. "Sometimes I look at Pen and see she's still little, and it reminds me I'm not old at all. Same thing when I catch sight of myself in a mirror. It's a real jolt to see I'm still young, because I feel about a thousand years old. There's not much I haven't seen or heard," she said, trying obliquely to give him some hint of the things Joe had done to her. She took a hard drag on her cigarette, her eyes on his. "You probably shouldn't get your hopes up about me, Dennis. I've been...used in some bad ways. I don't know if I'm ever going to get over it. There are days when it seems as if I will, and days when everything that's happened is like this mountain I've got to climb and I'm too tired to take one more step."

"Don't give up on us yet," he said, as if afraid she was going to dump him there and then.

"The thing is, I wouldn't want you getting hurt because I can't be the way you'd like me to be."

"I like you just the way you are. I'm not planning to change you."

He seemed almost too good to be true, and she wondered if she'd always be suspicious of the things men said and did. "How can you like the way I am? I sure don't."

He laughed and patted her on the arm. "Take it easy on yourself. One of these days you'll start believing there's a lot about you to like."

"You know what scares me more than anything else?"

"What?"

"That Joe's bound to come after me. Somehow or other he'll track us down. You can't imagine what he's like. Alma says I can get legal papers to keep him away, that I can't spend my life living scared. But I know no paper on earth could keep him away."

"Listen," he said, taking hold of her hand, "I really care about you and Pen. So do Alma and Eva. D'you think we'd just sit by and let something happen to you? You're not alone, Bobby. You've got friends here."

She took a final puff on her cigarette before putting it out. "I have this daydream lately," she said softly, wondering what harm there could be in telling him. They'd been so truthful with one another, and he'd said he liked her, that he cared about her and Pen. It had to be okay to admit she cared too, in her own way. "I picture the three of us together, you, me, and Pen, and I get a good feeling. I've had some of the best times of my life with you, Dennis. It feels like you're a real friend."

"I like your daydream," he told her, giving her hand a small squeeze. "I have one of my own that's a lot like it."

She looked at their two hands joined on the tabletop, then up at him, and said, "I never held hands with anyone but my grandpa and my aunt Helen." A blush rising into her cheeks, she lowered her eyes and laughed almost inaudibly. "I sound like such an idiot."

"You sound fine. And I like hearing you laugh. You're making progress, Bobby. It shows a bit more every time I see you."

"I sure hope so," she said. "I'm trying my best."

"I know you are, and everyone's rooting for you."

Eva and Alma sat and watched the intruder gulp down two cups of coffee between furious puffs of a cigarette. Every few minutes he got up and went to the window to look out, then he checked the time before sitting down again, the gun always in his hand. Each time he moved, the women could smell the sweaty tobacco odor he gave off. And as the minutes passed, the odor grew stronger. Alma thought that if evil had a distinct smell, this was it.

Eva wanted badly to do something, but there was nothing she could do, and her mounting frustration was like a weight bearing down on her. There was no way to warn Bobby, no way to get this man out of the house. Each time he went to the window she considered making a dash for the door, but she couldn't abandon Alma. She had no doubt this man would shoot her aunt in retaliation for any move she might make, and she wanted all of them to survive this encounter. Every time her eyes met her aunt's, Alma gave her an almost imperceptible shake of her head, signaling that Eva was to do nothing. So they sat, and waited.

And while they waited—the clock on the mantel ticking audibly, maddeningly—Eva vacillated ever more wildly, fervently wishing at one moment that she'd never allowed Bobby to set foot in the house, and deeply ashamed of herself in the next for entertaining such a thought. None of this was Bobby's fault; she wasn't to blame. But, God, if she'd never responded to their ad none of this would be happening. Eva had to concentrate hard simply to maintain some semblance of calm. Were she to be completely honest with herself, she'd have to admit that Bobby and her precocious little girl had enlivened the household, had given Alma back some measure of her former zest for life. Both their lives had been enriched by exposure to Bobby's simple goodness and affection. Yes, she had perhaps told more than Eva had wanted to hear. But Eva was entirely responsible for that; she'd practically begged Bobby to confide in her. One couldn't ask to see someone's personal photo album then complain about the quality of the snapshots. That was neither right nor fair. Bobby had bared her soul, seeking only understanding. Eva had denied her that. She'd never behaved so badly to someone who so little deserved it. She wanted desperately to apologize, to make amends. But how? And when? This madman was waiting to kill her. There had to be something she could do, *something*.

"How did you find her?" Alma asked him as he went again to look out the window. It was an academic question. She was fairly certain he'd killed to gain the knowledge. She was attempting to converse rationally with a murderer. Astonishing, petrifying. For a year her thoughts had been almost exclusively of death. Now, with the personification of death right there in her living room, she knew categorically that she didn't want to die.

Joe smiled again, that wide, animalistic grin that bared his teeth. "You don't want to know that," he said with a self-satisfied air, flopping back down in the armchair. "What you don't know can't hurt you, Grandma."

Alma's right hand tightened into a fist and she resisted the temptation to enter into a verbal sparring match. It would only exacerbate the situation.

He gave Eva another up-and-down once-over that caused the blood to pound in her ears, made her want to hurl the table lamp at him. This man was a visual rapist, and she feared doing anything that might tempt him to put his imaginings into action.

He stubbed out his cigarette and at once lit another, regarding Alma through the smoke. "This your house, Grandma?" he asked.

"What possible relevance can that have?" she said, keeping her tone of voice neutral, gazing back at him unflinchingly.

It took him a few seconds to catch the drift of her remark. Then, frowning, he sat forward on the edge of the chair and said, "I asked you a question, lady. Whose fucking house is it?"

"It's mine," Eva lied, hoping to deflect his attention from her aunt.

His eyes, when they turned, focused on her breasts, then slowly lifted to her face. "Yeah?" He started to smile. "Got yourself a rich husband, hunh?"

"That's right," Eva said, and looked pointedly at her watch. "He should be arriving home from the city anytime now."

Joe laughed and took another drag on his cigarette. "You wish, babe," he said. "Wherever your old man is, he's not about to show up here anytime soon. Think I'm stupid? I checked this goddamned place out for a day and a half. I didn't see no rich husband coming or going."

"He's been away on a business trip," Eva said icily.

Joe looked doubtful, his eyes going to the window, then returning to Eva. "Well," he said, "he shows up, he can join the party." He checked the time again, then got up and began pacing the width of the room, looking back and forth between the two women. "Who the fuck's that guy, anyway?"

"What guy?" Eva asked, wishing she could get her hands on one of the fireplace tools.

"The *guy*," Joe said, coming to stand over Eva, "that's fucking my wife. That guy."

"No one is fucking your wife," Alma said, articulating each word carefully. "Dennis is my physical therapist."

Joe snorted loudly and moved in front of the wheel-chair. "Fat lot of good he's done you, Grandma," he said, poking her left arm with his gun.

Responding instinctively, Alma smacked his face with her right hand.

He didn't hesitate, but drew back his hand and whacked her so hard she flew to one side and nearly toppled over, wheelchair and all.

Eva seized the opportunity to grab the table lamp by its neck and swung the base at him as he turned, deflected the blow with an upraised arm, caught hold of Eva's wrist, and quickly twisted her arm up behind her back. The pain was immediate and acute, bringing tears to her eyes.

"Don't mess with me, bitch," he said in a low throbbing voice. "I'll rip your fucking arm out at the roots." He gave her a push that sent her sprawling on the floor, grabbed the lamp, and heaved it behind the sofa, where it landed with a shattering crash. To make sure she got the point, he kicked her in the thigh, saying, "Try any more cute stunts and I'll shoot you. Now get your ass on that couch and stay put. As for you, Grandma," he turned back to Alma, who was holding a trembling hand to her face, "mind your fucking manners. You don't go hitting people," he said, jamming his face right into hers so that she could see the tobacco stains on his teeth and smell his faintly garlicky breath. "It's not nice," he added, then stood up and smiled again.

"I was thinking we could take Pen to the circus next Sunday," Dennis was saying as he steered the VW along the southbound on-ramp at exit 17.

"Oh, she'd love that. As long as it's okay with Alma," Bobby said, feeling the small car rock in the backdraft as a huge truck roared past in the inside lane.

"You know it'll be okay with Alma." He smiled over at her.

"I guess, but you never know. It sure would be a big treat for Pen. She's never been to the circus."

"Have you?"

"Once. Grandpa and Aunt Helen took me when I was about Pen's age. It's funny, you know. I remember being confused, because there was so much to look at. And the clowns made me cry. I thought they were sad. They had these teardrops painted on their cheeks, and their smiles were upside down. Even after Aunt Helen explained, I still couldn't laugh at anything they did. It's silly, but that's what I remember."

"Kids get some funny ideas," he said kindly. "I could never watch the trapeze artists because I was convinced they were going to fall. And I hated the wild animal tamers. I wanted the lions and tigers to eat them."

She laughed.

"No kidding," he said. "Those guys going into the cages and cracking their whips, waving chairs. It didn't seem fair."

He pulled into the driveway, put the car in neutral and got out his wallet. "Here's my card," he said. "I've been meaning to give you my number but I kept forgetting. I've got an answering machine, so you can always leave a message."

"Thank you." With an impish smile, she said, "Maybe I'll call you up one night for a telephone visit."

"That's the general idea," he said playfully, reaching for her hand.

Eva's shoulder ached and her thigh throbbed from the vicious kick he'd given her. But what hurt most was her self-esteem. She felt devalued, minimized by what was happening here. No one, not even in play, had ever struck her. Her mind kept recoiling from the fact of this man's having handled her so brutally.

It felt as if the three of them had been sitting in this room for days. Joe seemed to have taken up a permanent position by the windows, turning every other minute to check the driveway, the gun in his hand hanging by his side. She despised him, wanted him out of their home, out of their lives; she wanted him dead. How had Bobby managed to live with this creature for eight years? How had she survived all those weeks and months of torture? Just over an hour in this man's company had Eva thinking murderous thoughts and feeling horribly soiled. To think she'd held Bobby somehow responsible for the abuse she'd described! She looked over at her aunt, recalling the way Joe had struck her, and every muscle in her body went tight with fury.

She suspected that their lives would never again be the same because of this man, because of his invasion of their home, and she raged inwardly at this violation of their privacy, of their persons. She'd read about people like him but she'd never imagined she'd actually encounter one. Ian had been nothing like this. But maybe she was wrong. Maybe, given the proper circumstances, he'd have been precisely like this: a deranged bully, a small man whose only power lay in terrorizing women. Why was she thinking about Ian now? It didn't help.

Alma looked at Eva, watched her battling with her anger. It was ironic, Alma thought. This demented man holding them hostage was, in many ways, like the living embodiment of her stroke. The stroke had reduced her to a captive; this man now held them both captive. He was like a maverick blood clot that had exploded, short-circuiting their lives, drastically reducing their mobility, curtailing their freedom. And it had only just begun. He had come to do damage and he wouldn't leave until he'd satisfied that urge. She was filled with dread, and infuriated by her helplessness.

"Here they come!" Joe declared, peering out through a crack in the curtains. He stepped away from the window and looked first at Alma, then at Eva. To Eva he said, "You're going to go open the door and tell them to come on in, both of them." Eva opened her mouth to protest, and Joe said, "I'm going to be waiting right here with Grandma." He went over to the wheelchair and held the gun to the side of Alma's head. "Say or do anything funny and I'll take her out. Now go get them in here!"

Her body feeling impossibly heavy, Eva started for the door. She didn't want to do this. She wanted to fling open the door and scream at Bobby and Dennis to run for help. But she didn't dare. Alma's life was at stake. She knew this despicable man wouldn't hesitate to kill her. Quaking with fear and mounting anger, she unlocked the door and pulled it open. Dennis was opening the passenger door for Bobby. Eva couldn't seem to make herself speak. Behind her, from just inside the living room, Joe Salton whispered harshly, *"Get them here! Do it, or your mother's dead meat!"*

Oh, God! Eva wet her lips. Bobby was looking over questioningly.

"Could you both come in for a moment?" Eva said, her heart seeming to sink in her chest. She felt like a traitor.

"What's the matter?" Bobby asked, quickly crossing the driveway, at once thinking something was wrong with Penny.

Dennis followed her, assuming from Eva's distressed expression that Alma quite possibly had had another stroke.

Eva backed away from the door, moving to the living room, where, peripherally, she could see Joe standing directly in front of Alma, the gun raised. Oh, God, oh, God! She couldn't bear this, wished she were dreaming, wished this were another nightmare she could shove aside through sheer willpower.

Bobby was asking, "What's wrong? What's happened?" as she came through the door, Dennis at her heels.

"Surprise, surprise!" Joe Salton exclaimed with a happy laugh, both hands holding the gun steady, assuming a classic shooter's stance, knees slightly bent, elbows close together.

Don't let this happen! Eva prayed silently, the four of them watching the man with the gun as he thumbed off the safety catch with an audible click.

Thirty-Three

Alma summoned all her strength and heaved herself up out of the chair and lunged at Joe Salton, throwing him to one side as the gun went off with a great roar. Someone screamed. Fairly deafened and completely off balance, Alma was already falling when Joe swung around, gave her a mighty kick, swung back again, the gun like a pointing finger aimed at those still standing, and shouted, *"Nobody fuckin' move!"*

Penny was awakened by a big noise. It was so loud that it made her heart go very fast. Slipping out of bed, she ran barefoot to the bottom of the stairs, where she stood for a second, listening. Then she ran up the stairs and peeked into the kitchen. Nobody there. She could hear a man yelling in the living room. She knew that voice and it scared her. Holding her breath, she tiptoed through the kitchen and leaned into the doorway to look across the hall. One quick look. Her heart jumped and she was even more scared. She turned and ran as fast as she could back through the kitchen toward the apartment door.

She wanted to lock the door, but if she did her mom wouldn't be able to get in, so she pushed it almost shut, then scrambled down the stairs to where it was dark, the only light coming from the open bathroom door. Her thumb automatically popping into her mouth, she looked over at the stairs, trying to think what to do, her heart beating fast fast fast, worried about her mom and Granny and Auntie Eva. Dennis too.

She looked around, saw the telephone, remembered what Granny had taught her. She darted over and snatched up the receiver, pushed the numbers. When the lady answered, she whispered, "My daddy's here and he's hurtin' everybody. I don't know what to do." The words came tumbling out almost faster than she could say them, her heart going so hard she could barely catch her breath.

"Slow down now and say that again."

Penny repeated what she'd said, her eyes on the stairway, afraid to see the door fly open and Daddy come racing down the stairs after her. He'd hurt her, the way he did that last time when he'd been making lots of noise and it woke Penny up so she went to see and it made him mad so he hit her and threw her all the way across the room.

"What's your name, sweetheart?"

"Penny Salton."

"And how old are you?"

"I'm six. He's *upstairs* and he's got a *gun*. He hurted Dennis and my granny. He's gonna do bad things to my mom. You gotta make him *stop*."

"He's got a gun?"

"Yeah. He's shootin'. I'm *scared*."

"I know you are. Just talk to me. Okay? Do you know your address? Can you tell it to me?"

"Uh-hunh." Penny recited it, dancing from one foot to the other. "You gonna send policemen?"

"Yes, we are. You stay on the line with me now. Okay?"

"Okay."

"Where are you, Penny?"

"I'm downstairs."

"And where's everybody else?"

"They're up in the livin' room. Dennis and Granny're lyin' on the floor. Daddy *hurted* them. Send the policemen to make him *stop!*"

"Who else is there, Penny?"

"My mom and my auntie Eva." Penny felt as if she was going to have an accident and had to hold her knees very tight together. She kept her eyes on the stairway, clutching the receiver with both hands. "I don't want anything bad to *happen!*"

"Okay, sweetheart. I know. Just stay on the line with me. Okay? We're going to send help. Okay?"

"Okay. But *hurry!*"

Bobby knew she should've been terrified but somehow she wasn't. She'd gone far beyond terror, into a region of numb acceptance. From the moment she'd taken Penny and driven away from the house in Jamestown, she'd known something like this was bound to happen. It had only ever been a matter of time before Joe found her. She'd always believed he would. There was nowhere she could've gone where he wouldn't have found her. He'd warned her a thousand times that if she tried to run from him he'd kill her. She'd been a fool to think, even for a moment, that he wouldn't make good on that threat; to hope she and Penny could have a decent life somewhere new, without him. Her prime regret was that she'd caused this to happen in this house, to these people. Dennis was slumped in the doorway, shot. His hand was dripping with blood. The sight of that bloodied hand filled her with sorrow and shame. She didn't want him to die, especially not because of her. She wasn't worth anyone's dying over.

Eva moved to help Alma, but Joe, never taking his eyes from Bobby, snarled, "Stand still, bitch! She can stay there!"

"Don't hurt anybody else, Joe," Bobby said, her ears ringing from the gunshot, her voice sounding as if it came from a great distance. "They have nothing to do with us."

"Don't give me that shit! You think I don't know what you've been up to with that asshole? How long've you been sneaking around behind my back with that jerk?"

"He's just a friend," she said, knowing he wouldn't believe anything she said. All she could hope for was to get him out of the house before he did any more damage. He was going to kill her anyway. But maybe she could talk him into leaving here. If she had to die, at least she could try to spare these good people the sight of it. She glanced anxiously at Dennis, praying he wasn't too badly injured. This was all her fault; she wanted so badly to tell Alma and Eva and Dennis how sorry she was; she never meant to bring any of this down on their heads.

"What the fuck you think you're doing, taking off on me that way?" Joe raged, trying to keep track of everyone. The old broad was moaning and groaning behind him. For all he knew, she might try some other stunt. "You," he said to Eva, "get your fucking mother back in her wheelchair." He moved half a dozen feet to the right in order to keep his eye on them all. Too many goddamned people to keep track of here. He hadn't counted on that.

"He's yellin' and screamin'," Penny whispered into the receiver, wedging herself into the narrow gap between the sofa and the wall, hiding where she hoped nobody could find her. "When's somebody gonna *come*? You *said* the policemen were comin'."

"Soon, sweetheart. They're on the way now. You're doing just fine. Try to stay calm. I know you're scared, but you're doing real well. Stay on the line with me now, okay?"

"Okay, but tell them to *hurry*. I don't want him to hurt nobody else."

"They're on their way. They'll be there any minute. I promise."

"He's *bad*," Penny said passionately, "very, very bad. That's why we runned away from him."

"You ran away? From where?"

"From Jamestown, where we used to live."

"Jamestown, New York?"

"Yeah. When're they *comin'*?"

"Soon now. Don't worry. What grade're you in, Penny?"

"First grade. My teacher's Mrs. Corey. Oh!" she cried, startled. "He's shoutin' again! I want it to *stop!*"

"Does he know where you are?"

"Unh-uh. I'm hidin'."

"Good girl. You stay where you are. Help's on the way. Now tell me about the house, Penny. Do you think you could describe it to me?"

"Uh-hunh."

"Great. You're doing real well. Now tell me where the doors are. Okay?"

Alma had no strength left. The man's kick had caught her squarely in the chest, knocking the air out of her lungs. Now it hurt to breathe. Eva struggled to get her back into the chair. Alma wanted to help, tried, but couldn't, and Eva couldn't manage to move her. Eva's face was dark and twisted. Rage glowed in her eyes.

"I need help," Eva said angrily. "I can't manage alone." She wanted to fly at the son of a bitch, rip him to pieces. Containing her fury required a mammoth effort of will. But she didn't dare take any chances now. All she could do was try to help her aunt and hope Dennis wasn't too badly injured.

"Go help her," Joe told Bobby, waving her over with the gun.

Whispering, "I'm sorry," Bobby bent to help Eva lift Alma back into the chair. "I'm really sorry." She smoothed Alma's hair with a cold, trembling hand.

"It's not your fault," Alma gasped.

Tears welled in Bobby's eyes. She'd brought horror into this lovely home. Everything was ruined now.

"Shut the fuck up and get over here!" Joe ordered.

Bobby moved away from the wheelchair but kept her distance from him, looking over at Dennis, whose eyes were half-closed, his hand now hidden inside his coat. "Dennis needs an ambulance," she said.

"Who gives a shit! It wasn't for that fucking old broad that asshole'd be dead right now. I said get *over* here!"

Was Penny sleeping through this? Bobby wondered. Please don't let her wake up and come trying to find out what all the noise is about. If she stayed downstairs she'd be safe. Joe wouldn't even think of her. He was always forgetting about Penny. So far as he was concerned, Pen didn't exist. Stay asleep, Pen, she prayed; please stay asleep.

"You *hear* me?" Joe bellowed. "I *said* get *over* here! *Now!* Or I'll finish off your boyfriend." He again aimed the gun at Dennis.

Resigned, lowering her head, Bobby approached him. Maybe Dennis wasn't too badly hurt. Maybe everyone would be okay if she could only somehow get Joe away from the house.

He leaped forward and smacked her across the face.

"Leave her alone!" Eva shrieked. Her control was slipping away; she could feel herself on the verge of doing something wild. Her fingernails dug into her palms. Her arms quivered with tension. She had to find some way to stop this. She couldn't just stand by while another friend died.

"Mind your own goddamned business!" Joe warned, getting a handful of Bobby's hair and dragging her forward.

Her head pulled painfully to one side, Bobby said quietly, "I'll go with you. Just leave these people alone. They've got nothing to do with us."

"You don't *tell* me what to *do!*" he raved, threading his fingers deeper into her hair, pulling harder, dragging her down even farther.

In the brief silence there was a solid authoritative knock at the front door. For a moment Joe froze. Fuck! One of the neighbors must've heard the shot, called the cops. How the hell'd they get there so fast? All of a sudden now he was running out of time, and he couldn't decide how he wanted to handle this. He could take Bobby out right now, put the gun to her head and do it. He aimed at the top of her head, his finger sweaty on the trigger. He'd counted on it lasting longer, prolonging the whole thing. He wanted to enjoy the power. More knocking at the front door, harder this time.

"They're coming," the 911 lady said. "They're on your street now."

"Somebody's poundin' on the door."

"It'll all be over soon."

"But he's still yellin'."

"Don't worry, sweetheart. Everything's going to be okay."

Penny didn't think so. The police had come before, when they lived in the old house, and sometimes they took Daddy away, but he always came back and hurted her mom some more.

"You there, Penny?"

"Uh-hunh."

"Good girl. Just stay on the line with me. Okay?"

"Okay."

At the door a voice said loudly, "Police. Open up!"

"*Back off!*" Joe shouted. *Back off or I'll take them all out!*"

"Come on, man," the voice said through the door. "Just chill out and talk to us!"

"*FUCK OFF!*" Joe screamed, waving the gun at Alma, then Eva, maintaining a fierce grip on Bobby's hair.

Again pounding at the door. "Come on. Open up!"

Joe pointed the gun at the window and let off a round.

Glass shattered. The sound of running feet moving off. Silence. Now they all could hear the chattering of the police radio.

"He's shootin' again!" Penny cried.

"I can hear it. Stay where you are, Penny. Okay? We're sending in some special people to help. They're on their way. They'll be there any minute now."

"What special people?" Penny's heart was going too fast again, and she was really afraid she was going to have an accident. She had to go badly.

"A SWAT team. They're already on their way."

"What's a SWAT?"

The 911 lady began explaining. Penny's ear was starting to hurt from holding the receiver so hard.

Alma was getting her breath back. It still hurt when she inhaled or exhaled but at least she could catch a deep breath.

"Why not just give up?" she said quietly, in the lull.

Joe turned to look at her.

"There's no possibility of your getting away," she said reasonably. "Give up now before you do any more damage."

Joe looked astonished, as if a statue had come to life and begun speaking. "The *point,* Grandma, is damage," he said, half-smiling, giving Bobby's hair another yank for good measure. Bobby didn't make a sound. Tears dripped off the tip of her nose.

"Let go of your wife's hair," Alma said, keeping her tone low and reasonable. "You're not proving anything by hurting someone who's smaller and weaker than you are."

His smile dissolved. "Shut the fuck up!" he said, but with considerably less than his previous energy, responding instinctively to Alma's natural authority. This old

broad had guts. She reminded him of his second grade
teacher, Miss Hastings.

Someone was on a bullhorn outside. "PUT DOWN
YOUR WEAPON AND COME OUT OF THE
HOUSE!"

Joe's head turned. He let go of Bobby, gave her a little
shove, moved toward the windows, peered out to have a
look-see what was going on out there.

"Penny, do you think you can do something for me?"

"I don't know. What?"

"Do you think you can get upstairs to the kitchen and
open the backdoor to let in the officers?"

Penny thought about it, decided she had to do it even if
she was scared, and said, "Uh-hunh."

"Okay, sweetheart. You be real careful now. Okay?"

"Okay."

Penny put the receiver down and crawled out from behind the sofa. She hesitated for a moment at the bottom of
the stairs, listening. She thought she could hear Granny
talking. She started up the stairs, going as quietly as she
could, arrived at the kitchen door and very carefully
pushed it open, looked over in the direction of the living
room, then at the back door, then again at the living room.
The 911 lady said she should, so it had to be okay. She ran
tiptoe over to the door, tried to open it, but the chain was
on and she couldn't reach it. Mouth open, breathing hard,
she ran and grabbed hold of one of the chairs, trying to
hurry, but the chair was really heavy and she couldn't lift
it, had to push it over to the door. Then she climbed up and
got the chain off the door.

Somebody pushed the door open and another somebody picked her up, whispering, "Good girl. You'll be
okay now," and carried her out, running. It was cold and
Penny's teeth started chattering. The man carrying her was
all dark and she asked, "Are you a policeman?" and he
said, "That's right, honey," and kept running with her, all

the way to the street, where he opened a car door and set her down on the back seat. Another policeman put a blanket around her and said, "Sit here now, sweetheart. Okay?"

"You gonna get my mom?" she asked, watching out the window as a lot of dark men went running back to the house.

"Don't worry. We'll get her. She'll be real proud of you. You've done a great job."

Penny put her thumb in her mouth and watched anxiously through the car window.

Joe was busy at the window, shouting at the police officers outside, his hand with the gun swinging back and forth as he glanced around the room every few seconds, trying to keep it all together but coming unglued because he was losing it. Bobby waited until he turned again to the window, then ran over to Dennis and knelt beside him, asking in a whisper, "Are you okay?"

He nodded. "Playing possum. It's only a graze," he murmured, eyes on Joe. "Better get back over there."

"I'm sorry, Dennis."

"Sshhh. It's okay."

"What the fuck're you *doing?*" Joe screamed at her. "Get the hell over here *now!*"

She stood up, gauging the distance between herself and Joe, between herself and the front door. This had to end. As if unable to help himself, Joe's head turned again to the window, the gun making another undirected swing through the air. She looked over at Eva and mouthed, I'm sorry. Eva's hand flew up, as if to stop her.

He'd kill her anyway, one way or another, sooner or later. It was meant to end that way; she'd always known it. "I'm going out the door, Joe," she said loudly and clearly, then turned and stepped past Dennis, convinced he'd shoot her in the back, but she had to do whatever she could to get him out of this house. And she knew he'd follow her. He didn't care about anybody else here; he'd only ever cared about seeing her dead. Penny would be looked after; Alma had told her that. They were fine people; they'd give her a good life, better than she ever could.

She got to the door, put a hand on the knob, turned it, heart in her mouth, wind rushing in her ears. Footsteps pounded behind her. She didn't turn, wouldn't, couldn't. Opened the door. A roar from Joe—an incoherent bellow of rage. I love you, Pen, she thought, trying to swallow, but the fear wouldn't let her. Then, one on top of the other, two more ear-shattering detonations and she flinched, waiting for the pain, saying good-bye to Pen. I love you, I love you. Nothing.

She turned, not understanding, saw Joe stagger, a man with a gun in the kitchen doorway, and Joe still aiming the gun at her, still moving toward her. Another shot. Joe flew back, colliding with the wall, his hand with the gun falling, his body sliding down the wall, leaving smears of blood on the paint, his eyes astounded. They stayed that way, even when he stopped moving. She stood rigid, waiting for him to give her one of his evil smiles, waiting for him to get up and chase her into the night.

Dennis slowly stood, his hand still inside his coat, as police officers surged into the house followed by medics and more members of the SWAT team. Rooted in place, Bobby couldn't take her eyes off Joe. Then she remembered Penny and in a sudden panic darted to the kitchen, headed for the apartment. But one of the SWAT team officers stopped her with a hand on her arm, and she turned to look at him. He was speaking but she could scarcely hear him. She shook her head to hear better, eyes on his mouth, trying to make out what he was saying and at the same time trying to free herself of his grip, needing to get to Penny.

"She's outside, in a patrol car," the officer said again, more slowly and louder.

Bobby blinked rapidly, wanting to be sure of what she was hearing, her eyes leaving the officer's mouth, sliding past him to look into the living room where people were swarming over Alma and Eva. Ambulance attendants were leading Dennis out of the house. She looked again at Joe. Someone had thrown a blanket over him, cutting off his stupefied gaze. She felt a tugging at her arm and understood at last that the officer wanted her to go with him. Crazed with concern for Penny, determined to get to her the instant the police were done with her, she allowed herself to be directed out of the house and led down the driveway to where all kinds of police cars were parked every which way, blocking the road.

The officer opened the back door of one of the patrol cars, indicating Bobby should get in. She ducked down, looked inside. Penny, wrapped in a blanket, broke into a huge smile, exclaiming, "Mom!" and threw out her arms, the blanket sliding off her.

Bobby reached out, wrapped her arms around her little girl, closed her eyes, and held Penny tight to her chest. It was over. Once and forever, it was over. A sob shook her, and she held Penny even more tightly.

After

Penny was upstairs with Melissa in her bedroom, both of them occupied with the coloring books, markers, and crayons Bobby had brought back for Penny from Jamestown; coloring and listening to one of Melissa's Grateful Dead tapes. Alma was taking her afternoon nap. Eva had gone for a walk with Charlie. And Bobby was sitting in the kitchen opposite Dennis, mugs of coffee steaming on the table.

Bobby lit a Marlboro, trying to figure out where to begin. The truth was always best, she decided. "I thought maybe I'd never hear from you again. I thought maybe you wouldn't want to know about me."

"But I explained to Eva that the substitute was only temporary," he said, "until I could get back to work. And I couldn't call you in Jamestown because you forgot to leave me a number where I could reach you. Eva told me when you'd be back, so I waited, hoping you'd call again."

"I was kind of glad I only got your answering machine," she admitted. "I didn't really know what I wanted to say to you. I wasn't sure what you'd think."

"Bobby, nobody blames you for what happened."

"I feel as if they should," she said, her eyes on the steam rising from her coffee. "I'm trying hard not to feel that way, especially since everybody's being so nice about it, but..." She shrugged, thinking maybe she'd go see the psychiatrist Charlie had told her about. She needed somebody professional, somebody *official*, in a way, to tell her she hadn't done anything wrong. Then she might start actually believing it. But right now it was hard. She still had a lot of trouble accepting that Aunt Helen was dead, that she'd never see her again. She thanked God every day that Joe was dead; it felt almost wicked, how grateful she was to have him gone.

"Listen," Dennis said, putting a hand on her arm. "I think everybody feels the same way I do: that we got off lightly. Eva got a bruise or two, Alma has a couple of cracked ribs that're healing nicely, I got a minor flesh wound, and Pen wound up a bona fide heroine with her picture in the paper. It could've been a hell of a lot worse."

"I know that," she said, her voice huskier than usual. Pen had saved their lives. It was incredible.

"What're you going to do about everything back in Jamestown?" he asked. "I'm assuming you're planning to stay on here."

She looked over at the doorway, as if expecting to see Alma and Eva, a note of surprise in her voice as she said, "I was so sure they'd want us to go."

"I don't know why you'd think that," he said, trying a coaxing smile on her. "I *told* you: Nobody blames you. So what would be the point of upsetting the status quo? You've got an arrangement here that works."

Her arm moved, and he thought she was pulling away from him. But her hand, scarcely larger than Penny's, slipped into his. He knew right then that eventually everything was going to be okay.

She took another puff of the Marlboro and said, "Aunt Helen's lawyer's taking care of everything. He's arranging for the Salvation Army to take all the stuff from my old house. We only rented that place, you know. It wasn't ours. He's getting people in to clean it up so the owner can rent it again. It was a terrible mess." She shook her head, remembering the panic she'd felt stepping through the front door a week earlier. Just being in the house had scared her so much she couldn't wait to get out. She'd only stayed long enough to fill up a box with Pen's books and toys. Everything else she'd left. She preferred to do without rather than have any reminders of her old life. "The other house," she went on after a time, "the house I grew up in, I thought a lot about what I wanted to do. See, my aunt had insurance, a couple of policies. I never knew that. But the money'll come to me. And the dealership people, they gave me Aunt Helen's car, said I should keep it. Everybody's been so kind."

"I saw it outside," Dennis said, keeping a gentle hold on her hand. "I was wondering."

"They didn't have to do that," she said, tapping the ash off her cigarette, looking everywhere but at him. "But they said it was only right. They all came to the funeral." She had to stop for a moment and took a swallow of coffee to ease her throat. "So many people came. She had a lot of friends." She coughed, took another puff of her cigarette, then at last met Dennis's eyes. "I'm turning the property over to the shelter people so they can use it for a safe house. The lawyer said I was crazy, but if that's what I wanted, he'd make the arrangements. You think it's crazy?"

"No," he said, meeting her eyes. "Not a bit."

"I like to think maybe some other woman and her little girl will be safe in my house, maybe even sleep in my old room. It makes me feel better, thinking that. And I'm paying Eva back for fixing the window and replacing the hall carpet, painting the wall. She got all impatient. You know the way she does." She smiled for the first time since he arrived. "She started saying it was absolutely unnecessary. But Alma said, 'Let her do it.'" She imitated Alma's gruff bark, her smile growing wider. "And Eva said okay. But she still thought it was ridiculous. That made me feel a bit better, too." She lowered her eyes, her smile dimming, then raised them again. "I was so glad when you called. I thought maybe... Well, I guess I've already told you that."

"I wanted to give you some time to get settled back in here. And, anyway, I had to take it easy for a little while, until I got the stitches out. Now I'm almost as good as new. Want to see?" he asked, making as if to lift his sweater.

She flushed, smiled again, and said, "No!" her eyes going to the doorway, then returning to him. "You're being a real . . . really good sport about all this, Dennis."

"No, I'm not. I'm simply being realistic, like everyone else. There's no reason why anyone would want to hold you responsible for what Joe did. Although there's one thing I should say, and that is this: I didn't one hundred percent buy the picture you painted of him. In the back of my mind I kept thinking he couldn't be as bad as you made him out to be. But he was even worse than you said. I feel pretty guilty for not taking you at your word. Maybe it's one of those 'male' things I'm going to have to get over. You know? I just couldn't believe it."

"I told you one time you had to meet him to believe it," she said quietly.

"And you were right. I'm sorry. I'll never again doubt anything you tell me. Scout's honor. So, listen," he said.

"What?"

"My folks have a big bash every New Year's Eve, and I was wondering if you and Pen would like to come."

"I don't think I could," she said. "Eva's going to be out with Charlie, Melissa's meeting up with some of her friends, and somebody has to stay with Alma. Otherwise, I'd like to. A lot. I've been missing you the last little while."

"Well, that's all set then," he said happily. "Because I already talked Alma into coming with us. My folks said the more the merrier, so I'm bringing all three of you."

"Alma said she'd go?" Bobby was amazed.

"Yup. She said she and Pen could go off somewhere and have a nap if it got to be too late. Eva said we could use the van for the evening."

"I guess it's okay, then," she said, wondering how he'd managed to convince Alma to go. But maybe she hadn't needed much convincing. She'd been different since that night Joe came to the house. She'd started getting in touch with some of her friends, and the other night a couple of them had come to visit. She'd stayed up way past her usual bedtime, talking and laughing. And almost the minute Bobby arrived back from Jamestown, she'd started in, insisting Bobby sign up for some night courses. Bobby had said she would. Now she was pretty excited about it, looking forward to learning new things. "That's okay," she repeated, and gave Dennis's hand a squeeze. "I'm so glad to see you." He'd called just when she was thinking she'd probably never see him again.

"You've got to learn to have a little more faith in people, Bobby."

She'd have to do that, she thought. It was one of the things she'd talk about with that doctor friend of Charlie's when she went to see him. She had quite a list of things she wanted to talk about. But she was already beginning to feel a whole lot better. Alma had said flat-out that she was staying, that she and Pen could stay forever if they wanted to. And Eva, when she wasn't walking around with what Alma called her "zombie stare"—that blanked-out look she got because her mind was on the book she was writing in her head—was nice as she could be. And what was really amazing was that even though she'd expected to, she hadn't had one bad dream since Joe died. Not a single one.

HELP FOR VICTIMS
OF DOMESTIC VIOLENCE
IN THE UNITED STATES

The National Council on Child Abuse and Family Violence in Washington, D.C., provides a referral service to persons seeking information or community services related to domestic violence.

For information, call (800) 222-2000 between the hours of 8 a.m. and 5 p.m.

The National Coalition Against Domestic Violence is a grass roots coalition of battered women's service organizations and shelters that supplies technical assistance and makes referrals on issues of domestic violence. The following is a listing of Domestic Violence State Coalitions:

Alabama Coalition Against
  Domestic Violence
Montgomery, Alabama
(205) 832-4842

Alaska Network on Domestic
  Violence and Sexual Assault
Juneau, Alaska
(907) 586-3650

Arizona Coalition Against
  Domestic Violence
Phoenix, Arizona
(602) 495-5429

Arkansas Coalition Against
  Violence to Women
  & Children
Little Rock, Arkansas
(501) 663-4668

Central California Coalition
  on Domestic Violence
Modesto, California
(209) 575-7037

Northern California
  Coalition for Battered
  Women and Their Children
San Rafael, California
(415) 457-2464

Colorado Coalition Against
 Domestic Violence
Denver, Colorado
(303) 573-9018

Connecticut Coalition
 Against Domestic Violence
Hartford, Connecticut
(203) 524-5890

Child, Inc.
Wilmington, Delaware
(302) 762-6110

D.C. Coalition Against
 Domestic Violence
Washington, D.C.
(202) 662-9666

Florida Coalition Against
 Domestic Violence
Winter Park, Florida
(407) 628-3885

Georgia Advocates for
 Battered Women
 and Children
Atlanta, Georgia
(404) 524-3847

Hawaii State Committee on
 Family Violence
Honolulu, Hawaii
(808) 538-7216

Idaho Network to Stop
 Violence Against Women
Idaho Falls, Idaho
(208) 529-4352

Illinois Coalition Against
 Domestic Violence
Springfield, Illinois
(217) 789-2830

Indiana Coalition Against
 Domestic Violence
Lafayette, Indiana
(317) 742-0075
(800) 332-7385 (state hotline)

Iowa Coalition Against
 Domestic Violence
Des Moines, Iowa
(515) 281-7284

Kansas Coalition Against
 Sexual & Domestic Violence
Pittsburgh, Kansas
(316) 232-2757

Kentucky Domestic Violence
 Association
Frankfort, Kentucky
(502) 875-4132

Louisiana Coalition Against
 Domestic Violence
Baton Rouge, Louisiana
(318) 389-3001

Maine Coalition for Family
 Crisis Services
Sanford, Maine
(207) 324-1957

Maryland Network Against
 Domestic Violence
Annapolis, Maryland
(410) 268-4393

Massachusetts Coalition of
 Battered Women's Service
 Groups
Boston, Massachusetts
(617) 476-8492

Michigan Coalition Against
 Domestic Violence
Lansing, Michigan
(517) 484-2924

Minnesota Coalition for
Battered Women
St. Paul, Minnesota
(612) 646-6177

Mississippi Coalition Against
Domestic Violence
Biloxi, Mississippi
(601) 436-3809

Missouri Coalition Against
Domestic Violence
Jefferson City, Missouri
(314) 634-4161

Montana Coalition Against
Domestic Violence
Bozeman, Montana
(406) 586-7689

Nebraska Domestic Violence
and Sexual Assault Coalition
Lincoln, Nebraska
(402) 476-6256

Nevada Network Against
Domestic Violence
Sparks, Nevada
(702) 746-2700
(800) 992-5757 (state hotline)

New Hampshire Coalition
Against Domestic and
Sexual Violence
Concord, New Hampshire
(603) 224-8893
(800) 852-3311 (state hotline)

New Jersey Coalition for
Battered Women
Trenton, New Jersey
(609) 584-8107
(800) 572-7233 (state hotline)

New Mexico State Coalition
Against Domestic Violence
Santa Fe, New Mexico
(505) 624-0666

New York State Coalition
Against Domestic Violence
Albany, New York
(518) 432-4864
(800) 942-6906
(state hotline—English)
(800) 942-6908
(state hotline—Spanish)

North Carolina Coalition
Against Domestic Violence
Durham, North Carolina
(919) 490-1467

North Dakota Council on
Abused Women's Services
Bismarck, North Dakota
(701) 255-6240
(800) 472-2911 (state hotline)

Action Ohio Coalition
for Battered Women
Columbus, Ohio
(614) 221-1255

Oklahoma Coalition
On Domestic Violence
and Sexual Assault
Norman, Oklahoma
(405) 360-7125
(800) 533-SAFE
(state hotline)

Oregon Coalition Against
Domestic and Sexual
Violence
Portland, Oregon
(503) 239-4486 or -4487

Pennsylvania Coalition
  Against Domestic Violence
Harrisburg, Pennsylvania
(717) 234-7353

N-11 Calle 11
San Souci
Bayamón, Puerto Rico 00619
Contact: Rev. Judith Spindt

Rhode Island Council
  on Domestic Violence
Central Falls, Rhode Island
(401) 723-3051

South Carolina Coalition
  Against Domestic Violence
  and Sexual Assault
Columbia, South Carolina
(803) 669-4694

South Dakota Coalition
  Against Domestic Violence
  and Sexual Assault
Agency Village, South Dakota
(605) 698-3947

Tennessee Task Force on
  Family Violence
Nashville, Tennessee
(615) 242-8288

Texas Council on
  Family Violence
Austin, Texas
(512) 794-1133

Utah Domestic Violence
  Advisory Council
Salt Lake City, Utah
(801) 538-4078

Vermont Network Against
  Domestic Violence
  and Sexual Assault
Montpelier, Vermont
(802) 223-1302

Virginians Against Domestic
  Violence
Williamsburg, Virgina
(804) 221-0990

Washington State Domestic
  Violence Hotline
Naselle, Washington
(206) 484-7191
(800) 562-6025 (state hotline)

West Virginia Coalition
  Against Domestic Violence
Sutton, West Virginia
(304) 765-2250

Wisconsin Coalition Against
  Domestic Violence
Madison, Wisconsin
(608) 255-0539

Wyoming Coalition Against
  Domestic Violence
  and Sexual Assault
Casper, Wyoming
(307) 856-0942

HELP FOR VICTIMS
OF DOMESTIC VIOLENCE
IN CANADA

SOS Violence Conjugale is a 24-hour hotline that will refer you to emergency services and shelters throughout Canada. Call (800) 363-9010 from any location within Quebec except for the city of Montreal. If you are calling from Montreal or from any other province in Canada, the telephone number is (514) 873-9010.

The following is a list of Provincial Transition House Associations in Canada:

Alberta Council of Women's
  Shelters
Edmonton, Alberta
(403) 429-2689

British Columbia/Yukon
  Society of Transition
  Houses
Vancouver, British Columbia
(604) 669-6943

Department of Family
  Services
Winnipeg, Manitoba
(204) 945-7245

New Brunswick Coalition of
  Transition Houses
Saint John, New Brunswick
(506) 634-7570

Provincial Association
  Against Family Violence
St. John's, Newfoundland
(709) 739-6759

Family Violence Prevention
  Program
Yellowknife,
  Northwest Territories
(403) 920-6254

Transition House
  Association of Nova Scotia
New Glasgow, Nova Scotia
(902) 755-4878

Ontario Association of
  Interval and Transition
  Houses
Toronto, Ontario
(416) 977-6619

Prince Edward Island
  Transition House
  Association
Charlottetown,
  Prince Edward Island
(902) 368-7337

Charlotte Vale Allen

Fédération des Ressources
d'Hébergement pour
Femmes Violentes et
en Difficulté du Québec
Longueuil, Quebec
(514) 674-0324

Regroupement Provincial des
Maisons d'Hébergement et
de Transition pour Femmes

Victimes de Violence
Conjugale
Montréal, Québec
(514) 279-2007

Provincial Association of
Transition Houses in
Saskatchewan
Saskatoon, Saskatchewan
(306) 625-6175

New York Times Bestselling Author

ELIZABETH LOWELL

has done it again! Watch for

WARRIOR

Another compelling novel coming in April 1995.

Nevada Blackthorn had never been on the losing side of a battle. But when the hunter gets captured by the game, he quickly learns from Eden Summers that surrender can be so sweet....

"Elizabeth Lowell sizzles." —Jayne Ann Krentz

 MIRA The brightest star in women's fiction

MEL2

Award-winning romance author

LINDA HOWARD

This April, face some unexpected complications in

The Cutting Edge

Brett Rutland was an expert at catching corporate
thieves with cold, unerring precision. Then
he met beautiful and desirable executive
Tessa Conway. Life was perfect...until the day
Brett identified the embezzler within Tessa's
company.

Could their love withstand the ultimate challenge?

Bestselling Author

Jasmine Cresswell

May 1995 brings you face-to-face with her latest thrilling adventure

Desires & Deceptions

Will the real Claire Campbell please stand up?
Missing for over seven years, Claire's family has
only one year left to declare her legally dead and
claim her substantial fortune—that is, until a woman
appears on the scene alleging to be the missing
heiress. Will DNA testing solve the dilemma? Do
old family secrets still have the power to decide
who lives and dies, suffers or prospers, loves or
hates? Only Claire knows for sure.